Bournville

'*Bournville* is a wickedly funny, clever but also tender and lyrical novel about Britain and Britishness and what we have become. Told over a series of seven historical occasions – witnessed on different models of television set – it offers both a big picture window that opens out on the social changes between VE Day and the end of lockdown, and a small intimate window that reveals one family's struggle through three generations, their differences and secrets, and attempts or refusals to overcome them. Told with compassion, steadiness, decency and always a glint in the eye, this is a novel that both challenges and delights. For anyone who has felt lost in the past six years, it is like meeting an ally' Rachel Joyce, bestselling author of *The Unlikely Pilgrimage of Harold Fry*

'It is miraculous how, in his new novel, Coe has created a social history of post-war Britain as we are still living it. *Bournville* is a beautiful, and often very funny, tribute to an under-examined place and also a truly moving story of how a country discovered tolerance' Sathnam Sanghera, bestselling author of *Empireland*

'British novelists love to diagnose the state of the nation. Few do it better than Jonathan Coe, who writes with warmth and subversive glee about social change and the comforting mundanities it imperils' *Spectator*

'Epic in scope but personal in resonance . . . *Bournville* is poignant, rich and about the evolution of a nation as well as the evolution of a family . . . a book written with real heart' Elizabeth Day

'Coe tracks the fortunes of a family through snapshots of communal experiences, from the Queen's coronation through the 1966 World Cup to pandemic lockdown, in a moving, compassionate portrait of individual and national change' *Guardian*, Best Fiction of 2022

D1342615

'A compelling social history that's sprinkled throughout with Coe's inimitable humour, love and white-hot anger' *Evening Standard*

'For all the novel's satirical tang and historical sweep, it's at root a tender portrait of apparently simple folk trying to fathom the mystery of their own personalities' *Spectator*

'At heart *Bournville* is a novel designed to make you think by making you laugh, and the seriousness of the subject matter is tempered throughout by the author's piercing eye for the more ludicrous elements of human nature' *New Statesman*

'There is much to enjoy here, as in all Coe's novels . . . an intelligent criticism of our shared history since 1945' *Scotsman*

'A book of things blended together: comedy with tragedy, England's past with its present, and cocoa solids with vegetable fat' *Irish Times*

'Slips down a treat' *Daily Mail*

'Coe's interwoven paeans to the lives of those rooted in the very centre of the UK – *The Rotter's Club* and *Middle England* among them – blend comedy, tragedy and social commentary in enjoyably memorable fashion, and his latest, *Bournville*, is no exception . . . Coe's particular gift is to understand how nostalgia, regret and an apprehension of what the future will bring might make us more, not less, empathetic to the frailties of those around us' *FT*, Best Audiobooks of the Year

'This is another eminently readable Coe, full of believable characters and fizzing dialogue. And it couldn't be more timely' *Big Issue*

'Affectionate, full of good humour, and often moving, this is Coe at his best' *Crack* magazine

'Coe has the great gift of combining engaging human stories with a deeper structural pattern that gives the book its heft' *Guardian*

Bournville

A Novel in Seven Occasions

JONATHAN COE

PENGUIN BOOKS

PENGUIN BOOKS

UK | USA | Canada | Ireland | Australia
India | New Zealand | South Africa

Penguin Books is part of the Penguin Random House group of companies
whose addresses can be found at global.penguinrandomhouse.com.

First published by Viking 2022
Published in Penguin Books 2023
001

Typeset by Jouve (UK), Milton Keynes
Printed and bound in Great Britain by Clays Ltd, Elcograf S.p.A.

The authorized representative in the EEA is Penguin Random House Ireland,
Morrison Chambers, 32 Nassau Street, Dublin D02 YH68

A CIP catalogue record for this book is available from the British Library

ISBN: 978–0–241–51740–6

www.greenpenguin.co.uk

MIX
Paper | Supporting
responsible forestry
FSC   FSC® C018179
www.fsc.org

Penguin Random House is committed to a
sustainable future for our business, our readers
and our planet. This book is made from Forest
Stewardship Council® certified paper.

For Graham Caveney

Contents

Prologue

March 2020

The arrivals hall at Vienna airport was so quiet that Lorna had no difficulty picking her out, even though they had never met before. She had short brown hair and a boyish figure and brown eyes that lit up when Lorna peeped out from behind her gigantic instrument case and said:

'Susanne, right?'

'Hello,' Susanne answered, stringing out the word in a sing-song way, and then, after a moment's hesitation, she drew Lorna into a welcoming hug. 'We're still allowed to do this, aren't we?'

'Of course we are.'

'I'm so excited you're here at last.'

'Me too,' said Lorna, automatically. But it was true.

'Good flight?'

'Fine. Not too busy.'

'I've brought my car.' She looked with sudden apprehension at the gleaming black flight case that contained Lorna's double bass, and said: 'I hope it's big enough.'

Outside it felt almost cold enough to snow, and the street lights cast sparse coronas of amber across the night air. As they walked to the car park, Susanne asked more questions about the flight (did they check your temperature at the airport?), asked Lorna if she was hungry (she wasn't) and explained some things about the arrangements for the next few days. Lorna and Mark would be staying in the same hotel, but he was flying in from Edinburgh, and wouldn't arrive in Vienna until tomorrow morning. Their gig would start at around nine in the evening, and the next day they would take the train to Munich.

'I can't come with you to the concerts in Germany,' she said. 'Much as I would like to. The label just doesn't have the budget to pay for my travel. We're doing everything on a shoestring. Which is why you're being picked up in this, and not a stretch limo.'

She was talking about her own car, a ten-year-old Volvo estate covered with scratches and dents which did not inspire Lorna with confidence. Nevertheless, it certainly seemed big enough for the job in hand.

'This should be fine,' Lorna said, but when she took a closer look inside the car, she saw an unexpected problem. There was a baby seat in the back, surrounded by all the detritus of someone for whom childcare was the number one priority – wet wipes, food wrappers, plastic toys, soothers – but more worryingly, every remaining square inch seemed to be filled with rolls of toilet paper, plastic-wrapped in packs of nine. She reckoned there were about twenty packs in there.

'Sorry about these,' said Susanne. 'Let me just . . . Well, let's see what we can do.'

They began by trying to get the bass into the car through the boot lid, but it immediately encountered a solid wall of toilet rolls. Lorna took out about nine or ten packs and put them on the tarmac but they still couldn't slide the neck of the bass through all the packs of toilet paper on the back seat. So then they took the top layer of rolls off the seat and stacked them by the side of the car and between them managed to manoeuvre the bass deep inside, past the baby seat, so that its head was almost touching the windscreen and the boot lid would just about close. When they tried to pack all the toilet rolls around it, however, they wouldn't fit.

'Maybe if we took the instrument out of the case,' said Susanne, 'and filled the case with toilet paper . . . No, I don't think that would work.'

Eventually the problem was solved when Lorna sat in the passenger seat with the neck of the bass pressed up against her cheek, and Susanne loaded eight or nine packs of toilet paper onto her lap, in a tower which reached to the roof of the car.

'Do you feel safe?' she asked, anxiously, as she began to drive along the almost empty roads leading towards the centre of Vienna.

'Very,' said Lorna. 'They're like an air bag. If we crash into something they'll probably save my life.'

'You don't look very comfortable. I'm so sorry.'

4

'Don't worry, I'm fine.' After a moment or two, she said: 'Look, it's kind of . . . an obvious question, but why have you bought so much loo paper?'

Susanne glanced at her in surprise, as though the answer was self-evident. 'I just decided to stock up. I mean, maybe I went overboard a bit, but still . . . you can't be too careful, can you?' She drove on, negotiating a set of traffic lights. But she could tell that Lorna didn't really understand her explanation. 'Because of the virus, right?' she added, to leave no room for doubt.

'You think it's that serious?'

'Who knows? But yes, I think so. Have you seen the footage from Wuhan? And now the whole of Italy's been locked down.'

'Yes, I heard,' Lorna said. 'They're not going to do anything like that here, are they? I mean, there's no chance the gig tomorrow will be cancelled?'

'Oh no, I don't think so. It's already sold out, you know. It's not a huge venue – two hundred or so – but that's pretty good for jazz these days. And in the morning a journalist wants to speak to you, for a music website. So there's a lot of interest. Everything's going to run smoothly, don't worry.'

Lorna allowed the relief to show on her face. This tour was a huge thing for her. The first time she and Mark had taken their live set out of the UK; the first time anyone had paid for them to play more than one gig at a time; her first earnings from music in over a year. By day she was one of four women working on the reception desk of a fifteen-storey office block in central Birmingham. Her colleagues had a vague idea that she played music in her spare time but they would have been amazed to know that something like this was happening: that someone was paying for her to go to Austria and Germany, that she was being put up in hotels – that a journalist, for heaven's sake (even a journalist from a website), wanted to interview her. Lorna had been looking forward to the tour for weeks, living for it. It would break her heart if this weird little virus were to derail everyone's plans.

Susanne left her at the hotel and promised to come round in the morning, straight after breakfast. It was a budget place, some miles from the centre of town. The rooms were tiny, but Lorna was grateful just to be there. For half an hour or more she lay on her bed, thinking. She wondered whose idea it had been to equip such a small room with a strip light that couldn't be dimmed. She wondered why she had chosen to play an instrument that took up more space in the room than she did, and had almost got jammed in the lift. Above all, she wondered why anyone would react to the global spread of a virus by buying almost two hundred rolls of toilet paper. Was this really people's darkest fear: that one day, because of a terrible economic crisis, or a crisis of public health, or the onset of climate catastrophe, they might not be able to wipe their bottoms?

She looked at her watch. Nine-thirty. Eight-thirty in Birmingham. It would be a good time to call home. By 'home' she meant the UK, but she didn't plan to call her husband, Donny, who would be out with his friends by now. Nor did she want to call her parents, who were on holiday, taking advantage of the unexpected (and unwanted) expansion of their leisure time now that Britain had finally left the EU and all the British MEPs were out of a job. No, it was Gran who would be waiting to hear from her. Lorna had promised to Skype her as soon as she landed in Vienna. Gran, for whom every flight was a potential disaster, a plane crash waiting to happen, would be sitting at home in a state of low-level anxiety until Lorna called to say that she was back on *terra firma*.

She sat up on the bed and flipped open her laptop, a cheap purchase from the dodgy electronics dealer down the road from her flat, which so far had served her well. There was no desk or table in the room so she put a pillow on her lap and settled the computer on it, then clicked on her grandmother's Skype username. As usual there was no answer. There never was. Why did she keep trying to do it this way? You had to call her landline first. Landline and letter: Gran didn't trust more modern forms of communication, but she believed in the reality of these. She had owned a tablet for six years now – it had been an eightieth birthday present – but couldn't really work out how to use it. You had to call her landline, call her on Skype at the same time, and talk her through the process. You had to do this every time.

When the rigmarole was over at last, Lorna found herself look-ing at the usual view on her laptop screen: the top half of Gran's forehead.

'Can you hold it at a different angle?' she said. 'Tilt it down towards you.'

The image shook violently and tilted in the wrong direction. Now all she could see was Gran's hair, permed and tinted blonde as always.

'Is that better?'

'Not really.'

'I can see you all right.'

'That's because I've got the camera in the right place. Never mind, Gran, it doesn't matter.'

'I can see you.'

'That's good.'

'We can still talk anyway.'

'Yep, we can.'

'Where are you?'

'In my hotel room.'

'In Venice?'

'Vienna.'

'That's right. It looks very nice.'

'Yeah, it's pretty cosy.'

'How was your flight?'

'Good.'

'No problems?'

'No problems. How are you, Gran?'

'I'm fine. Just been watching the news.'

'Yes?'

'It's a bit worrying, actually. It's all virus this, virus that.'

'I know. They're talking about it here as well. The woman who picked me up from the airport had about two hundred loo rolls in her car.'

'About two hundred what?'

'Loo rolls.'

'How ridiculous.'

'Perhaps you should get a few spare ones.'

'Why on earth would I do that?'

'Or a few extra tins of baked beans or soup.'

'Rubbish. People do go over the top. Anyway, Jack usually does the shopping for me, or Martin. They can get me anything I want.'

'I suppose so. It's just that . . . nobody seems to know what's going to happen.'

'Do you think we'll get it over here? The virus.'

'They've got it in Italy.'

'I saw that. Everyone's been told to stay indoors. It'll be like the plague, won't it? The Black Death, and all that caper.'

Lorna smiled. This was one of Gran's favourite idioms. She used it all the time without realizing it. Only she could describe the Black Death as a 'caper'.

'You look after yourself, that's all,' Lorna said. 'Stay inside and take care.'

'Don't worry,' Gran said. 'I'm not going anywhere.'

*

The first two hours of the next morning were spent in a café next to the hotel, where Lorna had breakfast, did her interview, and then met Susanne for coffee. The interview was stressful: she had no experience of talking to journalists. The interviewer was a cheerful hipster in his early thirties who spoke perfect English and seemed to want to ask her more about Brexit and Boris Johnson than harmonics and walking bass lines. When she did finally drag the subject around to music, she ended up talking mainly about other members of her family: about her Uncle Peter, who played violin in the BBC Symphony Orchestra, and then about Gran, of all people. 'I think all my musicality comes from her,' she said. 'My grandmother, Mary Lamb. She's a wonderful pianist. Could probably have been a concert pianist, actually. But she became a housewife and mother instead, and ended up playing "Jerusalem" once a week at the local WI.' After that she had to spend some time explaining what the WI was, and was pretty sure that by the time the explanation was finished, her original point had been lost. It was a shame Mark hadn't been there. He had way more experience with this sort of thing, and was always so funny, and so irreverent, the mood would have been far lighter.

But Mark did not arrive at the hotel until 1.30, at which point he and Lorna immediately went looking for somewhere to eat. Most of the restaurants in this district were characterless, fast-food sorts of places. They walked for about ten minutes until they found something that looked more traditional: a gloomy interior with guttering candles and heavy oak tables and no translations on the menu. Weeks later, Lorna would remember the atmosphere that day in the restaurant, and in the city generally, as being strange, unsettled: there was an air of tension, as if it was slowly dawning on people that some change, some unseen, imminent event was about to knock their daily lives off kilter in ways that they did not yet understand and were not prepared for. The feeling of subdued apprehension was difficult to define, but palpable.

Lorna ordered a salad and a tonic water; Mark had a massive open sandwich and two lagers. She did worry about his eating.

'Don't look so disapproving,' he told her. 'I need to eat to keep my strength up. And Scotland's cold, you know. You need a lot of body fat to survive up there.'

She started telling him about the interview. 'He wanted to know how we met.'

Mark paused, his fork halfway to his mouth.

'I don't remember how we met,' he said.

'Yes, you do. You came to our college. We all had the chance to sit in with you.'

'Ah yes, that's right,' he said, looking much more interested in the food on the end of his fork.

'I was the best,' Lorna said, waiting for Mark to nod in confirmation. He didn't. 'At least, you said I was the best.'

'Of course you were the best,' he said, chewing.

'So then we went for a drink afterwards. You asked me which of your albums was my favourite and I said I'd never heard of you until today.'

'That I do remember. I was charmed by your candour and horrified by your ignorance, in equal measure.'

'And then we just . . . took it from there.'

'Taking it from there' had involved playing together for a few hours the following week, at the flat in Moseley where Mark had been staying at the time. After that they had started to make recordings, remotely – Mark sending her files from his home studio in Edinburgh, Lorna adding the bass parts at home. In this way they had amassed many hours' worth of music, which would eventually be distilled into one seventy-minute album for Mark's Austrian record label, and in the process they had evolved a style in which the slow, ambient drones that Mark coaxed meditatively out of his guitar were underpinned and enriched by Lorna's contributions on bass, which she approached as a melodic instrument, often using a bow. It was an extraordinary thing, for her, to go from promising student to recorded musician in such a short space of time, but the fact was that the collaboration worked – she and Mark had simply clicked, from the very beginning – and although the UK press was not interested and it was hard to get gigs at home, sales of their album in the rest of Europe had been respectable, and now here they were, in Vienna, on the first date of a six-day tour, doing their best to recreate the textures of those studio recordings in a live setting. That evening, as Mark did one of his solo spots midway through their set and Lorna watched from the side of the stage, she marvelled again at the way this man – this overweight, filthy-minded, carelessly dressed, altogether slightly seedy-looking man – could make music like an angel when it suited him, using his fingers and his pedals to make his guitar sound like an entire orchestra, filling the room with complex harmonies and overtones and fragmented lines of melody that held the young audience in a kind of ecstatic trance.

'Miserable lot of fuckers in there tonight,' he said to Lorna as they sat down to dinner afterwards.

'What are you talking about? They loved it.'

'I didn't feel we were getting much back from them,' he said. 'I've seen livelier crowds in a morgue.'

Susanne looked genuinely mortified, as if the behaviour of this audience was her own personal responsibility, so Lorna rushed to reassure her:

'Take no notice. They were a great crowd. It was a great evening. This is his way of showing gratitude, believe it or not.'

For dinner they had been joined by Ludwig, the owner of the record label. He had brought them to a restaurant called the Café Engländer, although there didn't seem to be anything very English about it: the food was Austrian, and came in generous portions, including a *Schnitzel* which, when it arrived, looked big enough to satisfy even Mark's appetite.

'Look at that,' he said, his eyes gleaming. 'Just take a look at that!'

Susanne and Ludwig beamed, proud that their national cuisine was meeting with such enthusiasm. Only Lorna, who had ordered a salad again, looked disapproving.

'You've got about three quarters of a calf there,' she said to him, in a low voice, so that the others couldn't hear. 'Someone like you shouldn't be eating something like that.'

'Someone like me?' he said, helping himself to potato salad. 'You mean someone fat like me?'

'I didn't say that. I would never call you fat.'

'Good,' Mark said. 'Because I'm not fat. According to my doctor, I'm morbidly obese.'

After performing with such intensity for almost two hours, Mark and Lorna would have preferred a light-hearted conversation, but this turned out not to be Ludwig's style. He was in his late fifties, with stylish grey hair, an austerely trimmed beard, a sharp mind and an elegant and precise way of speaking. Within a few minutes he was questioning them about the state of British politics.

'As you know, Mark, I am a committed Anglophile. I first came to London in 1977, the height of punk. I didn't like the music much but the attitude was captivating, to a young man who had grown up in Salzburg, an ultra-conservative city with no counterculture that I'd ever noticed. It was the time of the Queen's Silver Jubilee, I remember, and for a while it seemed everyone was singing either the national anthem or 'God Save the Queen' by the Sex Pistols. It was somehow wonderfully revealing of your national character that these two songs could be on everybody's lips at the same time. I think it was then that I also watched a James Bond film, *The*

Spy Who Loved Me, and listened as the audience cheered when his parachute opened and revealed a Union Jack. Again, so British! Flattering themselves and laughing at themselves at the same time. I stayed in London for three months and at the end of it I was in love with everything I found there: British music, British literature, British television, the sense of humour – I even started to like the food. I felt there was an energy and inventiveness in this place that you didn't encounter anywhere else in Europe, and all done without self-importance, with this extraordinary irony that is so unique to the Brits. And now this same generation is doing . . . what? Voting for Brexit, and for Boris Johnson? What happened to them?'

Before either Mark or Lorna could offer an answer to this difficult question, he continued:

'It's not just me. This is what we're all asking ourselves. You know, this is a smart country we're talking about, a country that we all used to look up to. And now you've done this thing that to us, as far as we can tell, diminishes you, makes you look weaker and more isolated, and yet you seem really pleased with yourselves about it. And then you put this buffoon in charge. What's going on?'

Mark glanced at Lorna and said, 'Well, where do you begin with that one?'

'I suppose for a start,' she said, 'you begin with the fact that London and England are not the same thing.'

'For sure,' said Ludwig. 'I understand that.'

'And England and the rest of the UK are not the same thing,' Mark added. 'I moved to Edinburgh for a reason.'

'I understand that too. But still, you're an Englishman at heart, right?'

'It's not how I'd define myself. It's not my core identity.'

'I don't think,' said Lorna, choosing her words carefully, 'that there's such a thing as a typical English person.'

'Well, I would like to find one, if I could,' said Ludwig. 'And when I found them, I would ask them two questions: this new path you've taken in the last few years – why exactly did you choose it? And why did you choose this man, of all people, to lead you down it?'

Just then Susanne's mobile phone buzzed. She picked it up to look at the message.

'Wow,' she said. 'Looks like you were just in time.'

'What do you mean?'

'It's from the venue. They're closing their doors, starting tomorrow, on the orders of the city authorities. No more public events. No more gatherings of more than fifty people.'

The others received this information in silence, at first. The mood was suddenly sombre.

'Well, that was bound to happen,' said Ludwig. 'They've been talking about it for days.'

'At least it's not a total lockdown, like Italy,' said Susanne.

'That will come,' Ludwig assured them.

'Where are we meant to be going tomorrow?' Mark asked. 'Is it Munich?'

'I'll contact the venue first thing in the morning,' said Susanne, 'and let you know what they say. But I'm sure there won't be a problem.'

Lorna dug into her salad and took a couple of mouthfuls of white wine. It was sweeter than she was used to, and slipped down like honey. She looked around the restaurant and reflected that this was such a beautiful moment for her: so different to her life in Handsworth, so different to her daily working life: a world of welcoming faces, kindred spirits, graciousness and *Gemütlichkeit*. She hoped that it wasn't going to be snatched away from her before she'd had time to savour it.

*

The next morning Susanne met them at the Hauptbahnhof, to see them safely onto the 8.30 train for Munich. She was starting to look worried. Mark and Lorna had five more dates on their tour: Munich, Hanover, Hamburg, Berlin and Leipzig. It seemed likely now that at least some of them would be cancelled, even though each of the different German states was taking these decisions independently, making its own judgement call.

'The trouble is, once one of them imposes restrictions, the others will feel they have to follow. And I'm not going to be with you to make sure things go smoothly.'

'We'll be fine,' said Mark. 'If the venues close we'll just have to wrap up warm and play outdoors. Do an acoustic set. Mark Irwin and Lorna Simes unplugged.'

'Oh, I'd be sorry to miss that!' said Susanne.

'We'll record it and you can put it out as a live album.'

She smiled bravely, and then made as if to say goodbye to Lorna with a hug, just like the hug with which she had welcomed her only thirty-six hours earlier at the airport. But at the last moment they both changed their minds, and instead performed the awkward gesture that was now becoming common, putting their elbows together in what felt like a distant echo of normal human contact. Mark was having none of it. He put his arms around Susanne and pressed her against his soft protruding belly and squeezed her for about ten seconds.

'Sorry, but no stupid virus should stop us from showing how we feel,' he said. 'You've been great. Invite us back whenever you can, yes?'

'Of course. Things will be back to normal again soon and then we'll have you back.'

'Great.'

He kissed her on the forehead and then he and Lorna began the arduous business of loading their gear onto the train.

It was a four-hour journey and Lorna loved every minute of it. The late-winter sun was bright, the landscape shifted and evolved as they crossed the border from Austria into Germany, and like a tourist she took dozens of photos of the snow-capped Bavarian Alps and the towns and villages nestling between their slopes. She sent a couple of them to Donny and to Gran, but neither replied. In the window seat opposite her Mark dozed, occasionally snoring and then waking up with a start. Lorna suspected that he hadn't got much sleep the night before. He hadn't come back to the hotel with her after dinner: instead he'd found some guy on a dating app and had gone off to a club to meet him. She chose not to enquire about what had happened after that.

Next to the sleeping Mark sat a trim, well-dressed woman who was leafing through a German copy of *Vogue* magazine. Lorna became fascinated by how difficult she was finding it to turn the pages, because she was wearing a pair of delicate fawn leather gloves. Even though it was warm inside their carriage, and the woman had taken off her coat and jacket, she kept these gloves on for the entire journey.

*

The virus continued to chase them across Germany. In Munich, Hanover, Hamburg and Berlin, their luck held: the venues remained open until their performances had taken place, although all four of them closed their doors the next morning. Every evening, the pattern was the same: soundcheck, followed by gig, followed by a quick meal with the organizers. At these meals the conversation would always return, eventually, to the virus, to the new measures announced by the state authorities, to the new phrases like 'social distancing' and 'herd immunity' which people were now using like experts, to the new epidemic of nervous jokes about hand-washing and elbow-touching and handshake-avoiding, to the frightening reports of lockdown in Wuhan, to speculation about how Italy would cope with its lockdown and whether other European countries would soon follow suit. These conversations were mainly casual and light-hearted, with an undertone of incredulous apprehension, a sense that the things they were talking about could not really be happening or about to happen. The venue owners were also wrestling with more immediate, practical concerns: how long these closures were going to last, how they were going to pay staff and rent, whether they had enough money in their bank accounts to see them through the imminent crisis. They were alarming conversations, when you thought about them, but wine and food and laughter and human warmth seemed to make them not just tolerable but enjoyable.

Berlin was probably the best gig of all. Mark's playing was particularly inspired that night. It was almost as if he knew this was going to be their last performance for a while, and rose to the occasion by losing himself in the music, surrendering to it completely, with a degree of absorption and self-forgetfulness that Lorna would not have thought possible.

His performance was generous, too: generous to her. As the bass player, her role could have been merely supportive, but he never let that happen, always made her feel like an equal partner. But tonight she knew that he was playing on a different level, and she wouldn't be able to match his patient, unhurried invention, his miraculous flow of ideas. That was OK. It was a privilege to be there alongside him. They were playing in a strange venue, the basement of a record shop in former East Berlin, not far from the Fernsehturm. There was only room for an audience of seventy or so, and the place was full to bursting. Once or twice Lorna found herself looking into the crowd of young Berliners as they stood so tightly packed together, and thought about them breathing in and out, touching each other, touching the chairs and then touching the chairs that had been touched by other people, even coughing occasionally, and she felt that she could visualize this tiny, deadly organism of which they had only just become aware jumping from one person to another, from host to host, in search of its next place of residence, its next opportunity to incubate and attack. At such moments she knew that her concentration was faltering and she was letting Mark down, breaking the pact of trust that existed between two musicians who were improvising on stage together. She would quickly pull herself together and try to start playing with renewed focus. Once or twice she and Mark would conjoin: their peaks of intensity coincided and then, just for a few seconds, something magical was achieved and for those precious moments audience and performers would be lifted, time was suspended, and a feeling of something like bliss spread throughout the room. These were the moments that she lived for, but sometimes you could play a whole set and it would never happen. That night in Berlin they were blessed; nirvana came fleetingly within their grasp, and when they went out for food afterwards everyone was still on a high.

But the next morning, when Mark and Lorna reached Leipzig, a message was waiting for them at the hotel. Tonight's gig, the last one of the tour, was cancelled.

They stood there in the lobby, feeling a bit deflated and stupid. Lorna clutched on to her enormous glossy instrument case, whose very size seemed more ridiculous than ever.

They called Susanne and she offered her sympathy. 'I did tell you this would probably happen,' she said. She offered to book them on a flight home that day but they knew this would involve extra costs that the record company couldn't afford.

'There's no need,' Mark said. 'We'll just hang out, and take the flight you booked for us tomorrow morning. Don't worry about us, we'll be fine. We'll go out and have a look around the city this afternoon.'

Lorna knew that this was what she should be doing, but she couldn't summon the enthusiasm for it. She understood that under the circumstances they were lucky, very lucky, to have almost completed the tour, missing out on only one gig, but still, the sense of anti-climax was strong. She let Mark go on his walk – who knew what alleyways it would lead him down – and stayed in her hotel room, flicking between channels on the TV until finally she decided to call Gran one last time. The news about the virus was quite worrying now. Lorna was actually starting to feel paranoid about catching it, about getting too close to people, shaking their hands, being breathed on. As for Gran, she was eighty-six, and although she was fit and well (apart from her aneurysm), still, if she were to catch it there was every chance it would hit her hard. She seemed to have quite a devil-may-care attitude towards health issues these days, and Lorna felt it was probably time to impress upon her the importance of being careful in the weeks ahead.

This time, for a change, the Skype tone rang out only three or four times before there was a response at the other end. And this time, for a change, it was not Gran's high, wrinkled forehead that loomed into shaky view, but the face of Peter – her father's younger brother – fully visible and centred perfectly on the screen.

'Oh, hello,' she said. 'I didn't know you were visiting.'

'I only decided this morning,' he said.

'Have you driven up from Kew?'

'Yes, got here about an hour ago.'

Her Uncle Peter lived alone in a small terraced house about half a mile from Kew Gardens in south-west London. It was a two-hour drive up to his mother's, but he did it quite regularly, once every two or three weeks. She had been widowed now for more than seven years and although she was at last getting used to it, he knew – and Lorna knew – that there were times when she still found the loneliness almost too much to bear. He felt it was his duty to come up and see her whenever he could.

'Did you want to speak to Gran?' he asked. 'I'll go and get her.'

Lorna was left staring at a screen which remained blank until a large and handsome feline, his pelt a lively collage of black and white patches, jumped onto the table and glared into the camera with accusing green eyes, before turning round and offering her an impudent view of his backside. 'Charlie, get off that table!' Peter could be heard saying, and a hand reached out to whisk the complaining creature, Gran's devoted companion, decently out of view. After that two faces filled the screen, which Peter had rotated to landscape. Gran was looking very pleased with herself. Her eyes gleamed with the happiness of being in the presence of her youngest son. There was an element of triumph in it.

'Look who turned up on my doorstep this morning,' she said.

'That's nice,' said Lorna. 'How long's he staying?'

'You'll stay the night, won't you?' Gran said, turning to Peter.

'Oh yes.' Then he asked Lorna, 'So where are you at the moment?'

'Leipzig,' she said. 'But the show tonight's been cancelled.'

'Oh no! Not because of the virus?'

'Everything's closing down here, all over Germany.'

'You be careful,' said Gran. 'Don't go breathing in any germs. And keep washing your hands. That's what we have to do, apparently. Keep washing our hands.'

'I've got a concert in two weeks' time,' said Peter. 'I wonder if that'll go ahead.'

'Are you still coming home tomorrow?' Gran asked.

'Yes.'

'I should think Donny will be happy to have you back safe and sound. What are you going to do with the rest of the day?'

'I don't know.'

'You should visit the family vaults,' said Peter, unexpectedly.

'What?'

'We've got family buried in Leipzig, somewhere.'

'We do?'

'Yes. That's right, isn't it, Mum?'

'Well, I don't know about that. But your great-grandfather,' she said, speaking directly to Lorna, 'was German.'

'Really?' said Lorna. 'Your father, you mean?'

'No, not my father. Grandad's father.'

Peter chipped in to correct her: 'Not his father. His grandfather.'

Gran looked confused for a moment, and then agreed: 'Oh yes. Grandad's grandfather.'

'So my great-great-grandfather,' said Lorna.

Gran turned to Peter for confirmation. 'Is that right?'

'That's right. You mean Carl.'

'That was him. Carl. Geoffrey's grandfather.'

'And he was from Leipzig?' Lorna asked.

'Oh, I don't remember that. He had a German accent. I could hardly understand a word he was saying.'

'Yes, he was,' said Peter, emphatically. 'I've been working on the family tree.'

'What was his name?' said Lorna, suddenly excited at the thought of visiting old churchyards and discovering the graves of forgotten ancestors.

'Schmidt,' said Peter. 'Carl Schmidt.'

'Oh,' said Lorna. 'That doesn't narrow it down much.'

'Not really. Bit of a needle in a haystack.'

'I think I'll probably just go to a museum or something.'

'Good idea.'

'Well, you be careful,' said Gran. 'And keep washing your hands, for goodness' sake.'

They said goodbye to Lorna and Gran went into the kitchen to make tea, the third pot of the visit already. Peter followed her and stood by the kitchen window while she busied herself with the mugs and the teabags. He looked out over the garden: the flower beds he had been told off for trampling on as a boy; the sloping rect-angle of lawn down which he used to toboggan whenever the snow had grudgingly consented to fall; the spreading sumac tree with whose skeletal branches and lime-green leaves he had grown so familiar throughout long afternoons of reading or daydreaming: an entire, miniature landscape he had known intimately since he was ten years old and which had barely changed at all in the succeeding forty-nine years. The family had moved here in 1971. Before that they had lived a few miles away, in Bournville, where his mother had been born and had spent her own childhood. She would never leave this house now, he was sure of that, even though it was far too big for her. 'I shall die here,' she had started to say, apparently think-ing that this event was more and more imminent. Close to her heart, an aortic aneurysm was growing. Little by little, millimetre by milli-metre, every year. It was inoperable, her specialist had told her.

'Will it burst?' she had asked him.

'Maybe,' he had said. 'In a year's time, or two years, or five, or ten. You might be lucky.'

'And what happens when it bursts?' she had asked.

'That,' he had told her, 'will be what we call a *lethal event*.'

Ever since then, she had referred to the aneurysm as her 'ticking timebomb'. There was nothing to be done about it, except to carry on with life, curse the fact that it prevented her from driving a car any more, and hope for the best. Or hope that something else car-ried you away first, maybe, because at her age, something was going to get you, wasn't it? Sooner rather than later. She had never thought about the future much, any more than she liked to dwell on the past: she lived life in the moment, a strategy that had served her well enough for most of a century.

Peter found it frustrating, all the same, this tendency of his mother to live only for the present. Recently he had fallen prey to an obsession with family history, something that had begun with the death of his father and gathered momentum after his partner had left him and he found himself living alone with too much time on his hands. He had been searching archives online and sifting through the paperwork in his mother's house whenever he visited, but the resource he really wanted to tap was her own memory, and that was proving to be hard work. Not because her memory was fading, but because the past was a subject which appeared to hold no interest for her. Any droplets of information he could extract were offered grudgingly, and yet she was the last survivor, now, of her generation, the only one living who could recall family stories going back to the 1950s and 40s. What could she tell him, for instance, of the forgotten Carl Schmidt, her late husband's grandfather, who had come to Birmingham in mysterious circumstances in the 1890s, and had lived there through two world wars – wars in which the main aggressor was his native country? What had his position been? What kind of man was he?

'Oh, I don't remember much about him,' she said. 'I was very young. He seemed very severe and frightening. I was scared to death of him.'

Sitting in an armchair by the bay window, with Charlie on her lap purring in his patch of sunlight, she reached across to pick up the *Daily Telegraph* which was folded open at the Quick Crossword.

'Come on,' she said. 'Seven across, "Fashionable" – six letters, beginning with T.'

This was a flagrant attempt to change the subject, and Peter wasn't having it.

'You must remember something,' he said.

' "Trendy",' said Gran, and pencilled it in.

'I mean – when was the first time you met him?'

She sighed, knowing that she would get no peace out of Peter when he was in the mood to press her like this.

'Well, I can remember *that*, of course.'

'When was it?'

'At the end of the war.'

'So, around 1944, 1945?'

'Oh no, I mean the very end.' She took a cautious sip of her tea, which was still too hot. 'Right when it was all over,' she said. 'VE Day, and all that caper.'

ONE

VE Day

8th May 1945

I.

The air did not smell of chocolate, but chocolate was in the air. Nobody needed to put a name on the factory that stood at the heart of the village. They simply called it 'the Works'. And inside this factory, they made chocolate. They had been making chocolate there for more than sixty years. John Cadbury had opened his first shop in the centre of Birmingham back in 1824, selling ground cocoa beans for hot drinking chocolate: a devout Quaker, like his brothers, he saw the drink not only as a nutritious component of breakfast, but as a healthy substitute for alcohol later in the day. The business had grown steadily, the workforce had expanded, bigger premises had been acquired and then, in 1879, his sons decided to move production out of Birmingham altogether. The area they chose largely consisted, at the time, of sloping meadowland. Their vision: industry and nature existing in harmony, symbiotic, co-dependent. At first the factory was small. A one-storey, red-bricked building, flooded with light on three sides by generous windows that allowed views onto the green spaces all around. Next to the factory were placed sports fields, gardens and a children's playground. From here, the city centre seemed remote. This place called itself a village and it felt like a village. Workers had to travel from miles around, arriving at the railway station that in those days was still known as Stirchley Street. This arrangement could not continue for long, given that by the end of the nineteenth century the number of people employed at the Works had risen from two hundred to more than two and a half thousand. In 1895 the company acquired more of the land surrounding the factory buildings, and soon the workers could enjoy further recreation grounds and a cricket pitch. But the Cadbury family's ambitions went beyond that. They imagined houses: affordable houses, well-built houses, houses with deep gardens where trees could flourish and fruit and vegetables could be grown. Quakerism, as before, was at the heart of their project, and their goal was 'the amelioration of the conditions of the working-class and labouring population in and around Birmingham by the provision of improved dwellings, with gardens and opened spaces to be enjoyed therewith'. Whenever it was possible, they bought up more and more pockets of land in this swathe of countryside to the south of Birmingham, determined that less visionary, more profit-hungry developers should not get their hands on them. And in this way the village grew, reaching outwards, extending, putting out shoots, blossoming in plant-like formations until it covered hundreds of acres and consisted of more than two thousand houses, many but not all of them occupied by Cadbury workers, and although it was soon surrounded and hemmed in on all sides by other, more ordinary suburbs, by Stirchley and Cotteridge and Small Heath and King's Heath and King's Norton and West Heath and Northfield and Weoley Castle and Selly Oak, still this village never lost its character. At its hub lay the village green. Close to the village green stood the junior school with its clock tower housing the famous carillon. Surrounding the school were Woodbrooke Road, Thorn Road and Linden Road, throughways which, however much traffic would fill them in the years to come, somehow always kept their sense of calm, a pastoral memory of shade and leafiness that was embedded in their very names.

What should it be called, this special place? You might have thought, for the people who named it, that with its almshouses and playing fields, its miniature boating lake and white-flannelled crick-eters, the village was built as an archetype – a parody, almost – of a certain notion of Englishness. The little stream which wound through its very centre was called the Bourn, and many expected that Bournbrook would be the chosen name. But this was a village founded on enterprise, and that enterprise was to sell chocolate, and even in the hearts of the Cadburys, these pioneers of British chocolate manufacture, there lurked a residual sense of the inferior-ity of the native product, compared to its Continental rivals. Was there not something quintessentially, intrinsically European about the finest chocolate? The beans themselves had always come from the far corners of the Empire, of course – nothing unBritish about that – but the means of turning them into edible chocolate had been invented by a Dutchman, and it was a truth universally acknowledged – if for ever unspoken – that it was the French, and the Belgians, and the Swiss, who had since brought the making of chocolate to a pitch of near-perfection. If Cadbury's chocolate was ever truly to compete on this field, it would have to be branded in such a way that it trailed in its wake an overtone of European refinement, Continental sophistication.

So Bournbrook, they decided, would not quite do. A variation was chosen. Bournville. The name of a village not just founded upon, and devoted to, but actually dreamed into being by chocolate.

2.

By Monday morning, 7th May, there was still no definite news. The war was over, it seemed, but the peace had not yet begun. People were getting restless, and impatient for an announcement. Were they expected to keep going into work? When would they be allowed to celebrate? After almost six years of sacrifice and deprivation, surely it wasn't asking too much to have a few sing-songs and bonfires, and for the pubs to stay open late? Chatting over the fence, Samuel's next-door neighbour Mr Farthing said it was a bloody disgrace, pardon his French, and Sam agreed and said the government was asking for trouble if it didn't allow them all to let their hair down and have a good time for a day or two. People would remember it when the election came around.

Doll had plenty of views about politics, but she was never asked to take part in conversations like this. While her husband and Mr Farthing were putting the world to rights over the back fence, she checked the time on the grandfather clock in the hallway and went to fetch her broom from the cupboard under the stairs. She was a creature of habit. At a quarter to eleven every weekday she always went out to sweep the front step, and had a very specific reason for doing so: because it was at this hour that the children at the school across the road took their morning break. She liked to get outside just before it started, so that first of all she had a few minutes to savour the habitual, resonant silence of Bournville at that time of the morning. Then she would hear the ringing of the teacher's handbell, and immediately afterwards, it would begin: the gradually rising babble of high-pitched voices, muffled and indistinct at first, then suddenly full-throated as the main doors of the school were thrown open and eighty-seven children thundered out into the playground. Doll loved the silence that blanketed her village for much of the day, but she loved the sound of the next fifteen minutes even more. She loved the sound of the children calling out each other's names, the shrill cries of over-excitement, the chanting of nursery rhymes and taunting songs and skipping games. Not that any of these elements could be heard distinctly, or separated one from the other: everything merged into one chorus, a lovely, chaotic medley of infantile voices (even though Doll also knew – and this added considerably to the pleasure of her listening – that her own daughter's voice was somewhere in there as well, even if she couldn't make it out). Standing on the front doorstep with her broom in hand, listening to the distant sound of children's voices, Doll felt that she was at once inhabiting the past, present and future: it reminded her of her own childhood, her own schooldays, more than thirty years ago, the little church primary school in Wellington, Shropshire, an ancient but vivid memory, but it also reminded her that these shouting and singing children would be the ones carrying the next few years on their shoulders, rebuilding the country after its six-year battering, laying the memory of the war to rest. Past, present and future: that was what she heard, in the sound of the children's voices from the playground at mid-morning break. Like a murmurous river, like the incoming wash of the tide, a distant counterpoint to the swish, swish, swish of her broom on the step, a disembodied voice whispering in her ear, over and over, the mantra: *Everything changes, and everything stays the same.*

*

Being a creature of habit, Doll came out onto the front doorstep at a quarter to eleven the next morning as well, even though she knew that there would be no children to hear this time. The schools were closed today. And yet Bournville's silence seemed more profound than ever – even on this momentous morning. The announcement had finally come on the wireless yesterday evening: two days of celebrations. But anyone who expected to see drunken rioting or impromptu dances breaking out on the pavements of these reserved, tree-lined streets, with their rows and rows of placid, imperturbable houses, would be disappointed. The roads were if anything emptier than usual. The silence if anything was more absolute. It was not broken, in fact, until Doll had finished her sweeping and was about to go back inside: at which moment she heard footsteps and, turning to see who they belonged to, saw Mr Tucker from number 18 walking by. He was wearing his bowler hat as well as his thickest worsted overcoat, in spite of the heat.

'Morning, Mr T,' she said, keen to chat. 'What are you doing in your work clothes this morning? Didn't anybody tell you?'

'They did not,' he answered, in his prim, perpetually indignant voice. 'I took the tram into Town just as usual, and it was only when I reached the office that I found out anything was amiss. The front door locked and nothing to explain why. A note pinned to the door would have been *something*. The work of a few moments.'

'That's a shame. What a wasted journey for you. I suppose they thought that everybody would have heard about it on the wireless.'

'I do not own a wireless,' said Mr Tucker.

'Ah well. Now you've got two days off and can join in the fun with everyone else. There'll be a bonfire at Rowheath tonight.'

'I shall find something better to do,' said Mr Tucker. 'It will not be difficult.'

He was about to go on his way, but even he had noticed that there was something unusual in Doll's appearance, and could not help being curious about it.

'Mrs Clarke – what, may I ask, is that thing on your head?'

He was referring to a sheet of newspaper, folded into a rough triangular arrangement and festooned with red, white and blue stripes in crayon, which was perched on top of Doll's auburn hair.

'It's a hat,' she said. 'Mary's been making them all morning. Shall I ask her to make one for you?'

'Thank you, no,' he said. 'I appreciate that this is a time for celebration, but still – there is such a thing as dignity. Dignity at all times.'

He walked on, tripping briefly over the root of the lime tree that had started to bulge out from beneath the pavement. Doll did her best not to laugh as he tried to pretend it hadn't happened and continued on his way. She watched his receding figure, reflecting that he was a mystery all right, but no trouble to anyone, living alone at number 18 and never making any noise or mess, keeping his garden nice and tidy and all his window- and door-frames freshly painted every two or three years. She was lucky with her neighbours, really. Bournville was a high-class neighbourhood. People there were a cut above, and this was important to Doll, who had never felt any contradiction between her three main articles of faith: her Christianity, her socialism and her snobbery.

She saw Mr Tucker unlock his front door, turning to cast one final disapproving look at her paper hat before vanishing inside. His footsteps had made hardly any noise, but now that he had gone, that absolute and eerie silence seemed to descend again almost instantly.

What a strange atmosphere the village had today. Everyone seemed unsettled, half-excited and half-exhausted, as if torn between joy that the war was over at last and the freedom to admit, finally, what an ordeal it had been and to sink into a weary depression by way of response. Doll herself felt restless. She was looking forward to the bonfire at Rowheath tonight but apart from that, what were they supposed to do? How was the day supposed to pass? Sam had been told to take the day off work and was currently in the living room, absorbed in the pages of Mary's comic. Going back into the house, she peeped around the living-room door at him and was irritated, at first, to see him lounging in the armchair, oblivious to her presence, his gaze fixed happily on a cartoon strip intended for ten-year-olds, but her feelings softened when she saw the smile on his face, the gleam of childlike enjoyment in his eyes as he followed the latest exploits of Desperate Dan and his prodigious consumption of cow pies. It made her happy to think that he was still a kid at heart, and he deserved a bit of silly pleasure after everything he'd been through in the last few years, all those nights spent on the roof of the Works watching out for fires over the city as the planes flew in, when he should have been snug and warm at home with her. (Most nights, instead of her husband lying in bed beside her, nestled against the curves of her body as he should have been, it had been Mary, curled into a ball and clutching Little Ted to her slowly rising and falling chest, lulling Doll into a reluctant sleep with the regular ebb and flow of her guileless, sibilant breath.) So instead of reproaching him, she merely said, in a teasing way:

'Catching up on your reading, are you?'

Sam put the comic down with a guilty start.

'You told me you were going to start reading history books. And have another go at *War and Peace*.'

'I am. Just as soon as I have a moment.'

Doll picked up the comic.

' "Korky the Cat",' she read, and then recited the verse at the beginning of the front-page strip. ' "Korky played a hunting game, And what do you suppose? He won the best prize of the lot, By following his nose." ' She dropped the magazine back into her husband's lap. 'A grown man reading stuff like that!'

'Is that what you came in for? To have a go at me?'

'No, I came to see where Mary had got to. I thought she was making hats.'

'She finished. She's gone out into the garden.'

'Well, she can't sit out there all day. She's got things to do.'

'For heaven's sake, woman,' Sam cried out in exasperation, 'it's a special day today. Everyone's supposed to be celebrating.'

'Well, Mrs Barker's coming at half-past five, the same as any other Tuesday. And I haven't heard Mary practise for days.' She walked over to the piano, opened up the lid of the stool and took out some sheet music. 'Look at this! She hasn't touched her Beethoven.'

Reluctantly, Sam laid the comic aside and rose to his feet.

'I'll have a word with her,' he said. There was no point in letting Doll do it. She would only get the girl agitated, and then there'd be a shouting match.

Pipe in hand, he strolled out through the hallway, the kitchen and then the small glass-covered area that they grandly referred to as 'the verandah' before reaching the garden. Mary was sitting beneath the apple tree, on the ungainly wooden bench Sam had designed and built himself a few years back and which, amazingly, had not collapsed or disintegrated yet. He was not especially good with three-dimensional things; drawing was his talent.

He sat down next to his daughter and lit his pipe, then handed her the tobacco tin and allowed her to put it to her nose and inhale the thick, heady aroma. She loved the smell of his tobacco.

'Don't you feel like reading?' he asked, nodding towards the unopened book sitting on her lap.

'I'm having great thoughts,' said the child, solemnly.

'Ah.' Sam puffed on his pipe two or three times, trying to get it started. 'Well, those don't come along every day of the week. What sort of thoughts?'

'I was wondering what would be the best way to kill him. Whether he should be hanged from a lamp post, or burned alive.'

Sam glanced at his daughter curiously. She was not usually prey to these sorts of sadistic impulses.

'Old Adolf, you mean? I don't think you have to worry about that. He's done for. Probably dead already.'

'No, not Hitler,' said Mary, with a dismissive snort. 'I don't care about *him*. I mean Beethoven. I want him to suffer.'

'Beethoven's long gone,' her father said. 'Anyway, what's he done to you?'

'He wrote that piece. That stupid *Écossaise*. Last week I practised it and practised it and it still didn't sound right, and this week I haven't done any practice at all and Mrs Barker's going to be *furious*. And why do I have to see her today anyway? I thought today was supposed to be a holiday.'

'It is a holiday. That doesn't mean everything has to come to a standstill. Life has to go on, you know. We've learned that, if nothing else.'

'I bet none of my friends have got piano lessons today.'

'Well, they aren't as good at playing the piano as you are. It's a responsibility, you know. When you're playing to packed houses at the Royal Albert Hall in a few years' time, you'll be glad you did your practice.'

Mary scoffed. 'I'll never be good enough to play at the Royal Albert Hall.'

Sam patted her on the knee. 'Just run inside and do a few minutes, will you? Then your mother will be happy and we can all have a quiet life.'

Mary stood up with a heavy sigh and trooped off. Samuel stayed on the bench, continuing to enjoy his pipe in the peace and quiet and then, a few minutes later, being entertained by the sound of his daughter and Beethoven engaged in mortal combat; but before long Doll appeared at the entrance to the verandah and started chivvying him again. This time it was the garden that required his attention, apparently, and under his wife's unforgiving gaze he was obliged to spend most of the next hour on his hands and knees, thinning seedlings, sowing cabbages and earthing up potatoes. It was tiring work, which left him breathless, sweaty and with two large soil-coloured patches on the knees of his trousers. He was just about finished when Doll, having finally left him to it a few minutes earlier, reappeared from the verandah with an unexpected visitor: her brother-in-law.

'Hello, Jim.' Sam struggled to his feet, wiped his hand on his trousers and held it out. 'This is a turn-up for the books. Has Gwen let you off the leash today, then?'

'In a manner of speaking. She's got three of the neighbours round and they're in the kitchen drinking tea and squawking away like a clutch of chickens. So I thought I'd escape and see if I can tempt you to a pint somewhere.'

'A pint?'

'Yes.'

'Of beer, you mean?'

'Exactly.'

Sam was embarrassed. 'Well, look, Jim, we've got nothing in the house. Doll doesn't believe . . .'

'I didn't mean here. I'm hardly going to invite myself round to your house and demand a drink, am I? I thought we could go to the pub.'

Embarrassment was replaced by shock at the audacity of this suggestion. It was the middle of the day. Obviously, Sam knew that the pubs were open in the middle of the day, but he would never normally think of visiting one; not under his wife's nose, so to speak.

'You wouldn't mind, would you, Doll?' said Jim, anticipating the objection. 'I mean, normally I wouldn't dream of throwing temptation in your husband's path. But today of all days . . .'

She was not happy about it, that much was obvious. At the same time, she was not really in a position to object. Doll revered her brother-in-law, was perhaps a little afraid of him. He was her older sister's husband and this gave him a great deal of moral authority. If he thought it was appropriate to go to the pub at lunchtime today, that was that. She would simply have to defer. The only concession she could demand was that her husband should return within the hour.

But that was never very likely to happen: not least because the nearest pub, in any case, was more than a mile away. There were no pubs in Bournville itself. They were not part of the ethos on which the village had been built. Almost a century earlier the Cadbury family had, after all, conceived of drinking chocolate as an alternative to alcohol. Their whole business was founded on the principle of temperance. And when the Bournville Estate had been handed over to the Bournville Village Trust in 1900, the deed of transfer had expressly stated that 'the sale, distribution, or consumption of intoxicating liquor shall be entirely suppressed'. If Sam and her brother-in-law wanted a drink, they would have to earn it by walking.

*

And earn it they did. By the time that Samuel returned home, a good quantity of drink had been sold to him, then consumed by him, and was now pleasantly distributed around his nervous system. Doll was not impressed. Her chagrin was palpable, but she didn't say anything to him directly, since that was not how things worked in this household. Mary's mother and father rarely quarrelled. Disagreements would arise, a minimum of oblique words would be exchanged, long simmering silences would ensue. But voices were never raised above the aggrieved, petulant tone in which Doll now said:

'You're cutting it a bit fine. It's almost three o'clock.'

'Why, what happens at three o'clock?'

She clicked her tongue. 'What happens at three o'clock?' she repeated. 'How many pints have you had? It's Mr Churchill on the wireless, that's what happens. How could you forget *that*?'

The radio was already turned on, and was pouring out light music at a discreet volume. As Sam lowered himself wearily into his armchair, Doll turned up the dial and called her daughter down from upstairs. 'The Prime Minister's going to make a speech!' she shouted. 'You don't want to miss this!'

They sat and listened to Mr Churchill in the same sort of respectful silence they might observe for the King or for the Reverend Chapman's weekly sermon. Mary found it very dull, and hard to concentrate on. For the first few minutes he seemed to be doing nothing but reciting the names of foreign generals and politicians and talking about the signing of treaties and agreements which also had foreign-sounding names. She noticed that her father's eyelids were starting to droop as the Prime Minister droned on. But then it started to get more dramatic: Churchill announced that '*Hostilities will end officially at one minute after midnight tonight.*' He reminded everyone that some of the Germans were still fighting the Russian troops but said that '*this should not prevent us from celebrating today and tomorrow as Victory in Europe days. Today, perhaps,*' he went on, '*we shall think mostly of ourselves. Tomorrow we shall pay a particular tribute to our Russian comrades, whose prowess in the field has been one of the grand contributions to the general victory.*'

When she heard this, Doll nodded sagely and said to her husband: 'That's true, isn't it? We would never have won if it wasn't for the Russians.' But Sam, under the unaccustomed influence of three pints of lunchtime beer, had fallen asleep and was snoring gently with his head thrown back and his mouth half-open. Doll shook her head, incredulous. For a moment it looked as if she was considering waking him up by kicking the soles of his outstretched feet but she thought better of it, and left him to doze.

'*The German war,*' the Prime Minister continued, '*is therefore at an end. After years of intense preparation, Germany hurled herself on Poland at the beginning of September 1939; and, in pursuance of our guarantee to Poland and in agreement with the French Republic, Great Britain, the*

British Empire and Commonwealth of Nations, declared war upon this foul aggression. After gallant France had been struck down we, from this island and from our united Empire, maintained the struggle single-handed for a whole year until we were joined by the military might of Soviet Russia, and later by the overwhelming power and resources of the United States of America. Finally almost the whole world was combined against the evil-doers, who are now prostrate before us. Our gratitude to our splendid Allies goes forth from all our hearts in this island and throughout the British Empire.'

Doll was pursing her lips and nodding her agreement again, while Mary thought about the word 'island' that Churchill kept using. She had never really thought of her country as an island before. When she heard the word it made her think of the book Auntie Gwen and Uncle Jim had bought for her last Christmas. It was called *The Island of Adventure* and her mother had been cross because she thought her daughter was too old to be reading Enid Blyton: now that she was starting big school in September she was supposed to be reading Shakespeare and Dickens and people like that. But she'd read the book anyway and really enjoyed it. It was about four children staying for the holidays with their aunt and uncle who lived in a clifftop house by the sea, near to a sinister island called the Isle of Gloom which was nearly always shrouded in mist. There were lots of mysterious things going on there which were finally revealed to be the work of a criminal gang, although the real villain turned out to be the children's servant, a Black man called Jo-Jo. Anyway, it had been a thrilling book and ever since then the word 'island' had always made her think of mystery and adventure. It was nice to be reminded that she actually lived on an island. It made her feel special.

The Prime Minister was close to the end of his speech. He concluded:

'We may allow ourselves a brief period of rejoicing; but let us not forget for a moment the toil and efforts that lie ahead. Japan, with all her treachery and greed, remains unsubdued. The injury she has inflicted on Great Britain, the United States, and other countries, and her detestable cruelties, call for justice and retribution. We must now devote all our strength *and resources to the completion of our task, both at home and abroad. Advance, Britannia! Long live the cause of freedom! God save the King!'*

These last three phrases seemed calculated to provoke an enormous cheer, but in that quiet, undemonstrative living room in Birch Road, Bournville, they met with a more subdued response. Doll nodded her agreement, Mary felt relieved that the speech was over, and Samuel had slept through nearly all of it. With one final recriminatory glance in his direction Doll rose to her feet and said, 'When your father wakes up, make him some coffee, will you? I've got work to do.' She padded upstairs and went into the back bedroom to start taking down the blackout curtains.

Mary stayed where she was, listening to the wireless. After the broadcast from Downing Street was over there was a programme called *Bells and Victory Celebrations*. There were reports from lots of different cities, all sounding remarkably similar: crowds cheering, church bells ringing out, snatches of song ranging from 'Roll Out the Barrel' to the Hallelujah Chorus. One of the reports came from the centre of Birmingham, only a few miles away, but as far as Mary was concerned it might as well have been coming from the other side of the world: the streets of Bournville were still quiet and empty and apart from the radio broadcast the loudest noise in their house was her father's snoring.

Before the programme was over, her mother called to her from upstairs. She wanted Mary to climb up into the attic and store away the blackout material she had now taken down from every window in the house. Getting into the attic involved pulling down the foldaway ladder that Sam had constructed, and which Doll did not trust to bear her own weight, or indeed that of any adult. Mary accepted the task willingly as she always enjoyed exploring the attic. It would even give her the opportunity to check on something while she was up there. Up in the attic, in the little space between the water tank and the sloping roof of the house, she kept a little box in which she had stored what she called her 'treasures'. These included her pocket diaries for 1943 and 1944, the four-leaf clover she had found in a meadow on her visit to Warden Farm (her Uncle Owen and Aunt Ivy's farm in Shropshire), a piece of shrapnel Tommy Hunter had salvaged from his front garden and traded her for a bag of liquorice allsorts, and a signed photograph of John Mills, the famous actor who had graced Bournville with his presence one magical day three summers ago, when he had come on a morale-boosting visit to the Works. After struggling up the ladder with the blackout material folded away in a cardboard box, Mary spent a happy few minutes in the gloom examining these trophies and wondering what she could add to them, when a rap on the front doorknocker, and the sound of her dreaded piano teacher's voice, reminded her that the day still held one terror in store for her. Reluctantly, she clambered back downstairs to confront her nemesis.

Mrs Barker, her piano teacher, had a lean and angular face which matched her clipped, astringent manner of speaking. Her voice was a harsh monotone which suggested anything other than a musical temperament. Despite this, she had an uncompromising respect for the great composers which Mary's interpretation of Beethoven's *Écossaise* failed to satisfy. There were four especially problematic, rhythmically inflexible bars which she made her repeat again and again, trying to coax a degree of expressive *rubato* out of her, and as poor Mary was pounding her way through them for the seventh or eighth time, she was surprised when she glanced out of the front window to see her father leaving the house *again*: this time in the company of a man she didn't recognize. They walked down the front garden path and out into the street together. Then they were gone. What could it mean?

When the piano lesson was over, Mrs Barker, after some severe commentary on Mary's performance, went into the kitchen to collect her payment. Mary followed. They found Doll bent over her most enormous saucepan, stirring furiously, her brow drawn into complex furrows of rage and disappointment. When she saw Mrs Barker she did her best to pull herself together, although the smile she offered would have chilled anyone to the marrow.

'Ten shillings, as usual?' she asked.

'That's right. Thank you.'

'I don't suppose,' Doll said, handing over a dog-eared ten-shilling note, 'that you'd like to stay for dinner?'

Mrs Barker looked surprised, and Mary looked horrified. What was her mother thinking?

'Well . . .' Mrs Barker appeared to hesitate, but they both suspected that the hesitation was performative. She had no family of her own, and most probably had been anticipating a solitary meal this evening.

'It's corned beef hash,' said Doll. 'Sam's favourite. I made it specially for him, but seemingly he won't be here to eat it.'

'He won't?' said Mrs Barker.

'He's gone to the pub,' said Doll. 'For the *second* time today.'

'I see. Well, in that case . . .' She drew an emphatic breath, as if she were about to take an irrevocable leap in the dark rather than simply accept a neighbourly invitation. 'How kind. I do like a bit of hash.'

'Good-oh. It won't be completely wasted then, after all the trouble I've taken. Mary, lay the table for three. The good cutlery, today. From the top drawer of the dresser.'

3.

Mary did not like eating with these heavy, silver-plated knives and forks, which only came out once or twice a year and gave everything they touched a bitter, metallic flavour. Nonetheless, the dinner was good: hot, savoury and satisfying. She thought it an awful shame that her father was missing it, and hoped that he wasn't feeling too hungry. But perhaps beer filled you up. Her mother and Mrs Barker had treated themselves to small yet unprecedented glasses of sherry before eating and had become positively chatty and familiar with each other. It seemed that her piano teacher was not quite the Gorgon Mary had taken her for, although her presence and conversation still gave the house a notably different atmosphere. If someone had asked her what her parents talked about over dinner, Mary would not have been able to answer, even though she ate with them every evening: she knew that words were exchanged between them, news imparted, sentiments expressed, but everything they said seemed so mundane that none of it managed to penetrate her consciousness, and she assumed that this was what all grown-up conversation was like. But Mrs Barker seemed to give the lie to this notion. She would say things like:

'Of course, this country will never be the same again after the war.'

'You don't think so?' Doll would answer, while her daughter registered, and marvelled at, the hinterland of judgement and worldliness conjured up by those two simple words 'of course'. 'But surely, that was the whole point of fighting – I mean, to preserve what we had.'

'Not just to preserve it. To improve it. To build upon it.'

Doll wasn't sure about this. 'I'm just glad that it's over,' she said, 'and our children are safe, and we can all sleep soundly in our beds again.'

'Am I right in thinking,' Mrs Barker said, spearing a cube of potato and popping it into her mouth, 'that you made a small contribution to the war effort yourself? You were employed at the Works for a while?'

'That's right,' said Doll. 'Just for a few months, a couple of years ago now. They were very short so they put out an appeal to the whole village. They'd turned over most of it to munitions by that stage. I was on the shop floor, helping to make bullets, pins for hand grenades, all sorts of things.'

'And how did you find it?'

'Oh, the job was very boring. And yet . . .'

'And yet?' Mrs Barker prompted. Her eyes gleamed expectantly.

'Well, I didn't mind it, I must say. Didn't mind it a bit.'

'You enjoyed spending time with the other women? The other girls?'

'Yes, there was that. But also, you know . . . It made a change. A break from routine. Of course, it was hard on Mary. She had to let herself in after school, make her own tea . . .'

'I didn't mind that,' Mary was quick to say. And it was true. The war had given rise to many episodes from which her memory shrank: her brief, unhappy evacuation to Gloucestershire was one of them; another, even more traumatic in its way, was a visit to the cinema in Selly Oak to see *Pinocchio*, a screening which was interrupted by an air raid, followed by a mass scramble for the exits, and a terrified run home beneath the drone of Dornier bombers overhead. Mary had had a horror of the film, and the story, ever since. But her mother's months working at the factory were not like that: Mary had not in the least minded those afternoons getting back from school to an empty house, retrieving the front-door key from beneath the flowerpot in the garden, stepping into its embracing silence. She had done her homework unsupervised, played whatever she chose to play on the piano, listened to the wireless as much as she wanted, spread jam as thickly as she could on her slices of white floury bread. It had been heaven.

'Well, there you are,' said Mrs Barker. 'Children are capable of being much more independent than we allow them to be.'

'Yes, but all those changes in the factory were temporary.

Everything will go back to how it was before, now. Back to making chocolate again.'

'Naturally. And they will still need skilled, intelligent workers. You could always find work there if you wanted to.'

Doll pursed her lips. 'I'm not sure how Sam would feel about that . . .'

'What could be nicer than the two of you walking to work together in the morning, hand in hand? And back again at the end of the day.'

Put like that, it was an appealing image, certainly. But Doll still felt that these tempting suggestions had little basis in reality.

'But someone has to look after the house. It's a lot of work, you know, keeping it looking like this.'

'I don't doubt it for a moment. But if you were earning a wage, couldn't you use some of the money to pay a cleaner? Perhaps Samuel himself could even help you with some of the heavier tasks, at weekends.'

At this, Doll could not stop herself from laughing. What had seemed a practical proposal for a moment had suddenly spiralled into pure fantasy.

'Sam! I hardly think so. He never does a thing about the house. Never has, never will. Only today he spent an hour sowing vegetables and then had to have a lie-down for most of the afternoon.'

'I thought that was because of the beer,' said Mary.

Doll glowered as she poured herself more water. 'Well, that didn't help.'

'I simply think,' said Mrs Barker, 'that you might give some thought to rejoining the workforce now that the war is over. I know that many of my friends – married women, all of them – are thinking about it. You might find that it adds an extra layer of satisfaction to your life. As for Mr Clarke . . .' She smiled indulgently. 'Don't be too harsh on him today. This is a unique occasion, Mrs Clarke. A real red-letter day. I think the wives of Britain can perhaps let their husbands off the leash for a few hours.'

'Who *was* that man, anyway?' Mary asked, before her mother could respond to this.

'What man?'

'The one he went to the pub with just now – the second time.'

'That was Mr Lamb,' said Doll. 'Frank Lamb. One of your father's friends from work.'

'Ah! Funnily enough I know the Lambs,' said Mrs Barker. 'They live on the Longbridge Estate, don't they? Next door to one of my sisters, as it happens. Are they close friends of yours?'

'Not really. Frank's quite pally with Sam at work. They play snooker together, and all that caper.'

'A nice couple,' said Mrs Barker. 'Poor Mrs Lamb, I'm afraid, has not always found the going very easy in the last few years.' Neither Doll nor Mary seemed to understand what she meant, so she added: 'She's half-German, you know. On her father's side. It's made things rather difficult with her neighbours.'

'I didn't know that,' said Doll. 'How very unfair. She can't help it, can she, if she's got a German father?'

'Exactly. But not everyone's as understanding as you are, Mrs Clarke.'

A substantial lull in the conversation followed this compliment. Then Mrs Barker looked at her wristwatch and said:

'Well, this has been a most unexpected treat, but I must be getting on. It's almost time for church.'

'Church?' said Doll, bewildered. 'On a Tuesday?'

'Yes. The Reverend Chapman is taking a special service. Had you not heard about it?'

'No, nobody told me.'

'Perhaps you'd like to come?'

'Of course,' said Doll, rising eagerly to her feet. She never missed an opportunity to go to church. She loved it in the same way that other women loved going to the pictures. 'Mary, get your hat and coat on.'

'Do I have to come too?' Mary said, her heart sinking at the very thought. This was a dreadful turn of events. In her desperation she made a reckless offer: 'Wouldn't you like me to stay at home and do the dishes?'

'They can wait,' said Doll. 'You can do them when we get

back. There should just about be time before the King's speech at nine.'

And then they quickly cleared the table together, pulled their coats on and left the house in an orchestrated flurry, Doll almost forgetting to lock the front door behind her in her haste, Mary lagging behind the grown-ups as they strode ahead along Birch Road, so eager were they both to give thanks to the God who had finally delivered them from the German evil.

4.

By five minutes to nine, the atmosphere in the Great Stone was getting pretty rowdy. In the lounge bar, Albert, the septuagenarian pianist, had exhausted his repertoire some time ago and now just seemed to be banging out 'Roll Out the Barrel' over and over again, but nobody minded: there was something about this song that people never appeared to tire of, or perhaps it was just that everyone was so drunk by now that they were singing any tune and any words that happened to come into their heads, no matter what he was playing. Meanwhile the centre of the public bar had been cleared of chairs and tables and a form of dancing was going on: someone had installed a portable gramophone and about two dozen patrons were jitterbugging enthusiastically, although they had to stop for a while when the two oldest dancers got tangled up in the red, white and blue bunting that had fallen loose of its moorings and was hanging perilously low over the dance floor. This caused one of them – the husband – to miss his footing and fall over, creating a domino effect which resulted in seven or eight dancers ending up on the floor in a shrieking tangle of arms and legs. The old man who had caused this collapse found himself pinioned beneath the body of an attractive twenty-year-old woman, a situation which gave him no displeasure at all, until she removed herself with a friendly laugh and pulled him to his feet and within a few seconds they were jitterbugging again, this time with each other until the wife intervened and reclaimed possession of her husband. Watching this little marital comedy unfold, the thrashing dancers cheered and roared with approving laughter.

Far removed from this atmosphere of boisterous celebration, Frank and Samuel sat opposite each other in the private bar, a small, wood-panelled, smoke-filled enclave adjacent to the lounge but quite separate from it. In this cloistered space they could of course hear the competing musics of Albert's piano and the raucous gramophone, but both were considerably muffled and did not disturb their conversation much; or wouldn't have disturbed it, anyway, if it hadn't already run its course and petered out. Frank was a taciturn man at the best of times, and as for Sam, for the second time that day his eyelids were beginning to droop under the influence of the four or five pints he'd sunk since arriving. Fortunately (perhaps) the pub had run out of beer about forty-five minutes earlier, and rather than move on to shorts the two men had been nursing empty glasses ever since. Tobacco and cigarettes filled the void well enough.

Now, in any case, came a distraction. Albert stopped playing. The gramophone was silenced. Tom the landlord clapped his hands and called for quiet from his position behind the bar. His son and a friend lifted the heavy wireless set up onto the bar's polished wood surface and turned it on. The dancers stopped dancing and went back to their seats if they had them, a few people cried out 'The King! The King!' and conversation quickly dropped to almost nothing. There were just a few murmurs of complaint, from those who weren't royalists or just didn't want their drinking interrupted.

'I don't want to listen to the bloody radio,' one man grumbled, loudly.

'It's the King, mate!' another patron called back.

'The K-K-K-K-King!' someone echoed, in a cruel imitation of the monarch's famous stutter. There was plenty of laughter at this, as well as a few reproving tuts and a cry of 'Shame!'

The preceding broadcast was not finished yet, and chatter among the pub's customers began to gather momentum again as it dragged on. Within a minute or two conversation had been resumed at a volume loud enough to drown out the voice of the BBC announcer, and to obscure the King's first words as he at last began his thin, lugubrious oration.

'Sssssshhhhhh!' went the general whisper around the public bar, and the chattering died down at once: all except for a woman who continued to prattle on over her gin and lime, until a ferocious, bald-headed man at the next table shouted, 'Fanny, His Majesty's talking. Show some respect and shut your bloody cakehole for once.' There was a bit of laughter and cheering, and then the King had the floor of the Great Stone to himself.

'*Today we give thanks to Almighty God,*' he began, '*for a great . . . deliverance.*' (The pause before 'deliverance' was agonizing, and caused many of the listeners to wince in embarrassment and sympathy.) '*Speaking from our Empire's oldest capital city, war-battered but never for one moment daunted or dismayed – speaking from London, I ask you to join with me in that act of thanks . . .*' It seemed that he would never arrive at the second half of the word. 'Come on, mate, out with it,' somebody shouted, and it was as if the King had heard, because over the crackling airwaves his lips managed to form, finally, the two closing syllables, '*. . . giving.*' A sigh of relief went up around the bar.

After that, he seemed to rally, and his speech gathered in confidence.

'*Germany,*' he continued, '*the enemy who drove all Europe into war, has been finally overcome. In the Far East we have yet to deal with the Japanese, a determined and cruel foe. To this we shall turn with the utmost resolve and with all our resources. But at this hour, when the dreadful shadow of war has passed far from our hearths and homes in these islands, we may at last make one pause for thanksgiving and then turn our thoughts to the tasks all over the world which peace in Europe brings with it.*'

'That's where my David is – Japan,' a man muttered. 'God knows what those bastards are doing to him out there.' And then louder, so everyone could hear: 'Fucking Japs! They're worse than the fucking Krauts!'

'Oi! Keep it down, you!' Tom admonished from behind the bar. 'And watch your language when there are ladies present and the King's speaking.'

Meanwhile the toneless monologue rolled on, unstoppable now.

'*Let us think what it was that has upheld us through nearly six years of suffering and peril. The knowledge that everything was at stake: our freedom, our independence, our very existence as a people; but the knowledge also that in defending ourselves we were defending the liberties of the whole world; that our cause was the cause not of this nation only, not of this*

Empire and Commonwealth only, but of every land where freedom is cherished and law and liberty go hand in hand. In the darkest hours we knew that the enslaved and isolated peoples of Europe looked to us, their hopes were our hopes, their confidence confirmed our faith. We knew that, if we failed, the last remaining barrier against a worldwide tyranny would have fallen in ruins.'

' "Our cause",' Frank repeated, ' "was not the cause of this nation only." Now, that's well said, that is. My father-in-law would appreciate that. Don't you think? Wasn't that well said?'

But Sam had not really been listening. The King's voice irritated him – not the stammer, but the fey, pinched vowels of the English upper classes, which sounded to him like a foreign language. Try as he might, he could never see why everybody (including his wife, who was a Labour voter like him) showed such deference and obeisance to this uninspiring man and his pampered family.

'There is great comfort,' the King continued, *'in the thought that the years of darkness and danger in which the children of our country have grown up are over and, please God, for ever. We shall have failed and the blood of our dearest will have flowed in vain if the victory which they died to win does not lead to a lasting peace, founded on justice and goodwill.'*

'Hear, hear!' Sam cried, feeling nonetheless that he should show some approval out of politeness to his royalist friend, and deciding that the words 'peace', 'justice' and 'goodwill' were easy enough to concur with, without compromising his principles.

'To that, then, let us turn our thoughts on this day of just triumph and proud sorrow, and then take up our work again, resolved as a people to do nothing unworthy of those who died for us, and to make the world such a world as they would have desired for their children and for ours. This is the task to which now honour binds us. In the hour of danger we humbly committed our cause into the hand of God and He has been our strength and shield. Let us thank Him for His mercies and in this hour of victory commit ourselves and our new task to the guidance of that same strong hand.'

Now there was a long pause, the longest yet, and it gradually dawned on the silent listeners that the speech was over.

'Blimey – he made it,' someone said.

'Good for him!' another of the customers shouted, and then

there was a loud scraping of chairs as everyone rose to their feet when the national anthem started up on the wireless. They sang the turgid melody with fervour and feeling, and most of them had tears welling up in their eyes before they reached the end of the first verse. At which point, Sam took a worried glance at his wristwatch, tapped Frank urgently on the arm and said: 'I told Doll I'd meet her at a quarter past. It's nearly that now. I aren't half going to catch it.'

'I'll come with you,' said Frank. 'My lot are going to Rowheath as well.'

They quickly slipped on their coats and began pushing their way through the crowd in the public bar. The singing was ragged now, and a bit tuneless, but no less deeply felt. Most people did not know the words to the later verses, so they were either improvising or just singing the first verse over and over again. Sam wondered how long everyone would stay in the pub now that the speech was finished and there was no more beer. The bonfire at Rowheath might prove a more popular attraction. They were not the only ones leaving, he noticed.

5.

Refreshed and invigorated not just by the Reverend Chapman's words but by the mere experience of being inside the church for thirty minutes, Doll had a luminous glint in her eye when they reached home, which even the King's halting and soporific performance on the wireless was not enough to extinguish. After that, she and Mary pulled on their coats again, locked up the house and fell in with the crowds heading towards the bonfire. Sunshine had broken through in the late afternoon and they were now at the end of a warm, mellow evening with just the slightest tinge of blue still left in the sky. As they turned into Woodbrooke Road and then headed up the hill towards the playing fields, Mary could not help noticing that some of the streets had made far more effort to mark the occasion than her own. There was still Union Jack bunting hung between the trees in Thorn Road, and in the next street there were trestle tables and benches set out on the pavement, strewn with the remains of cake and sandwiches, and with groups of neighbours still sitting around, chatting, draining the last of their beer bottles and singing the occasional fragments of song. Why, she wondered, did her own street have to be so placid and reserved, why did it have to give off a perpetual air of superiority, of considering celebrations like this to be somehow beneath it? The other thing she noticed was the light spilling from the windows of all the houses. Few people seemed to have drawn their curtains yet, and after so many years of blackout – years stretching back as far as she could remember, back to before her sixth birthday – there was a delicious novelty in the warm glow of all these lights, coming from every direction, each one slightly different from the other in texture, brightness and intensity. And out on the playing fields there would be even more light, even more warmth. The bonfire and the fireworks. She clutched her mother's hand more tightly still as she savoured these moments of anticipation and a shiver of daughterly love ran through her.

Her father was waiting for them, as arranged, at the corner of Heath Road and Selly Oak Road. He was not alone. The man he'd gone to the pub with was there as well, along with another woman and a much older couple. Mary's mother and father didn't kiss or hug when they met. This was not their style at all. Instead Doll looked her husband up and down – noticed the slight heaviness of his eyelids, the almost imperceptible sway of his body – and, drawing her own conclusions about the state he was in, clicked her tongue disapprovingly and waited to be introduced to the strangers. Since Sam failed to cotton on to this, there followed a silence of many seconds before Frank held out his hand and said:

'Hello, Mrs Clarke. You haven't met my wife, Bertha, I don't think? And this –' he turned towards the more elderly couple – 'is Mr and Mrs Schmidt. Bertha's mother and father.'

'Charmed, I'm sure,' said Doll, and found herself almost curtseying, so imposing was the figure of the tall, grave-looking man who now shook her hand and bowed slightly in her direction. He was wearing a black homburg hat which he raised as he bowed, revealing a high forehead and a thin shock of whitish hair. He also sported an immaculately trimmed moustache, a pinstriped three-piece suit and a silver fob watch, the chain hanging from his waistcoat pocket in a perfect semicircle. Commanding as he was, however, it was his wife who drew everyone's eye. She was almost as tall as her husband, and twice as broad. Words like 'stout' and 'well-built' could not have done justice to her bulk, which was shrouded in a shapeless cashmere overcoat and topped off with a cloche hat, an emblem of coquettish femininity which didn't seem to suit her at all. She clasped her husband's arm like a cat with a helpless mouse in its clutches, and watched him with an intensity in which adoration was mixed with fierce possessiveness.

This group now headed through the gates onto the playing fields, and began easing their way through the crowd, trying to get closer to the bonfire which was burning brightly in the distance. Frank and his wife were on the lookout for their son, Geoffrey, who was supposed to be there somewhere. Mary hoped that he would be friendly, because she was starting to crave the company of other children, but when they finally caught up with him, she was disappointed: he seemed friendly, all right, but far too old for her to latch on to. Sixteen or seventeen at least. He was with a bunch of young men who seemed to be of his own age or even older, and to make matters worse, most of them seemed to have been drinking. In fact they had bottles of beer with them now, as well as a large whisky bottle they were passing between themselves. Geoffrey, it was true, seemed a shy and quiet young man, who looked embarrassed to be seen with these friends or acquaintances. Tall and gangly, with shoulders sloping at the angle of a milk bottle, he kept himself at a few paces' distance from them, torn, it seemed, between aloofness and the desire to be noticed and included. As for the group's ringleader, you could tell who that was because he made more noise than the others, spoke more often and more aggressively, and had a more brazen swagger: his name, Mary later discovered, was Neil Burcot. Within a few seconds of her taking up position next to this rowdy bunch, he was already jeering and catcalling at another new arrival.

'Blimey, lads,' he shouted above the noise of the crowd and the barrel organ, 'look at this! Look at "Kenneth"!' He pronounced the name slowly, with an affected posh accent. 'Look at what he's wearing! Hey, Kenny, what's the idea? Turning up for a fucking bonfire with a fancy piece of ribbon round your neck!'

'Hello, Neil,' the object of these comments replied, with measured politeness. 'I thought it was a special occasion and worth making an effort for. Watch your language, by the way. There are ladies and children here.'

There was clearly a history of deep enmity between these two, because Neil's immediate response to this rebuke was to march up to Kenneth, stare him in the face and then, putting his hand to the flamboyant, canary-yellow cravat the other young man was wearing, he flicked it contemptuously to one side and said: 'Giving away a bit too much about yourself there, Kenny. We always thought you were a nancy-boy. Now we know it.'

Kenneth ignored this, and went over to greet one of the other members of the group who (under Neil's baleful gaze) shook him warmly by the hand and said: 'Hello, Ken, you're back then?'

'That's right. Got back last week.'

'Tripoli, wasn't it?'

'For a while. Final posting was Rome.'

'Italy, eh? Bet you've seen some things. Got some stories to tell, I reckon?'

Kenneth smiled. 'I'll save them for my memoirs.'

Mary was taking all of this in, open-mouthed. She thought that this man must be extremely brave to have travelled to these far-flung places and fought for his country. He was also very handsome, and she *loved* his yellow cravat. It made him look indescribably dashing, and she hated this other man for being so rude about it.

'Nuts!' Frank now declared, apropos of nothing apparently. His wife, Bertha, looked at him in surprise, as did Doll and Sam. 'There's a man over there selling nuts,' he pointed out. 'Hot salty peanuts. I'll go and get a few bags. Who wants one?'

'Frank,' his father-in-law said, reaching into his trouser pocket for some change, 'I cannot allow you to pay for all of us. Please let me make a contribution.'

'Nonsense, Opa. A few nuts aren't going to break the bank.' And with that, he headed off on his errand.

For Mary, one feature of this exchange was more striking than any other: Mr Schmidt's accent. She remembered, of course, that he was German, but for some reason she had not expected him to *sound* German. Or at least not quite so heavily and unmistakably German. And she was not the only person to have noticed: Neil Burcot looked sharply over at Mr Schmidt as soon as he heard him speak.

'Do you know those people, dear?' Bertha Lamb asked her son, as this group of undesirables continued joshing, talking, drinking and arguing, behaviour which did not quite qualify as antisocial, but seemed to be constantly on the verge of it. 'Surely they didn't go to the grammar school?'

'Some of them did,' said Geoffrey. '*He*' (pointing at Neil) 'was three years ahead of me, till he was expelled.'

'I see.'

'Just high spirits,' said Mr Schmidt, offering Neil a smile which was noticed but not returned. 'Isn't that what today is all about?'

His daughter looked doubtful. His wife gave his arm a squeeze which was strong enough to make him wince.

Just then a ripple spread through the crowd, a slow crescendo of wonderment as the first of the fireworks was set off and a few seconds later the blue-black sky exploded with noise and light. A medley of gasps and sighs rose into the air. Mary looked up at her father as more fireworks went off and thought she saw something strange in his eyes, a kind of double perspective, as if he was watching the display intently but remembering something else at the same time. Many years later, as an old woman, she would still have a clear memory of his unreadable face at that moment and she would wonder if he had been thinking of those other night skies he had witnessed during the previous few years, from his vantage point on the roof of the Works, the blackness being criss-crossed by searchlights, the drone of the aircraft overhead, the city rocked by the sounds of shelling and anti-aircraft fire, the battered townscape dotted with fires as far as the eye could see. And then these other benign explosions and showers of light and trails of heat and fire that in some ways seemed to be a festive parody of all that he must have witnessed. It had been hard to tell, in the years after the war, whether his mind ever dwelt on those long nights, those air raids. He never spoke about them. But strangely, Mary would always remember the fleeting mystery of how her father's beloved, familiar face looked that night far more vividly than what happened next, even though what happened next was altogether more dramatic.

The trouble began when another group of young men arrived, breaking through the crowd and approaching close to the bonfire. They appeared to be friends of Neil's because they shouted greetings to him as they passed. One of them was pushing a wheelbarrow in which was placed a crude effigy, a rough approximation of a human form, a grotesque torso sitting in a semi-upright position. The effigy bore no real resemblance to any human being alive or dead but it was immediately identifiable, because the ragged jacket thrown over its upper half sported a swastika armband, and in the midst of the nightmarish ovoid of its face, beneath a nose represented by a clothes peg, was a little rectangular moustache made from the bristles of some discarded broom or brush. As soon as people realized who it was meant to represent, the figure attracted an outbreak of jeers and catcalls which reached a peak as the wheelbarrow was pushed to its destination and its contents hurled onto the fire. The German Chancellor instantly went up in flames and the crowd – especially that part of it close to Mary and her family – went wild. Cries of 'Burn him! Burn the fucker!' rang out, causing Mr Schmidt to raise his voice and say: 'Gentleman, really! A little bit of decency in front of these young women, if you can!'

Perhaps it was the invocation of 'decency' that triggered him above all, but Neil lost his rag at this point. He rushed towards Mr Schmidt, brandishing a whisky bottle which was by now empty.

'Carl, watch out!' his wife shouted, but this was a mistake too.

'What did you say his name was?' Neil hissed. 'Carl's a German name, isn't it? Is your husband German?' There was no response from the elderly couple. 'Well – are you a Kraut or aren't you?'

'I am a naturalized English citizen,' Mr Schmidt began. 'I have been living in this country for more than—'

'You're a fucking Kraut is what you are,' Neil retorted. 'You've got some nerve turning up here tonight, when for the last five years you've been bombing the shit out of us and killing our lads abroad.'

'I have nothing to do with that,' Mr Schmidt insisted, 'I have—' But he was not allowed to say any more.

Mary could remember almost nothing of what happened after that. The smashing of glass, the sudden about-turn and disappearance of Neil as he and his friends ran off, and then Mr Schmidt laid out on the ground, blood leaking from a wound on his forehead, a wound which was staunched by Kenneth, who pulled the yellow cravat from around his neck and fashioned it into an impromptu bandage. After that she forgot everything. She had no memory of how she got home, no memory of how the cravat itself had come home with her, no memory at all of picking it off the ground which she must have done in the midst of the chaos and confusion. But there it was the next morning in the pocket of her dress. A strip of glossy yellow cloth, now mottled with dried bloodstains which formed an abstract decorative pattern down its whole length.

The wound, it transpired, had not been a serious one. Mr Schmidt was shocked rather than injured. His family could not persuade him to press charges. He did not want any fuss, he wanted to put the whole episode behind him. They tried hard to change his mind, but it was no use. He was a stubborn old man. Doll and Samuel, hearing the news from Frank a few days later, shrugged their shoulders and said that it was a crying shame, because thugs like that should be punished, but it was his own choice. After that the shape of the story gradually shifted and blurred as it took its place in the shared mythology of Frank, Bertha and the rest of their family, settling into some vague authorized version in which it was Geoffrey who had come to the aid of his grandfather. Only Mary recalled it differently – but who would ever believe an imaginative young girl? – cherishing her memory of Kenneth's heroism and gallantry, the proof of which she kept in her possession in the form of his bloodstained cravat, which she stowed away in her box in the attic along with her four-leaf clover, her signed photograph of John Mills, and all her other childish treasures.

TWO

The Coronation of Queen Elizabeth II

2nd June 1953

I.

After the engineer had left, Sam called Doll into the living room, and for a minute or two they just stood there, hand in hand, gazing in silent pride at the amazing new object in the corner. It was simple in design, consisting of two halves: in the upper half, a 17-inch screen, pale green-grey and slightly bulbous; in the lower half, a speaker cabinet, with two Bakelite dials mounted in the grille, one for volume, one for tuning. Between the two halves ran a narrow strip of black plastic, at its centre a small golden capital 'F' which announced that the set was manufactured by Ferranti of Manchester. This stylish device was all that they needed, apparently, to gain entry into the magical kingdom to which more and more British people had been flocking in the last few years: the community of television viewers. Now they, too, would be able to enjoy old-time music hall from the Stoll Theatre in London, watch the fashionable dance troupe the Television Toppers at 'some of London's most famous rendezvous', see the racing from Kempton Park and the women's hockey from Wembley Stadium, take a tour round the *Historic Houses of England*, learn about *Poultry on the General Farm* and discover how cricket bats were made in *King Willow*. Doll could obtain 'practical help for the housewife' from Joan Gilbert in *About the Home* while Sam absorbed the political wisdom of the contributors to *In the News*, and together they could expand their general knowledge by watching the popular panel game *Animal, Vegetable, Mineral?* And during the many hours of the day when BBC television was not broadcasting at all, the set could be hidden, its rosewood doors closing discreetly over the screen and the speaker so that it looked for all the world like a perfectly respectable cocktail cabinet. Doll liked this feature more than anything else, and spent a few happy hours experimenting with different vases and flower arrangements to place on top of it. The final result, she thought, was most attractive. You wouldn't even know there was a television there at all. Unfortunately the same could not be said for the outside of their house, which was now disfigured by a huge and ugly aerial that horribly interrupted the clean lines of the roof and the gable. She pleaded with Sam to do something about it but he insisted that nothing could be changed: it had to be positioned in exactly that spot and at precisely that angle.

While Doll retreated to the kitchen in order to nurse this grievance in her usual brooding silence, Sam went outside to look at the offending object again from the perspective of the front garden. Personally, he couldn't see what his wife was so upset about. True, the aerial was highly visible, but it was also a thing of beauty and modernity. Its gleaming metal and sharp angles announced to the world: yes, we live in a gracious house, but we are also New Elizabethans, coasting into the 1950s on a wave of technological change. Why did she object to that? Three years earlier, in December 1949, an enormous new television transmitter had been erected on top of a hill near Sutton Coldfield, about ten miles away, and it had been considered such a newsworthy event, and such a scientific miracle, that people had made special trips to visit it, turning it into a family day out. He and Doll and Mary had been among them, and while it was true that Doll hadn't seemed especially thrilled at the prospect, or especially impressed when she saw the transmitter itself, still it had (in his recollection) been a memorable excursion. Sam had been disappointed to have missed the Festival of Britain. He would have liked to take his family down to London, to visit the South Bank, to explore the Dome of Discovery with all its many and varied displays of scientific endeavour, and of course to see the Skylon, the wonderful cigar-shaped sculpture supported on steel cables that made it appear to be floating above the Thames. Somehow he'd not been able to persuade Doll and Mary to make that trip – he'd had to make do with reading about these things in the newspaper – but Sutton Coldfield was a good deal closer and the transmitter was, in its way, just as impressive an object as he imagined the Skylon to be. And their new television aerial made him feel connected to the transmitter and connected, via the transmitter, to Broadcasting House in

London and suddenly Bournville no longer seemed to be cut off from the wider world. Sam had a strong sense of people being newly drawn together by these electromagnetic waves rippling out from the capital to every city, town and village in the country. So he would not take the aerial down from the roof, or change its position to make it less conspicuous. It was a force for progress, and a force for unity. It was a force for good.

2.

Geoffrey's courtship of Mary had begun in the autumn of 1951, when she was still at school. Every morning they would find themselves taking the same bus together, she on her way to school, he on his way to the university campus. At this time Geoffrey was twenty-two and Mary was seventeen. His behaviour towards her was gentlemanly and courteous: no touching or trying to get fresh with her or anything like that. They would mainly just talk, and even then they never talked about anything serious. Sport, mostly, because they were both mad about tennis. Mary had grown into a fine, athletic girl. Somehow she pulled off the difficult trick of having broad shoulders – a strong, muscular upper body in general – while maintaining an hourglass figure and a grace and delicacy in her movements that attracted the attention of plenty of other men besides Geoffrey. She was school captain at lacrosse, a stalwart of the school tennis team and had recently enrolled as a junior member at Weoley Hill tennis club. As soon as he learned this, Geoffrey joined too. They played together there two or three times a week, at weekends and in the evenings if it was light enough. Their games, as so often happens, reflected their characters: Geoffrey was slow and guarded; intelligent and resourceful in his placement of the ball but handicapped by his cautious temperament. Mary was the opposite: strong, fast, impulsive, always looking for the quickest and most efficient solution to a problem, never given to analysis or to looking back on her mistakes. In a way they complemented each other well: Geoffrey's hesitancy made up for Mary's lack of reflection. After the games they would drink lemonade or lime-and-soda in the members' room and make eager, light-hearted conversation. In the early days Geoffrey would try to talk to her about his studies but they both became aware that everything he told her was going over her head. Mary had a quick, intuitive grasp of her own limitations: she knew what she could understand, and she knew what she would never understand, and what she could never understand she didn't want to hear about. It was enough for her to know that Geoffrey was studying Classics, and was very clever, and was writing a thesis about Virgil, or perhaps Ovid – one or the other – and on the very rare occasions when he discussed the two-year trauma of his recent National Service, he claimed to have survived it by spending evenings at his barracks translating passages from *Oliver Twist* and *Nicholas Nickleby* into Latin.

The other members of the club became so used to seeing Mary and Geoffrey together that they all assumed they were a couple even before they themselves realized that that was what they'd become. And so it had been natural enough for one of the lady members, Jane Sanders, to approach them one day – a day in July 1952 – with a request for a game of mixed doubles. 'My brother's up from London for a few days,' she said, 'and I've got to find something to do with him, so I thought I'd bring him along for a game on Friday evening. Will you take us on? I think we'd be a pretty even match.'

'I wonder what her brother will be like,' Mary said, as she and Geoffrey cycled home afterwards. To her the phrase 'up from London' implied a terrific degree of sophistication.

'Kenneth? I know him a bit,' he answered. 'He was at school, a couple of years above me. I don't suppose you remember, but he was there on VE night. The time there was that kerfuffle with my grandfather.'

Mary – who would have chosen a stronger word than 'kerfuffle', personally – could not help feeling excited at the thought of meeting the hero of that evening again. At least, she thought of him as the hero. She had the haziest, most unreliable memory of that night – it was seven years ago, after all – and yet one of the things that bothered her was not being able to remember the role that Geoffrey himself had played in it. Of course it had been very crowded, there had been no shortage of people to offer Mr Schmidt assistance, or to pursue the culprits off the scene, but even so, it puzzled her that she couldn't remember Geoffrey getting involved at all. Perhaps he had just been too slow to react, as he often was on the tennis court. Still, his own grandfather . . . That was the strange thing about it.

When the time came for their match against Jane and her brother, they beat them comfortably, two sets to love. In fact it was Mary who did most of the heavy lifting: Geoffrey was off form – he seemed more sluggish than ever at returning the ball, and Kenneth proved rather too good at getting him running around the court – and their margin of victory owed a lot to Jane's repeated mistakes. Afterwards, since it was a warm evening, they ordered their drinks in paper cups and took them down to the edges of the Bourn, the little river that drifted along the club's northern boundary, its cloudy brown-green water offering a home to the occasional stickleback, as well as a restful spectacle for tennis players.

Kenneth made a point of sitting next to Mary and compliment-ing her on her game. 'That's quite a backhand you've got there, young lady.'

'Thank you. D'you get to play much in London?'

'I'd like to, but there never seems to be time.'

'Kenneth's awfully busy,' his sister boasted. 'He's taking the world of journalism by storm.'

'Writing up cake sales and stories of old ladies calling out the fire brigade because their kittens are stuck up trees,' he said, with heavy self-mockery.

'Not any longer.' To the others, Jane explained: 'He starts with the *Evening Standard* on Monday.'

'Congratulations,' said Mary; but Geoffrey's response was to ask, rather sourly: 'Why d'you want to go into a dirty business like jour-nalism, anyway?'

'I don't think it's dirty,' said Kenneth. 'Not at all. I think there are a lot of interesting things happening in this country at the moment – social changes and so on, after the war – and journalism has an important part to play in that. Explaining the issues to people. Keep-ing them informed.'

Geoffrey sniffed. 'Seems a very idealistic way of looking at it, to me.'

'That's because you're only interested in what happened two thousand years ago,' Mary said. 'Ancient Rome, and all that caper.'

Geoffrey might have been prepared to let the subject drop, but this remark stung him into further comment: 'Anyway, I don't think the country *is* changing very much,' he said. 'Straight after the war it did look as if there was a danger that might happen, but now that we've got the right sort of government again, things are back on track.'

'A danger?' said Kenneth. 'Is that how you'd describe what the Attlee government was doing? Setting up a National Health Service? A welfare state? You think those things are dangerous?'

'Oh, come on, boys,' Jane implored. 'Don't start falling out over politics. Aren't there better things to talk about, on a lovely evening like this? Do you know anything about model boats, Geoff?'

'Model boats? Not really, why?'

'Because my charming sister,' said Kenneth, 'has roped me into taking her lad to Valley Park tomorrow morning, before I go back to the smoke. He'll be expecting someone who knows what he's doing, and I don't have a clue.'

'As a good journalist you'll bluff your way through it, I'm sure,' said Geoffrey.

'Why were you being so sharp with him?' Mary asked later, as Geoffrey was walking her home. It was after nine and another long summer evening was drawing to a close. The leafy streets of Bournville were still bathed in pale greenish light.

Instead of answering, Geoffrey said musingly: 'Jane's done all right for herself, marrying Derek Sanders. Brought herself up a notch or two.'

'A notch or two?'

'Up the social scale. She and Kenneth aren't really from round here, you know. They grew up in Cotteridge, in a tiny little terrace. I saw it once. Proper little back-to-back, it was.'

Well, listen to you, Mary thought. You and your parents still live in a bungalow. And a wooden one at that. But all she said was: 'Do you think they're common, then?'

'No, but I should say they were lower middle rather than middle

middle like us,' said Geoffrey. And added: 'He'll lose that Brummie accent down in London soon enough, you wait.'

Mary couldn't see that it made any difference whether you were lower middle or middle middle or anything else. And she hadn't even noticed that Kenneth had an accent. Geoffrey was being a real pain in the you-know-what this evening. What had got into him?

Beside the gate to her front garden they stopped, and Geoffrey put down their tennis bags so that he could take both Mary's hands in his own. She didn't resist, but her heart wasn't in it tonight.

'I meant to say,' Geoffrey went on, 'that I'm going motoring tomorrow. My cousin Sheila's coming over with her new fiancé in the morning, and we're going out to the Malverns. Taking a picnic.'

'Oh?' said Mary.

'His name's Colin. Colin Trotter,' said Geoffrey, as if this was relevant. 'I think I'm supposed to be vetting him on behalf of the family.'

'Checking on his accent?' she asked, teasing, but with an edge.

He ignored this question. 'Would you like to come too? Make up a four. It would be so nice if you came. Nice for me, that is.'

Mary hesitated. She had no plans for tomorrow. On the other hand, she had formed an intention – an intention so vague it could hardly be called a plan. And she was quite angry with Geoffrey.

'I'm sorry, but I can't,' she said. A lie was required. She was not very good at this, but she dreamed one up quickly. 'I promised Mum I'd go shopping with her in Town. Make a whole day of it. Lunch at Rackhams, and so on.'

'Oh, well, that's a pity.' He sighed, said, 'Oh, well,' one more time, and then leaned in for his goodbye kiss. There was a moment of confusion, as he went for her mouth and she offered a cheek and somehow he ended up planting one on her ear. Really, after six months' courting, they should have been better at this.

'Goodnight,' Mary whispered, blushing, and went all the way to her parents' front door before she realized that she'd left her tennis bag on the pavement, and had to go back for it.

That summer of 1952 was blessed with flawless weather, and the next morning, too, had been gloriously warm and sunny. It was a

Saturday in early July, and by the time Mary had wandered around to the model boating lake in Valley Park (not on her usual walking route, of course, but why shouldn't she?) the sun was at its zenith and the deep blue of the sky was reflected in the placid waters. The playing field behind the lake, and the tall oak trees cordoning off the mysterious grounds of Woodbrooke alongside it, created a backdrop so pastoral-seeming that you could easily believe you were in the countryside, with only the noise of traffic from the nearby Bristol Road to spoil the illusion. But even the traffic was light this morning. Bournville seemed to have an inexpressibly calm, almost enchanted atmosphere. There were a few people sitting on benches beside the water, and three little boats out on the lake itself, one of them belonging to Kenneth and his nephew, who were watching it helplessly as it bobbed away in the centre, becalmed and quite out of their reach.

'Morning,' Kenneth said, looking pleased but not especially surprised to see her. 'We're having a crisis here. This is Timothy, by the way. I'm glad you came by. Timing could have been better, though.'

'How are you going to get it back?' Mary asked.

'We just have to wait for a bit of wind, I suppose. Doesn't seem to be much at the moment, though.'

Timothy, unconcerned by the situation, wandered off to look at the ducks, while Mary and Kenneth took their place on a bench in the sun.

'My dad used to bring me here,' Kenneth said, tilting his head to catch the warming light. 'Before the war. It hasn't changed. Hasn't changed a bit.'

'I do love it here,' said Mary. 'But I can't believe you miss this part of the world very much. There must be so much to do in London, compared to here.'

'True,' he said.

'When did you move there?'

'Just over a year ago. You're right, it did seem to be where everything was happening. The Festival was just starting. All the new buildings going up on the South Bank. Skylon, and the Pleasure Gardens. Lots of exciting things going on.'

'Makes this place seem a bit of a backwater, I should think.'

'Not really,' said Kenneth. 'More of an oasis, maybe. It's very . . . cloistered here, isn't it? The people who live here are pretty privileged, but I doubt if they see it that way. Like the Londoners who live in Hampstead. People who've been lucky in life don't really like to be reminded of it.'

'You think that I'm lucky?'

'Of course. You could have been born anywhere, to anyone. But you pitched up here. And very nice it is too.'

Just then Timothy came running up to alert his uncle to the progress of their boat. It had finally been blown out of the centre of the lake and was making headway towards the furthest edge. Kenneth took his nephew's hand and together they ran off to retrieve it. Mary was left, at first, feeling rather stung by his remarks – she did not feel that her family was remotely 'privileged', and didn't care for the word at all – but typically she shrugged the feeling off, refusing to analyse it, and lost herself instead in the spectacle of the two of them bending over the water as they rescued their yacht. She could tell that Kenneth was someone who liked children and knew how to interact with them, and this ranked highly on Mary's list of desirable qualities in a man. They launched the boat again and this time seemed to have done a better job setting it on its course, and now it made a straight line towards Mary, revealing itself, as it came into view, as a well-crafted miniature, its hull painted a deep glossy red and its sails billowing gently in the wind. Timothy's eyes were fixed on it, gleaming with the pride of ownership, as he followed it around the perimeter of the lake.

Satisfied with the way things were going, Kenneth rejoined Mary on the bench. For a while neither of them spoke. Then Mary said, casually:

'Is Dartford near London?'

'Dartford? Pretty near, yes. About half an hour by train, I should think. Why?'

'That's where I'm going in September. There's a college of physical education there.'

'Physical education? As in PE?'

'That's right.'

'So you're going to be a PE teacher? That makes sense. I'm sure you'll be a very good one. How long will you be there?'

'Three years. So I imagine I shall be coming in to London rather a lot.'

Kenneth was slow to take the hint: but he took it eventually.

'All right, then,' he said, reaching into his pocket, 'in that case we should really meet up. That's if . . . I mean, you might want someone to show you the sights.'

He took a notebook from his trouser pocket and wrote down his address and phone number and tore out the page. Mary tried not to snatch it off him too eagerly.

'Thank you,' she said, and although the remaining time she passed with them went by far too quickly, and ended with nothing more thrilling than both nephew and uncle shaking her politely by the hand, she was not too despondent. She would be seeing Kenneth again in the autumn, and that was the important thing. As usual, she didn't stop to examine the reasons why.

3.

14th September 1952

Ma and Pa drove me down from Birmingham and we arrived at Dartford College at 3 p.m. What a dreary-looking place. My heart sank into my boots as soon as we went up the driveway. We unpacked my things and then after I had waved them goodbye I had to go upstairs and have a little cry in my room. Very embarrassing because in the middle of it in walked Alice, one of the girls I am sharing with. I am going to have to get used to not having any privacy here! Very different to having my own bedroom in Birch Road. Anyway she was very nice about it and there is another girl with us now called Laura who seems nice as well. I dare say we shall all be very jolly together once we get used to it.

27th September 1952

First visit to London to meet Geoffrey. It tipped down with rain unfortunately but that didn't stop us from having a lovely day. I met him off the train at Euston and after we had had a cup of tea and a piece of cake at the station we went to the British Museum. What an education, having G as my tour guide! He doesn't say much, but seems to know everything about everything. Then we walked back to the station and he spent so much time kissing me goodbye that he almost missed his train and had to run for it. I took the Underground to Charing Cross and then came back to dull old Dartford, feeling flat as a pancake. I miss him so much.

26th October 1952

Things have settled down here and I am getting quite used to the routine. The set-up is quite straightforward: they feed us, then we go outside and burn it off, then they feed us again, then we burn it off again, and so it goes on. The food is your typical stodge. Toast and cornflakes for breakfast, buns and doughnuts mid-morning, something hot and filling for lunch (mince and beans seems to be the cook's favourite), scones or teacakes in the afternoon then something a bit lighter at dinnertime like cheese or ham salad and then fruit. I would be putting on pounds if they weren't making me do so much exercise! Hockey, netball, tennis, running, volleyball. Heaven knows what we'll do when the nights start drawing in and it gets cold. Lots of gym I expect! No actual teaching practice yet, that starts next term.

London again yesterday, to see Geoffrey. This was the third time so far. We are starting to know our way around the city like a regular pair of Cockneys. We usually go to a museum or gallery and then for a walk in one of the big parks and then have some dinner before he goes home. Yesterday we pushed the boat out and went to Maison Lyons at Marble Arch. I had <u>coq au vin</u> – very adventurous! – and G had a mixed grill that was so big he couldn't finish it. Terrible sadness after he'd gone back as usual. Almost cried on the train back here but managed to pull myself together in time.

22nd November 1952

I had been meaning to write to Kenneth ever since I got here but could never quite get up the nerve. Well, I needn't have worried because this week he sent me a lovely postcard with the nicest suggestion. He said that he had a spare theatre ticket to a show in London and did I want to go with him? Did I? Just try stopping me!

He didn't tell me what the play was and I didn't find out until we got to the theatre – it was the new Agatha Christie that everyone has been talking about: <u>The Mousetrap</u>. Before the show we had real champagne in the bar (I didn't dare to ask how much it had cost – anyway Kenneth said he could put it all on expenses) but sadly there was no time for any dinner afterwards or I would have missed the last train back here. I had to make myself some cheese on toast in the kitchen which was a bit of a feeble end to the day but I was absolutely starving and anyway I didn't really mind because we had had such a lovely time. Kenneth is such a good conversationalist. He talks much more than Geoffrey does and is starting to know such interesting people. I could sit and listen to him for hours.

As for the play, I must say I was rather disappointed and thought it was pretty ropey, compared to her books. Very slow and obvious. I'm glad I saw it when I did because I imagine it will be closing before very long.

14th January 1953

Well here I am, back in the jug again, as they say. And feeling more homesick than ever, this time. What a lovely family Christmas we all had together, and so many wonderful times with Geoffrey. I will remember that day ice-skating at Rowheath for a long time. Now it is back to the grindstone and even though it's nice to see Alice and Laura again, I am awfully tempted to run down to the station and get the first train home. I wonder if this will ever get any easier? I just have to hang on to the thought that I will be seeing G again in ten days.

Ten days! At the moment it feels like a lifetime.

14th March 1953

What a day. I don't know how I'm supposed to write any of it down in a diary. My hands are shaking so much I can hardly hold my pen.

For one thing – none of it might have happened, if I had accepted Kenneth's invitation to go with him to a 'private view' at some gallery in Hampstead. It sounded like a fascinating thing to do and I was almost going to take him up on it, but then I couldn't really put Geoffrey off, I knew how much he was looking forward to seeing me and taking me to the Zoo. I met him off the train at 11.30 and we had the usual big stodgy lunch and then went to the Zoo, where there was a whopping great queue to get in. We had a lovely time anyway. Funnily enough Geoffrey would not come with me into the reptile house, he has a terrible fear of snakes and will not even look at them when they are safely behind glass. He has some odd ways about him sometimes. Then after the Zoo we went into the Park and sat beside one of the ornamental ponds and it was such a romantic atmosphere and it was at that moment that he said the last words I was expecting to hear: 'Mary darling, will you marry me?' he said, and my heart nearly burst. Of course I said Yes. So now I am officially engaged to be married!!! I really cannot believe it. I have spent the last twenty-four hours on Cloud Nine and everything seems totally unreal at the moment. Of course I rang up Ma and Pa and told them and they were over the moon as well, although Pa did ask me if I thought I was perhaps too young to be engaged but I don't think he meant it, I think he was just so shocked that he didn't really know what to say.

18th May 1953

Another nice day in London with Geoffrey. We went to the jewellery quarter to see about getting the ring made bigger because it is much too tight on my finger. This was a part of London neither of us had ever been to before and I rather enjoyed it but Geoffrey did not seem at all comfortable. In fact he was quite out of sorts by the time we got back to Oxford Street and when I asked him what was wrong he just said, 'Did you see how many coloureds there were on the bus?' Of course I had noticed but I didn't really think anything of it. I still don't see that it was anything to get upset about. Live and let live, I say! Afterwards we had rather a quiet afternoon in Hyde Park. It was very hot and sunny so we just lay on the grass and I made daisy-chains while Geoffrey read his book. I was a little bit cross about this but he had been on a waiting list at the library for six weeks to get it, so I suppose I can forgive him. It's called <u>Casino Royale</u> and is about a spy who is supposed to be very brave and sexy. Geoffrey certainly looked enthralled, and did not seem at all pleased when I put a big daisy-chain around his hair while he was reading it. I thought it made him look adorable but he didn't see the joke.

23rd May 1953

What to do about Coronation Day? Should I spend it in London with my friends, or back in Bournville with my family?

The good news is that Ma and Pa have got their television set in time. Apparently it was delivered just last week and they are so relieved because they heard that some people had been put on a waiting list for months and Radio Rentals were saying that they couldn't guarantee anybody a set in time for Coronation Day. Anyway, they have got it now – and it's a real beauty, Pa says.

But it does seem a bit crazy to go all the way back to Birmingham to watch it on television when the real thing will be happening right on my doorstep, so to speak. There's a whole gang here who want to go and be part of the crowd and they've asked me to go with them, and it's very tempting I must say. Just imagine what it would be like to see the Queen herself go by in her carriage!

On top of that, this morning I got a letter from Kenneth asking if I would be coming up to London on the day and saying that he would like to meet up with me if I did. It would certainly be nice to see him again. In fact I think that settles it.

Geoffrey will be disappointed if I'm not there, of course, but I shall write to tell him that he and his family are still very welcome to go round and watch it on Ma and Pa's set, since they don't have one of their own. They won't be the only ones taking advantage, I bet!

4.

Doll put the phone down and came back into the living room.

'That was Frank on the phone,' she said.

Sam, his eyes fixed on the screen, did not hear her.

'Watch out!' he shouted at the television.

'Watch out? Watch out for what?'

'There's a ruddy great shark down there,' he said.

Doll bent down and squinted at the image.

'What on earth are you on about? What shark?'

'There!' Sam insisted, pointing. 'At least, I think it's a shark.'

He was pointing at a monochrome square consisting entirely of different patches and blobs of grey, some of them light, some of them dark, the whole thing being visible only through a thick snowstorm.

'That's not a shark,' said Doll irritably. 'That's a man in a wetsuit. Frank just phoned, I said.'

'This French bloke,' Sam continued, ignoring this last piece of information for the second time, 'goes deep-sea diving and takes his camera with him. You wouldn't believe what he sees down there. They've found a ship that's been there for two thousand years. Two thousand years! Near the Île du Grand Conque.'

'The eel de what?'

'Grand Conque. It's off the French coast. Marseille. "Grand Conque", it's called. Probably means "Big Nose" in French.'

'I couldn't care less,' said Doll, and placed herself pointedly between her husband and the television screen. 'Why do I need to know about the Eel de Grand Conk? How's that going to help me? Obsessed, that's what you are. You'll watch any old rubbish on that thing.'

'Rubbish? How can you say that? Highly educational, this is.'

'For the third time, that was Frank on the phone. Bertha wants to know if she can bring her father with her.'

'Shift out of the way,' he said, waving his hand in irritation. 'Bring her father where?'

'Here, of course.'

'What does she want to bring him here for?'

'Oh, for crying out loud! They're coming on Tuesday! To watch the Coronation. I've told you a hundred times.'

'Oh yes.' Sam's tone of voice was different, suddenly. He sounded subdued and chastened. 'You did tell me that. Only . . .'

'Only what?'

'Well, it must have slipped my mind. Because I told Mr F from next door that he could come round. He's bringing Janet, and both the kids.'

Doll put her hands on her hips and stared at him, horrified.

'You did *what*? How are we going to fit them in? Four of them, plus Frank and Bertha, and Geoffrey, and Carl . . .'

'Who's Carl?'

'Bertha's father, the German! Plus the two of us. That's ten people. Where are they all going to sit? How are we going to feed and water them?'

Back on deck, Jacques Cousteau was talking to camera, probably explaining something about his most recent dive but in such a thick French accent that Sam was having difficulty understanding a word he was saying. Doll realized she had lost her husband's attention again, and was not going to get an answer to any of her questions. As usual, it seemed she would have to resolve her latest domestic problems unassisted. She sighed and left the room.

*

The next morning, she answered an unexpected knock on the door to find that her mother, Julia, was standing on the doorstep, carrying an all-too-familiar navy blue suitcase.

'Oh no,' said Doll, 'you haven't left him again, have you?'

'I've left him again,' said Julia, her voice shriller and more piercing than ever, a full-frontal assault on the ears.

'What's happened this time?'

'Eh? What?'

'Have you brought your deaf aid with you?'

'No. I lost it again.'

'Oh, Ma . . .'

'Well, are you going to invite me in, or do I have to stand out on this step all morning?'

Doll turned, walking heavily back inside in what amounted to a gesture of resigned invitation. Her mother followed. These separations from her husband were frequent but unpredictable, and usually resulted from some trivial disagreement which would be quickly resolved over the telephone after a short cooling-off period. Doll had long ago reached the conclusion that they were little more than a pretext for her mother to install herself in their house for a few days and enjoy some home comforts without the distracting presence of her husband. Doll would have accommodated her willingly enough in any case, but for some reason it suited her mother to arrange it this way. And indeed, this time, it seemed there was a further motive, because instead of following Doll into the kitchen, she made a straight line for the living room, where Sam was enjoying a few minutes alone with the cartoon strips in the back pages of the *Daily Mirror*.

'Hello, Grandma,' he said, rising to his feet. 'This is a surprise.'

'Is this it?' She peered down at the television set, and whistled in appreciation. 'Ooh, isn't it a beauty?'

'Is Doll making you a cup of tea?'

'It's very big, isn't it? Dominates the room.'

'Are you staying for a bit? Would you like me to take that case upstairs?'

'Go on, turn it on.'

Sam let out a sigh. Her hearing was obviously worse than ever. Either that, or she was interested in the new television set to the exclusion of all other things. 'There's nothing on now,' he told her. 'Not at this time of day.'

'Go on, turn it on,' she said, louder than ever.

'There's nothing on,' Sam repeated. 'Programmes don't start until the middle of the afternoon.'

'The middle of the afternoon? Well, that's no use to me. Take that case upstairs for me and I'll have a little lie-down before lunch. I'm worn out. What are we having? I fancy a bit of ham salad.'

5.

Mary had proposed meeting on the steps of the National Gallery, but Kenneth knew that this would have been impossible, and sure enough, on the day, Trafalgar Square and the steps themselves were unbelievably crammed with people. Some of them had been sleeping there all week to secure their places. Instead, he suggested a meeting point in a normally quiet side street close to Victoria Station. Mary arrived there shortly after ten o'clock, accompanied by her room-mates Alice and Laura, who were suitably impressed by this dashing young representative of the London newspaper world. Today he was once again wearing one of his cravats, not in yellow this time but a deep navy blue. Alice and Laura fell for him immediately. Together this ill-assorted quartet managed – following a devious route chosen by Kenneth in advance – to make their way towards Westminster Abbey avoiding the worst of the human congestion. Even then, it took the best part of fifty minutes to get anywhere near the Abbey itself.

'I say, what crowds!' Alice said, as they inched their way along Old Pye Street. 'You're awfully clever, Kenneth, to know your way around all the nooks and crannies like this. We'd have been quite stumped without you.'

'Well, I'm not a native,' he said, 'but I've learned to find my way around.'

Mary felt inexpressibly proud of having turned up this resourceful guide. Finally they reached Storey's Gate, the point beyond which they could proceed no further, and found that any view of the Abbey they might have hoped for was blocked by five or six rows of tightly packed spectators. There was an ocean of Union Jack flags, stretching as far as the eye could see.

'What a nuisance,' said Alice. 'We're not going to get much of a view.'

But Mary had an answer to that. From her bag she produced an intriguing, apparently home-made object: a long cylinder of cardboard, with little round mirrors fitted at both ends.

'Behold,' she said triumphantly, 'handmade – by Geoffrey the genius.'

*

Seated in the living room of his fiancée's parents, Geoffrey could not help wondering if Mary was making use of his ingenious present that morning. It had taken him most of last Friday afternoon to fashion that periscope, and although she had thanked him for it in her letter, he was not entirely reassured that she fully understood its purpose, or intended to take it to London with her. This was of a piece, perhaps, with his persistent sense of being slightly under-appreciated by Mary. An irrational sense, no doubt: here he was, after all, in her parents' house, along with his mother and father and grandfather, being made to feel as welcome as if they were all part of the same family. It was almost as if they were married already. And yet he realized that he would never quite feel sure of her until the vows were spoken and the wedding ring was on her finger.

By now there were seven people gathered around the television set in Doll and Sam's living room. It was crowded, but not impossibly crowded. Geoffrey's mother, Bertha, was at one end of the sofa, with the irascible Julia at the other, a cup of tea balanced on the arm next to her and, on her lap, a plate piled satisfyingly high with digestive biscuits. In between them sat Carl Schmidt, eighty-one years old now, wedged tightly between these two women and looking pretty cheerful about it. Indeed, ever since his indomitable wife, Nellie, had died the year before, his daughter and son-in-law had noticed a subtle but marked change in the old man, an unfamiliar light gleaming faintly in his eyes, an unaccustomed, private half-smile permanently forming at the corners of his mouth. He seemed to have recovered some of his zest for living, and to look about twenty years younger.

Frank and Samuel had taken the two remaining armchairs, Sam's positioned close to the set so that he could lean in and adjust the controls, since every few minutes the image would start shaking and wobbling to the point where it became unrecognizable. For some reason this happened whenever they put the kettle on or opened the fridge door. Doll had brought in three extra chairs from the dining room and had presented the best of them to Geoffrey, who as Mary's fiancé held the rank of guest of honour. Doll herself sat towards the back of the room, on an uncomfortable chair with a poor view.

It seemed wonderful, miraculous, to be able to watch all of this on television, to be sitting in Birmingham and witnessing these scenes at the very moment that they were unfolding in Westminster Abbey. In many ways, the television image was not a perfect substitute for reality; in others, it had certain advantages over it. For instance, the television audience had the benefit of a commentator to explain what was happening. As a passage of solemn processional music played in the background, the reverential tones of Richard Dimbleby emerged from the television speaker.

'The music fills the whole building as we wait. The whole scene laid out in its splendid colours. For now almost motionless. We watched it coming together almost like a mosaic, fragment by fragment of colour . . .'

'Almost like a what?' said Julia, at the top of her voice.

'Mosaic,' Sam repeated, slowly and emphatically. 'He's saying it's like a mosaic. Lots of different colours.'

'I wish he'd speak a bit louder. Can't you turn it up a bit?'

'He keeps talking about the colours,' Bertha complained. 'But we can't *see* the colours. You'd think he'd tell us what they are.'

The voice continued:

'. . . from the time very early this morning when the Abbey was almost empty to the time now when, in all its lovely pattern, the pattern of the cross below us, of which that throne is the centre, we are waiting. The serried ranks of the bishops, all in their cassocks and surplices . . .'

'The *what*?' said Julia. 'What did he say?'

'Serried ranks,' Sam repeated, spelling out every syllable, 'and cassocks and surplices.'

'Serried? What does that mean? What's a serried rank?'

'I have no idea. And don't ask me what a cassock is either, because I don't know.'

'A cassock is what bishops wear,' Frank offered, helpfully.

'Well, we all know *that*.'

'Where?' said Julia.

'Where? In church, of course.'

'No, I mean, where on their bodies do they wear them? Is that a cassock – what he's got on his head?'

'No, I thought that was a mitre.'

'I thought mitres were what they carried.'

'No, that's a crook. A bishop's crook.'

'Please, please!' Carl Schmidt suddenly called out with surprising passion. 'Can you all quieten down? We are missing the most important moments of the ceremony.'

Such was his tone of authority that everyone fell silent, and for the next few minutes the only thing to compete with the BBC commentary was the sound of Julia's remorseless progress through the pile of biscuits.

Sitting at the back of the room, Doll reflected that things were not going too badly so far. She could cope with this number of visitors. And the Farthings from next door were late. Perhaps they'd decided not to come after all. She was just beginning to feel comforted by this thought when there was a loud knock at the front door. She went to answer it and found herself confronted by six complete strangers: a man, a woman and four young children.

'Now I know what you're thinking, but there's no need to worry,' said the man, and held up a large paper bag, which was tightly filled with objects wrapped in greaseproof paper. 'We've brought our own sandwiches.'

★

The Coronation service itself was scheduled to last for almost three hours, so once Mary and her friends had all snatched a fleeting glimpse of the Queen entering Westminster Abbey (passing the periscope between them, with many admiring comments on Geoffrey's cleverness) there seemed little point in lingering at that spot. They decided to make their way to Hyde Park and try to position themselves so that they would have a good view of the royal procession passing by on East Carriage Road later in the afternoon. The sun was not smiling on London that day, and there was already a thin drizzle in the air, threatening to turn into a downpour. No matter. They laid a rug down on the grass, unscrewed the tops of their thermos flasks and poured themselves cups of tea. It would take more than a bit of rain to dampen the spirits of these young patriots.

*

The stranger turned out to be Mr Farthing's brother, who had driven over from Coventry with his entire family. Mr Farthing had invited him to the viewing party, it seemed, without troubling to mention this fact to the hosts. Luckily the six of them were perfectly happy to sit on the floor – as was Mr Farthing himself when he appeared ten minutes later with his wife and two daughters. So they all squashed together in a semicircle around the television set, and now there were seventeen spectators altogether.

The commentary continued:

'*And then, far to the right, in the south-western transept, there wait the peers of the realm. Sitting in their lovely robes, we watch them one by one and two by two entering this historic building on this great occasion, their lovely shoulder cloaks and capes of ermine, white, trimmed with gold, their coronets held in their laps.*'

'Ermine!' said Mrs Farthing. 'Just imagine how soft that must be.'

'Like stroking a big Persian cat,' her sister-in-law agreed.

'*And looking across the empty stalls, we see the front rank of the peeresses, who sit, their tiaras a-glitter and a-shimmer in their rows and rows, they sit facing their husbands the peers . . .*'

'Very poetic, isn't he?'

'Very. "A-glitter and a-shimmer".'

'Lovely tiaras, I must say. Do you think that's how they dress for breakfast? You know, the peer with his ermine, the peeress with her tiara, and it's all, "Pass the cornflakes, dear."'

Mrs Farthing was laughing at this until her husband gave her a gentle but emphatic nudge and frowned at her, a finger to his lips. She looked round and saw Bertha, Julia and Carl Schmidt staring at her from the sofa. She assumed a serious expression and turned back towards the television screen.

'. . . *and still the two empty chairs and the one young Duke, the prince of the blood who sits awaiting. The rich golden carpet spreads over the whole of the sanctuary, from where it joins the deeper blue carpet which hides the black and white chequered floor of the choir of the Abbey.*'

'Blue!' said Bertha. 'I was thinking it was red for some reason.'

'I'm glad he's telling us the colours now. Helps to imagine it more clearly.'

'. . . *We look now from the east, from above the altar, down across the theatre, and as it were straight down the length of the church. You see the deep blue of the choir carpet which spreads away out of our sight. And on each side of that deep blue carpet, in the carved oak choir stalls of the Abbey, there sit our distinguished visitors. If you look five or six stalls along at the back at the figure of that woman who just leaned forward and is reading – that is the splendid Queen Sālote of Tonga.*'

'Who?' said Julia loudly. 'Who's she? Where's she the queen of?'

'Tonga,' Sam informed her.

'An African! God preserve us.'

'Tonga isn't in Africa. It's in the Pacific.'

'Well, they're all Black, aren't they? Just look at her.'

'. . . *The queen who when she entered the Abbey earlier this morning dwarfed the two officers of the Guards who escorted her.*'

'Did you hear that? She's brought two dwarfs with her. Where are they, can you see them?'

'Oh, do be quiet. There are no dwarfs. Why would there be any dwarfs?'

'Well, you don't know what they get up to in Tonga.'

'. . . *A woman who serves the Commonwealth, and the only queen in this Abbey today in her own right other than the queens of our own royal family . . .*'

'Did you hear that?' Sam turned to address his mother-in-law at top volume, mouthing the words clearly. ' "She serves the Commonwealth." So it doesn't matter what colour she is, does it?'

'. . . *And so with bishops, peers, peeresses, and a great royal, diplomatic and state congregation, the seven thousand are made up.*'

'Blimey, seven thousand!' said Frank. 'That's a lot of people to get in one church, isn't it?'

There was another loud knock on the front door.

'We'll have that many in our sitting room soon, the rate we're going,' Sam muttered, and Doll rose apprehensively to her feet to see who the latest callers were.

*

At around one o'clock the rain started to ease off and Kenneth proposed a walk in Hyde Park. The procession would not be coming past for at least two hours yet, but Alice and Laura were worried about losing the favourable vantage point they had won by arriving early.

'Maybe you could keep it for us, then?' Kenneth suggested. 'Mary and I will just take a quick walk around the lake. Then it can be your turn.'

'Well!' said Alice, watching as they walked off into the distance. 'He didn't give us much choice about *that*, did he? I wonder what poor Geoffrey would say if he saw his fiancée wandering around London arm in arm with a dish like that.'

'Hidden depths, our Mary,' Laura agreed, shaking her head. 'Hidden depths.'

Mary was quite aware of the effect it had had on her friends, seeing her being whisked off for a sudden tête-à-tête. Kenneth, on the other hand, seemed oblivious to it. Taking the lead unobtrusively, and not responding in any obvious way to the fact that Mary had slipped her arm inside his, he steered a leisurely course past the drinking fountain and the bandstand, heading for the Queen Caroline Memorial at the western end of the Serpentine Lake. They were walking against the tide of people, most of them still hurrying in the direction of Park Lane and the route of the procession.

'Do you think Alice and Laura will be able to keep our places?' Mary asked, anxious now about missing out on a second glimpse of the royal carriage.

'Bound to. They seem pretty capable. Anyway, it's not the end of the world if we lose them, is it?'

Mary wasn't sure what he meant by this.

'Will you be writing a story about today?' she asked.

'Oh, they've got dozens of people covering it already. Only if I can find some angle that's a bit different. I tried to get them interested in the people living on my street who are having an anti-Coronation party, but they wouldn't buy it.'

'*Anti*-Coronation?' said Mary.

'Believe it or not,' said Kenneth, 'there *are* people who think this whole business is just a silly charade. It sounded rather jolly, actually, what they were proposing. Republican songs, card games with the king and queen taken out. I think they were going to stop short of a mock-execution.'

'I suppose it takes all sorts . . .' said Mary. '*You* don't think it's a silly charade, though, do you?'

Kenneth looked around him at the crowd, the thousands of people, the multitude of Union Jacks, the red, white and blue rosettes, the touts selling flags and pennants and every sort of patriotic trinket, and said: 'I don't know what I think, frankly. It's all a bit overwhelming. I dare say that people are still in need of pick-me-ups after what we all went through during the war but still, you know, I really thought it would go in the other direction. I thought Mr Attlee had found a way forward and we were all going to follow him down that path. But instead we booted him out, and now . . . now we have this. I mean, look at it! When did you last see anything like it? VE Day, I suppose.'

'The bonfire at Rowheath,' Mary said.

He glanced across at her. 'Oh, right – you were there as well, were you, that night?'

'Of course. That was the first time you and I ever met.'

Kenneth looked genuinely surprised. 'Really? I don't think so.'

'You don't remember Geoffrey being there?'

'Yes, I remember Geoffrey, of course. There was a nasty bust-up with his grandfather, the German.'

'Well, I was there too. I saw all that.'

He narrowed his eyes, musing. 'There was a little girl . . .' Turning towards her again now, he said in astonishment: 'That was *you*?'

Mary nodded. 'Didn't you realize?'

'No, I had no idea.'

'I thought it was so heroic, the way you helped him.'

'Did I? There was quite a crowd that night. Lots of people stepped in to do their bit.'

'You were the main one.'

Kenneth had spotted a rare vacant bench in the distance, and now suggested that they make for it. As they quickened their pace he said:

'Nasty piece of work, that bloke Burcot, the one who started it. He was in the same year as me at school. He ran off that night before I could say anything to him but a few months later I saw him again. He turned up one night and stood right next to me at the Hare and Hounds, cool as you like.' The bench was still empty when they reached it, and they sat down gratefully, although Mary could not help noticing, almost immediately, the sensation of cold and damp on her bottom. Never mind: it was lovely here, and they had a grand view of the choppy, metallic waters of the Serpentine. 'I could tell he didn't want to talk to me,' Kenneth went on, 'but I wasn't going to let him get away with that. I started by telling him he was lucky not to be in prison by now – which is perfectly true – but he scoffed and asked me what I expected to happen to a German who turned up at that sort of celebration. Of course, there were any number of answers I could have given, but I didn't really see the point. The thing was, I'd already met a lot of people like him – fought alongside them, in fact. Well, they were all a lot braver than he was, my pals in the army, but they had the same attitude. Tell them that you were fighting against Fascism – or even just fighting for democracy – and they'd think you were barmy. For them, it was all about self-defence: the Germans wanted to invade us, to take us over, and we were bloody well going to stop them. (Sorry, language. Mind you, theirs would have been a lot worse.) It was just us against them, you see. Well, there's nothing wrong with that, of course. They fought like heroes on that basis, you can't take that away from them. But they simply saw it as a war against the Germans: and to be honest, get them talking about politics and you'd find that some of them had views that weren't so far from the Nazis'. I'm sorry, but it's true. Maybe it shocks you.'

'No, not really,' said Mary. (She was intrigued, rather than shocked. Geoffrey never spoke to her like this.)

'It's just that I think there's an idea that some people like to have about the war. That it was a political thing. That everybody believed the real enemy was Fascism. And I'm not sure that's true. It's something of a myth. A myth that people on the Left are increasingly prone to.'

Feeling that a response was expected of her, but still not completely sure that she understood what Kenneth was talking about, Mary said:

'On the Left . . . that means the Labour lot, doesn't it?'

'As opposed to the Tories, yes.' Kenneth smiled, but somehow it was not a condescending smile. There was a lot of affection in it. 'You don't follow politics much, do you? Well, why should you? Why should anyone?'

'My parents are Labour,' said Mary, who for reasons she couldn't fathom was quite proud of this fact. 'They take the *Daily Mirror*, and so on. Geoffrey and his family aren't, though. True blue, they are. What about you?'

'Labour at the moment. But I don't think you should be defined by how you vote every few years. Let's see how things turn out.'

'I suppose as a journalist you have to be strictly impartial, anyway.'

Kenneth laughed. 'I don't think it really matters, at the level I've reached so far. But keeping an open mind is always a good idea, yes.'

*

Standing in the doorway of the living room, Doll surveyed the scene in front of her and reassured herself that, in spite of the appalling number of people who had turned up to claim the freedom of her house, the situation was more or less under control. Everyone had something to drink, and everyone had something to eat, thanks to her own hard work in the kitchen. In this she had been assisted by her niece Sylvia, who had arrived at about noon in the company of her parents, Gwen and Jim. Sylvia was twenty-nine now, and had a melancholy air about her: the man she was supposed to have married, a travelling salesman called Alex to whom she had been engaged for almost five years, had turned out to be a heel, a feckless liar with a string of other fiancées up and down the country. The truth had emerged only a few weeks earlier, and she had been mired in depression ever since, lost in near-silence, with a permanent, distant look of abstraction and disappointment in her eyes. Doll glanced at her now, perched in a corner of the living room on a stool which had been brought in from the kitchen, and could tell that although her gaze was fixed on the television, she was not really paying attention to the ceremony.

'What's the matter with her?' Bertha said to Julia, leaning across Carl to nudge her in the ribs.

The emollient tones of Richard Dimbleby were sounding out again from the television speaker:

'Now follows the singing of Handel's setting of the great anthem "Zadok the Priest". In the middle of this anthem the Queen will prepare herself for her anointing, the act which began with the invocation of the Holy Spirit. This is a most sacred part of the service, for it is the Queen's hallowing. Not until she has been anointed, as Solomon was anointed by Zadok, can she be crowned.'

'She's had a romantic disappointment,' Julia bellowed, louder than ever.

'Oh, the poor thing.'

'During the anthem, she will be divested of her crimson robe of state, and all her jewels, and will put on a simple white linen garment. In this garment of white, in such contrast to the splendours about her . . .'

'Five years, she waited for this fellow to make his mind up. Of course, we could all see it was never going to happen. But you cling on to your hopes, sometimes, don't you? You have to, when you're desperate.'

'. . . she will move for the first time,' Mr Dimbleby concluded, 'to King Edward's chair.'

At which point Sylvia vacated hers, and rushed from the room in tears.

*

'We really should be getting back to our vantage point,' Mary said.

'All right,' said Kenneth, 'you do that. But I think it's probably time for me to slip off.'

'Slip off? But you haven't seen the carriage go by. You don't want to miss that, surely?'

'I can live without it.'

If Mary was disappointed, it was not just because Kenneth was leaving, but because this was his reason.

'I'm not much of a monarchist, you know,' he told her, apologetically. 'I thought you might have guessed that by now.'

'But we *have* to have a king or a queen,' said Mary. 'It's tradition, it's English history, it's . . . it's everything.'

'Nothing very English about the current lot,' he said, laughing. 'They're more German than English. I'm not saying I don't love my country. I do love it . . .'

'Well, of course you do,' said Mary. Clearly she had no doubts on this score. 'You fought for it, didn't you?'

'Yes, I did,' said Kenneth. And hearing the change of tone in Mary's voice, he decided to seize the moment: for he had something far more important to express to her than his views on the hereditary monarchy. Taking her by the arm, he began to steer her along the path around the lake. Rain was beginning to fall again, quite heavily now, but neither of them had brought an umbrella. Mary fished a headscarf from her coat pocket and wrapped it firmly around her head. 'Listen,' Kenneth said. 'Before I go, there's something I need to ask you. I hope you don't think I'm being too forward.'

They strode onwards, in long silence, until Mary could stand it no more. 'Well, go on – out with it.'

'I know you've been walking out with Geoffrey, for quite some time now.'

'Yes?'

'Well, I mean, how do things stand between you? Are you serious about each other?'

Mary's heart missed a beat.

'Why do you ask?'

'Because I'd like to see a bit more of you. A lot more, in fact.' Inwardly trembling with nervous excitement, Mary said nothing at first, so he babbled on: 'I dare say you have a busy life, as a student, and all that, but—'

'We're engaged to be married,' she said then. And now it was Kenneth who was reduced to silence.

'I'm sorry,' she went on, 'I should have told you that before. I don't know why I didn't.'

'But . . . you're not wearing a ring,' Kenneth said.

'It's at the jewellers',' Mary told him. 'They're making it bigger.'

He fell silent again.

They were approaching East Carriage Road now, and it was starting to get very crowded indeed. They were hemmed in on all sides by people, pushing and jostling to catch a glimpse of the royal procession: shouting, laughing, singing snatches of everything from 'Rule Britannia' to 'How Much is that Doggie in the Window'. They were not ideal circumstances for a final conversation between two people in a state of emotional agitation. Kenneth decided that a hasty retreat was probably the best course of action.

'Look, I'd better make tracks,' he said. 'It's going to take me a while to get back to the office at this rate.'

'All right,' said Mary, unhappily.

'I'll write to you, shall I?'

'Yes, please do.'

(But he never did write to her.)

'And the next time I come up to town,' she added, 'perhaps we can see each other again.'

(But that didn't happen either.)

'Right-oh.' He kissed her on the cheek, a routine gesture which for some reason did not last the requisite second or two, but seemed to go on four or five times longer than it needed to, and which Mary had to bring to an end herself by pushing Kenneth gently away. He may or may not have said 'Goodbye' – afterwards she found it hard to remember – but within a few moments he was gone, swallowed up by the crowd, and had become quite invisible. She scanned the endlessly shifting mass of human bodies for a glimpse of his retreating figure, but there was no sign of him: instead she picked out Alice's ringlets of blonde hair, quite distinctly, and began the laborious task of pushing through the rows and rows of joyful, craning men, women and children until she could be reunited with her friends.

*

A reverential hush had descended upon the living room. The spectators were silent and the television, for the moment, was silent too, except for the background hiss and crackle, the almost inaudible carpet of white noise that had been accompanying the broadcast all day. Everyone in the room could sense that something significant was about to happen, even if they didn't yet understand what it was. Not, at least, until Richard Dimbleby's voice made itself heard again, and began explaining it to them:

'The Queen has received all the royal vestments. She now receives the priceless and beautiful Crown Jewels, culminating in the crown itself. But first . . . Her Majesty returns the orb, and the Archbishop now places upon the fourth finger of her right hand the ring, the ring wherein is set a sapphire, and within it, a ruby cross. This is often called the Wedding Ring of England.'

' "The Wedding Ring of England", ' Gwen repeated, almost in a whisper. It was an exquisite phrase.

'I wonder who calls it that,' said Julia. 'I never heard it called that before.' But even she was keeping her voice down now.

'A signal is given, and there enter the theatre from all sides the pages, bringing the coronets of those who have been taking part in the service . . . The moment of the Queen's crowning is come.'

Doll was standing behind the sofa. When she heard these words she felt the sting of tears behind her eyes, and reached for a handkerchief to dab at them. Her reaction did not go unnoticed by Geoffrey, who from his position on the other side of the room was watching the other nineteen viewers as they gazed, mute and bewitched, at the television set. He too was caught up in the drama of the moment, but his attention was directed not only at the images on screen, but at the effect they were having on these spectators.

For him, the moment at which the crown was placed on the new monarch's head was a moment of climax, a moment of release. Like everyone else, even with the help of the television commentary he had not really understood these final stages of the service; but to him they conveyed, nonetheless, a sense of correctness that was actually enhanced, not undermined, by their obscurity. Geoffrey had not cared for the atmosphere of the immediate post-war years: dangerous forces – rationalism, inclusiveness, egalitarianism – seemed to have been unleashed by the war, and threatened to shake the foundations of the old order. But now, this ponderous, arcane, incomprehensible ceremony felt to him like a breath of stale air, wafting its viewers back towards an earlier, more solid world, a world rooted not in dubious human values but made up entirely of dazzling abstractions and occult hierarchies. Before their very eyes even the Queen herself, this passive, inscrutable, twenty-seven-year-old woman at the centre of the ritual, had become no longer a human being in any meaningful sense but a mere symbol. And this was entirely right. This was her destiny.

Just look, Geoffrey said to himself, how everybody here is mesmerized by the solemnity of this moment, accepting its truth, its inevitability. Even (looking at Doll as he thought it) even the socialist! The old ways have won again. Tradition has won again. And so it will always be. England doesn't change.

It was not until the crown was resting safely on Elizabeth's head that he exhaled a long sigh – a sigh of relief, almost – and realized that he had been holding his breath.

*

'God save the Queen!'

'Long live the Queen!'

Alice and Laura shrilled out the phrases again and again, but they could still barely make themselves heard, so loud were the cheers and shouts and cries from the thousands of people pressed tightly around them. They were about two hundred yards from the balcony of the Palace. Too far to have anything other than a distant, indistinct view of the four people who were standing there: the infants Charles and Anne, waving bemusedly at the sea of upturned faces, and behind them, the royal couple, Philip and Elizabeth, their mouths locked into frozen smiles. Mary, peering through her periscope, was pleased enough: this was as good a view of the family as she had been hoping for all day, and it had taken a good ninety minutes pushing through the crowds to get this close. They could return to Dartford satisfied. And yet she did not feel like joining in with her friends' chorus of adulation. The compound of emotions this day had stirred up in her was too complex to find expression like that. The sight of that family of four on the balcony – just the sort of family she hoped and expected to have herself in a few years' time – filled her with pangs of hope, and on top of that she had Kenneth's surprising declaration (or near-declaration) to chew over. She would be almost silent on the train home to Dartford, ignoring her friends' over-excited chatter, and her dreams in bed that night would offer a wild, disorientating mixture of imagined scenes from the future lives of herself, and Geoffrey, and the country to which they belonged. Almost any scenario seemed possible.

THREE

The World Cup Final:
England v. West Germany

30th July 1966

I.

My dear Bertha,

I was delighted to receive your letter, and am enormously touched by your offer of accommodation in Birmingham on the days when Lothar and I will be visiting. Believe me, I was not 'fishing' for such an invitation when I wrote to say that we would be coming! It was simply that I do think it important to keep up these family connections, however remote they might be, particularly in the light of recent historical events, of course. In other words, I see this as an opportunity to make a contribution, however small, to the improvement of Anglo-German relations. And so Lothar and I would be very grateful to accept your proposal, and look forward very much to being welcomed into your home. I shall bring with me some photographs, documents and souvenirs of your father Carl's early life in Leipzig, which I hope you will find of interest and perhaps even some sentimental value . . .

2.

Halfway through the 1960s, and Mary is now thirty-two years old. She and Geoffrey have been married for eleven years. They have three sons, aged ten, eight and five. Geoffrey's career has taken an unexpected turn, and this rather cerebral Classics graduate is now the manager of a bank in Solihull. But he is happy in his job, and happy in his marriage. The whole family is happy.

Cousin Sylvia is happy too, by and large. Following her romantic disappointment she was lucky enough to meet another man during a long walking holiday the following summer, in Switzerland. His name was Thomas Foley and at the time he was a civil servant living in London. They married and for a while they lived in suburban Tooting with their baby daughter, Gill, but then Sylvia persuaded her husband to move to the Midlands and now they live in Monument Lane, on top of the Lickey Hills, just a few miles from Bournville. Mary and Sylvia are no longer just cousins but also good friends, despite the ten-year age difference between them. They meet once a week at least. Happy times.

Even the country is happy, after a fashion. The fifties had not been an easy decade for Great Britain. Post-war austerity had dragged on. Rationing seemed to go on for ever. The Empire began falling apart, and Britain's self-confidence with it. But now a little renaissance seems to be taking place: not economic, or political, but cultural. In a few days' time, John Lennon will tell the world that the Beatles are more popular than Jesus. The song of the summer is 'Sunny Afternoon', by the Kinks, currently at number one in the charts for the second week running. The two cousins have both seen the group singing it on *Top of the Pops*, which they watch every week with their children. They know all the groups: the Kinks, the Beatles, the Rolling Stones, the Hollies, the Who, Herman's Hermits, and Dave Dee, Dozy, Beaky, Mick and Tich. Every week they gaze in obscure longing at these long-haired, pretty young men miming for the cameras in their flowery shirts and wide collars: the songs seem like dispatches from another world, a world of melody and colour, freedom and weightlessness, ambiguity and transgression. One hundred miles away London, apparently, is swinging. Bournville? Not so much.

Today Mary and Sylvia have brought their youngest children to the miniature boating lake. The same lake where Mary met Kenneth and his nephew on a summer morning back in 1952; but she doesn't think about that now. That was all an impossibly long time ago. Both women are wearing short sleeveless dresses, sunglasses, straw hats. There is the gentlest of breezes, the wispiest of clouds flecking the sky. Other than that Bournville is defined, as always, by its stillness.

Neither Mary's son (Peter), nor Sylvia's (David), owns a model boat, or would know what to do with it if he did, but David has brought a plastic model of *Thunderbird 4*, which floats, after a fashion, so they set about amusing themselves with that, and Sylvia says:

'It's nice to see them playing together. They seem to get on well, don't they?'

'They do,' Mary agrees. 'I'm glad David's taken to Peter. He doesn't seem to have made many friends at nursery.'

'Oh? I wonder why not?'

'Shyness, I think. He's a timid little thing. Takes after his father.'

Sylvia glances at her. It's not the first time she has heard Mary say something like this: not critical of Geoffrey, exactly, but at the same time not altogether laudatory. It strikes her that they are married to very similar husbands: both frustratingly reserved and uncommunicative.

'I know Geoffrey's shy,' she says, trying to put a positive spin on things, 'but that's what makes you such a good couple. *You're* so friendly and outgoing. It might be a bit much if both of you were like that.'

'Hmm. Maybe. I just wish he wasn't so . . . Well, look at the way he is with Jack, for instance. The poor boy's *dying* to be taken to one of the World Cup games. But Geoffrey won't do it. Refuses point blank.'

'I heard it was turning out to be a bit of a damp squib,' says Sylvia. Part of the tournament is actually being played out on their doorstep – the Argentinian team, incredibly, is staying at the Albany Hotel in central Birmingham, and there are three matches scheduled to be played at Villa Park – but none of her friends (or even their husbands) seem to be talking about it much.

'Not in our household,' says Mary. 'Football mad, Jack is. Pictures and charts all over the walls in his bedroom. He can tell you the name of every England player and how many goals they scored last season. And all he wants is for Geoffrey to take him to one of the matches at Villa Park.'

'But why won't he?'

Mary shakes her head and sighs out the words, 'I don't know.' Then, after thinking it over for a moment, she says: 'Actually I do. You know what, I think he reckons it's common. Tennis and golf are for the likes of him, not football. And he won't drive to Villa Park because he thinks it's in a rotten part of town and something will happen to the car if he parks it there. He's a terrible snob, you know. I think he gets it from his parents.'

'Or his grandfather.'

'His grandfather?'

'I met him once, at your folks' house. On Coronation Day. He was terribly stiff, I remember.'

'Carl? Yes, he was stiff but – oh, he was all right, really. Quite a sweet and gentle soul, underneath.'

'If you say so.'

'I never really got to know him or anything, but just before he died we had quite a nice little chat. It was strange – he was ever so ill, and I was ever so pregnant with Jack – and Geoffrey told me that Mr Schmidt wanted to see me, so I went and saw him – he was sitting up in bed, in that same little house he'd been living in for fifty years, and he looked like death warmed up – but we talked for quite a while, half an hour or so, and he told me how happy he was that I was pregnant and Geoffrey was about to become a dad and what he wanted to tell me was that Nellie – that was his wife – always used to say that the time when her daughters were little children was the happiest time of her life, and he wanted me to know that, and he hoped the next few years would be like that for me.'

'Yes, that does sound nice of him,' Sylvia admitted. 'And have they been?'

Mary ponders the question.

'The happiest time of my life? I suppose they have, so far.'

3.

'Finished with that,' Martin says, in a perfunctory way, and tosses the comic onto his older brother's bed.

Jack looks up from his copy of the *Evening Mail*, from which he is carefully tearing out a page, prior to trimming it with scissors and pasting it into his World Cup scrapbook.

'Good this week, isn't it?' he says.

'It was all right.'

The comic in question is called the *Victor*. It is not really to Martin's taste. He has little interest in stories of Second World War derring-do. The exploits of 'Killer' Kennedy leave him cold. The adventures of Matt Braddock, VC – this week flying Beaufighters against German mine-laying aircraft – stir no passions in him. In this he differs from his older brother, who laps these things up with relish, week after week: stories of wartime heroics which, however much they may differ in circumstantial detail, can always be reduced to a primal contest between the gallant English and the dastardly Germans, and always with the same outcome: the Englishman, merely by virtue of being English, will always win against the German, however much the odds seem to be stacked in Jerry's favour. (In fact, the steeper the odds the greater the triumph, and the narrower the victory the sweeter it tastes.)

'There aren't many jokes in that thing,' Martin now elaborates. 'I thought comics were supposed to be funny.'

'Not all of them,' says Jack. 'Anyway – here's one. What do you call a German who's taking part in the World Cup final?'

'I don't know,' says Martin.

'The referee.'

His brother stares back at him blankly.

'I don't get it.'

'Because their actual team isn't going to get to the final.'

Martin ponders this. It doesn't really make sense. 'I thought their team was supposed to be good.'

Jack glares at him, then reaches for his scissors. 'Yes, they are good. It's just a joke.'

'Why are you cutting that story out, anyway?'

He cranes over the excised newspaper page and sees a blurry photograph of an unsmiling man in late middle age. The accompanying article informs him that the man is 'Mr Ronald Tucker of 18, Birch Road, Bournville, aged 55', who has been convicted of two counts of public indecency and sentenced to six months in prison.

'It's on the other side, idiot.'

Martin flips over the page and finds a story which certainly seems more likely to appeal to his football-fixated older brother. Here there are two photographs: a dark-haired footballer wearing the Argentinian kit, and an avuncular man in medical overalls, beaming at the camera and holding up some kind of surgical instrument. The headline reads: 'FOR ARGENTINA'S RATTÍN THE TOOTH HURTS.'

'Who's that?' Martin asks.

'Argentina's captain. He had a toothache so this bloke pulled it out. His surgery's just up the road from here.' He cuts off a little square of sellotape and begins sticking the page into his scrapbook. 'If I were him,' he continues, 'I wouldn't have given him an injection first.'

'Why not?'

'The Argies are filthy players. All they want to do is nobble the other side. They don't care how obvious they are about it. They're a disgrace to the game. The worst team in the tournament.'

'Worse than the West Germans?'

'They aren't dirty like the Argies.' He looks up. 'Is it true that we've got a German cousin?'

'Yes.'

'And we're going to meet him at the weekend?'

'Yes. Exciting, isn't it?'

'Not really,' says Jack. 'I don't think we'll have much in common. What are we supposed to talk about?'

'Well, football,' says Martin. 'I would have thought that was obvious.'

4.

The captain of the Argentinian team, obliged to have his tooth extracted by a dentist in the inner suburbs of Birmingham, is not the only footballer from overseas who finds himself getting to know the host country better than he was expecting. As the tournament develops and gathers momentum, England – which might be accused, in the post-war years so far, of being rather an inward-looking country – finds itself cautiously opening its doors to guests from other parts of the world, and different footballing cultures begin to rub up against one another.

The Italian team, on being presented with their accommodation in Durham University's halls of residence, promptly replace all the furniture. The mattresses, they tell newspaper reporters, are especially unacceptable.

The team from Uruguay arrive for their first training session at Hounslow sports centre only to find that it has been double-booked and is already in use by a local Scout group. The Uruguayans look on in some bemusement as these young pioneers play Manhunt and Leap Frog and run relay races with beanbags on their heads; then they head off in search of an alternative venue.

The North Koreans, billeted in Middlesbrough, complain that they cannot sleep because of the noise from Teesside airport. Playing host to these Communist visitors, however, has given local residents a new sense of connection to London and the other metropolitan centres: 'The people of Middlesbrough now feel that they are part of the country,' a spokesman says.

The most popular TV show in the country is *The Man from U.N.C.L.E.*, and the Russians turn out to be just as obsessed with it as the English are. En masse they visit a hairdressing salon in Durham city and demand 'Robert Vaughn haircuts'.

The Bulgarians need a team to practise against, and a group of volunteers from Manchester Town Hall are happy to supply one. Everyone thoroughly enjoys the match, which the Bulgarians win 12–1.

There is a minor scandal when the French team is accused of charging English fans for autographs.

It is reported that the Portuguese team, staying in Wilmslow, have brought six hundred bottles of wine with them, and several barrels of virgin olive oil, having assumed (correctly) that they will not be able to obtain palatable substitutes for these items in England.

The Spaniards have been instructed by their medical team not to drink British tap water as it will probably make them ill.

Meanwhile, veteran player Ron Flowers has been asked to name the advantages that the England team will enjoy by playing at home, and he has no hesitation in saying that the main one is 'being able to eat the right food'.

And whether this is indeed the reason, or whether there is some other explanation more related to their footballing skills, the England team have started to make respectable progress. An adequate nil–nil draw with Uruguay is followed by a 2–nil win over Mexico. Victory over France on 20th July at Wembley Stadium will secure them a place in the quarter-finals. People are starting to notice their much-improved recent performances, and it could be that this tournament is finally beginning to attract the attention not just of dedicated fans like Jack, but the whole country.

5.

Geoffrey reverses their car (an Austin A60 Cambridge, snowberry white, with embassy maroon side flash) out of the driveway.

The first few minutes of their drive from Bournville to West Heath take them down Birch Road, past the house where Mary was born and where she spent the first two decades of her life. It also takes them past number 18.

'That's where he lives,' Mary says, pointing through the window. 'Curtains are drawn, I see. Keeping a low profile.'

'Where who lives?' Peter pipes up, from the back seat.

'Just someone we used to know.'

Martin turns to his brother and whispers: 'He's going to prison.'

'Why? What did he do?'

'He kissed other men.'

Peter's eyes widen.

'Where?'

'I don't know – on the mouth, I suppose.'

Jack laughs. 'I don't think that's what he meant.' He leans over to his youngest brother and says: 'In the public toilets.'

His mother turns round to reprove them. 'All right, you lot, that's enough.'

'Mum, I don't under—'

'That's enough, I said.' She settles back in the passenger seat. 'Men like that are the lowest of the low. That's all you need to remember. The lowest of the low.'

This vivid phrase enters Peter's consciousness and lodges there. The words ricochet around his head for the rest of the journey, which he spends in thoughtful silence. The family car rattles its way along Turves Green, then turns into the Oak Walk. It is 12.45 on a Sunday afternoon, so the roads are quiet anyway. But even so, something changes, subtly but profoundly, when they turn off the main road. They are entering a district called the Longbridge Estate. (Years later it will become known as the Austin Village.) For Peter, the youngest of Mary's three sons, this place has an air of enchantment. His older brothers sitting beside him on the back seat – stolid Martin; impulsive, impatient Jack – don't seem to notice it, but this tree-lined road marks the entrance to a world which, in Peter's eyes, is even more special than Bournville itself. They leave behind the featureless houses, the newly sprouting high-rise blocks – the 1960s, in other words – and find themselves instead spirited away to a place of secrecy and magic. There are three streets here, running parallel to each other – Coney Green Drive, Central Avenue and Hawkesley Drive – connected by smaller roads which intersect in a series of grass-covered roundabouts where sycamores grow. Everything here is verdant, leafy, placid. Along each of the main roads you find the houses: but what strange houses they are! They are freshly painted, white, weatherboard bungalows, reminiscent perhaps of New England, the kind of bungalow you might imagine serenely overlooking the ocean on the shores of Rhode Island. How did they come to be here, in this south-western corner of Birmingham? They were shipped over, prefabricated, all two hundred of them, from Bay City, Michigan, in 1917, when Herbert Austin urgently needed extra accommodation for workers at his rapidly expanding car factory. Later on they began to be sold to young couples in need of convenient, reasonably priced housing: couples such as Frank and Bertha Lamb, who purchased their bungalow in Hawkesley Drive back in 1924 and live there still, forty-two years later, much to the fascination of their little grandson Peter who loves everything about this exotic home and its surroundings. He loves the light, plant-filled entrance porch, the sitting room with its fussy, old-fashioned furniture, the little kitchen at the back, dominated by a curvaceous American refrigerator, the little ladder of wooden steps at the back door where the house sits a few feet above the ground, creating a child-sized space which you can burrow into, hiding yourself, lying low and listening to the sounds of adult life above, the heavy footsteps on the floorboards, the muffled voices. He loves the long garden, with its densely planted vegetable patches on one side and sweet-smelling flower beds on the other, separated from each other by a paved pathway which is perfect for playing hopscotch. But all this is simply a prelude. For this pathway brings you, after twenty yards or so, to the real wonder of this place, its crowning glory: the shelter. The air-raid shelter, as the grown-ups call it, although Peter has only the haziest idea of what an air raid is or why his grandparents should once have had to build a shelter against one. The structure is beautifully camouflaged, the roof covered with turf and the wooden door painted the same grass green. (In years to come, looking back on his visits to this house, he will reflect that the shelter bore a striking resemblance to Bilbo Baggins's home in *The Hobbit*, a book he will briefly come to regard as the greatest ever written.) You descend to its subterranean depths by a flight of seven steps made of brick – a stairway constructed by Frank himself, in the fearful autumn of 1939 – and today, as always, Peter is so eager to visit it that the first thing he says to his grandmother is:

'Hello, Nana, can I go and play in the shelter, please?'

Bertha smiles at him, but Peter senses something disapproving in the smile.

'After lunch, I think. We have two guests here, you see, and you haven't even been introduced to them yet.'

Chastened, Peter waits to be told the names of the two strangers standing in front of him: a tall, pale, wisp of a man about his father's age, and a stocky, dark-haired boy a little shorter than Jack (although in fact he is two years older). The man is wearing a jacket and a bow tie, something Peter has never seen before, and the boy, absurdly, is wearing long shorts which come below his knees.

'So this is Volker,' says Bertha, presenting the wisp of a man. 'Volker is your second cousin once removed. And this is Lothar' (presenting the boy) 'who is your third cousin. They have come all the way from Gütersloh in Germany.'

The two guests hold out their hands. Peter is bewildered for a moment, but then guesses that he is meant to shake them. He holds out his hand as well. Then Jack and Martin hold out theirs. There is a confusing exchange: two German hands reaching out for three English hands, meeting, clasping, unclasping and then re-clasping in a sort of cat's cradle of fervent but awkward handshakes. Bertha looks on, beaming her approval.

'What a wonderful moment,' she says. 'The two sides of the family meeting at last.'

They sit down to lunch. All nine of them are tightly squashed around the little dining table, but Bertha has been adamant, all morning, that the whole family should sit together, and would not entertain the idea of adults and children eating separately. She has prepared a collection of cold plates. Always, when Peter comes to dinner at his nana and grandad's, he is strangely fascinated – and strangely repulsed – by the food on offer. He has never realized, before today, that his grandmother's cooking has a German slant, derived from her father, Carl, who had insisted on instructing his wife in the ways of preparing *Kartoffelpuffer* and *Spätzle*, *Eintopf* and *Rinderroulade*, a tradition which was also passed on to their three daughters. Peter has never understood that this explains the different flavour of the cold meat, either sweeter or spicier or smokier than the English ham his mother gives him at home, or the strange, lime-green, vinegary, wholly inedible pickles which are always piled on the side of his plate and which always remain there for the duration of the meal, untouched. And today the food is more Germanic than ever. There is sauerkraut, pungent yellow mustard, and dark brown, rough, grainy rye bread which bears no relation whatsoever to the thin white slices he is used to. He pecks at the food, horrified, and yet at the same time mesmerized by the enthusiasm with which Volker and his son are tucking in, emitting polite little grunts of approval, occasionally dropping compliments like: 'This is wonderful! Even better than we get at home.'

'Tomorrow,' Bertha says, 'I shall cook you a proper English meal. Steak-and-kidney pie. But today I wanted to give you something that would make you feel at home.'

Despite the success of the food, and the uniqueness of the occasion, conversation is not flowing as freely as everyone might have hoped.

'Is it a large town, Gütersloh?' Geoffrey enquires of his cousin.

'There are approximately seventy-five thousand inhabitants,'

Volker replies. 'It is a pleasant place. There is a park, a number of excellent shops, and houses are not too expensive. My parents moved there when I was eight years old, and my wife's family have been there for even longer. We like it very much and we have no plans to move.'

'She didn't want to come here with you, then?' Mary ventures.

'Pardon?'

'Your wife. To see the football.'

Volker laughs. 'Oh, no, no! She and Lothar's sister are quite content to stay at home, I assure you. Football is not their cup of tea at all.'

'How was the game yesterday?' Mary asks. She loves all forms of sport, even if football is not her favourite, and she feels much more interest in the progress of this tournament than her husband or her in-laws seem to do.

'It was nil–nil,' Lothar answers, in his excellent English. 'Quite boring, in fact. I was quite disappointed in our team. I thought they would have scored two goals or perhaps more.'

'What about Argentina?' Jack asks. 'Did they play by the rules?'

'There were many fouls,' says Volker. 'At one point there were six or seven players all arguing among themselves, the referee had to stop the match, and the Argentinian manager came running onto the pitch to complain. One of their team was sent off.'

'Typical!' says Jack. 'That was Albrecht, wasn't it?'

'He's been following the matches ever so closely,' Mary says, proudly. 'He could tell you the name of every player in every team.'

'Why didn't you go to the game yesterday?' Lothar asks. 'In your home city.'

'I didn't have anyone to take me,' Jack explains, his voice thick with grievance. 'Dad doesn't like football. The only person who used to take me to football matches was my grandpa. He used to take me to see Wolves and West Brom. But he and Grandma have moved away now. They live miles away, in the Lake District.' (Sam and Doll left Birmingham two years earlier, and have retired to Coniston, and Jack feels their absence keenly. It is not just a question of being taken to football matches. He misses his grandfather's humour, his warm, kindly presence, his way of interacting with children that has no trace of awkwardness or condescension. Jack has never made any secret of the fact that he much prefers Sam and Doll to his remote, austere paternal grandparents.) In a tone that is defiant, but does not carry complete conviction, he now says: 'Of course, I saw the match on television. You actually get a better view that way. And West Germany didn't play all that well, if you ask me.'

Before Lothar can respond to this, Martin butts in with:

'Why is it *West* Germany, though? Why isn't the whole of Germany playing?'

'Ah. Well, that is a long and complicated story,' says Volker. 'Germany has been divided ever since the end of the war, you see. Your own country and the United States had responsibility for the Western half. The Soviet Union controlled the East. Your great-grandfather, Carl, came from Leipzig, which is part of East Germany now. This is still where many of our relatives live. Luckily my parents moved to Gütersloh in the 1930s, so we are in the West.'

'Why is that lucky?'

'Because the East is not free. It's a Communist country. Everything that people do there is known to the secret police, and our relatives are not free to leave the country to come and visit us. Only for very special reasons like funerals, and even then they have to ask permission, and quite often it takes so long to be granted that it's too late.'

'And don't they have a football team?'

Volker smiles. 'Of course. But not a very good one.'

'My father says that Harold Wilson is a Communist,' says Jack. 'Don't you, Dad?'

Geoffrey is so embarrassed to have this bold opinion attributed to him that he literally squirms in his chair. He can think of nothing to say at first.

'Surely not,' Volker chides. 'The British Prime Minister?'

'Well . . .' says Geoffrey, finally. 'As near as makes no difference.'

'Believe me,' says Volker. 'I have visited East Germany. I've seen Communism in action. Your Prime Minister is no Communist.'

'Maybe not,' says Frank, coming to his son's defence, 'but he's in the pocket of the trades unions, and that's the last thing we need at the moment. The unions are far too powerful in this country already. That's one of the reasons Germany's doing so well, if you ask me. The unions aren't running the show.'

'Well, I'm not so sure . . .' Volker says, diplomatically.

'How do you account for it, then?'

'For *Wirtschaftwunder*? The German economic miracle?' He takes a sip of the Liebfraumilch that Frank has procured from the local off-licence, and winces slightly. 'Perhaps the danger of winning a war is that it gives you a sense of triumph and achievement – quite rightly – which makes you think you can afford to take things easy for a while. Whereas defeat, especially a defeat like the one we suffered, gives you no choice but to get back on your feet again and start rebuilding, straining every muscle in your body to do so. That certainly seems to be the philosophy of our Chancellor, Mr Erhard.'

A thoughtful silence follows this statement.

'Could you pass the butter, please?' Bertha now says, leaning towards Mary, and while this welcome distraction is in progress, Geoffrey leans in to Volker and says, confidentially:

'We don't really talk about that sort of thing, in this country, you know. Not politics, at the family dinner table. I should drop it if I were you.'

Volker takes a moment or two to digest this piece of advice – or rather, this instruction. Then, to Jack, he says pleasantly:

'Getting back to football, I happen to agree with you. We didn't play so well yesterday. Let's hope we do better on Wednesday.'

'You're going to that one as well, are you?' Jack cannot stop himself from asking.

'We are here to see *all* the matches,' Lothar boasts. 'Villa Park on Wednesday, and then, when our team wins that, we go to Sheffield, and then for the next match to Liverpool and finally we shall go to Wembley to watch our team win the final and take home the World Cup.'

Jack stares at him, his whole body welling up with hatred. He thinks: This boy will be going to Wembley? He will be going to *Wembley Stadium* to see the final, when I'm not even allowed to go up the road to Villa Park? He is consumed with rage.

'You're talking rubbish,' he says coldly. 'England are going to win the World Cup.'

Lothar snorts. 'Nobody believes that.'

'You won't even get into the final. Or the semi-final, or even the quarter-final.'

Instead of answering, Lothar takes the most disgusting food item on the table – a long green pickle, soaked in vinegar, which, being lurid green and somewhat flaccid, has the look of a radioactive slug – and pops the whole thing into his mouth. He chews on it with every appearance of satisfaction before swallowing loudly. Jack watches with disgust and wants to gag. He hates this boy now with a burning passion.

'Shall I help you clear the table, Nana?' Mary asks, rising to her feet.

'Oh, that's very kind, thank you.' Bertha turns to Volker. 'While we're getting the pudding ready, perhaps you could show Geoffrey and the boys the photographs you showed me yesterday?'

'Yes, of course.'

He retrieves a cardboard folder from a table on the other side of the room and for the next few minutes Jack, Martin and Peter have to pretend to be interested in these ancient black-and-white prints, some of them so faded that the images are all but impossible to make out, but which seem to consist mainly of hatchet-faced patriarchs who sport either long white beards or fantastic curlicued moustaches and whose attire ranges from the most severe and uncompromising formal wear to full German military uniform complete with medals and, in one case, a long and fearsome rapier. The three young boys feel no connection whatsoever with this gallery of Teutonic grotesques. Luckily, their bowls of tinned fruit salad arrive before too long and, after making them edible by dousing them in evaporated milk, they polish them off quickly and are free to leave the table at last.

All four boys now file out through the kitchen and squash together on the wooden bench at the top of the garden, except that there is not really enough room for Peter, who after failing to secure his place is obliged to sit cross-legged on the paving stones, in some discomfort. They can't think of anything to talk about but Martin has brought a little transistor radio with him so he turns it on and fiddles with the tuning dial until he has found the Light Programme. They are just in time to catch the last few minutes of a comedy show. Jack recognizes the voice of the lead performer and says, 'Ooh, it's Ken Dodd – he's really funny, he is.' More to prove his own point than because he actually understands the humour, Jack spends the remaining five minutes of the programme doubled up with laughter while Martin looks on in disdain and Lothar in bafflement.

'I do not understand any of this,' he says. 'What is happening? Why is the audience laughing?'

Jack turns to Martin and asks: 'Who says the Germans have no sense of humour, eh?' When Martin doesn't reply, he delivers the punchline anyway: 'Just about everybody!' Nobody laughs but himself, but he laughs enough for the four of them. Then he says to Peter: 'Where are you going?'

Peter has risen to his feet and is setting off down the garden path. The next programme has come on and it frightens him: it's a concert by the George Mitchell Minstrels, otherwise known as the Black and White Minstrels, and although of course he cannot see them, it's enough to be reminded of their horrible blacked-up faces which scare him whenever they appear on television, with their freakish expressions and their white-lipped rictus grins. Besides, he cannot wait any longer to go into the shelter. Once he has descended the steps and heaved open the door that complains loudly on its rusty hinges, he turns on the naked bulb suspended from the roof: it casts a dim light over the garden implements and sacks of vegetables that are ranged on the floor. There is a wide wooden shelf running the length of the wall, all the way from the door to the back of the shelter, and after roaming up and down the space a few times, considering his options, Peter sets about converting this into an impromptu racetrack for the two Dinky cars he carries everywhere in his pocket. Tins of paint, oil cans, a ball of twine, even a few shallots from a little hessian bag are all pressed into service, forming a series of obstacles around which he painstakingly pushes the cars, all the while keeping up a running dialogue in his head, imagining a conversation between two BBC sports commentators. He makes engine noises out loud, and vocalizes the gasps and cheers of the rapturous crowd. So absorbing does he find the game that he loses all sense of the passing of time, and does not even notice when Jack comes down the steps and joins him in this gloomy haven, breaking rudely into his fantasy world with the words:

'What are you up to, tiddler?'

Peter snatches the cars from the shelf and whirls around, looking guilty even though he has been doing nothing wrong.

'Just playing.' He puts the cars back in his pocket. 'Where are the others?'

'They were having this *really boring* conversation,' says Jack. 'And now they've gone for a walk, which is even more boring. D'you fancy a game of cards?'

Peter is surprised, and pleased. His oldest brother, whom he worships, does not normally make invitations like this. The problem is that he doesn't know any card games. Jack tries to explain the rules of Knockout Whist and Pontoon to him, but they are too complicated. They end up playing Snap. Peter feels guilty, and ashamed, that he isn't old enough or clever enough to play a real card game with his brother, but Jack doesn't appear to mind. He seems preoccupied. A frown is etched on his brow, and he doesn't focus very well, allowing Peter to win four out of the first five games. Peter is uneasy. His brother is clearly not himself this afternoon. Something must have upset him. Peter was not paying attention to the conversation during lunchtime – he has a habit of drifting off, of detaching himself from any situation that seems too complex or too uncomfortable or simply too dull – but he guesses it has something to do with their new cousin. Whatever the reason, it is alarming. Peter hates to see his brother out of sorts, and would do anything in his power to make things better for him. It cheers him up, slightly, that after a while he seems to recover his concentration, and wins the last four games in a row.

Jack is just shuffling the cards again when they hear footfalls on the steps. It is Martin and Lothar. They have finished their walk and they come bearing gifts.

'Look,' says Martin, 'Nana gave us this to share.' It is a bar of Cadbury's Bournville chocolate. The plain, dark sort. 'And Lothar's brought some chocolate with him from Germany.'

'For us?' says Jack.

'If you like,' says Lothar, none too warmly.

'OK then, let's see what the difference is.' Jack takes the bar of Bournville chocolate from Martin, breaks off two rows, and gives half a row to each of the other three boys. 'Now bear in mind,' he says to Lothar, 'that English chocolate is the best *in the world*. And Cadbury's make the best chocolate in England. Both our grandfathers worked for them, and Nana worked for them, and all her sisters worked for them, and . . . basically, this is the best chocolate you will ever get in your life.'

Peter is surprised to hear his brother say this. He knows for a fact that Jack does not really like plain Bournville chocolate. He never buys it, and almost never eats it when it's offered to him, because he much prefers Dairy Milk. He says Bournville is too bitter and too strong. But now he very ostentatiously bites off a square of chocolate and closes his eyes while eating it, as if the taste is driving him to ecstasy. Mmm, he says. Mmm, that tastes so good. Go on, Lothar, try some, try some of the best chocolate in the world.

Lothar breaks off a square and pops it into his mouth casually. He chews, swallows, and says:

'It's a little bit greasy for my taste. But it's all right, I suppose.'

'*All right?*' says Jack. 'You're telling me that Cadbury's Bournville chocolate is just all right? You obviously don't appreciate quality. Come on then, let's see what you lot have to offer.'

He takes the German chocolate bar from Lothar's hand. It has a lilac wrapper, decorated with an attractive picture of a farmer guiding a solitary cow through an Alpine meadow. The word *Milka* is emblazoned in white, and beneath it, the legend *Hochfeine Alpenmilch-Schokolade*. Jack unwraps it and sniffs it, as if it might be toxic. Apparently satisfied, he breaks off four pieces, as before, and hands them round.

Everyone puts their piece into their mouth at the same time. Martin says nothing, but Peter is immediately enthusiastic. This chocolate is wonderfully creamy and light and flavoursome. In fact it is easily the nicest chocolate he has ever tasted. 'Really good!' he says. 'Can I have some more?' But, turning to Jack with his hands stretched out, he is confronted by a horrifying sight. Jack's face is convulsed, and with his hands to his throat he starts making choking noises. His face goes bright red and he spits the half-consumed square of chocolate out onto the floor of the shelter.

'Ugh!' he cries. 'Horrible! Revolting! It tastes like . . . like . . . Well, I don't know *what* it tastes like. It's the most horrible thing in the world. Are you trying to poison us?'

'Poison you? Are you crazy?'

'No, I'm not crazy. I know what you're like.'

'How can you know what I'm like? You've only just met me.'

'You Germans are always trying to poison the English. It happened only last week.'

'Last week? What are you talking about?'

'Last week "Killer" Kennedy was captured by the Nazis and they tried to poison him. They offered him a cup of tea and it had poison in it. He pretended to drink it but then spat it out.'

'I'm not a Nazi.'

'You're a Hun, aren't you?'

'I don't know what that means. I never heard that word before.'

'Well, this is how "Killer" Kennedy deals with Huns.'

Jack seizes the ball of garden twine from the wooden shelf and starts to unwind it. His movements are quick and efficient but in truth Lothar is so bemused that he could have taken all the time in the world.

'Come on,' Jack says to his youngest brother. 'Let's tie him up. Let's see what kind of secrets we can get out of the filthy *Schweinhund*.'

Peter understands what is going on now: it is a game. Jack wants to play a game with Lothar, acting out one of the stories from his *Victor* comic. He holds on to the ball of twine while Jack wraps it around Lothar. Lothar puts up with this for a few seconds, but then he tries to resist, at which point Jack pushes him roughly to the floor.

'*Schweinhund! Dummkopf!*' he shouts.

'Ow, that really hurt!' says Lothar, who has fallen heavily on his ankle and twisted it.

'Never mind that,' says Jack. His enemy is only half-tied up, so he pinions him to the floor by straddling him and holding him by the wrists. 'Tell me everything, you filthy German coward! Tell me all your secrets!'

'Yes, tell us everything!' Peter repeats in his shrill voice, kicking Lothar's left thigh feebly.

'Well,' says Lothar, 'I can tell you one thing.' Very quickly, and without any apparent effort, he has slipped free from his skimpy bonds, flipped Jack over and has him pinned to the floor on his stomach, with his arms twisted behind his back. 'At school I study judo, and I have a blue belt. And if you *ever* lay a hand on me again – and this,' (he turns around to address Peter, who is watching him mesmerized) 'this applies to you as well – if either of you ever lays a hand on me again, I shall destroy you. I'll destroy you both.'

He shoves Jack flat against the floor, stands up, dusts himself down and then walks back up into the daylight with measured, composed steps. After a moment of stunned reflection, Martin follows him.

That leaves Jack and Peter. Jack sits up on the floor and rubs the back of his hand, which has been grazed and is bleeding slightly. He looks accusingly at Peter.

'Well, you didn't help.'

'Sorry. It was only a game, anyway.'

'That's right. Just a game.'

He gets up and limps towards the stairway. Peter follows. Before long, all four boys are back in the sitting room, where the grown-ups are finishing their coffee. Frank and Volker have resumed their discussion of Britain and Germany's industrial performance. Mary is looking restless, and ready to leave. Bertha is smiling a triumphant smile. Everyone is getting along. Everyone is happy. The family meeting has been an unqualified success.

6.

Wednesday's two matches are both important. At Villa Park in the afternoon, watched by Volker and Lothar, West Germany defeat Spain by two goals to one. At Wembley Stadium in the evening, watched by Jack on his parents' unreliable, embarrassingly small television set at home in Bournville, England defeat France by two goals to nil.

The Spanish manager is overcome by shame at his team's defeat. In what is widely regarded, by the British press, as an absurd display of Mediterranean histrionics, he breaks down in tears and tells the assembled reporters: 'I quit. I'm retiring from football. Tonight I'm finished with the game. Spain's defeat has been too much for me.'

Not to be outdone, the Italian manager, whose team has also been knocked out, addresses a different crowd of reporters and tells them: 'I haven't spoken to the players yet, because they are too upset. What is the use of talking to them? They are like a family without parents. But for me it is worst of all. No one can understand how bad this feeling is. In the state I'm in at the moment, I'm not prepared to give opinions on individual players or the match itself.'

But these memorable outpourings of Continental emotion are soon overshadowed by the ructions attending on the quarter-final match played between England and Argentina on Saturday 23rd July. Thirty-five minutes into the game the Argentinian captain, Rattín, is sent off for repeatedly questioning the West German referee's decisions. At first he refuses to leave the pitch, and play is suspended for seven minutes while he argues with the referee and a number of Argentinian officials and FIFA representatives join in the dispute. At one point it looks as if the whole Argentinian team is going to walk off. Geoff Hurst scores the game's only goal in the seventy-eighth minute, but the Argentinian players are adamant that they would have won if they had not been reduced to ten men, and at the end of the match there are ugly scenes: the referee is jostled by members of the team as he makes for the tunnel, with one of them appearing to raise a fist, at which point policemen and tournament officials have to intervene. One of the FIFA officials involved says afterwards that he saw the referee being 'kicked and jostled' by Argentinian players: 'I took one of their players by the shoulder to turn him round, so that I could note his number. It was number twenty, Onega, and he spat in my face. I have seen players disappointed after losing – in tears even – but this was mass hysteria. It was frightening. The scuffles continued down the tunnel into the dressing rooms.'

In an interview after the game the England manager Alf Ramsey says: 'Our best football will come against the team who come out to play football and not act as animals.'

Infuriated by this comment, the Argentinians say that Mr Ramsey will be barred from entering their country until he apologizes. His words are 'beneath him and beneath us', says Juan Santiago, leader of the Argentinian World Cup delegation. 'Either he was not in a normal state of mind or drugged.'

Their manager, Juan Carlos Lorenzo, says: 'Now all we want to do is get out of England and go home. The World Cup has been spoiled for us.'

It is reported that in Buenos Aires, armed guards have been drafted in to protect the British Embassy because anti-English sentiment is running so high. The Argentinian newspaper *Crónica* says: 'The English stole the game. They are still the pirates that pillaged the Caribbean and stole the Malvinas.'

Mr Ramsey will later withdraw his comments, saying there was 'no excuse' for them.

The result still stands, however, so England are through to the semi-finals. So are West Germany, who have defeated Uruguay 4–0 at Goodison Park in Liverpool. Both teams win their semi-final games, eliminating Portugal and Russia from the tournament. Which means, incredibly, that the 1966 World Cup final, on 30th July 1966, will be played between England and West Germany at Wembley Stadium.

This fixture will, of course, be freighted with painful and recent historical associations, but drawing attention to this fact would surely be a breach of English tact and good manners.

On the morning of the match, Jack opens his father's copy of the *Daily Mail* to read the views of their football correspondent, Vincent Mulchrone. 'West Germany may beat us at our national sport today,' Mr Mulchrone writes, 'but that would be only fair. We beat them twice at theirs.'

7.

'Why don't you all come over?' Sylvia says on the telephone. 'Thomas is away, and Gill and I aren't interested, so David's got no one to watch the match with. He'd love it if your boys were there. And our set's so much bigger than yours. We could sit in the garden or go for a walk on the Beacon while the football's on.'

And so, on World Cup final day, after an early lunch, the snowberry-white Austin Cambridge comes out again, and Geoffrey drives the whole family over to Sylvia and Thomas's house in Monument Lane, at the top of the Lickey Hills.

It is a substantial home which they have furnished in a modern style, very different to the traditional, conservative decor favoured by Geoffrey and Mary at their semi-detached house in Bournville. Mary sometimes forgets that Thomas is not from the Midlands, originally. He grew up in Surrey and worked in London from an early age: even during the war, she believes, he was employed as some sort of junior civil servant in Whitehall. After Sylvia had met him on holiday and married him they lived in London for a while – Tooting, or somewhere like that – and they both remain much more au fait with the capital than she is nowadays. Thomas often goes there on business and sometimes he and Sylvia go down together for a weekend, visiting those shops, those streets, those landmarks with which Mary was briefly familiar during her time in Dartford, but which now seem as distant and unreal to her as the boulevards of Paris or the canals of Venice. There is a new shop on the King's Road, apparently – she has read about it in the *Sunday Times* colour magazine – which is called Habitat and which specializes in modern, minimalist, Scandinavian-style furniture, and although Sylvia has not actually bought anything from there apart from a couple of rugs and a toothbrush-holder, clearly it has had a profound influence on her, because her home has none of the clutter, the bric-a-brac, the family souvenirs, the china ornaments, the ranks of framed photographs that Mary likes to fill her house with. Indeed, whenever Mary crosses Sylvia's threshold she feels that she is entering an alien landscape. The dividing wall between sitting room and dining room has been knocked down to make one single, airy living space, but the boldness doesn't stop there, because in addition, the dividing wall between the dining room and the *kitchen* has been knocked down, so that the whole ground floor of the house has in fact become one big room, with vast, plate-glass French windows overlooking the garden and the hills beyond. The original staircase to the first floor has been removed and replaced with a set of modern polished wooden cantilevered steps, adding even more of a sense of light and space. The furniture is sleek and stylish (and, Mary thinks, rather uncomfortable), the hi-fi system (upon which Thomas likes to spend the evenings listening to his collection of obscure classical records) is by Bang & Olufsen and, best of all, there is a television set (manufactured by ITT) with clean, elegant lines and a screen much larger and clearer than any Mary has ever seen before. Sylvia has already laid out cushions in a circle around the set for David and the three Lamb brothers to sit on while watching this afternoon's game.

There are snacks and finger food arranged in multicoloured plastic bowls, Martinis for the grown-ups, lemon and orange squash for the children.

This is the first time that Mary's boys have visited Sylvia's house. Martin and Peter take it in their stride, but Jack cannot conceal his admiration. He wanders around the big downstairs room, gawping at the hi-fi and the television set and the spectacular view, looking with a mixture of bafflement and longing at the few well-chosen ornaments, such as the gleaming silvery model of the Atomium from the Brussels World's Fair of 1958. Mary watches him, and knows what he is thinking: all of this is better than what we have at home. These people have more money than us. I want to live in a house like this. If not now, then one day.

Outside, the rain has passed, and it is a warm if grey afternoon. Luckily the garden furniture has been kept dry by the sun umbrella, so Sylvia, Geoffrey and Mary can sit with their Martinis and Gill, aged nine, joins them at the big round table with her lemon squash and her Nancy Drew book.

At Wembley Stadium the rain has passed too, about half an hour earlier, but it has left the pitch damp and heavy: good news for the England team, who are used to these kinds of conditions. Jack is delighted. While the national anthems are playing he scans the faces of the crowd in the background, but the picture is far too blurry to make out any details, and he fails to spot Volker and Lothar, although he knows they must be there somewhere.

Then the Swiss referee blows his whistle, and the match is under way.

'It's started!' Jack calls out to his mother in the garden.

Normally, perhaps, Mary would have been reluctant to abandon Sylvia to the company of her husband, whose conversation can often be dry, and sometimes non-existent. But today he appears to be positively sparkling. Admittedly he is talking on a subject close to his heart: how she might best manage her finances. Sylvia has been spending too much, she says, and running up an overdraft, but Geoffrey tells her that his bank now has a solution: a new facility called a 'charge card', a little shiny piece of plastic which you simply have to present in any shop in order to secure a month's free credit. Listening to him, Mary is reminded of how attentive and sympathetic her husband can be, especially when talking to a woman, and (to her occasional surprise, given his enthusiasm for ancient languages) how excited he sometimes gets when talking about innovations and new technologies. Sylvia, in any case, seems quite enthralled, so Mary has no qualms about leaving them together in the garden, and rushing inside. Soon she is sitting cross-legged on the floor with the children, and is absorbed in the progress of the game.

The first few minutes are tense. England make most of the running, and have a good number of shots at goal, but twelve minutes into the match, disastrously, it is Germany who score first. Ray Wilson, playing at left back, tries to head the ball clear after a German attack, but succeeds only in passing it directly to German striker

Helmut Haller, who takes immediate advantage by shooting it straight past the diving English goalkeeper, Gordon Banks. Mary, Martin and David all groan and hold their heads. Peter, who still doesn't fully understand the rules of football, looks a bit confused. Only Jack seems unfazed.

'OK, it's a setback,' he says, 'but in a way it could be a good sign. Since the war, any team that scores first in the World Cup final has always ended up losing.' It's the kind of fact that he seems to keep at his fingertips these days. His audience is impressed, and reassured.

Sure enough, his confidence appears to be justified. A mere six minutes later, Geoff Hurst, the English centre forward, has equalized. Bobby Moore has taken a rapid free kick, setting Hurst up for a powerful header which easily gets past Tilkowski, the German keeper. One-all. The crowd at Wembley goes wild. And so, in its quieter way, does the crowd sitting around Sylvia's television set.

It is still one-all at half-time, when Mary goes back out into the garden.

'It's very exciting in there,' she says. 'You're missing out.'

'We'll come and watch the second half,' says Sylvia. 'But Geoffrey and I have been having the most interesting chat.'

'Oh?' says Mary, curious. Surely her banking arrangements couldn't have occupied them for more than forty-five minutes?

'He tells me,' Sylvia says, 'that you're thinking of moving house.'

'Oh. Well – yes, I suppose we are.'

Mary, to tell the truth, is still very happy in Bournville, but Geoffrey has recently started to voice his dissatisfaction. He has not made his reasons very specific. He will say general things like, 'The area is changing too fast', or even 'going downhill'; offer vague suggestions such as 'we need to get away from the centre of Birmingham, it's not the same as it used to be'; talk about overcrowding and the need to have neighbours who are more 'our sort of people'. He talks about being closer to nature, to the hills, about getting plenty of fresh air and going for long country walks: all ideas which Mary finds deeply appealing. But she is resistant to change and it will be a few more years before he gets his way.

'I've been trying to persuade him that you should move out here. So that we can be neighbours.'

Mary likes this idea, too. The three of them are still talking it over when the second half of the match begins, and Mary goes back inside.

It is raining again at Wembley now, a light rain which does not threaten to halt the match, although the pitch is certainly getting muddy. Umbrellas have been opened all around the stands. England attack ferociously, and there are a number of heart-stopping near-misses, which cause Mary and the boys to scream out in frustration.

Finally Sylvia, Geoffrey and Gill have to come inside to see what all the noise is about. Before settling down on the sofa, Sylvia pauses for a moment or two to take in the scene. She looks at Mary sitting on the floor, with the four boys around her, all with their eyes locked on the screen, and realizes that Mary is in her element: surrounded by children, wrapped up in sport. It is an image of perfect happiness. When they have both grown old and their children have long since reached adulthood, this is still how she will always love to remember her cousin.

Twelve minutes from the end of the match, there is a sudden miracle: Martin Peters scores England's second goal, intercepting a cross from Bobby Moore and driving it past Tilkowski at just five or six yards' distance from the posts. The German keeper has no chance. 'Yes! Yes!' Mary and Jack shriek, and now there is not a single person in the room who does not tingle with the unforeseen, incredible intimation that England might be on the verge of winning. Twelve minutes to go. Twelve minutes between their team and the ultimate glory.

It is almost too hard to watch. But nobody can take their eyes away from the television. Eleven agonizing minutes go by, but everything still seems to be on track. The West Germans fail to break through the English defence.

Then, with just one minute to go, the referee makes an extraordinary decision. Jumping up to head the ball clear, and leaning over one of the German players in the process, Jack Charlton is considered to have committed a foul and a free kick is awarded.

'That was never a foul!' Mary protests. 'How was that a foul? All he did was—'

'Shut up, Mum!' Jack says. 'They're going to take the kick any second. They won't hang about.'

The kick is indeed taken very quickly, by Lothar (that hated name!) Emmerich. The ball enters the English penalty box somewhat haphazardly and there is some scrambling around for possession, but suddenly a defender, Wolfgang Weber, has it and he drives it into the net at close range. An equalizer. An equalizer in the final minute! The German fans at Wembley can hardly believe their luck and in the midst of their cheering and jumping up and down Jack imagines Volker and his loathsome son celebrating together somewhere on those stands, their arms wrapped around each other in a tight, ecstatic embrace. Numb with despair now, he glances across the room at his own father, who is gazing phlegmatically at the television, accepting this monstrous turn of events with the same gloomy stoicism with which he seems to accept all of life's disasters and disappointments.

'What happens now?' Sylvia asks.

'Extra time. They play for another half-hour.'

'I'll go and put the kettle on.'

'There isn't time! They've already started.'

On the point of getting up from the sofa, Sylvia sinks back onto it and then leans forward intently, caught up now in the drama of the moment. Within the first four minutes of extra time, England have had three shots at goal: the first from Alan Ball, pushed over the crossbar by the keeper, the second from Bobby Charlton, which Tilkowski saves on the line, and the third from Roger Hunt, a shot from twenty yards which goes just wide. Each attempt draws gasps first of anticipation, then of disappointment. But the next one is even more dramatic. Some nimble approach work from England ends with the ball being passed to Hurst, who slips it past his marker, turns and shoots. The shot defeats Tilkowski, but then hits the bar, and bounces down over the line – or onto it, no one can tell. As it bounces back, in any case, a German defender kicks it clear.

'GOOOOAAAAALLLL!' Jack shouts at the top of his voice.

'Was it?' says Mary. 'Was it a goal?'

There is confusion on the pitch now. At first it seems as though the referee is waving play on, but then he goes over to consult the linesman. The BBC commentator doesn't know what to say.

'That was never a goal,' says Martin.

'Never,' David agrees.

'It bloody well was!'

'Jack!' his mother chides. 'Watch your language, in front of family.'

Jack ignores the reproof, because the referee has come to a decision, and it is a sensational one: the goal is allowed. He turns smugly towards his younger brother and his cousin, and points an accusing finger at them.

'Three–two!' he chants. 'Three–two, three–two, three–two! It *was* a goal, you see. Our country scored a goal, and you two didn't believe in it. Traitors!'

'Oh, don't talk rubbish,' says Martin, irritated beyond words by his brother's triumphalism.

'We're going to win!' Jack shouts, leaping to his feet and performing a premature victory dance. 'England are going to win the World Cup!'

'Sit down and shut up,' says Martin. 'There's another quarter of an hour to go yet. Anything can happen.'

And indeed, the way this match has been unfolding, he is quite right. Anything seems possible this afternoon. And there will be one more surprise, but it won't be a German equalizer this time. In the very last seconds of extra time, when some of the crowd are so sure that the game is over that they are already running onto the pitch, Bobby Moore angles a skilful long pass to Geoff Hurst, who slams it into the back of the net with the last kick of the day.

'GOOOOAAAAALLLL!' Jack shouts again, and this time everyone else joins in his celebration, although Martin cannot stop himself from saying, 'Well, that was a bit flukey. The ref had blown his whistle.'

'No, he hadn't! What's the matter with you? Why do you have to keep nit-picking? Don't you want us to win?' Jack shakes his brother by the shoulder: '*England have won the World Cup, mate.* Don't be such a wet blanket all the time.'

'I still don't think that third one was a proper goal.'

'God almighty . . .'

Jack can still not get through to his brother, and it is at this moment, for the first time in his life, that he understands there is a deep philosophical divide between them. Meanwhile his little brother and David, who seem to be on the point of becoming fast friends, have run outdoors and are already kicking a football around, trying to replicate the highlights of the match with Sylvia's back garden standing in for the pitch at Wembley. Jack cannot believe that they are not interested in staying around to see the greatest moment of the afternoon: the moment at which Bobby Moore takes the golden Jules Rimet trophy and holds it aloft in front of the roaring crowd and in front of the Queen. For years to come it will be remembered how he courteously wiped his sweaty palms on his shorts before shaking her hand, in order not to defile her virginal white gloves. Would the West German captain have thought of doing that? Of course not. Only the British know how to behave!

Half an hour later, as the family drives home through the outer suburbs of Birmingham, the streets already filling with people coming out to celebrate, carrying cans of lager and jugs of beer, Jack replays the last two goals over and over in his mind. What fills Martin with reservations about the victory is the very thing that thrills him the most: England have not just won, but they have won, in effect, by the thinnest of margins, with one of the winning goals being disputed and the other actually coinciding with the final whistle. Just like 'Killer' Kennedy or Matt Braddock, VC, they have defeated the Germans at the last minute, thwarted them against all the odds and escaped by the skin of their teeth. The triumph is theirs, and theirs alone.

Winner takes all: it's the perfect system, he decides, for sport and for life.

Martin, meanwhile, absorbing everything that goes on around him with his customary methodical wariness, sees his father directing his mother's attention to a little building on the corner of the street, and hears him saying, as they drive past:

'*That's* the kind of thing I'm talking about. Remember when that used to be a perfectly nice little corner shop?'

'It still is,' Mary answers.

'Yes, but look at those signs in the window. What language even *is* that?'

On the street, the shop's owner, wearing a turban, is picking up a wooden box full of exotic-looking vegetables which Mary cannot identify, and carrying it back into the shop. A group of four young men and one woman, already looking a bit the worse for drink, stumble past him chanting, '*England, England, England!*', almost bumping into him and knocking the box to the ground.

Delighted at this spectacle, Jack winds down the back window of the car and cries out to them:

'*Two World Wars and one World Cup!*'

They roar with laughter and give him the thumbs-up, as two of the men raise the woman onto their shoulders and start to carry her the rest of the way down the street.

8.

Dear Mary,

It was a great pleasure to meet you and your family in Birmingham last month. Lothar and I shall treasure a very precious memory of our lunch at Bertha's beautiful house.

Our time in England was very enjoyable and interesting, and it is especially satisfying that we have connected at last with our English family. Of course the 'icing on the cake', as I've heard you say, would have been victory for West Germany in the World Cup! But you cannot have everything in life. On the day, we both felt that the better team won.

I could sense your eldest son's disappointment that he was only watching the matches on television rather than in person, so with him in mind, Lothar and I purchased two souvenir programmes of the final at Wembley Stadium. You will find one of them enclosed. Please pass it on to Jack with Lothar's compliments, in memory of their first (but I very much hope not their last) meeting.

With warmest regards,
Volker

*

The joy of possessing a real programme from the 1966 World Cup final is tempered, for Jack, by his resentment at the warm-hearted gesture it represents on the part of his German cousins. Nonetheless, it has the potential to become a treasured possession, if he keeps it in pristine condition: but a few weeks after receiving it in the post he will deface it by adding Hitler moustaches to the photographs of all the German players. After that the programme will be stowed away in an old trunk, will survive a series of house moves, but will not see the light of day again until Sunday 27th June 2010, when Jack and his twenty-one-year-old son, Julian, are watching England's second-round World Cup game against Germany: a disaster for England, leading to a 4–1 defeat. When Frank Lampard's shot at goal hits the crossbar and clearly bounces across the line, only for the goal to be disallowed by the referee, the reverse echo of 1966 is unmistakable. Afterwards Jack tells his son the whole story of that famous match, and retrieves the souvenir from a spare bedroom by way of illustration. But Julian, seeing what his father had done to the players' photographs all those years ago, is distinctly unamused. In fact he is horrified, and makes no attempt to hide it. Only then will Jack, embarrassed by the actions of his younger self, quietly throw the programme away.

FOUR

The Investiture of Charles, Prince of Wales

1st July 1969

From: David Foley
Sent: Friday, July 22, 2005 11:42 AM
To: Peter Lamb
Subject: Llanbedr

Dear Peter,

It was a few weeks ago that you wrote to me, so I'm sorry
for the slow reply. First things first: you asked if I had any
photographs that could go into the album you're making for
your parents' golden wedding. I could only really find one, but
it's a good one: our two families on holiday together in Llanbedr,
in the summer half-term of 1969. There are eight of us, sitting
outside your caravan (I suppose my father must have taken the
picture), post-barbecue, looking very happy and pleased with
ourselves. The five children in the foreground, grown-ups sitting
behind. It's an especially nice one of your parents: your mother's
smile lights up the picture as always. (And you are holding on to
her for dear life, as always. Clutching on to her legs, in this
instance.) I've attached it to this email. I'm afraid the file is pretty
large – almost 2 MB! Hope it doesn't cause your computer any
problems downloading it.

Incidentally, do pass on my congratulations to your mum and
dad. Fifty years' marriage is quite an achievement. My parents
might have got there too, I suppose, had Mum not passed away
so early. However, I always thought your parents had a slightly
more solid marriage than mine did. Mum and Dad had quite a few
difficulties over the years – were already having them, in fact, when
we all took this holiday together. But of course you wouldn't have
noticed anything like that, at such a young age.

Actually, I found this photo more than three weeks ago, straight after you wrote to me, and it prompted me to send you a message right away, but the resulting email turned out to be so long I only just finished it last night. It developed into quite a detailed reminiscence about that week. I'm sending it to you now as another attachment, with some misgivings I must admit. I hope I haven't been too candid: some of it might be a bit difficult for you to read, I think, but as you know my credo as a writer has always been to tell the truth as directly as possible. (*FUCK ALL THIS LYING*, as the great B. S. Johnson said.) I hope, too, that my memory hasn't distorted things too much: it was thirty-six years ago that all this happened, after all! But I'd already started keeping my famous diaries by then, so I know at least that the dates and times are accurate. The thing is, I've always wanted to write something about that week, about us and Sioned, and the reservoir at Capel Celyn, because it's always stayed so fresh in my mind, and now you've inspired me to do it. You said you were going to make a little speech at your parents' anniversary party, so if there's anything in this account that you want to pinch and use for that purpose, just go ahead. I hope it all goes off splendidly, anyway. You will have a lovely time down there with all the family, I'm sure. That part of Devon is beautiful at this time of year.

Much love,
David

*

Following which, Peter immediately clicked on the attachment, and read:

Capel Celyn
A reminiscence by David Foley

*

So, Peter, this is what I remember:
It was the summer half-term, 1969. I was ten years old and you

were almost eight. This was the second year I had been keeping my diary. Every Christmas, from 1967 onwards, I would be given (among other things) a Letts Desk Diary as a present from my parents. I kicked the habit in the 1980s, but have recently taken it up again, so now I have almost twenty of these volumes, their multicoloured spines and golden lettering looking down on me from the shelf above my desk as I type these words. So I can give with absolute certainty not just the date of our departure (Saturday 31st May) but even the time: ten in the morning. We travelled in a convoy of three cars. Your father had traded in his Austin Cambridge by then, and had bought a solid, light blue 1800 – on the basis, I suppose, that it would be powerful enough to tow your new caravan. So he and Jack set out together in that, pulling the van behind them. Your mum, in her zippy little Hillman Imp, followed in the middle of the convoy, accompanied by Martin and yourself. Bringing up the rear were the four of us, squashed together in my mother's Morris Minor. In the last couple of years Dad had started to make quite serious money in the advertising business, and off the back of this he had bought himself a Jag, but on this occasion we left it behind at home. I expect he wanted to use it during the week when he came back, and besides, he wouldn't have trusted Mum to drive it unscathed around those narrow Welsh country lanes.

My diary, which is full of the most mundane detail, tells me that we made two stops on that journey. The first one was at Llangynog in the Tanat valley, where we had a loo break. This was where we also made a switch in the travelling arrangements: you and I, you may remember, were pretty fast friends at this point, and I requested a transfer to your mum's car so I could sit in the back with you. Martin, meanwhile, decided to join his father and older brother towing the caravan. You, your mother and I were the ones who set off first, up that steep incline which takes you into the outskirts of the Snowdonia national park, where the landscape suddenly becomes wild and open, and the main hazards for drivers are the sheep ambling across the narrow, winding road. I was fascinated by your mother's driving. Both my parents were cautious drivers, braking as they drove around bends, changing down into low gear whenever they approached junctions or traffic lights. Your mother had no time for any of that. She drove as fast as she possibly could and zoomed around those hairpin bends with the practised confidence of a Formula One driver. If the car in front of her was moving too slowly she overtook it at the earliest opportunity, not always at the safest moment either. Within a few minutes your caravan and my family's car were miles behind, a distant memory. Therefore, when we arrived at Llyn Celyn, the reservoir which lies four or five miles beyond Bala, we had some time to kill before the others caught up with us.

We had stopped by the side of the reservoir for a picnic. There was no particular need to do this: we were less than an hour from our destination near the coast. But it was one o'clock, the hour for lunch, and your mother was a stickler for family mealtimes. She had made several packs of cheese and cucumber sandwiches, wrapped in tin foil, and she had also brought packets of crisps and flasks of tea, and the time to have all this was now, not an hour later or half an hour earlier. Still, it was only polite to give the others time to join us, and while we were waiting, she led the two of us down to the water's edge.

Now, I should say a word or two about my slightly odd relationship with your mother at this point. Not only was I related to her (I suppose she is my first cousin once removed, although you may remember that we always called her 'Auntie Mary', just as you all called my mother 'Auntie Sylvia') but she was also my PE teacher at school. And so, in an odd way, I knew her better than you did: or at least, that part of her life which was invisible to you, which you probably never even thought about (because our parents' working lives are of no interest to us as children, none whatsover), was something I was very familiar with. She was not just my PE teacher, in fact, because the part played by 'Mrs Lamb' in the life of our school was much greater than that. She also gave piano lessons, played the piano at assembly in the mornings and sometimes read stories to us at the end of the day.

Now and then, however, difficult situations would arise from the fact that my schoolteacher was also a family member: for instance, if it should happen that I committed some offence and she was obliged to punish me. It's true that there was little real danger of this, because I was almost pathologically well behaved. Still, I can certainly remember one occasion on which the dilemma presented itself. Like many of my peers, I fell periodically under the spell of the most malign and disruptive boy in the school, whose name was Tony Burcot. He was darkly charismatic, much feared and a born mischief-maker: except that this phrase doesn't really do justice to his behaviour, which towards the end of our time at primary school went well beyond mischief into bullying, criminality and, on at least one occasion, sexual assault. Most of the boys in our class took turns to be his semi-reluctant sidekick, and it was during my period of service that an odd thing happened: one day, a number of notices appeared in the bathrooms and other strategic locations around the school telling everyone that there was a SERIOUS WATER SHORTAGE and everyone should be careful to use ONLY THE MINIMUM AMOUNT OF WATER for handwashing and drinking and ON NO ACCOUNT TO LEAVE THE TAPS RUNNING after using them. Naturally, this presented an irresistible temptation to Tony Burcot, who made it his business during morning break to go from bathroom to bathroom – girls' as well as boys' – turning all the taps on, and I was drafted in to help. But then, in a double stroke of bad luck, we were caught red-handed not just in the worst possible place – the junior girls' toilet – but by the worst possible person – your mother, who happened to come in just as we had completed our act of sabotage. It was one of the most painful moments of my young life, and is still etched on my memory. Tony and I were clearly partners in the crime, so there was no question of your mother showing favouritism by letting me off with a friendly word of reproof: I had to take the full force of her official disapproval. The mortification of it was unbearable: not the words that she spoke to me, but the painful knowledge, shared equally between us, that this was all a terrible falsehood, that only the previous weekend I had been at the pictures with Mrs Lamb and her three sons, and next weekend our two families were planning a Saturday outing to Silverstone to see the motor racing. On no account would she ever speak to me this way in situations such as those: she would not think to criticize or reprimand me even in the gentlest manner, out of consideration for my mother. Yet now here she was, telling me off, treating me and the evil Tony Burcot as if we were of the same kind. It was all a lie and a sham. She named our punishment – staying behind after school to pick up litter – and for the rest of the day my face burned with the shame of it: until, in an act of kindness which was so very typical of her, she put me out of my misery by finding a quiet moment to take me aside before the last lesson of the afternoon, and saying: 'You know that I had to do that, don't you?' I nodded, unable to meet her gaze, and then asked her an odd, barely relevant question, which had for some reason been nagging away at me for the last few hours: 'Why isn't there enough water anyway?' She explained that there was a problem with the local supply: it had been on the Midlands news, there had been an accident, a fracture, a broken pipeline at West Hagley – the location stuck in my mind for some reason – but I wasn't to worry about it, it would soon be mended and everything would be back to normal, and after that I felt much better, and then she took me outside to where my classmates were gathered on the stretch of grass beside the playground, twenty or thirty children ranged in a circle around her chair in the late-afternoon sunlight, so we could listen to her read aloud from *Tom's Midnight Garden*, which she did with tremendous verve and expression, bringing the characters to life, sometimes (I suspect) even enhancing the story with her own embellishments and digressions. She was – and, as I'm sure you could tell me, probably still is – a wonderful storyteller.

And, coming back to the matter in hand, what a story she told us that afternoon in Wales, Peter! Do you remember?

She led us down to the shore of the reservoir, down a rough little path which wound between the rocks and the trees, and then, after looking out over the water for a while, she said:

'Isn't it lovely, lads?'

We nodded. It was a picturesque spot, and I think I was just coming to the age where I was starting to appreciate the beauties of the natural world. On the other hand it was, after all, just a reservoir: nothing really to get too excited about.

'You'd never guess, would you,' she said, 'that there was a whole village down there, beneath the water?'

And now we both took notice. Your mother could see that she had our attention, and continued:

'Oh, yes. There's a whole village beneath this lake. An underwater village. Houses, shops, a church. The church is the main building, right in the middle. The steeple's so high that it almost sticks out of the water sometimes. Next to that you have the butcher's, the baker's . . .'

'The candlestick maker's?' you chimed in, remembering the nursery rhyme.

'Of course. All the shops are on the same long street, and at the end of the street you have the village square, with the clock tower, and the bandstand . . .'

'Do people live there, underwater?' you asked.

'No, the people left a long time ago. The whole village is deserted. Abandoned. That's what gives it such a strange feeling.'

'Maybe there are ghosts down there.' (This was my contribution.) 'The ghosts of the people who used to live there.'

'Quite possibly,' your mother said. 'You can see shadows under the water sometimes. I always used to think it was reflections of the clouds, but maybe you're right. Maybe it's the ghosts of the villagers.' She turned to see the effect these words had had upon us, and apparently satisfied, she said: 'Anyway, I suppose we'd better get back up to the car. The others'll be here in a minute, and they'll be wanting to eat.'

She began climbing back up towards the car park, but we didn't follow her at first. Neither of us wanted to leave that place. You were gazing out across the water, with a kind of mesmerized look in your eye. For my own part, I was staring down into the depths, trying to catch glimpses of those shapeless, abstract spectres which your mother's tale had raised in my imagination. Far in the distance, away to the left, stretched a thin plateau of rock and, just in front of it, an impressive grey cylindrical structure rising from beneath the surface of the reservoir. These were, of course, the gravity dam that contained its waters, and the straining tower. But I did not know this at the time, and took little notice of these man-made addenda. I was far too busy thinking about this wonderful submerged township and its watery inhabitants.

'Shall we go back up?' you said eventually. 'We don't want them to eat all the crisps before we get there.'

And so we ate our picnic, and drove on to our destination, but we didn't talk much in the car, being far too preoccupied with the story we had just heard and the wholly unexpected detour your mother had taken us upon: a voyage down to a lost, magical kingdom, thronged with the eeriest phantasmal images.

*

The caravan site which your parents had booked was nothing more than a field. A field in the middle of nowhere. Nonetheless, it was very beautiful. To get there, you entered Llanbedr from the direction of Harlech and took a left turn by the Victoria Inn. Within a few hundred yards you found yourself driving along an amazingly narrow road which ran at first beside the river Artro. Looking back, I can only marvel at your father's skill in negotiating this route without incident while towing a caravan. No wonder he was looking pleased with himself when he pulled up. Setting up the caravan on its pitch, connecting it to the spare car battery he had brought (he was always ingenious with things like that, I remember) he was full of jokes and high spirits. Being in an isolated spot with family and friends seemed to bring out the best side of him.

The field you were in belonged to a farmer whose house stood a few hundred yards away, nestled in a little hollow beneath some trees. And this was where our two families parted company, temporarily. We had rented the farmhouse for a week. The farmer himself (his name was Glyn) would be living all week with his wife and daughter in a small outhouse which he had converted into basic accommodation so that, during the summer months, he could rent out the main house to English holidaymakers anxious to sample something of the Welsh bucolic idyll. Letting caravanners plonk their vehicles down in his field seemed to be a relatively new sideline for him, and one which had not yet really taken off: that week, your family would be his only customers. Then again, he had not exactly gone out of his way to provide the necessary facilities. There was no running water – for that, you had to come to the house, and use the standpipe in the farmyard – and the waste disposal unit (human waste, that is) simply consisted of a large rectangular hole in the ground, covered over with a few planks nailed together. After you had all been in residence for a day or two, I'm afraid to say that this hole began to give off a noticeable odour.

*

On Sunday 1st June, I woke up late – some time after nine o'clock – and lay in bed listening to a medley of agreeable sounds carried my way by the morning breeze: the chirruping of thrushes and starlings, the bleating of sheep, the distant babble of the river, and the first movement of J. S. Bach's third Partita for Solo Violin in E major, BWV 1006.

It was you, of course, who was responsible for the latter. You were already a prodigy on the violin, and your mother would not allow you to miss your daily practice, even staying in a caravan in the back of beyond. I got out of bed, threw some clothes on and went out into the farmyard, from where I could see your field, and was confronted by a surreal but impressive sight: your music stand had been set up outdoors, next to the caravan, and there you were, standing in front of it in the morning sunshine, entertaining the sheep with a note-perfect performance of Bach's demanding score. Well, I don't know much about classical music (and didn't know anything then), but it sounded good to me: good enough that I was annoyed, intensely annoyed in fact, to hear it being interrupted by the sound of a portable radio being switched on. I wheeled around and there was the farmer's daughter, Sioned, sitting on a step with this radio on her knee. It was playing a song I disliked intensely at the time, and have disliked ever since – 'My Way', by Frank Sinatra. A maudlin, over-the-top ballad that set my teeth on edge with the first verse and then dragged on interminably to its bombastic conclusion. I decided to go over and give Sioned a piece of my mind.

'I hate that song,' I told her.

We had never spoken to each other before, so this was an abrupt way of introducing myself, but it didn't seem to bother her.

'Me too,' she said.

'Turn it off then.'

'No. There'll be something better on in a minute.'

'I can't hear my friend playing his violin.'

'I know. That's why I put it on. It sounds like he's strangling a cat.'

She seemed about the same age as me (actually she was a year older) and had brown hair which tumbled down to frame her pale, freckled face with natural ringlets. Despite the hot sunshine she was wearing a thick woollen jumper which gave off a strong but pleasant smell of farm animals. Her expression was challenging and she seemed not at all put out by my presence here, slap in the middle of her family home.

'I like the Beatles,' she said. 'Do you?'

'Yes,' I said. Everybody liked the Beatles.

She started singing the first verse of 'Get Back' and I joined in, and then we sang the chorus together. But I fell silent when I realized a man had appeared behind us, making me self-conscious. Emerging from the outhouse, he gave a nod of recognition to Sioned, took me in with a quick, appraising stare, then walked across the farmyard towards the metal gate. He took out a pack of cigarettes and lit one, then leaned against the gate, smoking and looking out across the fields.

'That's my uncle,' said Sioned. She lowered her voice slightly, even though he was well out of earshot.

'Does he live with you?' I asked.

'He lives all over the place,' she said. 'Wherever he can get a free meal, Mum says. He's been with us for more than a week now.' She narrowed her eyes and added: 'I bet those aren't even his cigarettes.' And then, with an abrupt change of subject: 'You're from England, aren't you? Which part?'

'Worcestershire,' I said. This was my standard answer, learned from my mother, who was such a snob that she never liked to admit her house actually had a Birmingham postcode.

'I don't know where that is.'

'It's in the middle.'

'I've never been to England. Don't want to, especially.'

'I don't blame you. Why would you? It's much prettier here.'

'You get bored with that after a while. We're so far from every-thing. We have to drive half an hour just to get to the cinema. I'd like to live in a big city somewhere, like Aberystwyth.'

'Where's that?' I asked. I had never heard of Aberystwyth.

'Not far from here. It's got a university and everything. I've been there . . . two or three times. You should see it! The shops! There are hundreds and hundreds of them.'

'Birmingham has lots of shops,' I bragged, not wishing to be outdone.

'Not as many as Aberystwyth, I bet.'

'Well, at least you're close to the sea here.' She looked at me, uncomprehending, so I added: 'For swimming in.'

At which, Sioned snorted. 'That's just something people do when they come here for their holidays. I hardly ever go swimming. My parents are farmers. They farm the land. It's hard work. All this –' she gestured around – 'isn't just for looking at, you know.'

At that moment the back door of the farmhouse opened. No one came out at first, but we could hear voices coming from the kitchen: the voices of my mother and father, in the middle of an argument.

'. . . never tell me *anything*,' I could hear my mother saying.

'Oh, what rubbish,' my father answered.

'I don't know if there's any point in us being married at all, if you won't talk to me.'

'You're being hysterical about this, as usual.'

That seemed to put an end to the discussion, as far as my father was concerned. He came out of the house and stood for a moment or two in the doorway, trying to regain his composure. He looked around him, taking in the scene – including the presence of Sioned's uncle – then noticed Sioned and me sitting nearby and, turning on a visibly forced smile, wandered over to the step where we were sitting.

'Getting to know each other?' he asked, to which neither of us could think of an answer. 'What a beautiful day,' he continued, and we couldn't think of an answer to that either. Then, pointing over towards the gate, he asked Sioned a much simpler question: 'Who's that man?'

'My Uncle Trefor,' she said. 'My mum's brother.'

'Does he live here?'

'Sometimes.'

He nodded, looked down at us one more time and said, pointlessly, 'Well. Carry on,' then strolled over in the direction of the gate. I watched him as he left and wondered – as all children have wondered, down the centuries – why my parents had to be so odd and why they insisted on parading their oddness whenever I was in the company of other kids. My face burned with embarrassment, but Sioned did not appear to have noticed anything untoward. She turned her attention to re-tuning the radio, which was just as well, because now my father started to behave even more strangely. He went over to speak to Trefor, but the sounds that came out of his mouth made no sense to me. It took me a moment or two to understand that he was talking in a foreign language. He only said a couple of words, but then Trefor looked at him in surprise and replied in the same language. I guessed that they were speaking Welsh. Welsh! Since when had my father spoken Welsh? He was full of surprises, that was for sure. Soon there came another one, because Trefor offered my father a cigarette and to my astonishment he accepted, put it in his mouth and allowed Trefor to light it for him. This was unbelievable. Not once, not once in my whole life, had I ever seen my father smoking. There were no ashtrays in our house, and guests who wanted to smoke were invariably asked to go outside in the garden to do so, even if it was night-time and raining. So what on earth was going on?

Before I'd had time to think any more about this, however, Sioned – unable to find anything worth listening to on the radio – stood up and made an irresistible proposition:

'Do you want to come and see the snakes?'

'There are snakes?' I asked, running along behind her, because she was already striding off in the direction of the field with your caravan in it.

'Wait and see,' she answered.

'Can my friend come too?' I asked. 'My friend Peter.'

'Why not?' Sioned answered. 'Anything to stop him playing that violin.'

And so we took a slight detour, and interrupted your practice mid-cadenza. As soon as she heard the music stop your mother popped her head out of the caravan door to protest, but I said to her, in what I hoped was a disarming way: 'We're just going to see the snakes, Auntie Mary. Peter will be right back.'

We were on our way before she had time to reply.

That was my first sight – I think yours too – of grass snakes in the wild. How Sioned knew they would be there for us to see I don't know. But there they were, in the lane that ran alongside your field, on a patch of drystone wall that was overgrown with grass: three snakes, a mother and two children probably, basking in the morning sun, sleepily entwined with one another. Their skins were a pale green-brown that blended in perfectly with their background. They took no notice of us at first, but graciously allowed us to observe them for five minutes or more, as they wound and unwound themselves around each other in comfortable, drowsy coils. It was only when I became bored and tried poking at the mother with a stick retrieved from the side of the road that they took offence and slithered languidly away into the surrounding bracken, never to be seen again.

*

After that, for the next two or three days at least, Sioned became an unofficial member of our family. She came with us on all our trips, whether we were going to the beach, or driving up to Llyn Cwm Bychan (which we called 'the Echoing Lake') to eat our latest picnic, or walking up to the grey medieval slabs which pave the Bwlch Tyddiad pass (which we called 'the Roman Steps'). Neither of our fathers had taken the week off work, so they had driven back to Birmingham on Sunday night in your dad's 1800, and would not return until Friday evening to take us home. This meant that, with the addition of Sioned, the gender balance in our party was now equal; although my memory is that my sister showed no interest in befriending her, and it was the three of us – you, me and Sioned – who became a threesome, a tight-knit trio who were rarely out of each other's company for those first few blessed days of warmth and sunshine.

The spell cast by your mother's story of the underwater village had started to fade slightly, but then it was revived one afternoon (Wednesday afternoon, my diary tells me) when we were taken to Harlech to visit the castle. Sioned was not with us that day – she had gone to Wrexham to spend a couple of nights with her grandfather – so you and I explored the ruins by ourselves. It was while we were climbing the steps to the top of the gatehouse that a vision came to me. 'What if there was a *castle* there?' I said.

'A castle where?' you asked.

'Under the lake.' You looked unconvinced, frankly, so I tried to bring the scene to life by painting a word-picture. 'A great big ruined castle. A family of sea serpents live there. I mean, lake serpents. You can see them coiled around the old pillars . . .'

'Like those grass snakes,' you said.

'Exactly. And there's an underground room full of treasure.'

'What sort of treasure?'

'Coral,' I said, decisively. 'Because that's the most precious thing, in the underwater world. Not gold, or silver, or diamonds. Coral.'

We stood on top of the gatehouse and looked out over the water, across the Irish Sea and towards the Llŷn peninsula. I don't know about you, but my imagination was beginning to race, like a steam engine that as yet had no railway carriages to pull.

'We should write all this down,' I said. 'We should write a story together.'

You looked doubtful.

'A story? What about? What would happen?'

I didn't have an answer to that at the moment, but further inspiration came later that evening from an unexpected source. After Harlech Castle we drove to Porthmadog, had an early supper of fish and chips (delicious) while sitting on the harbour wall, and then went to the cinema. It was a revival of *Thunderball*, the James Bond movie. At this time it was quite common for these films to be re-released every couple of years: cinema managers who were struggling to attract an audience with the latest films – those big musical flops like *Hello, Dolly*, say, or *Paint Your Wagon* – could always rely on filling the house with one of these strange, adolescent, sado-patriotic fantasies that for some reason had cast a hypnotic spell over the nation throughout most of the 1960s. Both your mother and my mother were in love with Sean Connery and seemed to find nothing more appealing than the idea of being brutally ravished by him in a hotel bedrooom during one of the spare moments between his fistfights with enemy henchmen or the latest casual assassination he had carried out with his trusty Walther PPK. Averting my horrified eyes from the screen during one of his bouts of lovemaking I glimpsed our mothers' faces in the smoky light of the cinema and have never forgotten those expressions of helpless, almost anguished longing, their eyes misted over, their mouths hanging half-open in the dreaminess of their lust. Disturbing though this spectacle was, however, it distracted me only temporarily from the thrilling momentum of the film, which resolved itself in the final thirty minutes into a series of underwater battles. Watching the wetsuited enemies slaughtering each other in these murky Caribbean depths, their identities hard to distinguish, each combatant merely a black, amphibious silhouette trailing streams of bubbles from his breathing apparatus, I found myself thinking again of the submerged village at Llyn Celyn, and began to envision the climax of the story we might set there.

We awoke the next morning to a heavy downpour which showed little sign of abating after breakfast. Undaunted, our mothers proposed a trip to Aberystwyth for a morning's shopping. As before, you and I sat together in your mother's car. It is not a short drive, from Llanbedr to Aberystwyth: most drivers would do it in about an hour and a half, but she managed to shave at least ten minutes off that time with her usual tactics of accelerating up to seventy on the straight stretches, hurtling around corners without using her brakes and resolutely overtaking slower vehicles even in the most hazardous conditions (and today the sheets of rain did nothing to deter her). By the time we screamed to a halt in a seafront car park, you and I were breathless with excitement and, given that the others were still some way behind, we had plenty of time to visit a kiosk selling sweets and chocolate bars. You bought yourself a sixpenny bar of Dairy Milk. I rather snobbishly abstained.

(I should explain about that, perhaps, in case you never realized it. We had a very elitist attitude to chocolate in our family. Back in the 1950s my father had spent some time in Belgium, and had developed a taste for Belgian chocolate. And that was the only kind of chocolate we ate in our house. I know: this was pure heresy, in the city of Cadbury's. Dad would bring a few slender bars back home from some fancy shop in London after one of his trips down there, which meant that Gill and I never got to eat chocolate very often at all. I know that your mother, on the other hand, would buy you a little Cadbury's chocolate bar every day. You told me once that these bars would be waiting for you after school. On the mantelpiece at home there were studio photos of you, Martin and Jack, and every day when you got back from school there would be a chocolate bar next to each of these framed portraits. I remember you telling me this and how envious it made me feel. And of course a few years later I rebelled and while most teenagers were experimenting with drugs and alcohol, I was mainlining Fruit & Nut, Bar Six and Curly Wurlies.)

Later on, as we were wandering the streets of Aberystwyth in the rain, I remember we walked past some of the university buildings and my mother said to yours:

'This is where he lives at the moment, isn't it? Perhaps he's in there right now.'

This suggestion seemed to give them both a frisson of excitement, and when I asked who they meant by 'he', your mum told me that it was Prince Charles, the Queen's eldest son and the heir to the throne. She had read in the newspaper that he was currently living in Aberystwyth, studying at the university in preparation for his investiture as Prince of Wales in a few weeks' time.

'Studying?' I asked. 'Studying what?'

'Welsh history, I suppose,' your mother answered. 'You know – Owen Glendower and all that caper.'

I didn't really share in their excitement, I have to admit. Who cared if some stuck-up prince was a few hundred yards away, poring over Welsh history books in a university library? I was more enthusiastic about our visit to a local stationery shop, stationery being one of my weird new passions. I bought myself a smart A4 notebook with narrow ruled lines and a nice watercolour painting of Harlech Castle on the cover. I was particularly enamoured of this painting, following our visit to the castle the day before, and somehow – after only half-hearing our mothers' conversation about Prince Charles – I had got it into my head that this was where his investiture would be taking place. Of course, it was Caernarfon Castle I should have been thinking of, but perhaps to a young boy (especially an English boy) one Welsh castle is much like any other.

That afternoon, back in Llanbedr and back at the farmhouse, as the rain continued to cascade, I summoned you to my bedroom and told you that we were going to start writing the story together. I showed you the first page of the notebook, upon which I had already written:

THE UNDERWATER VILLAGE
by David Foley
with Peter Lamb

These words were accompanied by some very fine illustrations of submerged cottages surrounded by mermaids and sea horses, but for some reason these were not what caught your attention.

'My name's not nearly as big as yours,' you objected.

'Of course not. It was my idea to write the story.'

'Are we going to write it together?'

'Yes.'

'Then why doesn't it say "by David Foley *and* Peter Lamb"? Why does it say *"with"*?'

I thought about this for an impatient moment, couldn't come up with an answer, and said: 'Look, we're never going to get it written if you keep asking stupid questions. Let's just get on with it.'

And for the rest of that afternoon, that's exactly what we did.

And the next morning. By Friday lunchtime our masterpiece was completed. Nothing much that I have written since then has come so quickly, or so easily. The finished story was twenty or twenty-five pages long, which is pretty good going, I think, for a collaborative effort between two young boys like us. After a good deal of perhaps over-elaborate scene-setting, in which a fair amount of time was devoted to describing seaweed trees and the school of great white whales who carried passengers on their backs and served as the community's public transport system, we moved on to the main story. This concerned the residents of a rival village from another nearby lake, who had invaded Capel Celyn and were laying siege to it (it was never specified how they had got there, a journey that presumably involved travelling by land). Their aim was to get their villainous hands on the reserves of coral which were stored in a well-guarded treasury beneath the ruined castle. Needless to say this invasion resulted in a number of underwater battles which were described at inordinate length in sentences like: 'He fired his death-ray gun and the bullet struck his target in the heart, sending blood everywhere which attracted a shoal of deadly sharks.' In the end, however, the doughty villagers of Capel Celyn saw off the invading hordes, peace was restored, and all was well again.

That afternoon, after lunch, we gave the notebook to your mother and sat on the sofa at one end of the caravan, tense with anticipation while she read it from start to finish. Afterwards she was generous in her praise. I've no idea what she really thought of it, and she had a few pertinent criticisms to make ('rather violent, in parts, isn't it?' – a bit rich coming from a fan of the James Bond films, I must say) but, as always, she had a genius for making children feel prized and appreciated. It is a measure of this genius, I suppose, that while I had no interest at all in what my own mother had to say about the story, your mum's verdict was enough to give me a glow of authorly achievement that lasted all evening.

And that evening, in fact, brought further joyful developments. For one thing, the sun came out again at last. For another, our fathers returned from Birmingham, arriving at about seven o'clock, in plenty of time for a barbecue supper. And not long after they had appeared, Sioned came back from Wrexham. As you, your father and I were walking up the farm driveway, Glyn's car overtook us and pulled up in the farmyard. Sioned leaped out and ran towards us and gave us both a big hug. I have to say that I found this gesture almost overwhelming. I was not used to girls showing me physical affection. Then she put her hand in mine and dragged me along the path with her, while you ran behind, trying to keep up. We sat down on our usual step and without saying more than a few words to us she took out a present her grandfather had given her, a pack of cards with pictures of different woodland animals on the back, and we began playing Knockout Whist. Meanwhile Sioned's father started unloading some things from the car, and then Trefor came from the outhouse to help him and immediately they began talking to each other in Welsh. This left your father in an agony of embarrassment. He had come all this way with us specifically to see Glyn – to pay him for the week's use of the field, as it happened – and yet he did not seem to know how to get his attention. It was painful to watch him hovering beside them while these two men ignored him and carried on with their conversation as if he wasn't there. Finally Glyn took pity and acknowledged his presence and your father began his approach with the dreadful words, 'Evening, squire!', affecting some sort of terrible *faux*-demotic which bore no relation to how he normally talked – or how *anybody* normally talks, because who calls anyone 'squire'? – and then he made some sort of equally awful remark about how he'd come to hand over his 'pound of flesh', which was such an inappropriate expression that Glyn seemed at first to have no idea what he was talking about. In the end, anyway, he managed to get his meaning across and the transaction was concluded. Afterwards he would complain to your mother about how the two men had spoken in Welsh as a way of excluding him, and she would concur, having had (she claimed) the same experience in the local shops:

'They start talking it as soon as you come in,' she said. 'Just to make you feel uncomfortable.'

'They don't like us, you know,' your father told her, and she protested:

'But why? What have we done to them? We've been keeping ourselves to ourselves, haven't we?'

'I don't mean you and me,' he explained. 'I mean *us*. The English. The Welsh just don't like us.' But it was far more the case, in my memory, that this man who always seemed so relaxed, so likeable with his own family – or with anybody he knew well – simply didn't know how to talk to two strangers, especially two from a very different social class to his own.

Forgive me, Peter, for dwelling on this detail. I have no wish to make fun of your father for his social awkwardness. But I think as you get older, as you enter middle age as you and I are now undoubtedly doing, you start to become interested in the mystery of your own self, and the key to that mystery is the relationship between you and your parents. I don't understand my own father. I have never understood him. When I was a young child – at the time I am writing about now – he came and went, in and out of our lives, seemingly as the fancy took him. At the beginning of the decade he worked in the PR department at Phocas Industries in Shirley, where they made electrical components for cars, but after a few years he left and helped to set up the Birmingham office of a big ad agency. Their main office was in London so, from then on, he took lots of trips down to the capital, but not just to there: they also seemed to have a lot of contacts in Eastern Europe, so he was always flying off to Hungary, East Germany, Czechoslovakia. He'd come back from these trips bearing weird presents and souvenirs from Eastern Europe (for us) and classical records on the Supraphon label (for himself). Gill and I loved getting these gifts, of course, but they were simply tokens: they didn't make us feel that there was any real warmth or closeness between us. Dad was reserved with his children, reserved to the point of coldness, but in his case I always felt that this was a choice he made – he could be friendly enough with people when he wanted to be – whereas your father's quietness always seemed to me an obvious sign that he was shy and unsure of himself in the presence of strangers. And the reason I'm telling this story now, revisiting that trip to Wales (one of the reasons, anyway) might be that there's something about that week – something, specifically, about the difference between Dad's way of behaving towards Glyn and Trefor, and your father's way – that tantalizes me, that makes me think (or hope) that it holds the key to his character, to the secrets that I suspect he hoards and keeps locked away still.

As perhaps we all do.

The starkest demonstration of this difference came the next morning, when my mother, Gill and I were in for a surprise. We were under the impression that we would be driving back to Birmingham at 10 a.m., travelling in convoy with your family as before, but then my father told us to stop packing and announced that we would not, in fact, be leaving until the evening. The reason? He had ingratiated himself with Glyn and his brother-in-law so thoroughly that they had decided to go fishing together. It was another beautiful sunny day and they were heading off up the Artro armed with fishing rods, ham sandwiches (provided by Sioned's mother) and twelve cans of Double Diamond bitter.

My mother responded to this development with cold fury.

'You just do whatever the hell you like, don't you?' I heard her say, and it was a shock, because I had never known her use a word like 'hell' before. 'What are the rest of us supposed to do all day?'

'Take the children to the beach,' said my father carelessly. 'We'll meet back here later this afternoon and go home around six.'

My mother registered the cool, almost contemptuous note of authority in his voice. 'It seems we might as well not exist,' she said, 'as far as you're concerned.'

They said more things like that to each other, but I don't remember them so well. Of course I may have misremembered these ones too. What I do remember is the feeling – the entirely new and chilling feeling – that there might be something seriously awry in the relationship between my mother and father, that something I had until now taken for granted, as the background and indeed the foundation of my young existence, was not as I had imagined it to be; that it had the potential to falter and crumble or perhaps even collapse altogether. (And I was not so far off the mark, because later that summer Gill and I were packed off to my grandparents in Shropshire for a few weeks, while my parents went away somewhere – France, I think – to start repairing their marriage. Which seemed to work, up to a point, because after that, in my memory at least, things were somewhat better between them.)

Anyway, all that is by the by. In the meantime, my mother, Gill and I got a bonus day at the seaside, accompanied by Sioned who as usual chose to come along with us, to spend the day in the dunes behind the nearest beach: the long sandy one that runs the length of Mochras (Shell Island, to the English). It was here, in those same dunes, while Gill and my mother were swimming in the sea later that morning, that Sioned pinned me to the ground, lay full length on top of me, kissed me on the mouth, and told me that she was going to marry me. She did not ask me to marry her, note: she told me that this was what was going to happen. I had no choice in the matter, not that I was anything other than flattered and delighted. And yet funnily enough I don't recall how I answered her.

Emboldened, in any case, by the new bond of trust and intimacy between us, I decided to allow Sioned the privilege of reading our story. I had brought the notebook with me in our beach bag, along with the towels and the swimming goggles, the Frisbee and the cricket set. I handed it over to her in a ceremonious way, and she looked suitably impressed when I told her that it was my own com-position (I may have omitted to mention your input), that I intended to be a writer in adulthood and in fact I was a writer already. And then I left her to it, and went for a walk along the beach, hugging to myself the sweet knowledge that the girl I loved was, at that very moment, in the process of learning that her young fiancé was noth-ing short of a creative genius.

I walked the length of the beach, following the curve of the pen-insula (it is a peninsula, not an island) until I reached the point where the beach turned rocky, and there I lingered for a while by the rock pools, looking for shrimps or crabs or any other signs of marine life. I decided to give Sioned at least forty-five minutes to read the story, because something like that shouldn't be rushed. The text was dense, and full of fine writing, and there were the illustrations to admire as well. So I walked back very slowly, right at the water's edge (it was almost high tide), sometimes wading in up to my calves.

The water was cold, and I had no particular wish to swim. As the morning drew on the beach was getting crowded, and the air shrilled with the cries of children, playing their ball games, throwing themselves shriekingly into the water, calling to get their parents' attention. A timeless sound. I mean that literally. Past, present and future: that's what you hear, in the sound of children's voices. An airborne whisper that tells you: *Everything changes, and everything stays the same.* And I can still hear those voices now, along with the wash of the sea as it broke gently upon the beach, and the cries of seagulls wheeling above me. I can picture myself as I was that morning: wearing a striped T-shirt and navy blue shorts, standing in the sea almost up to my knees, thinking . . . God knows what. Thinking nothing much, I dare say, but impatient for the admiration that Sioned was about to pour over my head.

When I returned to our pitch in the dunes, my mother and Gill were back, having finished their swim and dried themselves off. Sioned was sitting slightly apart from them, her knees drawn up to her chin. She was munching on an apple. I noticed that she had put the notebook back in our beach bag.

'Well?' I said, throwing myself down beside her.

'Well what?' she said, taking another crunchy bite.

'Did you read the story?'

'Yes.'

I waited for the first words of praise. They didn't come.

'And . . . ?'

'I thought it was the stupidest thing I ever read in my life.'

I stared at her. It was hard to believe that she had actually spoken those words. Impossible, at first.

'Wh –?' I faltered. 'What do you mean?'

'Do you know anything at all about Capel Celyn?' she asked. 'Do you even know where it is?'

'Of course I know where it is. We stopped there on the way here last week. We had a picnic.'

'Oh, so you spent about ten minutes there, did you?'

I didn't answer. Then she asked me what I thought was an irrelevant question.

'Do you know what my grandpa's house in Wrexham is like?'

'No, of course I don't.'

'It's horrible. It's a horrible little modern house surrounded by other horrible little modern houses on a big estate. The walls are already cracking and the roof leaks and the window in the bedroom where I sleep is so small and high up in the wall that it's like staying in a prison. He hates it there. Moving there made him so unhappy that all his hair fell out.'

'What's this got to do with my story?' I asked.

'Well, where do you think he used to live before they moved him?'

'Before who moved him?'

'The council.'

'I don't know – where did he live?'

'Capel Celyn, of course.'

Even now, this was not the answer I had been expecting. In fact, it made no sense to me.

'You mean he used to live underwater?'

'God in heaven, you must be the thickest person I ever met. It wasn't underwater a few years ago. They threw all the people out and flooded it. They flooded the whole valley.'

She kept saying 'they' without explaining who she was talking about. It was very annoying.

'Who did?' I asked.

'The English. *You*. Your lot.'

This also seemed to make no sense. 'Why would they do that?'

'Because they wanted to make a reservoir. To supply water for England.'

I thought about this for a few moments and had to admit: 'That's not very fair.'

'No, it isn't. And it certainly wasn't fair that my grandpa, who lived in that village for his whole life, had to leave home and go and move to a horrible new house in Wrexham. So all this stuff about ruined castles full of treasure and people riding around on sea horses is just –' she searched around for the right words, but all she could manage in the end was – 'just a load of old rubbish, frankly.'

I sat there in silence. This was awful. It was worse than the worst thing that had ever happened to me. Having the piss taken out of me by Tony Burcot and his gang, or being told off by your mother at school. For a minute I thought I was going to cry.

'But if that was true,' I said – not wanting any of it to be true – 'surely people would be more angry about it.'

'Oh, people are angry about it, all right. It's just that you lot never get to hear about it. The only time you ever come here is for your holidays. But people are angry, don't worry about that. You should hear my dad and my Uncle Trefor talking about it. And Capel Celyn isn't all they're angry about. It's the whole thing.'

'What do you mean, the whole thing?'

'Everything to do with the way you lot treat the Welsh.'

'I wish you'd stop saying "you lot". *I* don't –'

Sioned ignored me, and continued: 'This stupid business of making Prince Charles the Prince of Wales for a start.'

'But Prince Charles *is* the Prince of Wales,' I said.

'Well, and whose idea was that? We never asked him to be our prince. If there has to be a Prince of Wales why can't he be a Welshman? Why does he have to be English?'

Now that she put it that way, I couldn't really think of a good counter-argument.

'We're sick of being pushed around and bossed around and having our water stolen and everything else. And having him crowned prince is just about the last straw.'

'Aren't you going to watch it on television, then?' I asked. 'When they make him prince?' I thought that everybody in the whole country was going to watch it on television.

'They'll probably make us watch it at school,' said Sioned. 'But *I* shan't watch. I shall close my eyes and put my fingers in my ears.' She had worked herself up, by now, to a fine pitch of indignation. 'And I *don't* like your silly story and I don't like *you* any more either. And I'm *definitely* not going to marry you. That's right off, that is.'

To prove the point, she went over to speak to Gill – to whom she had barely addressed a word all week – and before I knew what was happening they had both got up and were running along the beach together with my Frisbee and starting to throw it back and forth to each other. They were both very bad at it, I couldn't help noticing. But that was small consolation, on the whole, for having had my literary ambitions so eloquently ground to dust, not to mention having been party (albeit in a completely passive way) to what was probably the shortest engagement of all time.

*

I don't retain a very clear memory of the day itself. 1st July 1969, I mean. My diary, as usual, gives some of the details. Coverage of the investiture began on BBC One at 10.30 in the morning, and continued for the next five and three-quarter hours. I can't believe that many people watched the whole thing. I do remember that the entire school was herded into the assembly hall at some point, perhaps late in the morning, to watch the proceedings on television. I was torn between two conflicting impulses. On the one hand, I had absorbed enough of Sioned's righteous indignation to make myself sceptical of the pantomime that was about to unfold, and I liked the image of myself as cynic, outsider, rebel: the one who would prick the pomposity of it all with a caustic aside, delivered *sotto voce* to my schoolfellows. On the other hand, as we made our way to the assembly hall I could not resist boasting about the fact that, only one month earlier, I had been to the very castle where the ceremony was going to take place, and I described in some detail the climb to the top of the gatehouse and the view it afforded of the Irish sea. When I saw that the location was a different castle altogether, one that I didn't recognize at all, I felt very embarrassed and shut up about it from that moment on.

The poor quality of the black-and-white image, lacking in clarity and contrast; light from the assembly hall windows reflected on the television screen, making it even harder to see what was happening; the thick dust coating the wooden floorboards upon which we were all kneeling or sitting cross-legged: these are my most vivid memories of that day. Plus a vague sense, I suppose, of history being made: knowing that schoolchildren up and down the country had also had their lessons suspended, and were sitting in their own dusty assembly halls, watching equally unimpressive televisions. Sioned would be one of them, of course. As Prince Charles delivered his address to the nation in careful, measured, expressionless Welsh, I could imagine her cringing, and in sudden solidarity with her I screwed my eyes tight shut and put my fingers ostentatiously in my ears. Not for long, though. Pretty soon my resolve cracked and I opened my eyes to look around and see who had noticed this idiosyncratic act of rebellion. Everyone's eyes were fixed on the television, or they were lost in childish worlds of their own, tracing pictures in the dust with their fingers, staring out of the windows and dreaming of the open air and escape. Nobody had noticed. Nobody, that is, except your mother, Auntie Mary, Mrs Lamb, who was sitting with the rest of the staff to one side of the television set, wearing her gym clothes, frowning at me and wagging her finger in a teacherly, reproving way.

Behind the gesture, though, there was love; even a certain complicity. And her eyes were smiling. Just as – now that I come to think of it – they nearly always were.

FIVE

The Wedding of Charles, Prince of Wales, and Lady Diana Spencer

29th July 1981

'How can I rise if you don't fall?'

– Robert Wyatt, 'The British Road'

I.

27th July 1981

Martin was sitting up in bed, a notebook on his knees and a biro poised between his fingers. Surrounding the bed were half a dozen tea chests and cardboard boxes. They hadn't had time to start unpacking the bedroom things yet, but despite the chaos, the tiny room was cosy. He liked the sloping ceiling above the bed, and the fact that he could talk to Bridget without raising his voice, even though she was in the bathroom cleaning her teeth. He liked the knowledge that when he woke up in the morning, summer light would already be pouring in through the east-facing window. Above all, he liked the fact that he was living in Bournville again, less than half a mile from the house where he had spent the first twelve years of his life. It felt like a proper homecoming.

At the top of a new page he had written 'HOUSEWARMING / ROYAL WEDDING PARTY'. They still hadn't decided which one it was. Well, it was both, really, that was the point. Underneath he had already made a fairly comprehensive guest list. His mother and father. His surviving grandparents, Doll, Sam and Bertha. His brothers, Peter and Jack. Jack's current girlfriend, Patricia. And now there was the question of their new next-door neighbours.

'So did you ask the Taylors if they wanted to come?'

'Yes.'

'What did they say?'

Bridget appeared in the bedroom doorway, her toothbrush still in her mouth, her lips foamy with toothpaste.

'Well, I spoke to Heather, and told her we were having some friends and family around to watch Charles and Diana's wedding, and did they want to come.'

'And?'

'She said the royal family were bloated parasites, feasting on the putrid corpse of a broken social system.'

'Shall we take that as a no, then?'

'I think so.'

'How were they otherwise?'

'They seem very nice. She lent me her secateurs so I can have a go at that creeper at the back of the house.'

She went back into the bathroom. Spitting and gargling sounds ensued.

'What about the people on the other side? What are they called again?'

'Gupta. Sathnam and Parminder. They seem very friendly. Said they'd definitely come round.'

'Good,' said Martin, adding them to the list. He looked up and sucked moodily on the end of his biro. An unwelcome thought had occurred to him, with respect to how his father might behave around this couple, but he kept it to himself.

'So how many does that make?' Bridget asked.

'That's ten. Not counting us.'

Bridget emerged from the bathroom and squeezed into bed beside him. Her skin was warm even through the fabric of her T-shirt and pyjama shorts.

'Going to be a bit tight, isn't it?' she said.

'Well, not everyone might turn up on the day. Dad said something about playing golf instead.'

'What? Your dad's got to be there. Did he really say that?'

'Oh, I don't know. Maybe I misheard. To be honest, I don't really care if he comes or not. He's hardly the life and soul.'

Bridget regarded him curiously. 'You've been really down on him these last few days.'

'Have I?'

'Ever since you saw him on Thursday night.'

Martin drew a line under the guest list and beneath it wrote a new word: 'CATERING'.

'What are we going to give these people to eat and drink, then?'

'Did something happen?' Bridget persisted. 'Did you have a row or something? You came home in a terrible mood that night.'

'I told you,' said Martin. 'The film was rubbish. It was a waste of time.'

'It was a Bond film,' said Bridget. 'You love Bond films. It can't have been that bad. Everyone else seems to like it.'

Martin sighed. 'He just pisses me off sometimes, that's all.'

'Roger Moore, or your father?'

This provoked a smile, at least. 'Dad. He's turning into such a grumpy old sod.'

'Your dad isn't old. What is he, fifty?'

'Fifty-two.'

'Well, you tell him from me that he's got to come. Tell him that I shall be very upset if he doesn't.' When Martin didn't answer, she said: 'You are still talking to him, aren't you?' To which he also didn't reply. 'For God's sake, Martin, what happened on Thursday?'

'I don't want to talk about it, all right?'

He snapped the notebook shut, put it on the bedside table and turned off the lamp. Lying down with his back to Bridget, he felt her hand snake around his waist, sliding downwards and heading purposefully between his legs. But he didn't respond even to this tempting overture.

2.

If Martin had a credo, it was moderation in all things. In 1976 he had left his grammar school in King's Norton with a moderately good set of A-level results. He had gone on to Lancaster University to study French and German, languages in which he showed a moderate proficiency. In 1980 – after a four-year course which had included a moderately enjoyable year abroad – he had graduated with a moderately good 2.1. His lecturers had found him quiet, sensible and easy to teach, and they had forgotten all about him the moment he left. After Lancaster he returned to the Midlands, moved in with his parents for the summer, and began scouring the job adverts in the *Birmingham Post* for something that would match his talents. These were the early days of Margaret Thatcher's government and unemployment was spiralling out of control. However, Martin was confident that he could find what he was looking for: a career that would bring him personal satisfaction, a sense of contributing to the public good, and financial reward. All in moderation, preferably.

His search ended up taking him back to the Cadbury Works which had loomed so large in the neighbourhood in which he'd spent his childhood. He spotted a notice advertising a vacancy in the Staff Recreations Department, working as deputy to the General Manager. It was a lowly position but he thought it might suit him, at least as an entry point. A more assertive person might have put greater emphasis on his academic credentials, but in his application letter Martin made only passing reference to these. He was lucky enough, however, to be granted an interview and eventually to secure the job, at a salary which was modest enough to start with, but promised to increase in moderate increments. So it was that on Monday 13th October 1980, feeling moderately nervous but also moderately excited, he found himself being driven to Barnt Green railway station by his mother, on a blue-skyed autumnal day bright with promise and possibility.

Mary and Geoffrey, having moved out of Bournville ten years earlier, now lived in a house halfway up Rose Hill, a broad main road which cut through woodland on either side to climb a steep incline, leading drivers away from the outermost suburbs of Birmingham and into the fringes of the Worcestershire countryside. At this time of the morning the road was busy with a steady flow of cars taking workers down the hill to the British Leyland factory at Longbridge for the eight o'clock shift, but Mary was undaunted by this and reversed her car into the stream of traffic in a swift, determined manoeuvre. Having tailgated the car in front of her as far as the Cofton Hackett roundabout, she swung right, away from the other commuters, and was then able to accelerate to a more comfortable fifty-five miles an hour. Martin found himself gripping the door handle and wondering why his mother insisted on taking every journey at breakneck speed.

'We're early,' she said, as they approached the junction with Fiery Hill Road at a quarter to eight.

'I'm not surprised,' said Martin.

'Come on then, I want to show you something,' his mother said, and instead of turning towards the station she drove on into Barnt Green village itself, where she pulled up outside a little modern semi-detached house with a 'For Sale' sign standing in its scrap of front garden. 'What do you think?' she asked.

'For you and Dad?' said Martin, surprised. He could see that their current house was perhaps too big for them, now that Jack had left home and Peter was at music college and his own return was merely temporary. But this seemed extreme.

'No – for Grandma and Grandpa. I want them to move back down here. They're getting on now, and they're too far away, living up there.'

'Up there' was Coniston, in the Lake District. For the last sixteen years this had been home for Doll and Samuel, ever since he had retired from Cadbury's in 1965. But a location which at first they had embraced eagerly, filling the early years of their retirement with walks on the hills, boating trips and scenic lakeside drives, had in the last few years become difficult. They did not like being several hours' drive away from their only daughter, and Sam's health was deteriorating. First it had been his prostate. Now he had developed a persistent cough, and breathlessness.

'Grandpa doesn't have cancer, does he?' Martin asked.

'We don't know,' said Mary. (But her suspicion was that her father had lung cancer, and when Martin asked the question something arose, unbidden, from the depths of her reservoir of memories: the smell of his tobacco jar. It was a smell for ever associated with her childhood, with the garden of the house in Birch Road. How she had loved to take that jar from him and put her nose right up to the tobacco, breathing in its smoky, infinitely comforting aroma.) 'He needs tests. And he needs to be down here, so we can get him to the Queen Elizabeth where they'll know what to do with him. So I was thinking of moving them into this place. What do you think?'

To Martin, the house looked depressing. He thought of his grandparents' cottage in the Lake District, the view over Coniston Water, the many holidays that he and his brothers had spent there throughout the 60s and 70s, and could not imagine them returned to this pinched, mundane setting.

'I suppose it'll suit them,' he said. 'They'll be close to you, anyway.'

'Quite,' said his mother. 'This way I could be with them in five minutes instead of four hours.' She thrust the car into first gear, performed a nimble three-point turn, and they were off again. 'I'll put an offer in this morning,' she confirmed, leaving Martin in a state of wonderment, as so often before, at her ability to live as she drove: quickly and decisively, with barely a glance in the rear-view mirror.

*

When Martin arrived back at Barnt Green station after his first day at work, Mary was there again, waiting for him in her car.

'What are you doing here?' he said. 'I was going to walk.'

'Walk? That'd take you hours.'

'You can't come and pick me up from the station every day.'

'Why not? I don't mind. It's just like it was a few years ago, when you were still at school.'

Yes, Martin thought: that's exactly the problem. And it made his heart sink even more when he got home, flopped down into an armchair with a copy of the *Evening Mail* and heard his mother calling from the kitchen:

'Don't forget your egg!'

He looked around. 'What egg?'

'By your picture!'

Sure enough, in front of his framed portrait on the mantelpiece, his mother had placed a Cadbury's Creme Egg. Martin picked it up and took it into the kitchen.

'What's this?'

'It's a Creme Egg.'

'Mum, I'm not ten years old any more.'

'You're never too old to eat chocolate.'

'And I work at Cadbury's now. I'm surrounded by chocolate. The whole place smells of chocolate. I'm literally breathing chocolate all day long. The last thing I want to do when I get home is eat chocolate.'

'Well, just save it for later if you don't want it now.'

Before he had time to reply, the doorbell rang.

'That'll be your brother. He said he'd pop round this evening. Go and let him in, will you?'

Jack was still in his work suit, although he had loosened his tie and was carrying his jacket over his shoulder.

'Evening, bro,' he said. 'How's the world of cocoa solids treating you?'

'Well, as first days go,' Martin began, 'I must say—' But his brother had no interest in hearing the answer to his question, and pushed quickly past him on the way to the living room. His mother came out to greet him and kissed him tenderly on the cheek.

'Hello, love – fancy a Creme Egg?'

'Yes, please.'

He spread himself out on the sofa, peeled the wrapping off the egg and polished it off in two satisfied mouthfuls.

'Guess who's coming to the factory next week?' he said to his brother, while his mouth was still full of chocolate.

'Prince Charles,' Martin answered.

'Oh – she told you, did she?'

Martin nodded. 'She did mention it. You know, just in passing, about fifty or sixty times. Will you actually get to meet him, though?'

The factory in question was, again, the British Leyland plant at Longbridge, where Jack was currently employed as a trainee sales executive. For the last few months all of his work had been intensively focused on the launch of a new model, the Austin Metro, which had a huge amount riding on it: the very survival of the company, in some people's opinion. The advertising agency tasked with promoting this model had chosen a patriotic theme, harking back to Britain's role in the Second World War. Newspaper ads had been appearing since the late summer, assuring motorists how much they would love driving the new Metro by using the strapline, 'This could be your finest hour.' Prince Charles would be honouring the factory with his presence on launch day, while Margaret Thatcher would visit the Metro stand at the British Motor Show a few weeks later. The theme of the whole campaign was national renewal, a subject on which the Prime Minister herself was known to be especially passionate. The moribund, economically disastrous, strike-bound days of the 1970s were gone; Britain was no longer the sick man of Europe; it was no longer considered embarrassing to talk up your country, to express patriotic pride, to insist that Britain's glory days were anything but over: this was the keynote of Mrs Thatcher's rhetoric, and British Leyland was rising to the occasion with a new car that would restore faith in the national motor industry.

'The TV adverts start tonight,' Jack told his brother. 'Halfway through *Coronation Street*.'

'Is that what you've come round for?' said Martin. 'To make us all watch an advert?'

'You won't want to miss this. I've seen it and it's bloody fantastic. It'll bring a lump to your throat, I'm telling you.'

Before this exciting premiere took place, Mary and Geoffrey and their two sons had dinner and interrogated Martin about his first day at work. He didn't tell them much. Despite all the talk of national renewal, Britain was still beset by problems related to the rise in oil prices, and an instruction had recently come down from government that all local authorities should lower the temperature of their public swimming baths by two degrees centigrade.

'So Ted – that's my new boss – and his second-in-command spent most of the morning trying to decide if they should do it as well. If they should lower the temperature in the staff swimming pool. You know, to set an example, as part of the Cadbury's ethos. Or should they keep it at the same temperature, to show everyone how lucky they were to work at a firm like Cadbury's and not have to use the public baths. And in the afternoon, when they decided, I had to write a little announcement about it for the *Bournville News*.'

There was an expectant pause.

'And . . . ?' Mary asked.

Martin looked up from his apple crumble.

'And what?'

'And what did they decide?'

'Oh. They decided to lower the temperature.'

He had not thought to finish off the anecdote, because to him, the ending was anticlimactic. By far the most interesting thing to have happened on his first day at work was something he did not mention to his family, but which preoccupied him now. Dining alone at one of the long communal tables in the main canteen, eating his lunch of lamb chops and mashed potato, he had noticed a group of four women sitting a few yards away from him. Noticed one of them in particular. Noticed the way that she smiled privately to herself while the others were talking; noticed the way her gaze flickered towards him every now and then; noticed the curve of her cheek and the dark brown of her eyes, almost the exact colour of Cadbury's Dairy Milk. But he had not spoken to her, and the only thing he knew about her for sure (because he had heard one of the other women speak it) was her first name.

Jack looked at his watch and rose to his feet.

'Come on,' he said. 'It'll be on in five minutes.'

They decanted themselves to the living room and turned on the television, which was tuned, as usual, to BBC One. Pushing the third button to switch over to ITV, Martin felt that he was performing an almost transgressive act, so rarely was this channel watched in his parents' household, and so strong was the atmosphere of unspoken paternal disapproval when it was. They found themselves confronted by *Coronation Street*, a programme which regularly attracted audiences of twenty million people but which none of them had ever watched even for a few seconds. They had no idea of the names of the characters on the screen, or what it was that they were talking about. Martin turned the volume right down and they watched in puzzled silence until the 'End of Part One' caption announced the beginning of the commercial break.

The Metro advert was the second to appear.

'This is it! Here we go,' Jack said proudly, crossing his legs and folding his arms.

At first, when the advert began, Martin thought that he was watching an old British war movie. The first shot showed a fleet of four military landing craft lined up threateningly alongside a stretch of coast. A narrator's menacing voice intoned:

'*Some of you may have noticed that for the past few years Britain has been invaded – by the Italians, the Germans, the Japanese and the French.*'

The word 'invaded' was almost spat out, with a brutal emphasis on the second syllable. The bows of the ships swung open and down their ramps came an army of Fiats and Nissans, Citroëns and BMWs. But before the audience had had the chance to become overwhelmed by terror at this spectacle, the image changed, dissolving into a factory production line, along which a succession of half-completed cars rolled, prompting the narrator to declare:

'*Now we have the means to fight back. The new Austin Metro.*'

There followed a torrent of statistics about the car's aerodynamics and petrol consumption, but it was the visuals, not the words, that held everyone's attention: as a fleet of the plucky new vehicles sped along the motorway, a crowd of spectators stood watching it from a bridge, cheering and waving Union Jacks. As the cars entered a picture-postcard village, they had to brake to a halt to allow some grey-haired farmer to lead two ponies across a ford: an idyllic English pastoral scene. The music on the soundtrack suddenly became louder and more recognizable – it was an orchestral arrangement of 'Rule Britannia'. The cars proceeded through the village, down a narrow cobbled street festooned with red, white and blue bunting. Standing in front of a massive Union Jack, an elderly gentleman – his chest hung with medals, clearly a veteran of the war – stood to attention and saluted. A brass band played. The villagers waved handkerchiefs from their windows as the cars passed by . . .

'Jesus Christ,' said Martin.

Jack looked at him sharply. 'What?'

'It's a bit much, isn't it?'

It was almost over. '*The new Austin Metro*,' the narrator proclaimed. '*A British car* . . .' (he paused for effect) '*TO BEAT THE WORLD*.' And on these words, the squadron of cars reached their destination: the white cliffs of Dover where, beneath a triumphant sunset, they gathered in a small platoon on the clifftop to keep watch for any return of the invading hordes.

'That doesn't look very safe,' said Geoffrey, noticing the proximity of two of the cars to the cliff edge.

'They lost one, apparently,' said Jack, with a smile of satisfaction. 'Slipped off and fell all the way down to the beach. Luckily there was no driver inside. Well, what do you think?'

His father simultaneously reached for his whisky glass and for one of his characteristic non-committal turns of phrase. 'Very memorable.'

'Was that the man off *Dad's Army*?' Mary asked, thinking of the decorated veteran. 'He looked just like – what's his name – Corporal Jones.'

'I don't think so. Just some actor they hired for the day.'

'Well, it's very good,' she assured him. 'I'm sure you'll sell hundreds of them after people have seen that.'

'We had all the local dealers in to watch it last week.'

'And?'

'They loved it. They *bloody loved it.*'

Martin was silent for a few moments and then, realizing that he was expected to say something too, asked a question: 'Beat it at what?'

'Come again?' said Jack, in the act of refilling his beer glass.

'The bloke said that it was a car to beat the world. Beat it at what?'

'Don't be thick,' said Jack. 'Beat it at . . . making cars, of course. Manufacturing.'

'It's not like it's a contest, though, is it? It's not like it's a football match.'

Jack sighed. 'You're so naive. Of course that's what it is. That's *exactly* what it is. You've heard of competition, haven't you? What do you think we're planning to do, give these cars away for charity?'

'No, but . . . "Beat the world." It's kind of a weird phrase, isn't it? A weird sort of mentality. Us against them.'

'Martin,' his brother said, patting him on the back, 'get real. The sixties are over. The *seventies* are over. We have a new Prime Minister, or hadn't you noticed? And she doesn't believe in any of that hippy-dippy rubbish. From now on, us against them is the way it's going to be. A zero-sum game. Put something on the scales and what happens? One side falls and the other side rises. It's the natural order of things. And if the world's going to be divided into winners and losers, I know which side *I* want to be on. We've all got to make that choice. You'd better make it too – and quickly, before you get left behind.'

Later that evening, as Martin was sitting up in bed reading, his mother came to say goodnight.

'I wouldn't take too much notice of your brother,' she said. 'He's all bluff and bluster.'

'I know.'

'He doesn't mean any harm. He's a good lad.'

'I know that too.'

She kissed him on the forehead and added, just before leaving the room: 'I baby you a bit, don't I?'

Martin smiled. 'Just a bit.'

'I can't help it. It's terrible when your kids grow up. The whole house feels empty. It's so nice to have you back.'

Martin was on the point of telling her that he wouldn't be here for long, but he couldn't bring himself to do it. He said: 'Well, I'm here now, and Jack is close by, and Peter keeps in touch, so . . . you're not doing too badly.'

'I know, love. Goodnight.'

After she had gone, Martin thought about the intense, wistful look that always came into Mary's eye whenever her youngest son was mentioned. She loved each of her boys equally, he was sure of that, she'd never had a favourite, but still . . . Somehow there was a closeness between his mother and Peter that he and Jack could never aspire to.

Well, family life was full of mystery. Martin turned off the light, lay down on his side and closed his eyes, murmuring the name 'Bridget' to himself before falling asleep.

3.

For Martin, having access to his own full-sized colour television seemed even more miraculous than renting his own house. He had set the alarm for six-thirty and promised Bridget that after a quick shower he would start making sandwiches for the guests, but when she came downstairs just after seven she found him lounging on the sofa, oblivious to her presence, his gaze fixed on a cartoon intended for young children.

'Catching up on your viewing, are you?'

Martin sat up with a guilty start.

Bridget was about to make another sarcastic comment, but the action unfolding on the screen caught her attention and she sat down beside him.

'Oh, I used to love *Tom and Jerry*.'

'It's not one of the old classics,' he said. 'I think this one's from the sixties. It's terrible.'

'And yet here you are, watching it.'

Martin took the hint, and rose to his feet. 'Sandwiches.'

'I'll come and give you a hand.'

They left the television on, and from the kitchen they could hear the wedding coverage starting: it began at a quarter to eight, more than three hours before the marriage ceremony itself was due to take place. For the next ninety minutes there was endless discussion of Lady Diana's dress, and reports from Balmoral Castle and Caernarfon Castle, where nothing much seemed to be happening. Martin and Bridget busied themselves preparing food and moving chairs into the living room.

At nine-thirty, earlier than invited, Mary arrived. She came with her parents, Sam and Doll, having collected them from their new house in Barnt Green. They had been living there for a few weeks, and hadn't taken to it at all. Martin thought they looked frail, depressed, and very, very elderly. Even so, they were happy to see him, and made no secret of their curiosity to meet Bridget. Doll shook her formally by the hand, but Sam was warmer. 'All I've seen of you,' he said, 'is one picture. Is it too soon for me to give you a kiss?'

'Ooh, I don't think so,' said Bridget, offering her cheek. 'It is a special day, after all.'

Sam puckered up and put his wrinkled lips against the smoothness of her cheek. Doll glared at him and afterwards, when they were alone in the living room, she said: 'What did you have to kiss her for? You always take things too far, you do.'

Mary gave Bridget a quick hug and asked if there was anything she could do to help in the kitchen. Meanwhile Martin brought coffee for his grandparents, and tried to get them settled. Already, now that there were five people in the house, he had become aware of how very small it was. Even the furniture seemed too small for Sam, who sat stiffly and awkwardly in the armchair, clutching tightly on the handle of his mug of coffee as it rested on his fragile knee. When Peter and Geoffrey arrived they brought Bertha with them: normally Sam would have got up to embrace her – for all their differences, he was very fond of his old friend's widow – but today he couldn't summon the energy.

'Hello, Sam,' she said, leaning down to brush his cheek with her own. 'Haven't seen you for a while. Not since Frank's funeral.' Turning to his wife, she said, more brusquely: 'Doll.'

'Bertha,' Doll replied, in the same tone. Neither of them could remember when or why relations had soured between them, but they had. Bertha sank onto the sofa, out of breath. 'I'll say hello to Martin in a minute.' Craning forward, she could see through the living-room door into the kitchen. 'I suppose that's his girlfriend, is it?'

'Yes,' said Doll.

'Have you met her? What's she like?'

'She seems very polite. Sam kissed her, and she didn't complain or anything.'

4.

One day, a few months after Martin had started work at Cadbury's, somebody, somewhere, going through the card index files that made up the factory employees' database, noticed an interesting fact: that a graduate in Modern Languages, who spoke fluent French and fluent German, was languishing in the Staff Recreations Department, his talents wasted. A series of internal telephone calls followed, an informal interview was arranged, and before long Martin found himself being offered a new job: Deputy Assistant to the Export Manager, with special responsibility for the Scandinavian territories.

'Why Scandinavia?' he asked, on his first day.

'Why not?' said his new boss. His name was Paul Daintry, and he seemed very friendly.

'Well, because I speak French and German. So I would have thought France and Germany would be the obvious places.'

'A strong point, well made,' said Paul. 'I suppose we'd better tell him, hadn't we, Kash?'

'Kash' was Kashifa Bazaz (Assistant to the Export Manager, with special responsibility for the United States). She was the third occupant of the large, pleasant, open-plan office that looked out over the managers' car park and, beyond that, one of the cricket pitches. Paul had been sitting in a relaxed pose, feet crossed and resting on his desk; now he stood up and walked over to the picture window.

'It's not quite as simple as that, you see,' Kashifa said. 'The trouble is we have the EEC to reckon with.'

'How do you mean?'

'Do you like Cadbury's chocolate, Martin?' said Paul, wheeling round and addressing him directly.

'Yes, I love it.'

'Bet you grew up with it, didn't you?'

Martin nodded.

'Of course you did. We all did. It's part of our childhoods. Part of who we are, as a country. Something that holds us all together. The taste of Cadbury's Dairy Milk chocolate. Lovely. The nectar of the gods. However, our Continental friends and neighbours take a different view, don't they, Kash?'

'Sadly they do.'

'Go on then, you tell him.'

Kashifa leaned forward at her desk. 'The EEC,' she said, dramatically, 'does not consider Cadbury's chocolate – or indeed any British chocolate – to be chocolate.'

Martin stared back, uncomprehending.

'They say that it contains too much vegetable fat, and not enough cocoa butter.'

'But . . . Well, that's just a matter of taste, isn't it?'

'Unfortunately not,' said Paul. 'The whole idea of the European Economic Community is that the people who belong to it will observe the same standards. And as far as chocolate is concerned the Brits, apparently, do not come up to scratch.'

'We don't export to France or Germany,' said Kashifa.

'Or Belgium or Spain or Italy or . . . well, you get the picture.'

'But that's outrageous,' said Martin. 'What can we do about it?'

'Not a lot,' said Paul. 'We can lobby Brussels. Try to get the law changed, which involves going through endless votes and committee stages. This has been going on for eight years and I can see it going on for another ten. In the meantime, well . . . flog as many chocolate bars to Sweden and Norway as you can.'

A momentary sense of gloom descended on the office, as the three of them contemplated this gross injustice and their apparent powerlessness to do anything about it.

Then Paul picked up the copy of the *Daily Mail* which was lying on Kashifa's desk and looked at the front page, which showed a picture of Prince Charles and Lady Diana Spencer beneath a headline announcing their engagement.

'Still,' he said. 'It's not all doom and gloom, is it? Look at these two. Young love – just the tonic we all need at the moment.'

And this, Martin would soon realize, was typical of his new boss. Nothing dampened his spirits for long: he worked hard to keep his colleagues cheerful, and to maintain a lively atmosphere in the office. Later in the week he suggested that they should all go out for a drink and a meal on Friday evening. He also invited the two typists from next door, and when Kashifa said that she was already supposed to be going out with a friend who worked in the legal department, said, 'No problem – bring her along too. Or is it a he?'

'No, it's just a girlfriend,' Kashifa said. 'You'll like her, she's really good fun. Her name's Bridget.'

*

At first Martin thought she had decided not to come. Their night out began at a pub called the Clifton on Ladywood Road, and although there were more people there than he had expected – one of the typists, Durnaz, had invited several of her cousins, most of whom seemed to have brought their boyfriends or girlfriends – Bridget was not among them. After an hour or so they walked the half-mile to Stoney Lane, where Kashifa and Paul stopped off at a mini-supermarket to buy beer and wine. Apparently the restaurant they were going to wasn't licensed. Despite everyone else's high spirits, and the pleasure of finding himself in a part of town he'd never visited before – where most of the shop signs were in Urdu, and the air was sweet with the smell of unfamiliar spices wafting from food stores and restaurants – Martin was beginning to despair when he spotted Bridget's familiar figure waiting for them outside a curry house called Adil's, which seemed to be their final destination. Inside they found even more of Kashifa's friends and were soon squeezed onto benches at a glass-topped table for twelve. He was several places removed from Bridget, but they were all packed so tightly together that he had plenty of opportunity to speak to her, if only he could think of anything to say. Everyone else seemed to know exactly what to order and he was too embarrassed to admit that he didn't know anything at all about Kashmiri food, and that when he was growing up his mother's idea of making a curry was to take the remains of yesterday's chicken, cover it with flavourless sauce made from a packet and throw in a handful of sultanas. Eventually one of Durnaz's cousins helped him out by suggesting a lamb masala spiced with nutmeg and whole black cardamoms: it came, like all the other dishes, sizzling in the pressed steel bowl it had been cooked in, and he was told to eat it without cutlery, scooping out delicious fiery mouthfuls with chunks of naan which were themselves beautifully light and moist. He thought it was the most wonderful food he had ever tasted in his life. When he asked what kind of cooking this was, he unwittingly sparked off an argument because Kashifa said it was called Balti and someone else said they'd never heard that word before and she must be making it up, and then Kashifa became very indignant and said she knew exactly what she was talking about, she even knew the person who had *invented* this kind of food, he used to work at this very restaurant and his name was Raheem and he was her sister-in-law's aunt's brother-in-law, and then somebody else said rubbish, Balti (because they had heard the word as well) was invented by another chef entirely, her uncle's best friend, Bhaskar, who worked at the Diwan restaurant on the Moseley Road, and it became clear that the origins of this new kind of cuisine, which had only been around for a year or two, were already lost in mythology.

By now everyone was full of food and the wine and the beer were flowing freely and the next subject for argument was the engagement of Prince Charles and Lady Diana, which had been seized upon by most people as a tentative shaft of sunlight at the end of a bleak and cheerless winter, but Durnaz was now saying that the dynamic between the couple gave her the shivers and thirteen years was way too big an age difference between husband and wife.

'There's something creepy about him,' she said. 'I can't put my finger on it. I don't think she knows what she's letting herself in for.'

'Rubbish,' said Paul Daintry, and announced to the table at large, with great authority: 'It's like a fairy tale, for a woman like her, marrying a prince. It's what every woman dreams of.'

'Not me,' said Kashifa. 'Give me a man my own age, thank you very much. Anyway, did you notice what he said, when that interviewer asked if they were in love with each other? "Whatever 'in love' means," he said. Not very romantic, is he?'

'If you ask me,' said Bridget, 'he looks like he'd rather be having it off with her brother.'

The women roared with laughter while the men – reared on a diet of TV comedy that understood women to be the butt of jokes, rather than the ones who made them – looked embarrassed but tried to laugh along as best they could. In fact Martin was delighted not so much by the comment itself as by Bridget's delivery. He had discovered, by now, that she was from a Glaswegian family, and was loving the musicality of her Scottish accent.

Martin shared a minicab back to south-west Birmingham with Bridget, Paul and Maureen, the second of the two typists. As they left this energetic and unfamiliar part of town behind, cruising along the Bristol Road and into Northfield with its dreary array of fish and chip shops and burger bars and Sainsbury's supermarkets, he began to feel subdued, even a little depressed. After weeks of seeing Bridget only in wordless glimpses at the canteen, he had finally spent an evening with her but there had been no special connection, no thunderclap. She seemed to get on better with the others than she did with him. He sat in a corner of the cab, nursing this morose thought while Maureen enthused about what a great time they'd all had.

'That was brilliant,' she said. 'We should do it every week.'

The suggestion seemed excessive to Martin, and he was unable to stop himself from saying:

'Well, every month, maybe.'

There was a short silence, but Bridget couldn't hide her amusement for long.

'Ah yes,' she said, speaking to the group in general but also, at the same time, to Martin in particular. 'The voice of reason . . .'

Martin looked across at her as she said it. Her smile was challenging, the note of delicious irony in her voice unmistakable. Their eyes met for a long, long moment.

5.

The sun blazed down on St Paul's Cathedral as Mrs Thatcher climbed the red-carpeted steps, her husband, Denis, following a few paces behind.

'What on earth's she wearing?' Doll said. 'She looks like she's turned up for a funeral.'

Bertha disagreed. 'I think she looks very smart. Striking just the right tone.'

'But why's she all in black?'

'That's not black. It's navy blue.'

'She shouldn't be there at all,' Sam maintained. 'Look at the way she's smirking.' He started shouting at the television: 'What about the unemployment figures, eh? What about the millions on the dole?'

'Pipe down, for goodness' sake,' his wife said. She glanced nervously across at Geoffrey, but he was – typically – pretending not to have noticed this burst of socialist outrage.

'Come on, Dad,' said Mary. 'Enter into the spirit. It's not as if she can hear you, is it?'

'I wish she could. I'd give her a piece of my mind.'

Meanwhile Martin's next-door neighbours, Sathnam and Parminder, had arrived, each carrying a tray laden with food. Martin took them both straight into the kitchen, where the trays were placed on the kitchen table alongside what already looked like the makings of a substantial banquet.

'These look *fantastic*,' said Bridget. She peered more closely at the plates. 'Just talk me through what we've got here.'

'These are just some samosas,' Parminder explained, pulling back the cling film. 'I didn't make them too spicy, because not everybody likes that. And here we have paneer tikka, and some tandoori aloo. These are vegetable kebabs. And in the bowls you'll find some raita and some green chutney – home-made.'

'Everything is home-made,' said Sathnam proudly.

'That's amazing,' said Bridget. 'Thank you so much. Why don't you go to the other room and find yourselves somewhere to sit? We'll just get these ready to bring through.' To Martin, after their guests had made their way to the living room, she whispered: 'Are your family going to eat any of this stuff?'

'God knows,' said Martin. 'Grandma doesn't even like French dressing on her salad.'

'Well, it's a good job we made lots of sausage rolls.'

Sathnam and Parminder had entered the sitting room but nobody noticed them come in at first. Everyone's eyes were fixed on the television, on the steps of St Paul's, on the cheering and waving crowds, on the London sunshine.

'Ooh, look,' said Bertha. 'Nancy Reagan's arrived.'

Not recognizing the name, Doll glanced across at Bertha and was therefore the first person to notice the presence of the new guests. She struggled to her feet and shook Parminder's hand.

'Hello, Nancy,' she said. 'It's very nice to meet you.'

6.

21st April 1981

The day he returned to work after the Easter weekend, Martin came home in the evening to find a stranger in the family house: a young, attractive, female stranger, who seemed to be there as the guest of his father, of all people.

'Who's that with Dad?' he said to Peter, who was home from college for the Easter holidays and currently sitting at the kitchen table, reading a paperback copy of a John Fowles novel, his ears covered by a pair of enormous headphones which were plugged into a Sanyo cassette recorder. Over by the cooker their mother was puzzling over the instructions on a packet of spaghetti, as she prepared to cook spaghetti Bolognese, a new and exotic addition to her culinary repertoire.

Peter took his headphones off. 'What?'

'Who's that woman next door with Dad?'

'His secretary.'

Martin had not even known that his father had a secretary. (Like Peter and Jack, he was relentlessly incurious about his working life.)

'Her name's Penny,' his mother added.

'Well, what's she doing here?'

'No idea,' said Peter.

'He's showing her that new gadget of his,' Mary said. 'The computer.'

'Very pretty, I must say,' said Martin, stealing some further looks through the kitchen doorway.

'Aren't you supposed to be going out with your new girlfriend tonight?' Peter asked, pointedly.

'Yes, I am. That doesn't mean I can't say anything about another girl being pretty, does it? Don't you think she's pretty?'

'I'm not that interested one way or the other, to be honest.'

Peter put his headphones back on without further comment, and then, on the pretext of collecting their used teacups, Martin went into the living room to see what was going on between his father and the mysterious secretary. He found them seated at the coffee table, which had been moved in front of the television set and upon which had been placed Geoffrey's new portable computer. This had been purchased at a shop in central Birmingham on Saturday afternoon and brought home in a mood of great excitement which the other members of the family had not been able to match. It was called the Sinclair ZX81 and consisted simply of a small black plastic box equipped with forty alphabetical and numerical pads which looked (but did not feel) like a typewriter keyboard. In order to see what you were typing, you had to plug it into a television set. At the moment Penny appeared to be trying to compose a letter on the screen. Martin could see that she had got as far as today's date and 'To whom it may concern' and 'Thank you for your letter of'.

'These keys are really difficult to use,' she was complaining.

'I'm sure you'd get used to it,' Geoffrey said. 'Anyway, this is a very early design. Everything's bound to be improved in the next year or two.'

'I'd much rather just use a typewriter,' she said. And then added, 'Hello,' to Martin, with a smile, as he reached down for her teacup.

'Have you finished with this?' he asked.

'Yes, thanks. I'm Penny.'

'Martin.'

Her smile turned flirtatious as she glanced towards the three framed portraits on the mantelpiece. 'I know,' she said. 'I recognized you. The good-looking one.'

Martin, who had never flirted with anyone in his life, did not know what to say to this.

'Why the chocolate bar, by the way?' she asked, referring to the Cadbury's Double Decker which was placed in front of his picture.

'Oh, I don't know what that's doing there . . .' Martin stammered, picking it up and moving it to the sideboard in rather a pointless way.

Geoffrey was impatient to continue explaining: 'The thing is, with a computer like this, you'll only have to write this letter *once*. Then you get the computer to memorize it, and the next time you need to send one, all you have to do is change the name. Think of the work it could save you!'

'How does it memorize a letter, then?'

'Ah – now you see, that's the clever part. It uses a tape recorder. A cassette recorder. Martin, where's your brother's tape recorder?'

'He's listening to it in the kitchen.'

'Go and get it then, will you?'

Peter protested loudly at the suggestion that he should interrupt his enjoyment of Prokofiev's Third Piano Concerto so that his father could continue this pointless scientific demonstration, but in the end he offered his sullen acquiescence, and took the machine with him into the next room. Afterwards, he went upstairs to his bedroom to continue reading his John Fowles novel, and he would not give this episode any more thought until thirty-two years later: not until the spring of 2013, when Mrs Thatcher had died and Britain had been to war with Iraq, when Princess Diana had died and the global financial system had almost collapsed, when the Twin Towers had been destroyed and the Berlin Wall had come down and Peter was sitting upstairs in his lamplit study in Kew, aged fifty-one, writing the eulogy for his father's funeral, and he would be flattened by a sudden, long-delayed feeling of guilt: guilt that none of them – not himself, or Martin, or Jack, or even Mary – had ever really listened to their father or taken him seriously when he tried to interest them in new technology. He had long since given up trying to stir their enthusiasm for Latin or Greek, but really, why had he never been more successful with his other hobby-horse? Hadn't he bought Peter (at great expense) a Sony Walkman, explaining that from now on he wouldn't have to carry a heavy tape recorder around with him whenever he wanted to listen to music in private? Hadn't he rented a top-of-the-range video recorder for the family because he thought this was the future of entertainment even though he never watched television himself? Hadn't he been obliged to bring his secretary home with him to demonstrate the labour-saving possibilities of the Sinclair ZX81 because his family couldn't have cared less about it? Why, Peter wondered that night, had they never paid any attention to him? Perhaps because Geoffrey always found it so difficult to assert himself, to communicate his own enthusiasms, given that Mary was the dominant personality in the family and she herself, throughout their married lives, never tried to understand the things that her husband found so interesting, so pressingly important. Whatever the reason, that night – the night of 17th April 2013 – he found himself looking back to the early 1980s and felt a pang of sympathy for his dead father, so full of quiet excitement back then, so full of a sense of budding possibilities that he hadn't known how to express or how to share. Up in that lamplit study, in that little house in a backwater of Kew, the thirty-two years between then and now suddenly seemed to collapse, the flow of time was halted . . .

*

But that was thirty-two years in the future. Going back even further, thirty-six years into the past, on VE night, 1945, Martin's grandfathers, Frank and Samuel, had sat side by side in the private bar of the Great Stone Inn: a small, wood-panelled, smoke-filled enclave adjacent to the pub's lounge but quite separate from it. In this cloistered space they had smoked their pipes and cigarettes in companionable near-silence and listened to the victory speech of King George VI on the radio. They could not be aware of it, but Martin and Bridget occupied exactly the same seats on the night of 21st April 1981, the night Geoffrey brought his secretary home with him to demonstrate the workings of the Sinclair ZX81, the night they went to the cinema in King's Norton to see *Chariots of Fire* and, not yet feeling ready to say goodnight and return to their separate homes, decided to go for a drink just before closing time. But they did not sit opposite each other in that private bar, as Frank and Samuel had done. They sat close beside each other on the banquette, their shoulders touching, their thighs pressed tightly together. They

sipped their drinks slowly and appreciatively, and in between sips
they kissed each other, and looked into each other's eyes, and lost
themselves in each other's smiles. Conversation between them was
slow, and gentle, and whispered.

'Enjoy the film?' Bridget asked.

'Yes, I did,' said Martin. 'I really enjoyed it.'

'Good, wasn't it?'

'Very good.'

'I love the music.'

'I love the music too.'

'We should buy it.'

'Yes, we should.'

'Vangelis. I never heard of him before.'

'Greek.'

'That scene on the beach . . .'

'With them running . . .'

'And the music . . .'

'That was beautiful.'

'What do you think was the message?'

'The message?'

'Do you think it had a message?'

'Believe in yourself.'

'Follow your dream.'

Having spoken this phrase, Bridget smiled, and added:

'Or maybe not, in your case. Being the Voice of Reason, and
everything.'

Martin said, with mock-indignation:

'I have dreams.'

'Modest ones, I'm sure.'

'You think I'm boring?'

'No. I think you're fascinating. I've never met anyone quite so
deliciously . . . sensible.' Stroking his hand, she said: 'When did you
last do something really impulsive, Martin? Something unexpected?'

And now Martin surprised her by thinking the question over, and
answering: 'Today, as a matter of fact.'

'Today?' She drew back slightly. 'Really?'

'Yes, really.'

She waited for him to elaborate, her smile growing broader. When he remained silent, she said: 'OK, I'll buy it. What did you do?' There was still no answer. 'You signed up for flying lessons, and you're going to become a pilot?'

He shook his head.

'You've handed in your notice at Cadbury's, and you're going to go and work on a kibbutz for six months.'

Martin shook his head again.

'OK, I give up. What, then?'

Martin drew a deep breath, and announced:

'I've joined the SDP.'

A full five seconds passed before Bridget put down her wine glass and burst out laughing.

'You did *what*?'

'Today,' he said, quietly but with proud emphasis, 'I became a fully paid-up member of the Social Democratic Party.'

'And that –' said Bridget, after taking it in – 'that's you following your dream?'

If it were possible to drink in a defensive way, Martin now demonstrated how it was done, by taking a defensive sip of his Guinness.

'Very much so,' he said. 'You don't support the Conservatives, do you?'

'Not particularly.'

'So who are you going to vote for in the next election? Labour?'

'I hadn't thought about it. There isn't going to be one for a while, is there?'

'Well, let me tell you – you *can't* vote Labour. They've been completely taken over by extremists. But now there's an alternative. This new party – it's the most exciting thing to happen to British politics for . . . well, for as long as I can remember. They're realistic, they're pragmatic, they're . . . what are you looking at me like that for?'

Bridget's expression was indeed ambiguous. It was hard to tell whether she wanted to collapse into laughter again or throw herself on top of Martin and ravish him on the table.

'You're beautiful when you're angry, that's all.'

'I'm not angry.'

'All right then, you're beautiful when you're mildly enthusiastic about something.'

He looked at her, feeling wounded but at the same time extremely happy.

'You're making fun of me, aren't you?' he said, and she nodded. 'I don't mind, though.'

'Why don't you mind?' Bridget asked, leaning in even closer towards him.

'Because ... Well, because I've fallen in love with you,' said Martin.

The words hung in the short space between them for a few seconds, pregnant and irrevocable. He waited for her response. He could not solve the mystery in her eyes, which gazed back at him steadily.

'Didn't you hear me?' he said. 'I said that I've fallen in love with you.'

'Me too,' said Bridget, and finally rewarded him with a long and tender kiss, before adding: 'Whatever "in love" means.'

7.

'Morning all,' said Jack, breezing into the living room with his current girlfriend in tow. 'Sorry we're late. We came by carriage but one of the horses fell over and sustained a nasty injury to the fetlocks. Very painful, that can be. Brings tears to your eyes.'

A lot of the time nobody really understood Jack's humour but everyone – the older family members in particular – seemed to be cheered up by it, feeding off his high spirits. Somehow he seemed to lift the energy levels of everyone in the room: much more than Peter did, anyway, because he had brought along his bulky cassette recorder and his even bulkier headphones and was already sitting in a chair in the corner, hunched over, listening to music while reading *The Glass Bead Game* by Hermann Hesse, ignoring the images on the television and the conversation around him altogether. Seeing his youngest brother shutting himself off from the celebrations in this way, Jack snatched the headphones from his head and said:

'Come on, you, make a bit of an effort. You can listen to Mozart any time you want.'

'It was Samuel Barber, actually,' said Peter, glaring at his brother angrily.

'Leave him alone,' Mary said, ruffling her youngest son's hair. 'You're all right, aren't you, poppet?'

If anything, this gesture seemed to annoy Peter even more than his brother's words had done. Reluctantly, maintaining an expression of studied contempt, he turned his attention to the television and consented to watch along with everyone else.

'Is it all right if I plonk myself here?' Jack's girlfriend said, sitting down on the arm of the sofa next to Parminder. 'I'm Patricia by the way. Look at all those people! Where is this, Westminster Abbey?'

'St Paul's Cathedral,' Parminder answered.

'The man doing the commentary just said there were three thousand guests,' said Mary.

'This is one thing we do really well in this country, isn't it?' said Jack.

'Wasting millions of pounds on pointless ceremonies, you mean?' said Peter.

'Oh, give it a rest, Lenin.'

'No wonder there've been so many riots in the last few weeks.'

'Jesus, I wish I'd left your headphones on, now.' To Patricia, he said: 'Do you fancy a drink? I'll go and see what's on offer. Service in this establishment is dreadful, I must say.'

He wandered into the kitchen, where Martin and Bridget were still hard at work preparing the food.

'Hello, lovebirds,' he said.

Martin – who was slicing up a cucumber – offered a grunt of welcome while Bridget submitted herself to one of the rather too energetic hugs in which Jack seemed to specialize.

'What do I have to do to get a couple of beers round here?' he asked.

'Help yourself, they're in the fridge,' said Martin. 'Sorry, we're nearly done. I'll give you a tour of the place in a minute if you want.'

'A tour?' said Jack, laughing as he bent over the fridge. 'No offence, mate, it looks very nice and all that, but isn't that a bit like offering to take someone for a hike round the inside of a phone box?'

'It may be small,' said Bridget, 'but we're both very happy with it.'

'Sounds like the secret of a successful marriage to me,' said Jack, unable to suppress a smirk as he reached up for two beer glasses and in the process noticed, with appalled fascination, the careful, measured progress his brother was making through the cucumber. 'Blimey, you'll never get it finished like that,' he said, taking the knife off him. 'Here, let me have a go.'

He began tearing through the vegetable in a series of rapid chopping movements and within a few seconds had sliced into his index finger. Kitchen towel was fetched, cold tap water was run over the wound and blood was wiped from the surrounding area.

'Slowly but surely is always the best way,' Martin reminded him. 'Or don't you remember our last snooker match?'

8.

It had been Jack's idea to invite Grandpa back to the Works one Friday afternoon.

'It'll take his mind off things,' he told Martin over the telephone. 'And bring back some nice memories, with any luck.'

Sam and Doll had not moved into their new house yet – the sale seemed to be taking ages, for some reason – but they had said good-bye to the cottage in Coniston. Their furniture and possessions were packed away in a storage unit and they had moved, for the time being, into Jack's old bedroom at their daughter's house on Rose Hill. Everyone knew that this was an interim arrangement, but even so, Sam was finding it difficult. He did not get on especially well with Geoffrey and resented having to accept hospitality from him. He had become sullen and taciturn. He had pain in his joints, in his lungs, in his groin. Doll herself was of little practical help so the burden of caring for her father and keeping his spirits up fell largely upon Mary, who these days also had a demanding job teaching at a special needs school. She too was beginning to look tired and fraught. So she considered this a thoughtful suggestion on Jack's part.

'Let's take him to the social club,' Jack added to his brother. 'He said he used to go there a lot, back in the old days.'

And so, at four o'clock on Friday afternoon, they found themselves standing on either side of their grandfather, grasping his arms gently and helping him to climb the wide staircase leading up to a spacious, high-ceilinged, sequestered room tucked away in one of the factory's quietest corners. Here ancient Venetian blinds, layered with dust, filtered out most of the afternoon sunlight, heavy lamp-shades softened the already weak glare from the overhead lights, and the air was thick with swirls of cigarette smoke and the smell of tobacco. At the centre of the room stood two billiard tables, their pale green baize and mahogany frames echoed in the faded wall-paper with which the room was decorated, and the worn-out furniture placed around its edges. These were the only licensed premises in the whole of Bournville, and between the two largest windows was a bar behind which a young man in a white tuxedo, with slicked-back hair and a world-weary expression, stood polish-ing glasses. Most of the tables were empty. There was a quartet of men playing cards, another man staring inscrutably into space as he sipped a pint of bitter and a brave lone woman reading a newspaper over a gin and tonic. One of the billiard tables was already occupied, so Martin made for the other and began to set up the balls for snooker. Jack took three cues from a rack on the wall and offered one of them to his grandfather, but Sam shook his head:

'No, I'm just going to watch.'

'Are you sure?'

'Yes, my eye isn't what it used to be.'

'Can I get you a drink anyway?'

'Pale ale, please. Just a half.'

The game began slowly. That is to say, Martin started it, spending more than a minute on his first shot, and then, after Jack had briefly tried and failed to pot a red, taking another five minutes to complete a three-shot break (red-blue-red) that won him a mere seven points.

'Good God,' Jack said, sipping on a double Scotch, 'we're going to be here till midnight at the rate you're playing.'

'Are you sure you don't want a go, Grandpa?' Martin said, offer-ing Sam his cue.

'I'm fine. I might try a few shots later. It's just nice to be here.' He looked around him happily. 'By heck, I spent a few hours here in the forties and fifties. And it hasn't changed much since then, I can tell you.'

'There was something I meant to ask you,' said Martin. It was his break again, after Jack had potted a red and then carelessly missed an easy pink, and he was walking around the table, giving himself various perspectives on what promised to be a fairly simple shot.

'When you worked here back then, did we sell much chocolate to the Continent?'

'To the Continent? Well, I don't know. That wasn't my department. I was a draughtsman. I was doing technical drawings, working on the machines. Why do you ask?'

'Because these days,' said Martin, nudging a red into a pocket, and moving on to the brown, 'we're not allowed to sell chocolate to Europe.'

'Not allowed? Who by?'

'The EEC. We don't put in enough cocoa butter, apparently, and we use too much vegetable fat.'

'Unbelievable,' said Jack. 'That'll be the bloody French, I suppose. Or the Germans. Probably both of them. Are you going to pot that thing or just look at it for the next half-hour?'

'Don't rush me,' said Martin. He struck the cue ball gently and with a satisfying click it made contact with the brown and knocked it into a corner pocket. But he missed the next red.

'Frank would have been the person to ask about that,' his grandfather said. 'But I've got a feeling it goes back to the war.'

'Most things go back to the war,' said Jack.

'How come?' said Martin.

'Well, you couldn't get the cocoa butter back then, you see. It was in short supply. So they had to change the recipe of the Dairy Milk bars. "Ration Chocolate", they called it. Less cocoa, more fat.'

'And they changed it back when rationing was over?'

'Well, I'm not sure that they really did. By then people were used to it. They'd started to like it. The taste of it kind of reminded them of the war, I suppose.'

'Why would anyone want to be reminded of the war?'

'Because Britain was great back then,' said Jack.

Martin, in the act of potting another red, glanced up at his brother. It always amazed him that he could come out with statements like this, without qualification, without really thinking what he was saying. He realized that it was Jack, out of the three of them, who had inherited their mother's impulsiveness, her ability to navigate the world by instinct. So far it had served her fairly well. Would it do the same for him?

'Your trouble,' Sam told his eldest grandson, 'is that you're always in too much of a rush. You need to take a bit more time over things. Look before you leap, so to speak.'

This was not a comment on his political judgements. They were all in the car park again now, and Sam was referring to his grandson's snooker technique: he had lost to Martin by three frames to two, largely by making a series of hasty unforced errors.

'Oh, you'll never get anywhere like that,' said Jack. 'There'll always be some bloke one step ahead of you.' They had arrived by the side of Martin's car, a 1976 Austin Allegro in avocado green. 'Dear oh dear, look at this old crock! Is that what you're driving these days?'

'It's all I can afford,' said Martin. His new job had come with a rise, but not a very big one. Still, he was proud of the fact that he owned his own car now. 'And it does the job. Gets me from A to B.'

Jack's car, a shiny new Austin Metro, as recently endorsed by both Margaret Thatcher and Prince Charles – and currently driven by Lady Diana Spencer, if the rumours were to be believed – was parked a few yards away. With a brisk fraternal handshake the two brothers said goodbye, and Martin drove his grandfather the few miles back to their shared temporary home.

*

Taking Sam back to the Works seemed to have had the desired effect. Over dinner that evening, he was in unusually good spirits. To make it even more of a special occasion, Doll had stirred herself out of her torpor to cook a roast dinner for the family. As usual, the meat had been cooked to a point where it was unrecognizable. When Grandma cooked, the only way you could reliably identify the animal you were eating was by the sauce you were given on the side: mint sauce meant lamb, apple sauce meant pork, and horseradish meant beef. Today was apple sauce.

Sam was wolfing it down. 'This is delicious,' he said. 'Well done, Ma.'

'Nice to see you've got your appetite back,' said Mary.

'Today was a tonic.' As he spooned more apple sauce onto his plate, he added: 'The only disappointing thing was that I didn't get to meet Martin's lady friend.'

'Well, none of us have had that pleasure yet,' said Mary, an undertone of genuine grievance in her voice.

There was a glint in Sam's eye as he said: 'I'm beginning to think she doesn't exist.'

Everyone was happy to see his teasing manner come back again, even Martin.

'Of course she exists,' he said, entering into the spirit.

'There's no evidence,' Sam pointed out.

'OK.' Martin stood up. 'If you want evidence, you can have it.'

He went to the little cloakroom under the stairs, fumbled around in his jacket pockets and returned with a small colour photograph.

'Here you are everybody, meet Bridget,' he said, and handed the photograph to his mother.

Mary took the picture and looked at it intently for a few moments. She gave the impression that she was about to choose her words carefully.

'What a pretty girl,' she said at last. And then, turning to Martin: 'I thought you said she was from Scotland.'

'She is. Glasgow.'

Mary passed the picture to Geoffrey. He pulled out his glasses from the pocket of his shirt, put them on, looked at the picture, took his glasses off, put them back in his shirt pocket and passed the picture on to Doll without saying anything. His face was a mask, unmoving and expressionless.

Doll held the photo up close to her eyes, then moved it slightly further away, squinting until it came into focus, and then said, looking at Martin but speaking to the table in general:

'Goodness, she's as black as the ace of spades.'

'All right, Ma,' Mary said, intervening quickly. 'There's no need to spell it out.'

Doll continued to hold on to the photograph until Sam ran out of patience and said, 'Am I allowed to look at it?' at which point she passed it over to him. He looked at the photo only briefly before handing it back to Martin with the words, 'Well done. Looks like you've got a cracker there.'

'Do you treat her the same?' Doll wanted to know. 'I mean . . . do you treat her the same as you would any other girl?'

'What a daft question,' said her husband.

Martin thought so too, but he smiled and answered it as politely as he could. His grandmother was almost eighty, after all, and had grown up in a very different time, and he knew that anything she said – daft or not – would always be well-intentioned. He was more worried about his father's response. Geoffrey had still not uttered a word.

9.

Geoffrey remained silent, even as Lady Diana climbed the steps to the church and his wife turned to him for support.

'He wasn't, was he?' she insisted.

'What?'

'What Jack called him. A lefty.'

'Who? What are we talking about?'

Mary let out a long sigh of frustration. It was increasingly difficult to tell, with her husband, whether he was being wilfully obstructive or just didn't listen to the conversations that were going on around him. Both interpretations of his silence were infuriating. This particular argument had been kicked off by Jack and Peter who, rather than sitting back and watching the ceremony, entering into its spirit of celebration and national unity, had done nothing but needle each other for the last few minutes. It had started when Peter alluded once again to the contrast between this royalist pomp and circumstance and the riots that had been taking place all month, up and down the country – in Brixton and in Toxteth, in Sheffield and Nottingham, Leeds and Wolverhampton, Handsworth and Moss Side. What kind of a country, he wanted to know, could allow these two worlds to exist side by side?

'Ah, OK,' Jack said, 'so you were watching *Newsnight* the other night too, were you? Because you're just parroting that lefty journalist they had on.'

'Ken Fielding,' Peter said, 'talks a lot of sense.'

'Rubbish. I heard what he had to say and it was just comfort food for *Guardian* readers.'

'That's not the paper he writes for,' said Peter.

'Did you say Ken Fielding?' Mary said. 'Kenneth Fielding? On the television?'

'Yes, what about him?'

'I used to know him. He was born round here, you know. Cotteridge. In fact, your father and I both knew him. We used to play tennis with him and his sister.'

'He's lost his Brummie accent, then.'

Mary's voice dropped, and it was no longer clear whether she was talking to the others in the room or merely to herself. 'Good old Kenneth. Haven't seen him for *years* . . . Oh, I'm so glad he's made something of himself.' Then, speaking directly to her eldest son: 'I wouldn't say he was a lefty, though. Not back when I knew him, anyway. Would you, Geoff?'

And when she failed to get not just the support she was hoping for, but any kind of answer at all, she surprised everyone – including herself – by getting up and leaving the living room and going to sit in the garden.

Meanwhile, Lady Diana was entering the cathedral, clutching her father's arm, her impossibly long white train stretched out behind her, followed by two tiny flower girls who added suspense to the occasion by looking dangerously close to stepping on it. The young bride, whose nervousness was visible even behind her veil, then began to walk up the aisle, embarking upon what the florid BBC commentator chose to call '*the longest and happiest walk she will ever take*'. On hearing this phrase Peter, too, decided that he'd had enough, and stomped out into the fresh air and the late-morning sunshine, against which he immediately had to shade his eyes.

'Come and sit here, love,' said Mary, patting the space beside her. She was sitting on the little wall that divided the garden into two at its midway point. There was no garden furniture. Peter went and sat beside her.

'Didn't you want to watch it?' he asked.

'Oh, I'll go back inside in a minute. I just fancied . . . a breath of air, that's all.' She put her arm through his and said, reflectively: 'I wish you'd told me Kenneth was on the television the other night. I would've liked to have watched it.'

'I didn't know you knew him.'

'What was he wearing?'

Peter glanced at his mother, finding this an odd question.

'I don't remember.'

'Was he wearing a cravat?'

'A cravat? I don't think so.'

'He used to put one on sometimes, if it was a special occasion. I wondered if he still did. I suppose it would look a bit old-fashioned now . . .' Half to herself, she continued: 'I used to see quite a bit of him, actually, back then. When I was a student. I suppose I had a bit of a crush on him and, well . . . and vice versa.'

Peter was not used to hearing his mother talk like this, and did not know how to react. Sometimes he felt that they understood each other perfectly; at other times – such as now – they seemed miles apart. On a rational level, on the surface, he could see that he had grown away from her and they now had almost nothing in common. But there were still sometimes moments of connection between them which contradicted that. In January, in the depths of winter, she had come down to London to visit him at the Royal College of Music and he had taken her to a concert featuring his fellow students. His father hadn't wanted to come, choosing to stay in his hotel room all evening instead. The piece being performed was Howells's *Hymnus Paradisi*, which neither Peter nor his mother had heard before. The seats in the concert hall were close together and because it was cold in there his mother did not take off her fake fur coat, so that they were forced into a physical proximity which Peter was happy enough, once the music had started, to relax into: it was like balling himself up against some warm, soft, infinitely comforting woodland creature out of a child's storybook. In this semi-infantile state he surrendered to the music, not knowing what to expect, and found that he was listening to one of the most moving pieces he had heard in his life. He knew that Howells had written it following the death of his son, but this work, he could feel at once, was about more than death, about more than one individual tragedy. In the piercing dissonances of the first movement, in the crystalline, vulnerable melody sung by the soprano in the second, he could hear an expression of grief at every loss that he or anyone else had ever experienced – loss of innocence, loss of childhood, of opportunity, of hope – until the music built into a howl of grief at the simplest and cruellest fact of all: the passing of time itself. As his scalp tingled with the terrible beauty of the music, he shifted closer still to his mother's body and knew that she was feeling the same things, and that these moments they were sharing, consigned to the past though they already were, would never be forgotten, not by either of them. Afterwards, when they came out of the concert hall, they found that snow had started to fall in the streets outside and as he walked with his mother back to the hotel, they linked arms and when he looked down fleetingly to see the snowflakes landing on the sleeve of her coat it seemed like another of those indelible moments, and the closeness between them seemed absolute, unbreakable. And yet now, in the back garden of Martin and Bridget's new house, he was embarrassed to feel her arm through his, and to be invited to share in these awkward confidences about some past entanglement that could mean nothing to him. Luckily he was saved from having to offer a response by the arrival of Bridget and Parminder, bearing the tray of samosas. The four of them sat on the wall and nibbled on the snacks.

'Jolly nice,' said Mary, a note of uncertainty in her voice. 'Quite spicy.'

'What's going on in there?' Peter asked. 'Is she still walking up the aisle?'

'It's going to take her at least ten minutes.'

'You could do wonders with this garden,' said Mary.

'Yes, we have plans,' said Bridget, 'lots of plans. It was the garden that made us decide to take it, really.'

'The house is nice, though. Small, but nice. I think you'll be very happy here.'

Bridget smiled. 'I think so too. We knew we wanted it as soon as we saw it. It was love at first sight.'

10.

At lunchtime, as arranged, Martin went to find Bridget in her office. She was on the telephone to her mother.

'Mum, everything is absolutely fine,' she was saying. 'I don't live anywhere near Handsworth. You've been to my flat. It's perfectly safe. Nobody is rioting in Balsall Heath.

'Of course I'm OK.

'No, I'm not coming home.

'Anyway, it'll probably kick off in Glasgow soon. It seems to be happening everywhere.'

After putting the phone down she smiled sadly at Martin and said: 'Parents.'

It had been almost three months since the first Brixton riots. Over the weekend, however, further unrest had flared up in the Toxteth area of Liverpool, in Wolverhampton, Leicester and Coventry, and in Handsworth, which was about seven miles from the Cadbury Works. As with all such events, no one could quite understand why the violence had erupted at this particular moment, in these particular places: some combination, no doubt, of poverty, unemployment, desperation, bad policing, bad community relations and the specific targeting of Black and other minority groups – it was easy enough to reel off a list of possible factors, but not so easy to see why it was happening now, or why, once it had started, it was spreading out so rapidly from flashpoints like Toxteth and Moss Side to so many other parts of the country. With unemployment standing at two and a half million and still rising, the Labour leader, Michael Foot, made a number of speeches laying the blame on Mrs Thatcher and her policies. Even her allies felt that the Prime Minister's first two years in office had been a disaster, and did not expect her to be back for a second term.

'I suppose we should thank our lucky stars,' Martin said, as they drove through the streets of Bournville a few minutes later, 'that we're not affected by any of that.'

From the passenger seat of his avocado-green Austin Allegro, Bridget glanced at him in surprise.

'Any of that?'

'The rioting, I mean.' Martin braked to a halt outside a small, semi-detached cottage in Pine Grove, and announced: 'Here we are.'

'Wait a minute,' said Bridget, laying a hand on Martin's arm just as he was about to undo his seat belt. '*You* might not be affected. Don't generalize about me. When we were growing up my brothers couldn't walk a hundred yards through Govan without being pulled over. It was the same for everybody. Anything that messes up relations between us and the police affects my family, and ends up affecting me. You do get that?'

He held her gaze for a second or two and said, 'Yes, sure. Of course I do.'

It was the first time he had felt any tension between them. But Bridget did not allow it to last. She gave him a forgiving kiss on the cheek and said: 'Come on, then. Let's go and inspect this palace of delights.'

A young, pallid estate agent was waiting for them on the doorstep. He offered nervous greetings to Martin and Bridget, only one of whom knew exactly why they were there. She simply thought that he wanted her opinion on a house he was thinking of renting. Martin, however, had an ulterior motive.

'It's very nice,' she said, as they explored the two compact bedrooms on the first floor.

'Small, but cosy.'

'Furniture's not too bad, as well. All looks fairly new. How much are they asking?'

'Two hundred and forty a month.'

Bridget's eyes widened.

'Can you afford that?'

'No, I can't.'

'Ah. So what are we doing here, exactly?'

'Maybe *we* could afford it,' he said, putting his arms around her, 'if we moved in together.'

She took a moment or two to absorb the implications of this. 'You're saying that you want us to live together,' she said, 'because then we could split the rent?'

'Mm-hm.'

Bridget disengaged from his embrace, walked over to the bedroom window and sighed. 'As usual, Martin, you really know how to sweep a girl off her feet.'

'Well, that wouldn't be the only reason, of course. I mean, I'd like to . . . It would be nice if we could . . .'

Bridget was peering intently out of the window.

'I've always fancied doing a bit of gardening,' she said. 'You could put a nice little flower bed down there. And a vegetable patch.'

'This could be your bedroom,' Martin stumbled, 'since it's a bit bigger.'

'You could grow potatoes in that . . .' she continued. 'Or parsnips. Do you like parsnips? I love parsnips.'

'That's unless you wanted to share a bedroom, of course. I mean, that's up to—'

Bridget wheeled around.

'OK,' she said. 'Let's do it.'

Martin was stunned. 'Really?'

'Really.' Her tone was crisp and decisive. 'But don't think it's got anything to do with you.' She walked back towards Martin, gave him a perfunctory kiss on the mouth, and said, 'I'm doing it for the parsnips. Remember that.'

II.

29th July 1981, 11.40 a.m.

Something about the wedding ceremony seemed to be driving people out into the garden. Jack and Patricia were the next two to emerge from the back doorway. There was no longer any room on the low wall where the others were sitting, so they squatted down on the little square of parched and patchy grass.

'I can't stand the tension in there,' said Patricia. 'They both look so nervous.'

'Well, you can't really see what she *looks* like,' said Jack, 'because of the veil. But you're right, I think she's terrified. She got his name wrong.'

'Got his name wrong?' Mary repeated.

'Yes, instead of Charles Philip she called him Philip Charles. When she was saying the vows.'

'Perhaps she thinks she's marrying his father,' said Patricia, and giggled.

'I hope that doesn't mean the marriage is null and void,' said Mary. 'It doesn't mean it's null and void, does it?'

'I wouldn't worry about it, Mum,' said Martin, who had now come out into the garden too, along with Sathnam. 'I'm sure the Archbishop of Canterbury knows what he's doing.'

'Prince Charles just made a mistake as well,' said Sathnam. 'Did you notice? He said "thy". I'm pretty sure he was supposed to say "my". He was supposed to offer her "my" worldly goods and he said "thy" instead.'

'Blimey,' said Jack, 'at this rate they'll have to scrap the whole thing and do a replay.'

'It does make you wonder,' said Bridget, 'whether they're the cleverest people in the world.'

'Thick as two short planks, the pair of them,' said Peter. 'That's the classic British mistake, isn't it, to think that people must be intelligent just because they've got a posh accent?'

'For your information,' said Jack, 'when he came to visit the factory I found him very intelligent. Asked a lot of questions, very on the ball. Knew all about transmission and carburettors and that sort of thing.'

'How exciting that you got to meet him,' said Parminder.

'Well, it was only for five or ten minutes. But the man isn't stupid, I can tell you.' Following the story of this impressive encounter, Jack could tell that he had everyone's attention, and he could never resist a good audience. 'Which reminds me – here's a good one. How do you keep an Irishman busy all day?' Nobody volunteered an answer – indeed, some of them didn't seem to realize that this was the set-up for a joke – so he provided it himself: 'Give him a piece of paper with "Please Turn Over" written on both sides.' His own laughter drowned out the laughter of everyone else; not that there was much of that, although Sathnam and Parminder did chuckle a bit, out of politeness. Martin's response was to say:

'I don't know if I ever told you this, Jack, but there were only two students on my course at uni who got a First. Do you know what they had in common?'

'No, what?'

'They were both Irish.'

Jack stared at him blankly. 'I don't get it.'

'I'm just pointing out to you,' Martin said, 'that there's nothing stupid about the Irish, as a nation. Nothing at all.'

'Oh my God, it was just a joke. You have heard of jokes, haven't you?' Turning to Bridget, he said: 'I don't envy you living with him, really I don't. His sense of humour was surgically removed at the age of five.'

'Martin has a sense of humour,' Bridget said, loyally. 'Don't you, love?'

'Well, true, he has joined the SDP, I'll give you that. That shows he'll do anything for a laugh.'

And this, inevitably, led them on to politics. Martin told them that the SDP was the only serious opposition party in Britain because the Labour Party had been taken over by extremists, and Peter said that Michael Foot wasn't an extremist, he was a very principled man, and not just principled but erudite, because did they know that he'd written a book about Jonathan Swift and also the introduction to the Penguin edition of *Gulliver's Travels*?, and Jack said, Great, that's just the sort of thing that'll keep the Transport and General Workers Union in line, when are you going to come down from cloud cuckoo land and join the rest of us in the real world, anyone could see he was just a silly old man in a donkey jacket, and Parminder said, Forgive her, she didn't mean to be impolite, but she thought this was a very superficial thing to say, you should not judge people by how they look or what they wear and you should not be rude about someone just because they are old, and Jack said he didn't mean to be disrespectful but—

—and at that point Geoffrey came into the garden and asked them what they were all doing outside.

'Your parents are wondering where you've gone,' he said to Mary.

'We're just having a breather,' she said. 'It's lovely out here.'

'You're missing all the music,' he pointed out. This was addressed not just to Mary but to Peter as well. 'I thought you were keen on music.'

'Yes, you're right,' said Jack, rising to his feet. 'We shouldn't be missing this. It's a historic day.'

'So was *Kristallnacht*,' said Peter.

'Oh, that's charming, that is. I can't tell an Irish joke, but you can get away with something like that. Go on, get inside, you little smartarse.'

Mary and Peter went indoors, followed by all the others. All except for Martin and Geoffrey, because just as Geoffrey was about to go inside, Martin called him back and said:

'Can I have a word with you, Dad?'

His father turned. They had not spoken to each other all day.

'It's about last Thursday.'

12.

23rd July 1981

A visit to the cinema in Porthmadog, one evening in the early summer of 1969, had marked the start of a family tradition. Since that day, when all three of Mary's sons had fallen under the spell of *Thunderball*, they had measured out the 1970s in James Bond films. *On Her Majesty's Secret Service* was the first one they had seen as a family, in the spring of 1970. Martin in particular was captivated by its pristine snowscapes, by the notion of an Alpine hideaway populated entirely by beautiful women, and by the unexpected, devastating melancholy of the film's final scene. Mary had complained that George Lazenby was not as sexy as Sean Connery, and was relieved when Connery returned for *Diamonds Are Forever*. They saw it one Saturday afternoon in central Birmingham, a wintry day in mid-January 1972, and although fans would not judge the film kindly in the decades to come, to escape for two hours from the freezing drizzle that whipped along New Street into the sunshine of the Nevada desert and the glamour of Las Vegas was blissful. *Live and Let Die*, released in July 1973 and consumed by the Lamb family on their caravan holiday near Plymouth the next month, saw Roger Moore replacing Sean Connery, at which point Mary abandoned the franchise. She thought he was too old, too English, too posh, insufficiently serious and insufficiently masculine, and from then on, watching these films would be a ritual shared only between the men of the family. *The Man With the Golden Gun* made a perfect post-Christmas treat in December 1974, at the end of a year which Jack, Martin and Peter had thoroughly enjoyed, but Geoffrey had found alarming: oil prices had soared in the wake of the Yom Kippur war, the trade unions had flexed their muscles, the IRA had killed twenty-one people in a Birmingham pub and a Labour government had been elected. Under the influence of these developments Geof-frey slipped into a mood of chronic apprehension, and the film itself was not involving enough or memorable enough to snap him out of it. But two and a half years later came *The Spy Who Loved Me*, and with this instalment Bond truly came to the rescue of his country. It was released, in fact, at a moment of fleeting, sunbathed national optimism. The Queen's Silver Jubilee (twenty-five years since she came to the throne! *Twenty-five!*) had been celebrated with sou-venirs, street parties and boisterous singing of the national anthem even as the Sex Pistols' 'God Save the Queen' was climbing almost to the top of the charts. It was somehow wonderfully revealing of the national character that these two songs could be on everybody's lips at the same time. The jubilee celebrations were succeeded in early July by two miraculous events: Virginia Wade winning the women's singles championship for Britain at Wimbledon, and Peter Lamb passing his Grade 8 Violin exam with distinction. Geoffrey and the boys were already feeling chipper, then, when they filed into the dress circle of the Odeon New Street one balmy night towards the end of that month. The cinema was packed. Buoyed up by the news of recent weeks, the audience's first big laugh of appreciation – along with a scattered round of applause – came after just two minutes, when Bond had already been enjoying his first sex of the film and, on being told by the lucky female in question that 'I need you, James,' answered, 'So does England,' with a charmingly rueful smile. But the audience response to this line was nothing compared to what came next. Escaping his pursuers on skis and hurling him-self over the edge of a snowy precipice, Bond went into freefall and was well on his way to certain death when the backpack he was carrying opened out into a life-saving parachute and this parachute revealed itself – joy of joys – to consist of an enormous Union Jack. The crowd in the cinema went wild. People were rising to their feet, punching the air and raising cheers that filled the auditorium and probably spilled into the street outside. After that, every man in the audience was entirely in Bond's hands and for the next two hours they followed his latest mission to save the world with uninter-rupted, worshipful concentration. When he and the beautiful

Russian spy were pulled out of the water in the closing scene – cocooned in a glass bubble, wrapped around each other and kissing languidly, their nudity concealed only by a white fleece blanket – and Bond explained to his astonished superior that he was 'Just keeping the British end up, sir,' there was another throaty eruption of laughter and cheering. It was a line that delighted Jack in particular, chiming as it did with a peculiar admixture of qualities that had come to define him as he reached adulthood: a combination of nationalism and facetiousness. (And for years afterwards, whenever he wanted to hint to his friends or his brothers that he had recently been having sex, he would always wink at them and say that he'd been 'keeping the British end up'.)

After that *Moonraker*, extravagant and colourful as it was, could only be an anticlimax. And indeed, Peter did not come to see that one, being the first of the brothers to turn his back on the family ritual, announcing that as far as he was concerned James Bond offered nothing but puerile jingoism and his new preference was for European art films. And then in June 1981, when *For Your Eyes Only* opened, Jack also went rogue, and chose to see it with his girlfriend, Patricia, in the first week of release, leaving just Martin and Geoffrey to carry on the tradition. Which they were, all the same, determined to do. Despite having lived under his roof again for the last few months, Martin had felt a distance opening up between himself and his father, and this seemed a good opportunity to try closing it. They could see the film together – just like in the old days – go for a drink afterwards, perhaps even have a chat about Bridget. Maybe under the healing influence of Roger Moore, some cartoon violence, some implausibly beautiful women and a series of suave one-liners, Geoffrey would shed his current reserve and they could have a heartfelt, serious conversation about the blissful new direction Martin's life was taking. Feeling confident that the strategy would work, he proposed a Thursday evening towards the end of July. His father agreed and booked two tickets for the Solihull cinema.

*

The programme was due to begin at 6.45. Martin arrived on time and entered the cinema foyer, but couldn't see his father anywhere.

After he had been waiting for a few minutes, a young woman arrived. She was very pretty, and looked vaguely familiar, and to Martin's surprise, she headed straight for him.

'Hello,' she said. 'Remember me?'

Not having a great memory for faces, he struggled at first to put a name to this one. But then it clicked into place.

'Oh . . . Yes . . . Penny, isn't it?'

'That's right. We met at your dad's house.'

It was his father's secretary.

'He'll be here himself in a minute, as a matter of fact,' said Martin. 'Are you coming to see the film too? You can sit with us if you like, or . . . no, you're probably meeting someone.'

'I am. I'm meeting you.'

'Me?'

'Geoffrey had to work late. He didn't want the ticket to go to waste so he asked if I wanted to come instead.' Martin looked . . . not crestfallen exactly, but certainly surprised, so she added: 'He said to tell you that he's really sorry. He knew you were looking forward to it.'

Martin nodded. 'Ah well.'

'You don't mind, do you? That I'm here, I mean.'

At this point he realized, slightly too late, that he was not being very polite, or showing much gratitude: it was nice of her, after all, to turn up and keep him company like this. She'd probably had plans of her own, and put them on hold for his benefit.

'Not at all. Shall we go in? The trailers'll be starting in a minute.'

They armed themselves with popcorn and cartons of Kia-Ora and found two good seats in the stalls. The lights were still up and there was muzak playing over the speaker system. For a few minutes they made awkward small talk. Martin learned that Penny lived in nearby Dorridge, had been working at the bank ever since leaving school at the age of eighteen, that she shared a flat with two girlfriends and had nothing but praise for his father, who was liked by everyone who worked for him, she said, especially the women, because he always treated them with respect unlike Andy, the chief clerk, whose hands were all over the place. In return Martin gave her just a few nuggets of personal information but didn't mention Bridget (somehow it didn't seem the right thing to do), and was halfway through a perhaps unnecessarily detailed account of last week's local SDP meeting when to his relief – and to hers, most likely – the lights went down and the supporting programme began. As well as the trailers, there was a large number of adverts to sit through, most of them low-budget ads for local businesses. Penny made fun of these by whispering a series of jokey, disparaging comments in Martin's ear. He did his best to reply in the same light-hearted spirit, but again it felt odd, and inappropriately intimate, to be swapping these breathy pleasantries with a woman who wasn't Bridget, and he was glad when the main feature started and they could watch it in silence.

Reviews of *For Your Eyes Only* had suggested that it was a more serious film than its predecessors, an attempt by the producers to recreate the grittiness of the Sean Connery era. Martin, whose taste for fantasy was – like his taste for everything else – moderate, approved this change of direction. It was time that Bond moved into the 1980s, definitely. During the title sequence, with its silhouettes of naked young women performing various provocative gyrations, he felt obliged to turn towards Penny and say, 'They should really have knocked this sort of thing on the head by now,' but she didn't seem to share his objections: 'I think it's sexy,' she said, and indeed during the first half of the film she laughed far more loudly than Martin did at Bond's laconic assassinations and absent-minded sexual conquests, not to mention the feeble quips and innuendos that accompanied them. During the second half, Martin became distracted from the film itself by something which he thought he was imagining at first, although he was gradually, and alarmingly, disabused of that idea: namely, that Penny had shifted in her seat and leaned in to him, so that her leg was pressed up against his, with their thighs enjoying especially close contact. He didn't know quite what to do about this. To turn away, and impose a distance between them, would also mean acknowledging the reality of the situation, which he was reluctant to do. So they watched most of the second half of the film in this position, Penny's leg supple and relaxed, Martin's stiff with tension.

She turned to him and said, as the credits were rolling, 'That was good, wasn't it? Fancy a drink?'

'Well . . .' He looked at his watch. 'It's getting quite late.'

'What are you talking about? It's nine-fifteen. Come on, just a quick one.'

She hooked her arm through his and more or less dragged him out of the cinema and into the nearest pub. He ordered half a Guinness and she asked for a large vodka and Coke. Then, seconds after they had sat down and taken their first sips, she leaned forward, told him that he looked like Oliver Reed, and kissed him on the lips.

Martin pulled back and said, 'Look, Penny, I don't mean to be rude, but what's going on?'

'I thought you fancied me,' she said. When he neither confirmed nor denied this suggestion, she explained: 'That's what your dad said, anyway. He said that when I came to your house you told everyone that I was pretty.'

Martin cast his mind back to that evening. Yes, he *had* said that she was pretty. He'd said it to Peter, who had presumably passed it on to his father, who had presumably passed it on to Penny. But why?

'Did he also tell you that I was seeing someone?'

'Yes, but he said that it wasn't serious.'

Martin went very quiet. In fact, he fell completely silent for some time. He understood, finally and with horrible clarity, the plan his father had put into action.

Penny looked at him and could see that his expression was grim.

'Oh,' she said. 'So it *is* serious.'

Martin nodded. 'We're moving in together on Monday, as it happens.'

'Oh,' she said again. 'Does your dad know that?'

'Yes.'

'Oh,' she said, one more time. 'That's a bit weird, then. I mean, he's set us up on a date. That's what this is, isn't it?'

'I suppose so.'

'Why would he do that? It's not very fair on you.'

'Or you. It's not very fair on either of us.' As the full import of his father's actions came home to him, Martin clenched his fists in anger. It was all he could do to stop himself from slamming them on the table. 'I'm so sorry,' he said at last. 'You've had a wasted evening.'

'Not really,' said Penny. 'I enjoyed the film. Didn't you?'

Martin smiled at her, wishing that he could cheer her up some-how. She had seemed so bright and lovely when she'd first walked into the cinema foyer a few hours ago, and now she looked miser-able. He reached out across the table and clasped her hand. After that they finished their drinks, and he drove her back to her flat. For some days now, there had been a persistent knocking from the engine of his car. On the way home tonight it got worse. He had no idea what it signified. James Bond would probably have known what to do about it; but then, James Bond never drove a 1976 Austin Allegro.

13.

From the kitchen window, where she was washing up plates and mugs, Bridget could not just see Martin talking to his father; she could hear every word they were saying. She heard Martin's account of what had happened last Thursday evening; she heard his father's apology, or half-apology. She went upstairs for a while, and sat in the back bedroom. It took everyone a while to notice that she was missing. When she heard Mary saying, 'Where's Bridget? I haven't seen her for ages,' she stood up and wiped her eyes, then came back downstairs and rejoined the family in the living room.

*

The television screen showed the balcony of Buckingham Palace. The wedding ceremony successfully concluded, the royal party returned. The two conjoined families lined up on the balcony, chatting, smiling, waving at the crowd packed around the Victoria Memorial statue. Half a million people. Central London at 1.10 p.m. on 29th July 1981.

*

Charles and Diana kiss. Flashbulbs pop. Tomorrow's papers have their front page. 750 million TV viewers are watching around the world. Among them, a family gathered round a television set in Bournville, Birmingham B30.

*

PETER

Listen to that lot. Just listen to them. What are they cheering for? Why are we supposed to feel happy for these people? Why should the nation, as a whole, feel happy for them? I may throw up.

MARTIN

Well, I told him what I thought. That's something. Now he knows how serious it is and he can bloody well come to terms with it. If he's capable of doing that. He's going to have to change. He's going to have to change or he will become bitter and detached and weird because this is the direction of travel now, the world is moving on, moving forward, and if people like him can't deal with it . . . Oh, that was a nice kiss. Very nice. Good luck to them both.

JACK

They're in love. They really are in love. That's good to see. You can't help feeling a bit cheered up by that. I reckon this is the turning point, for us, for the country. The first couple of years have been rough but we're going to be on track from now on. Bit of money to be made if you know what you're doing. You just need to have your wits about you and grab your chances when you can. And have the right person to share it with, helping you out. Don't think that's going to be Patricia, sadly. Sorry, love. It has been fun though.

PATRICIA

I hope you know what you're letting yourself in for, girl. I wouldn't like my first kiss to be in front of all those people. I don't think it would be easy to be a royal but the perks are pretty spectacular. As for this family here, they've really been getting on my tits this morning. But I reckon Jack's gearing himself up to dump me anyway. Maybe I'll get in first.

SATHNAM

Good neighbours are important. I have a good feeling about these people. Decent people. We'd better have them back to ours before long. We can cook them something nice. There will be bad times ahead for Martin soon. The old man, Samuel, is not well. He looks like Dada Ji did a few weeks before he died. His grandsons are fond of him, all three of them, you can see that. The young one, Peter, is very quiet. I think perhaps he has a secret. Jack – I have met men like Jack before. Always laughing, always joking, but sometimes people like that are hard underneath. Sentimental, too. Look at him – he loves all this stuff with Charles and Diana. He can't get enough of it. Well, I suppose there's nothing wrong with that. This monarchy stuff is all a lot of nonsense really but perhaps there's no harm in it. People need spectacle sometimes. Bread and circuses and all that. Anyway, it's over now so we'd better be polite and go home in a minute, we mustn't outstay our welcome.

PARMINDER

Can we go home now, please? We've been here for three hours. Three long hours.

MARY

I stood there. That's exactly where I stood. Almost thirty years ago. And they were there on the balcony, too. The Queen and Philip. The same balcony. Amazing to think about it, isn't it. Thirty years! She's worn very well, I must say. I hope that I've worn as well as she has. Oh, she's talking to Diana now. Chatting and laughing with her. That's nice. That's lovely to see. I think she really likes her. Well, of course she likes her, her son's in love with her, isn't he? That's a mother's impulse. As long as she makes your boy happy, that's all that matters. And I've never seen Martin looking so happy. Geoffrey'd better come round to her. What an old stick-in-the-mud he is. I mean, I always knew what his views were – I've known that from the beginning – but I did think he would change. Everybody changes, don't they? Even if it happens slowly. If you don't change I don't see how you can survive.

GEOFFREY

Namque Iunia Manlio,
qualis Idalium colens
venit ad Phrygium Venus

iudicem, bona cum bona
nubet alite virgo,

floridis velut enitens
myrtus Asia ramulis,
quos hamadryades deae
ludicrum sibi rosido
nutriunt umore.

quare age huc aditum ferens
perge linquere Thespiae
rupis Aonios specus,
nympha quos super irrigat
frigerans Aganippe,

ac domum dominam voca
coniugis cupidam novi,
mentem amore revinciens
ut tenax hedera huc et huc
arborem implicat errans.

Ah, Catullus!

BERTHA

*What a nice kiss. That's the future king, that is. And she's the future
queen. Queen Diana of England. I wonder if I shall live to see it. Lord,
I get tired easily now. I shall sleep for two or three hours this afternoon,
the sooner the better. I hope Geoffrey plans to drive me home.*

DOLL

Get well. Please get well again. Don't leave me here, alone.

SAM

*Oh, it's hard to think about anything but the pain. This bloody pain
which never goes away, just waxes and wanes. You try to put a brave*

face on it because that's what they expect of you. I know the lads expect me to be all smiles and cracking jokes. Well, it isn't easy. There comes a point in life where you just don't see the funny side any more, and I've reached it. Maybe I'll be lucky. Maybe I've got a few more years in me yet. I'll tell you one thing I don't need to see again before I die, mind you. Another bloody royal ceremony. The Coronation was bad enough, but this one, hell's teeth! She loves it, though: the one thing I was never able to change Doll's mind about, she loves the royals. Don't ask me why. I suppose I could understand it when we were young but now, after all this time, I really thought people would have seen through this shower of spongers. I thought the war would have changed everything, but maybe not. It changed things for a while and then gradually, bit by bit, we've gone back to how things were before. That's how I see it anyway. What do I know? Nothing, probably. You get to eighty and it turns out you haven't learned all that much. Just that life goes on and you have to make the best of it till it stops.

BRIDGET

Yes, but families like this . . . they never really accept people from outside, do they?

I mean, really accept them.

SIX

The Funeral of Diana, Princess of Wales

6th September 1997

I. Liturgy of Crystal

'Let's play another game,' said Gran.

'Why?' said Lorna. 'Don't you like this one?'

'I do, only we're running out of things to say. So instead of "I spy with my little eye", what about "I hear"? "I hear with my little ear"?'

Lorna thought this over. It seemed like an acceptable suggestion. 'All right.'

She frowned, and did her best to concentrate. She listened very carefully to the sounds around her. It was a quiet morning. It was a quarter past seven, and at the moment, they were the only three people on the beach. Even the seagulls hadn't arrived yet. There was the lightest of breezes, and the rhythmic swash of waves breaking on the pebbles: so small and so gentle, in fact, that they could hardly be called waves at all.

Lorna – seven years old at this time – had woken early, ahead of her brother and her sister and her cousins. The only other people awake so early were her gran and her Uncle Peter. At Gran's suggestion, they had piled into her car and driven to the beach: a chance to enjoy it before the crowds arrived. It was the last Sunday of August and this part of the south coast was swarming with holiday-makers. They could walk and play or talk for an hour or two and then with luck, when they returned to the house, everybody else would be up and breakfast would be on the table.

Peter, sitting on a rock a few yards away from his mother and his niece, was wearing headphones and listening to music on a Sony Discman. He had one three-minute track on repeat: 'Liturgie de cristal', the opening movement of Olivier Messiaen's *Quatuor pour la fin du temps*. Again and again he listened to the first few bars: the familiar, unearthly melody on clarinet, underpinned by dense piano chords, and then the entry of the violin, swooping and whirling . . .

'I hear, with my little ear,' said Lorna at last, 'something beginning with W.'

Of course, Gran had been expecting this. What else was she going to say?

'Ooh, I don't know . . .' she said. 'Could it be "wind"?'

Lorna inclined her head and listened intently.

'There isn't any wind,' she said.

'Yes, there is. It's very faint.'

'It's not wind.'

'Whispering?'

'What do you mean, whispering?'

'Well, when we swish our feet against the sand, like this, it makes a kind of whispering noise.'

Peter could hear his mother's voice faintly, behind the music. These lightweight headphones let in a lot of extraneous sound. He tried to focus on the violin part. That elaborate trill, high up on the top string: it was a nightmare to phrase properly. He'd botched it so far in every rehearsal. He wound the disc back ten seconds, and listened to it one more time. And then another. This performer – Erich Gruenberg, a violinist Peter idolized – was coming in a fraction ahead of the beat. Perhaps that was the way to do it.

Meanwhile Lorna had tired of the game and was paddling at the very edge of the sea, which lay tranquil and greyish-blue beneath the risen sun. A few miles across the water, the chalk cliffs of the Isle of Wight rose up, at their feet the three rocky outcrops known as the Needles, one of them host to a solitary lighthouse. Lorna, however, had no eye for this bigger picture. Her gaze was fixed on the sand beneath the water: every so often she would bend down suddenly to pick up a shell or a pebble, and when she had a handful of these she would bring them over to Gran, who had now placed herself on the rock next to Peter, spread out a towel on her lap and was drying and sorting the collection, occasionally holding an especially fine specimen up to the sunlight and examining it closely.

'They're a lovely colour, aren't they?' she said to her son.

Peter heard the question, but pretended that he hadn't; a stratagem that didn't work.

'Come on,' Mary said, 'I know you can hear me. You're only here for a couple of days. Can't you take those things off and talk to your mother for a few minutes?'

Removing the headphones, he said: 'I'm not listening to this for fun, you know. I have to play this piece in six days' time.'

'I'm aware of that.'

'Well, you know how difficult it is. You listened to it yesterday.'

'I know, and I've never heard such a tuneless racket in all my life. I don't envy you one little bit.'

Peter thought about this, about the fact that someone blessed with his mother's musical understanding and intuition should designate Messiaen's masterpiece a 'tuneless racket'. Why, he wondered, had her tastes never matured? Why did she remain, in some ways, locked in a perpetual childhood, far more at ease playing with her grandchildren than talking with her sons and their wives on topics suitable for adult conversation? Sometimes he found this quality disarming; other times – such as this morning – it annoyed him. Even now, for instance, he was struck by the absorption with which she was sifting through Lorna's pebble collection, as if it were an assembly of precious gemstones.

'Aren't they a lovely colour, I said?'

He leaned in and took a look before saying, in an offhand way,: 'Very nice.'

'I don't mean these,' said his mother. 'I mean Lorna, and Susan, and Iain.'

For a moment he didn't understand; or rather, couldn't quite believe what he was hearing.

'The kids, you mean?' he said. 'Martin and Bridget's kids?'

'Yes, I think they're a lovely colour. Not quite Black and not quite white. Somewhere in between.'

Taken aback, and not knowing what else to say, Peter mumbled: 'Well, they're nice-looking children all right.' He gestured towards Lorna. 'She's a very pretty girl, I've always said so.'

'Yes, but just imagine if everyone in the world was that colour. That would solve all the problems, wouldn't it?'

It was unusual, very unusual, for his mother to come out with any kind of political opinion, and this one was so unexpected that he didn't feel inclined to criticize it; which, in any case, he would have found difficult to do. Sometimes he thought his mother's naivety knew no bounds; at others, he thought she was the repository of a kind of primitive wisdom. At the moment he was thinking both of these things. But their conversation went no further in any case. Just then the calm of the scene was shattered when a vehicle drove onto the rocky promontory above them and scrunched to a loud halt on the loose chippings. Looking up they saw that it was a black SUV, just like the one belonging to Jack and his wife, Angela. And indeed it was Angela who jumped out of the car, which she had evidently driven from the house at great speed, and without locking it she came running down the flight of wooden steps which led to the beach. As she approached, Mary and Peter could see that she was out of breath, and pale, and had some terrible news to impart. It seemed at first that she was too distraught to speak.

'Ange?' said Peter. 'What's happened?'

Stopping in front of them and pausing only to inhale deeply, Angela put her hands to her cheeks and announced, in a shaky voice:

'She's dead.'

II. Vocalise, *for the Angel who Announces the End of Time*

'She's dead.'

At first neither Peter nor Mary knew who she was talking about. The use of that simple pronoun, 'she', made it clear that Angela could only be referring to someone known to all of them: a close family member. Peter's thoughts went immediately to his wife, who had chosen not to come away with them all this weekend. Instead, she was in France for two weeks, with a group of friends. (Well, that was what she'd told him. He wasn't sure that he believed her.)

'In a car crash,' Angela continued. 'Last night. In Paris.'

'Not Olivia?' Mary said, jumping to the same conclusion.

'Not, not Olivia,' said Angela – impatiently, almost. 'Not Olivia, of course not. I mean Diana.'

She thought that she had stunned them into silence. In fact, they were just puzzled.

'Diana?' Mary said. 'Diana Jacobs? No . . . not Diana. I mean . . . I played eighteen holes with her, just last week.'

'Do you mean *Princess* Diana?'

They all turned around, because there was Lorna, gazing up at them with wide eyes. Angela looked at her for a moment, then smothered her in a rapt, tremulous hug.

'Oh, my darling,' she said. 'My sweet darling. I'm so sorry.'

Lorna enjoyed the hug for a little while, then pulled away. Mary, meanwhile, had recovered her power of speech enough to say:

'What happened? A car crash, did you say? In Paris?'

'That's right. Late last night, or early this morning. She'd been out for dinner with Dodi, the Ritz or somewhere. They were trying to get back to their hotel, all these photographers were chasing them, they were going through all these tunnels . . . Oh!' She buried her head in her hands. 'It sounds horrible.' Once the spasm had passed, and she looked up, she saw that Peter had put his head-phones back on. '*What* are you doing?'

Resignedly, Peter pressed the pause button on his Discman and said, 'I'm supposed to be listening to some music.'

Angela stared at him with a mixture of amazement and disgust, then turned away. 'Do you want to come back to the house?' she said to Mary.

'No, it's all right,' Mary said. 'I'll stay here with Peter for a bit. Thanks for driving out here, though, and telling us the news.'

'I had to let you know,' said Angela. 'I knew you'd want to hear as soon as possible.' Addressing Lorna, finally, she said: 'What about you, sweetheart? Do you want to come back to the house with your Auntie Ange? See your mum and dad?'

Lorna thought about this. 'Will breakfast be ready yet?' she asked.

'Not yet. No one's had the time.'

'I think I'll stay here then,' said Lorna. 'With Gran and Uncle Peter.'

'OK, love.' She kissed Lorna on the forehead, and wiped away some tears from her own cheeks, then ran away back along the beach, and up the steps to the car. She drove off in a hurry. Jack would probably be telling their own children by now.

*

Charlotte and Julian were sharing a bedroom at the top of the house. Jack drew back the curtains which covered the little case-ment window and shook his children gently out of their sleep. Very soon they were sitting up in bed, alert and wide awake. He told them that Princess Diana had died. Charlotte did not know how to react at first, but when she saw that her father's eyes were filled with tears she fell against him and rested her head against his chest and her shoulders began shaking. Julian's lower lip started to tremble and then, not to be outdone, he too slipped into his father's embrace and for a while the three of them remained like that, on Charlotte's bed, clasping each other tightly: lost in a shared, mysterious grief that was noisy and tearful at first, then quite silent.

*

When Bridget came down the stairs in her dressing gown, she could see through the door to the study that Geoffrey was already out of bed, dressed and reading his spy novel. The house he had rented for the week was a solid, expansive Victorian property, with generous grounds screened off from the nearby village of Keyhaven by a protective wall of oak and chestnut trees. It must have cost him a fortune, although she knew that Jack, Martin and Peter had all chipped in as well. The study was particularly pleasant, with a heavy rosewood armchair placed next to the largest window, offering a view over the well-tended rose garden and towards the tennis court beyond.

'Morning, Geoff,' Bridget said, brightly. 'Can I get you a cup of coffee?'

'Got one, thanks,' he said, without looking up.

Bridget withdrew and made for the kitchen, where her elder daughter, Susan, was pouring herself orange juice. The first thing she said to her mother was:

'Has Uncle Peter been messing with this radio?'

'I very much doubt it. Why, what's wrong with it?'

'What is this *garbage* on Radio One?'

A doleful piece of classical music was streaming out from the radio on top of the fridge. It came to a halt a few seconds later and the DJ's voice, uncharacteristically solemn, announced:

'That was the *Adagio* in G minor by Tomaso Albinoni. We've put aside our usual playlist today on Radio One, and instead we'll be playing music that's more in keeping with today's news, out of respect for Princess Diana, who, as you will already have heard by now, died this morning in Paris. Next up: "Nimrod" from the *Enigma Variations*, by Sir Edward Elgar . . .'

Susan and Bridget looked at each other, incredulous.

'Diana?' said Bridget. 'Dead? Did you know about this?'

Susan shook her head.

'Come on, let's turn the television on. And go and get your brother out of bed. Tell him to come down here. Diana! I can't believe it.'

Within a few minutes Bridget and her two older children were sitting together on the sofa in front of the television set, gripped by the rolling news coverage, by the footage from the accident scene in Paris, the aerial shots of Kensington Palace in central London where crowds were already starting to congregate. Gradually the other family members came to join them in the sitting room. Even Geoffrey, drawn by the urgency of the reporters' voices, slipped into the back of the room and quietly drew up a chair behind the sofa. He did not say anything but, like the others, for the rest of the morning he could not take his eyes away from the screen.

★

It was late in the afternoon. Angela and her children were still inside, watching the news on television. Everyone else had gathered around the tennis court, where games were being played in varying combinations, with Mary usually deciding the composition of the teams. At sixty-three she was still full of life and energy, and although she had retired from teaching now, there was nothing she liked more than marshalling her family into various sporting activities – especially the young children. And, despite her age, she was still the best tennis player in the family by some margin (although Bridget had been known to display an impressive backhand). At the moment Mary was playing alongside Susan, whose brother, Iain, was partnered with Geoffrey: an uneven contest, as Geoffrey was slower on the court than ever, not least because of a recent hip operation. Winning, however, was not really the point: the family was together (all apart from Olivia), the sun was throwing long shadows across the grass court, there was a salty tang to the soft breeze blowing in from the sea half a mile away, and a jug of lemonade was there for the sharing. Jack, Martin and Bridget were sitting by the side of the court in adjacent deck chairs. Bridget had a book open on her lap – *The Twilight of Otters* by Lionel Hampshire, which came with the magic words 'Winner of the Booker Prize' emblazoned on its front cover – but it did not really seem to be engaging her attention, and she was half-asleep in the sun. Jack and Martin were casting a critical eye over the game as they sipped on their lemonade.

'Not a bad serve your boy's got there,' Jack said.

'Has his moments,' said Martin.

'Nice weekend, though, eh? Shame you've got to go so soon.'

'Yes, it has been nice. Mum and Dad have really enjoyed it, I think. Clever of him to find this place.'

'Well, yes . . .' said Jack, but there was a sceptical note in his voice.

'What's the matter, don't you like it?'

'This?' He gestured around him. 'I love it. This, to me, is absolutely the best of England. Afternoon tea on the lawn, the gentle thwack of the racket on the tennis ball . . .'

'So?'

'So they've got it for a few days. That's it. And yet Dad's a brilliant man, we both know that. And he worked hard his whole life. They should be *living* in a place like this, not renting it for a week.'

'What's your point?'

'Just makes me sad, that's all. All those years dealing with money, and he never really understood how it works. How money creates more money, if you know what you're doing, if you've got—'

'A ruthless streak?' Martin guessed.

'I was going to say a spirit of enterprise.'

'So you think our father's life has been a failure, is that what you're saying?'

'What I'm saying,' said Jack, 'is that by the time I retire – probably sooner – Ange and I are going to own a house like this.'

'Good for you,' said Martin. 'Invite us to come and stay in the guest cottage every now and then, won't you?' Iain now approached them, very pleased with himself, waiting to be congratulated on breaking Gran's serve and winning the set. 'Well done,' his father said, shortly. 'You'd better go and pack now.'

'Already?' said Iain, aghast. 'Can't we stay longer? I love it here.'

'Your mum said she wanted to be off by six o'clock,' said Martin. 'Have you forgotten that you're going back to school tomorrow?'

*

'I don't get it,' said Iain, screwing up his T-shirts and swimming trunks and cramming them into a holdall. 'Uncle Jack's children go to private school, right?'

'That's right,' said Bridget, standing up to get Lorna's underwear out of the wardrobe and almost banging her head on a low beam.

'But they go back to school *after* us. A week after.'

'It's not fair,' said Lorna. 'They get to stay here with Gran and Grandad all week.'

'But you have to pay for private school, don't you?' Iain persisted.

'You do,' said Bridget.

'So they should be having *longer* terms than us, not shorter. Otherwise it's just a waste of money.'

'Not going to argue with that,' said Bridget, looking around for unpacked items.

'Did Princess Diana go to private school or public school?' Iain asked now.

'They're the same thing,' said Bridget. 'Private schools and public schools are the same.'

'Really? I thought we went to a public school.'

'No. You go to a state school.' She could see that he didn't really get it, but she didn't have the time or energy to explain at this point. 'Anyway, I don't know what school she went to, offhand. But I expect it was private.'

'If she was the people's princess,' Lorna said, 'she should really have gone to the same sort of school as everybody else.'

'Good point, honey.' She noted how readily the phrase was already coming to her daughter's lips, even though it had been coined by Tony Blair only a few hours earlier. They had all watched him making his speech outside the church in his Durham constituency. It had been an impressive performance: sincere enough, no doubt, but also sure to boost his popularity among sceptical voters.

Giving up on his attempt to understand the British education system, Iain turned to a more urgent subject: 'Mum, can I sit in the front with you on the way home?'

'Sure,' said Bridget.

'What about Dad?' Lorna asked.

Bridget squatted down beside her. 'I told you, honey. Dad's not coming home with us tonight. He's got to go to Belgium tomorrow, so he's staying the night in London with Uncle Peter.' Seeing her daughter's face fall, she added: 'It's only for a few days.'

'It's not that,' said Lorna. 'It's just that he's so much better at driving than you are.'

*

Sunday evening traffic meant that Peter and Martin's journey back to London took almost three hours. To start with they listened to the radio, but the coverage of Diana's death was relentless, no matter which station they tried. Stuck in a three-mile tailback on the M3 just outside Basingstoke, they gave up and Peter asked Martin to put the CD of *Quatuor pour la fin du temps* into the car stereo. They listened to the short first movement in silence, and then halfway through the *'Vocalise, pour l'ange qui annonce la fin du temps'*, as the violin and cello played its searching melody in unison over Messiaen's 'blue-orange' piano chords, Peter said:

'This is Gavin's favourite movement. He says it sounds like Ravel and Webern writing something together.'

Martin didn't have the expertise to comment on this comparison. 'Remind me who Gavin is again?' he asked.

'He's the guy who turns the pages for Chiara, our pianist. Well, that's his main job. He's been helping out with other things at rehearsals as well.'

'Did you know him before? Is he a friend of yours?'

'Not really, why?'

'This is the third or fourth time you've mentioned him, that's all.'

'Oh.'

Peter stared ahead at the stationary traffic. He contemplated changing lanes, but instinct told him that it wouldn't be worth it.

'Have you heard from Olivia?' his brother asked.

'Not since Friday. There'll probably be a message on the machine when I get back.'

'You should get one of these,' said Martin, holding up his mobile phone.

'Kill me first,' said Peter, shifting into gear and moving the car forward a few yards.

'This MP I'm meeting in Brussels on Tuesday,' Martin said. 'Remind me again how we're related to him?'

'Paul Trotter? We're cousins. Well, I suppose . . . second cousins. His grandmother was Nana's sister. Auntie Ida. Why, are you going to bring up the family connection?'

'Maybe. It might give me some leverage.'

'You've been going to Brussels a lot recently. Do you like it?'

'It's not really a question of liking. I never see anything of the real city. I get a taxi straight off the train to the Parliament buildings. Then it's usually solid meetings for the next few days.'

'And how are you getting on? Have you persuaded those dastardly Continentals to see sense yet?'

'We're making a bit of progress. Bloody hell, though, it's an uphill struggle with anything where the European Union's concerned.'

'You deserve a medal or something.'

'Perhaps they'll put me in the New Year's honours list one day.'

Peter laughed. 'They should do that,' he said. 'A knighthood at least – for services to British chocolate.'

III. The Abyss of Birds

When Martin had first been sent to Brussels in 1992, the chocolate war had been rumbling on for almost twenty years. At its heart lay a conflict between two different traditions of chocolate manufacture. Some countries – Belgium and France being the most vocal – insisted on a strict definition of 'chocolate', meaning that if any product were to be marketed as such, its chocolate component must consist of 100 per cent cocoa, unadulterated by any form of vegetable fat. Otherwise, they maintained, alternative names such as 'vegelate' would have to be used. Meanwhile, countries with a less purist approach – including Denmark and the United Kingdom, both of which had joined the EEC in 1973 – protested strongly, and refused to change their methods of production which they insisted had been followed for decades. Ever since the Second World War Cadbury's had diluted the cocoa in their chocolate with a small amount of vegetable fat (typically no more than 5 per cent) and the British public had developed a taste for it. They resented the way in which the French, the Belgians and the other purists sneered at their chocolate, calling it 'greasy' and claiming that it was suitable only for children, not for the mature palate.

But a single market required the adoption of common standards. In 1973 the EEC began the process of trying to establish these standards for chocolate, with an attempt to draft a Chocolate Directive: one which was classified (in the arcane and impenetrable language of European policy-making) as a 'vertical' directive, since it aimed to address all the issues relevant to a particular type of food. The attempt was not successful, and an impasse was quickly reached. Cadbury's (and the other makers of so-called 'industrial' chocolate, such as the Scandinavian countries) refused to change their recipe, whereupon Belgium, France, Italy, Luxembourg, Germany and the Netherlands each placed individual prohibitions on the import of chocolate from these countries. For the next two decades, Cadbury's, Terry's, Rowntree's and others would find themselves shut out of these lucrative markets. So much for the free movement of goods.

By the early 1990s, Martin, now a senior figure in the export department, had come to see this as an intolerable situation. So had his bosses. They proposed that he should set up a base in Brussels and begin to do some serious lobbying. He rented a company flat on Rue Belliard, not far from the European Parliament and, more importantly, not far from the Place du Luxembourg, a bustling square colloquially known as the Place Lux, filled with bars and cafés where journalists, lobbyists and MEPs tended to gather in order to make contacts, do deals and exchange valuable gossip.

It was – in Martin's opinion at any rate – an exciting time to be in Brussels. The different member states of the EEC were hurtling towards ever closer union. Two breathless years would see the signing of the Maastricht Treaty, the launch of the single market, and the creation of the European Economic Area. Next on the horizon was the adoption of a single currency. Although he was not certain that this final step was entirely in Britain's interests, Martin was staunchly Europhile by temperament and welcomed most of these developments. The hostility being shown towards Britain's – and his own – favourite kind of chocolate did not deter him: this was a mere blip, the sort of stumbling block that was only to be expected on the road to harmonization, and he believed that polite advocacy and patient negotiation would end in a solution being found. But Martin soon came to realize that he was at odds with the majority of the British observers he would find gathered in the bars of the Place Lux, and particularly with the journalists. Here, the consensus was that things were moving too fast; that Britain was being asked to give up too many of its core freedoms; that the EU was nothing but a racket cooked up by bureaucrats to give themselves power; worse, that it was all a plot by the French and the Germans to take over Europe; and finally, of course (always a clincher with the British contingent) that Maggie had been right, and the cowards in her own party had forced her out because of it. These were the arguments he heard being rehearsed again and again over bottles of Chimay Bleu and steaming bowls of *moules frites*.

Martin soon got into a routine of staying two or three nights a week at the Brussels flat, where he would spend the evenings writing endless papers on the chemical constituents of British chocolate and the legal ramifications of treating it differently to the versions made in France or Belgium. (In this he was often assisted by Bridget, whose legal expertise proved useful: she would pore over the documents at home in Bournville after the children had gone to bed, and send him lengthy faxes breaking down the issues in forensic detail.) During the day, he organized meetings with MEPs, with members of the Commission and with other representatives of the 'industrial' chocolate makers. He didn't particularly enjoy hanging out with the British press pack, but that was part of his brief as well, and in doing so he noticed that, more and more often, one particular name was beginning to crop up in conversation. Most of the journalists were of a standard type: edging into middle age, cynical, world-weary, thoroughly fed up at being stuck in Brussels reporting on the workings of the EU, but still resolved to make a reasonably conscientious job of it. But word started to reach Martin of a pack member who was quite different: he had a wild mop of blonde hair and drove around Brussels in a red Alfa Romeo pumping out heavy metal on the car stereo, he knew the EU inside out because he had spent much of his childhood in Brussels, he had been to Eton and had been President of the Oxford Union, and he had decided to survive the tedious business of reporting from Brussels for the *Daily Telegraph* by treating the whole thing as a joke, by playing fast and loose with the facts and spinning every story as though the workings of the European Parliament were part of an elaborate conspiracy to thwart the British at every turn. His newspaper employed him as a reporter but he was not a reporter at all, he was a satirist and an absurdist, and he was clearly enjoying himself so much, and making such a name for himself, that all the other journalists were consumed with envy and were all busy working out how they could become like him, and an indication of the almost mythical regard in which they held him was that they never referred to him by his full name, only his first name. They simply called him 'Boris'.

Martin never actually met Boris, not to have a proper conversation. Whenever he arrived at a bar Boris always seemed to have just left, and whenever Martin left a bar he was always told the next day that Boris arrived just after. Boris was always on the go, never still for a moment, always in a hurry, always in a mess, always late, always under-prepared, always over-committed, always in demand and always out of reach.

'You never can pin him down,' Martin was told by Stephen, who wrote for the *Independent*.

'He makes his own rules. Then, if he decides he doesn't like his own rules, he breaks them,' said Tom, who wrote for *The Times*.

'Life to him is simply one big cosmic joke,' said Philip, who wrote for the *Guardian*. 'He doesn't take anything seriously.'

'Actually, there is something he takes extremely seriously,' said Angus, who wrote for the *Mirror*. 'His own ambition.'

'His appetites are prodigious,' said Daniel, who wrote for a gloomy Sunday broadsheet. 'And I'm not just talking about food.'

'The thing is, he'll probably die of a heart attack before he's forty,' said James, who wrote for a mid-market tabloid. 'God, I wish I was him!'

It was James, in fact, who had really latched on to Martin during those early months, in the autumn of 1992. He was fascinated by everything to do with the chocolate war. He was fascinated by the way that it crystallized the antagonism between the British and the French. He was fascinated by the way it exposed the absurdities of the single market. He was fascinated by the way that everyone seemed to have an emotional relationship with chocolate. He was fascinated by the idea that non-cocoa fats had been introduced into British chocolate because of wartime rationing, and concluded from this that what the British loved about their chocolate was that it 'tasted of the war'. But there was one thing about this subject that attracted him more than any other: the fact that Boris hadn't written about it yet. He saw this as an opportunity to endear himself to his editor by writing a big, juicy, double-page piece which would tap into every one of his readers' passions, all the passions that found them at their most vulnerable and easiest to manipulate: patriotism, wartime nostalgia, longing for childhood, resentment of foreigners. He summed up precisely what was going to be so irresistible about this story in one memorable phrase: he was going to 'out-Boris Boris'.

As far as Martin could see, James's research for this piece was not extensive. Martin himself was the only source, and the information-gathering consisted of one half-hour interview – or rather, an informal chat, over a couple of gin and tonics – in a bar on the Place Lux, followed by one or two phone calls to clear up some details which even James's editor (notoriously accommodating when it came to factual accuracy) thought needed checking. The piece appeared the following week, and Martin suspected it was not going to be a nuanced appraisal of the chocolate negotiations when he saw that it was published under the headline, 'BRUSSELS CHOC HORROR – THEY'VE GOT US BY THE SHORT AND CURLY-WURLIES'.

'Barmy Brussels bureaucrats,' the article began, 'could be on course to BAN the Great British chocolate bar if they get their way.'

Well, this was not true, for a start. But never mind. What next?

'Meddling Euro MPs with too much time on their hands are thinking of reviving the famous Chocolate Directive of 1973, which led to the French and the Belgians turning their backs on British chocolate and even claiming it shouldn't be called chocolate at all.

'What a load of Continental codswallop! *Sacré bleu! Quel snobisme!* Britain's world-beating chocolate is loved everywhere from Moscow to Caracas, and a Cadbury's Double Decker bar is as much a part of the British way of life as a London double-decker bus.'

Martin bought a copy of the paper from a news-stand on the Rue de Trèves. He was on his way to yet another meeting at the Place Lux, one which promised to be difficult but, if all went well, potentially very helpful. He had recently struck up a good rapport with a French MEP called Paul Lacoste, who had agreed to introduce him to a chocolatier from Paris who was passing through Brussels for a few days. Maybe, over a few drinks, they could begin to understand each other and perhaps even find some common ground. His mood of optimism was dented, however, when he read the first few paragraphs of the story. After reading another couple of sentences he screwed up the paper and threw it in the bin. He could feel himself blushing to be associated with such nonsense. He walked on towards the square, trying to reassure himself that the damage wasn't too great. His colleagues back at the Works would see it, for sure, and probably tease him a fair bit for being so naive as to cooperate with someone like James. But the paper in question wasn't widely read in Brussels, and with luck, the article would go unnoticed: it was such a classic example of British Euroscepticism that most people would dismiss it with a shrug. Even more likely, they wouldn't read it all.

On this warm evening in early October, Paul Lacoste and his guest, the chocolatier Vincent, were sitting at an outdoor table enjoying a cooling beer. On the table in front of them were two newspapers, both open at James's article. They nodded at Martin when he arrived, but otherwise did not greet him especially warmly.

For the first twenty minutes, nobody mentioned the article. Martin and Vincent did their best to be civil to each other. The meeting began with an exchange of gifts: of chocolate bars, to be precise. Martin had brought with him a gift pack containing some of Cadbury's most popular products: a Flake, a Dairy Milk bar, a chocolate frog (Freddo), a Picnic, a Boost and a Wispa, each one wrapped in brightly coloured plastic, and proclaiming its identity with its own individual logo in loud primary colours. Vincent, on the other hand, passed Martin a single, slender bar, wrapped in plain brown paper, on the front of which, in the simplest and most discreet of fonts, were printed the words, *Chocolat Artisanal Français Cacao Pur*.

'It is almost,' Vincent said, 'as if you and I are not engaged in making the same thing at all.'

'Well, maybe that's the point,' said Martin. 'If you think our products are so different, why should our chocolate pose any threat to you?'

'Because a lot of people prefer your chocolate to my chocolate, that's the problem.'

'And why would they do that?'

'Because they're idiots!' said Vincent, pounding the table in fury.

'Or perhaps because vegetable fat, and extra milk, are very pleasant additions to chocolate, and the British have a taste for them.'

'The British! Fuck the British! Your chocolate is as bad as your journalism.'

It was the first time James's story had been alluded to. Now that the subject had been raised, it could hardly be avoided.

'You seem to be quoted rather extensively in this article, Mr Lamb,' said Paul Lacoste.

'I only read the first few lines,' said Martin. 'I'm sure that whatever I'm quoted as saying bears only a distant relationship to what I actually said.'

'Well, apparently you said that, "The French and the Belgians need to get off their high horse—"'

'And what does this expression mean?' said Vincent. '"High horse"? Some kind of racist joke about the French eating horses?'

'It's a very common English idiom,' M Lacoste explained, and continued: '". . . come off their high horse and accept that the EU is about free trade if it's about anything at all. There is an easy way to choose which is the best kind of chocolate – let the market decide!"'

'Yes, well, I did mention free trade,' said Martin. 'But that wasn't what I talked about, mainly. I was talking about the *idea* of Europe. The idea that we Europeans no longer need to fight each other because we're finding far more rational and peaceful ways of sorting out our differences.'

'Well, if you really used the word "idea",' said M Lacoste, 'that explains why that part of your answer wasn't quoted. We all know that the English hate ideas.'

'No, I don't accept that,' said Martin. 'That's a tired old stereotype too.'

'And like all stereotypes, it has an element of truth. This is what we all like about the Brits, in fact! Your pragmatism, your common sense. The perfect counterweight to French pretentiousness. You know the famous joke about the French and the British, which everyone tells here in the Parliament? Some committee meeting is taking place, and the Brits come up with a very workmanlike, pragmatic solution to the problem in hand. But the French members just look at them and say, "Well, of course, that's all very well in practice. But how will it work in *theory*?"'

Martin laughed. Vincent, who seemed to have lost his sense of humour – if he ever had one – didn't join in.

'This is what works so well about the "idea of Europe", as you call it,' M Lacoste continued. 'For so many countries to find common ground takes a long time, and it involves a lot of arguing over somewhat ludicrous details, but we get there in the end and the Brits make a very helpful contribution. However –' he picked up the newspaper again, holding it between thumb and forefinger with some disdain – 'I cannot say that I find your journalism very helpful.'

Martin raised his hands in surrender. 'Look,' he said, 'I'm not going to put up a defence of that piece.'

'It's not the chauvinism,' said M Lacoste. 'It's not the scepticism. Do you know what I really don't like about this? It made me laugh. It did, in spite of myself. In a way, you know, there is something so vulgar and outrageous about it that it almost becomes witty. This is what is so characteristic of British journalism, and this is what makes it so dangerous. Making people dislike the European Union is one thing, but making them laugh at it, making them see it as a joke . . . well, that is a very powerful line of attack. The most powerful of all, in fact. You know where it comes from, don't you, this mischievous way of writing about Europe? You know who started it?'

Martin nodded. 'Of course.' He didn't need to say the name.

'Well, all I would say, Mr Lamb, is watch out for this fellow. He has the potential to cause a great deal of trouble.'

'I dare say you're right,' said Martin. 'Nevertheless, I remain hopeful. People are growing tired of the chocolate war. Change is afoot. Of course, everything here in Brussels and Strasbourg moves at a snail's pace—'

'Now you're doing it again,' said Vincent. 'Why this expression? Another so-called joke about our cuisine?'

'Not at all,' said Martin. 'I simply meant that everything here happens very slowly, as Monsieur Lacoste pointed out. And yet, despite this, things change. Progress is made. And I think there is going to be progress made on chocolate, some time in the next two or three years. I predict that the Directive will come back to Parliament again and this time people are going to make it work.'

*

REPORT on a meeting of the
Environment and Consumer Affairs Committee
at the European Parliament, Brussels, on 2 July 1996

Author: Martin Lamb

CONFIDENTIAL, f.a.o. Senior Management only

Background: Following intensive representations by members of CAOBISCO, BCCCA and other industrial bodies, the European Parliament is finally beginning to reconsider the famous Chocolate Directive of 1973, which in the last two decades has created huge difficulties for Cadbury's selling its products in certain European countries. The Parliament is now taking advice from three committees: Environment and Consumer Affairs; Development; and Agriculture. Today the Environment and Consumer Affairs Committee convened in order to consider the various proposals and suggest amendments.

The meeting: A considerable number of MEPs attended, and a considerable number (as usual) were absent. The French, who arguably have the most at stake in this dispute, had the largest number of absences. (N.B. the Tour de France started on 29 June.)

I would describe the meeting as lively. It was not always easy to follow the different interventions, as at least seven different languages were being spoken and the translators – who were excellent, as always – had some difficulty keeping up. Among the main points, however, were these:

Monsieur Jean-Pierre Thomine (France) raised the possibility that to extend the use of non-cocoa vegetable fats in chocolate would adversely affect the foreign exchange earnings of cocoa-producing countries in the developing world. MEPs from Austria, Belgium, Germany, Greece, Italy, Luxembourg, the Netherlands, Portugal and Spain concurred. Ms Victoria Keaton (UK, West Midlands) said that she thought the impact would be minimal, and MEPs from Denmark, Finland, Ireland and Sweden agreed. Herr Robert Fischer (Germany) proposed that an impact study should be carried out. MEPs from Austria, Belgium, France, Italy, the Netherlands, Portugal and Spain concurred while MEPs from Denmark, Finland, Ireland, Sweden and the United Kingdom disagreed and Greece and Luxembourg offered no comment.

Señor Jorge Herralde (Spain) said that the issue of labelling was crucial. Consumers should be informed about the products they are buying. Labels should specifically state when chocolate contains non-cocoa vegetable fat, as this would be a novelty in some of the 'pure chocolate' member states. Labelling of chocolate, he suggested, should be brought into line with the provisions of the general Food Labelling Directive. Denmark, Finland, Ireland, Sweden and the United Kingdom disagreed and while Austria, Belgium, France, Greece, Italy, Luxembourg, the Netherlands and Portugal agreed, they could not agree on the wording of the labelling. Austria, Greece, Italy, Luxembourg, the Netherlands and Portugal thought the label should say 'contains non-cocoa vegetable fat' while France and Belgium thought it should say 'not real chocolate'. Nor could they agree where the label should be placed. France, Belgium, Germany and Luxembourg thought it should be in large letters on the front of every bar; Spain, Portugal and Italy thought it should be in small letters on the back of every bar; and Greece and the Netherlands proposed a compromise whereby it should be in medium-sized letters on the side of every bar.

Herr Thomas Graf (Germany) raised the issue of 'quality' chocolate which has a higher set of minimum requirements for cocoa and milk. Some chocolate bars in Germany, for instance, are designated 'Vollmilchschokolade' and Herr Graf was adamant that such products should contain no non-cocoa fats at all. Mr Konstantinos Papastathopoulos (Greece), who was taking his own handwritten notes of the meeting, asked Herr Graf how to spell 'Vollmilchschokolade', and Monsieur Henri Baptiste (Belgium) who was also taking his own handwritten notes of the meeting, asked Mr Konstantinos Papastathopoulos how to spell Konstantinos Papastathopoulos. The issue of 'quality' labelling was left unresolved.

Madame Christine d'Alembert (France) made the by-now familiar suggestion that chocolate containing non-cocoa fat should not be called 'chocolate' at all. This was swiftly rebuffed by Ms Victoria Keaton (UK, West Midlands), who pointed out that it flew in the face of a clear jurisprudence from the European Court of Justice. She reminded the committee of the Béarnaise sauce case (26 October 1995), in which the Court judged that when products are essentially similar in all their characteristics, a change in the sale name is not appropriate. Monsieur Thomine pointed out that Béarnaise sauce was not chocolate. Ms Keaton replied that she was aware Béarnaise sauce was not chocolate, and what was his point? Monsieur Thomine said that the case she had cited was irrelevant, because there were no British companies manufacturing inferior Béarnaise sauce and trying to export it to other European countries as real Béarnaise sauce. Ms Keaton asked him if he understood the nature of legal precedent, or was that an unknown concept in France. Monsieur Thomine asked her if she understood the nature of good food, or was that an unknown concept in Britain. At this point the meeting became unruly and the committee chairman had to call it to order.

Finally Monsieur Bertrand Guillon (France) made the suggestion that if non-cocoa fats were to be allowed in chocolate, a proper scientific method for their detection should be employed. This proposal was welcomed by Austria, Belgium, Germany, Greece, Italy, Luxembourg, the Netherlands, Portugal and Spain, while Denmark, Finland, Ireland and Sweden also agreed that it seemed fair and they would raise no objections. Once again Ms Keaton rose to her feet and pointed out that no such detection method existed, it would not exist for several years, and that this was therefore nothing but a ruse to maintain the status quo and exclude British chocolate from

European markets. She described it as a 'typical French trick', leading Monsieur Guillon to say that she was being hysterical and should leave the chamber. Ms Keaton refused, saying it was not in the British nature to surrender unlike some countries she could mention, and that her father had not fought in the Battle of Britain to have French chocolate forced down his throat, to which Monsieur Guillon replied that his father had not fought for the Resistance in order to eat fatty chocolate that was only suitable for children. Before either Member could make further contributions, the committee chairman declared the meeting closed and congratulated everyone on a fine example of pan-European cooperation.

Conclusion: The long and arduous progress of the Chocolate Directive through the EU Parliament has barely begun, so we should not be too downhearted by the fact that, with their insistence on a detection method for non-cocoa fats that does not yet exist, the chocolate 'purists' scored a minor win today. In my opinion this is merely a temporary setback for the cause of British chocolate: it will neither survive a full vote in the European Parliament nor win the approval of the Commission. In short, there is plenty of road to be travelled yet, and in my view there remain grounds for us to be ~~optimistic~~ cautiously optimistic.

*

On the morning of 1st September 1997, Martin slept late at his brother's flat and was awoken at nine o'clock by the still unaccustomed sound of his mobile phone ringing. It was a call from Paul Trotter's diary assistant.

'I know you had a meeting with him in Brussels tomorrow afternoon,' she said. 'But he's cancelled his trip. He's going to be in London all week instead. Can we reschedule?'

Martin explained that he was catching the Eurostar at two-thirty that afternoon and would be away in Brussels for most of the week.

'He can squeeze you in this morning,' the woman said. 'He could give you half an hour at twelve o'clock, how does that sound?'

Better than nothing, Martin thought, and three hours later he was standing outside 1 Parliament Street in Westminster, where Paul – along with many other members of the prodigious intake of new Labour MPs following the landslide election in May – had his office. Martin was buzzed in and directed to a small, almost windowless room on the third floor, a room which Paul appeared to share with two other MPs who fortunately hadn't showed up today. It was a chaotic scene, with three desks wedged into a tiny space, each of them piled high with papers. In the middle of his desk Paul Trotter had somehow managed to make space for a chunky Toshiba laptop, upon which he was tapping away furiously when Martin arrived.

'What's it like out there?' he asked, after standing up to shake his visitor's hand.

Martin thought for a moment, trying to get the measure of this question, and said: 'Oh, it's . . . pretty warm. Not as sunny as down on the south coast, where I was yesterday, but still—'

'Not the weather,' said Paul. 'What's the *atmosphere* like? Are the crowds getting pretty big?'

'Well, yes, there did seem to be more people on the Tube than usual,' said Martin. 'A lot of them had flowers with them. I'm not sure why. Something to do with Diana, maybe?'

Paul stared at him, as if trying to work out whether he could possibly be saying this for real. 'Of course that's the reason,' he said. 'This week is going to be . . . well, amazing. We're going to see things we've never seen before in this country. Did you see Tony on television yesterday? Wasn't he incredible? "The people's princess." What a phrase.' He sat back down at his desk, looked at his laptop screen and said, half to himself: 'How do you compete with that?'

He seemed to have become distracted by the words he'd been in the process of writing. Martin took a seat opposite him – not that he'd actually been invited to do so – and watched as Paul's gaze flicked back and forth across the screen. He looked very young, although he could hardly have been more than six or seven years younger than Martin himself. His cheeks were pale and smooth, as if he hadn't started shaving yet, and there was an element of almost childlike concentration in the furrow of his brow. Spontaneously, Martin said:

'Did you know we were cousins, by the way?'

Paul looked up. 'Hm?'

'You and me. We're cousins. Second cousins, actually.'

'Really? Are you sure about that?'

'Quite sure. We have the same great-grandfather. Carl Schmidt. He was German. Our grandmothers were sisters.'

'I can't say I go in much for family history,' said Paul. 'We look back too much in this country: fixated on the past, that's the source of all our troubles. New Labour isn't going to make that mistake. Tony looks to the future.'

'Well, I'm all for that,' said Martin. The attempt to forge a family connection seemed to have fallen flat. He didn't really know what angle he should try next. 'It's a shame you had to cancel your trip to Brussels,' he said, for want of anything better.

'Well, how could I not? There was no choice. You couldn't possibly leave the country in a week like this.'

'What were you hoping to do while you were out there?'

'I just wanted to get a feel for . . . you know, if there were any matters coming up in Europe at the moment that affected my constituency. Talk to some MEPs, sound things out . . .'

'Ah! Well, I expect quite a lot of your constituents work in Bournville, is that right?'

'I thought that was a theme park now,' said Paul, who once again was looking at the screen and didn't seem to be listening very carefully. 'Hasn't the factory closed?'

Martin couldn't help but let out a sigh of exasperation. 'Of course it hasn't closed,' he said – although it was true that the shop floor and his own offices now shared premises with a tourist attraction called Cadbury World. (An aberration, in his opinion, and a great bone of contention with his children, because he and Bridget would not allow them to visit it, much to their resentment since they were well aware that Jack's children had already been twice, and were rumoured to have come home laden with free chocolate.) 'They're still making chocolate there and they're still employing lots of people and that's just what I wanted to talk to you about. The European Union. The chocolate war.' Getting no response from Paul as yet, he pressed on: 'As you probably know, in six weeks' time there's going to be a crucial vote in Strasbourg on the proposed amendments to the Chocolate Directive. So there's a lot of activity. Things are really hotting up.'

'Hotting up, are they? Good, good . . .' Paul pressed the backspace on his laptop a few times, deleting several words, and then, after typing in some more, he sat back and said, with a frown: 'What *is* the chocolate war, exactly?'

Martin was discouraged by this question, but gamely launched into a concise résumé of the dispute that had bedevilled European chocolate makers for the last twenty-four years. Even now, however, he could sense that he wasn't grabbing Paul's attention. Trying to give the subject a more personal dimension, he said:

'You probably have fond memories of the chocolate you ate when you were a child. And that's all we're trying to protect, at the end of the day. Great British brands like Dairy Milk . . . Cadbury's Milk Tray . . . Roses . . .'

'Roses . . .' Paul repeated, musingly. The word seemed to set off a train of thought. In a swift and decisive movement he picked up the phone on his desk. 'Janice,' he said, 'can you order a dozen red roses to be delivered here this afternoon? I'm going to take them to the gates of Kensington Palace later. Make sure the papers know, will you?' He hung up, turned to Martin, and sighed heavily. 'Can you believe it, though? Can you really believe that she's gone?'

'Yes,' said Martin, nodding along. 'It's very sad.'

'Will you be taking some flowers yourself?'

'Well . . . I wasn't planning to. I mean, it's not as if I knew her or anything.'

'But we all knew her.' Paul leaned forward, passionate now. 'We all knew her and loved her. She was the princess' (his voice started to wobble) 'of all our hearts.' The phrase seemed to impress him. He let it hang in the air for a moment or two, savouring it, and then immediately started typing again.

'What *is* that you're writing?' Martin asked.

'This Friday I'm giving a speech to the East Midlands branch of the Royal Association of British Dairy Farmers. My speechwriter delivered it last week but of course now I've got to rewrite the whole thing.'

'Really? To make it about Diana?'

'Obviously.'

'Do you think you could maybe put in a few lines about chocolate as well?'

Paul gave a dry laugh as he continued typing. 'Not exactly relevant, is it?'

'European sales of British chocolate are highly relevant to dairy farmers, I would have thought.'

'Not everyone is as obsessed with chocolate as you seem to be.'

'I'm not obsessed. It's my job.' Martin pulled a couple of sheets of paper out of his briefcase. 'Look, I've got some figures for you here. The global chocolate industry is worth thirty billion pounds a year, and Europe accounts for about half of that—'

Paul cut him short. 'I'd like to help you, Martin, really I would, but you have to see it from my point of view. I have to keep things strictly on-topic here.' He paused and looked up again, as a sudden thought struck him. 'I don't suppose we know if Diana had a favourite chocolate bar?'

Beginning to sense that this meeting was a waste of time, Martin was about to make his excuses and leave when Paul's telephone rang. After a brief conversation, Paul put the receiver down, closed the lid of his laptop and stood up to shake Martin's hand. 'Well,' he said, 'this has all been very fascinating but I'm going to have to go. There's a guy from the *Spectator* waiting downstairs who wants to take me out to lunch.'

They rode down in the lift together, and during their descent Paul revealed a little more about his lunch companion.

'He's writing a piece about all the new Labour MPs, I think that's the plan,' he said. 'Which is a bit ironic, actually. I think what he was really hoping was that people would be writing profiles of *him* by now.'

'Oh, why's that?' Martin asked.

'Because he stood in the election too. Rather hilariously, the Tories put him up in some rock-solid Labour stronghold in North Wales, of all places. Of course he didn't stand a chance. Old Etonian, Tory, went to Oxford, English establishment through and through. Hardly going to impress a bunch of Welsh farmers who hate everything that comes from England and spend most of the day up to their ankles in sheep shit.'

'So now he's gone into journalism?'

'Oh, he's been doing it for ages. Spent a fair number of years in Brussels, apparently. Made quite a name for himself taking the piss out of the EU.'

By now Martin knew exactly who Paul was talking about. Sure enough, when they left the building, there waiting for them on the pavement was the familiar stout figure in his ill-fitting, slightly too-tight suit, with the usual alert, wary, ironic glint in his eye and the over-cheerful greeting which seemed to be something between an expression of undying friendship and a declaration of war. Martin said goodbye to them both, and while he looked around for a taxi to take him to Waterloo, he watched Boris's unmistakable mop of blonde hair as it bobbed away along the street until it was swallowed up, finally, by the crowds: the dense, gathering crowds of mourners who were by now making their way in their thousands towards the gates of the palace, bearing their flowers and gifts and handwritten cards.

IV. Interlude

In the town of Llangollen, in the county of Gwynedd, overlooking
the River Dee, stands a fine old pub called the Corn Mill. And it was
in this pub, on 2nd May 1997, that two journalists had met for a
lunchtime drink. It was the day after the general election. Llangollen was part of the constituency of Clwyd South. It was a new
constituency, created for this election, but the result had never been
in any doubt. As always in this part of the country, the people had
voted for a Labour Member of Parliament. His name was Martyn
Jones, and he had won 22,901 votes. Coming a poor second, for the
Conservative Party, was a new candidate, Boris Johnson, who had
won 9,091 votes.

'Well,' said the first journalist, placing two pints of bitter on the
table. 'That's all over, then.'

'I don't think,' said the second journalist, taking her first sip, 'that
we'll ever see another contest quite like that.'

'The poor man never stood a chance,' said the first journalist.

'Poor man?' said the second journalist. 'Not exactly how I'd
describe him.'

'Oh, come on,' said the first journalist. 'You have to feel a little bit
of human sympathy.'

'And why's that?' said the second journalist. 'If a man is delusional
enough, and arrogant enough, to put himself forward in a place
which has voted Labour for a century . . .'

'It's not arrogance, though, is it?' said the first journalist. 'More
like the luck of the draw. I'm sure he would have preferred to stand
somewhere else.'

'Are you telling me you didn't think that man was arrogant?' said
the second journalist.

'Now I didn't say that,' said the first journalist.

'I've never in all my life,' said the second journalist, 'seen a more textbook example of English entitlement.'

'And yet . . .' said the first journalist.

'And yet?'

'And yet the funny thing is . . .'

'The funny thing?'

'. . . that people didn't hate him.'

'They didn't vote for him either.'

'No, but in a strange way they liked him.'

'Did you like him?' asked the second journalist.

'No, I wouldn't say that exactly.'

'I'm glad to hear it.'

'And yet . . .' said the first journalist.

'There it is again,' said the second journalist. ' "And yet . . ." '

'Yes. And yet there was something about him. A certain charm.'

'Charm?'

'A certain charisma.'

'Charisma?'

'He didn't take himself seriously,' said the first journalist. 'That was endearing.'

'I didn't find myself endeared,' said the second journalist. 'And why would anyone take him seriously?'

'He learned a bit of Welsh,' said the first journalist. 'That showed commitment.'

'Anyone trying to get elected here would learn a bit of Welsh,' said the second journalist. 'And his accent was terrible.'

'Of course his accent was terrible,' said the first journalist. 'He knew that. He made a joke about it. And people laughed.'

'I can't think why,' said the second journalist.

'I suppose because it gave them something in common with him.'

'Are you out of your mind? He went to Eton. He went to Oxford. He lives in London. He writes for the Tory newspapers. What the hell does he have in common with people round here?'

'He knew that what he was trying to do here was ridiculous. Absurd. He'd been given an impossible task and he was trying his best but he knew that he was doomed to fail. A lot of people feel like that, no matter where they live, or what their background is.'

'Feel like that about what?'

'About everything. About life.'

'Well, now he goes back home, to a big house in London and a well-paid job on a newspaper. Not much in common with the people of Llangollen there, is there?'

'I know what you think,' said the first journalist. 'You think that just because people here have voted Labour all their lives, and their fathers before them, and their grandfathers before them, they will vote Labour for ever. But it doesn't work like that. For one thing, the party they just voted for is not the same one they voted for twenty or thirty years ago.'

'I'm aware of that.'

'Things change,' said the first journalist.

'And everything stays the same,' said the second. 'The people of this constituency will never vote Tory. Not while there are men like him in the party.'

'Would you care to make a bet on that?'

'Certainly.'

'A hundred pounds?'

'Let's not bring money into this. That's so sordid.'

'What then?'

The second journalist smiled. 'If it ever happens, I'll give you a blow job.'

The first journalist laughed. 'Well, now I've heard everything. Deal.'

'Shake on it.'

They shook hands.

'Got time for another half?' said the first journalist, who had moved to this town only recently, from Newport, in the south, and whose name was Aidan.

'Just a quick one,' said the second journalist, who had grown up on a farm not far away, near the village of Llanbedr, and whose name was Sioned.

V. In Praise of the Eternity of Jesus

The Coffrini Trio

St Cuthbert's Church, Philbeach Gardens,
London SW5

7.30 p.m., Saturday 6th September 1997

Chiara Coffrini, piano
Peter Lamb, violin
Marcus Turner, violincello

with
Camille Ducreux, clarinet

Programme

Gabriel Fauré
Trio in D minor, Op. 120

*

Interval

*

Olivier Messianne
Quatuor pour la fin du temps

They were rehearsing in Chiara's flat on Wednesday afternoon, and it had been going well. For almost ninety minutes Peter, Marcus and Camille worked on the short '*Intermède*', which involved complex cross-rhythms and unison playing that called for the utmost precision. Then, as they broke for tea, Gavin opened up one of the two boxes containing the programmes which had arrived that morning from the printers', and that was when they noticed the mistake.

'We'll have to send them all back,' said Marcus. 'The tossers have spelled his name wrong.'

'Such a shame,' said Chiara, looking at the rest of the programme. 'It looks really good.'

'It's my fault,' said Gavin. 'I'm so sorry. I should have gone there in person, not done it over the phone. Do you think they'll be able to reprint them in time?'

'Maybe,' said Peter. 'But we'd better see to it this afternoon. What time do they close?'

'Five-thirty,' said Gavin. 'We've got an hour. I'll get round there now.'

'I'll come with you,' said Peter.

Neither of them, strictly speaking, needed to stay until the end of the rehearsal: the next movement, '*Louange à l'éternité de Jésus*', was a long duet for piano and cello, and would keep Chiara and Marcus busy for the rest of the afternoon, while Camille was happy to take over page-turning duties at the piano. So Peter and Gavin left together, and took the Tube to Fitzrovia where the printer grudgingly admitted that the misspelling of the composer's name was his own fault. 'I'm sorry,' he said, 'but it's been so hard to concentrate on anything this week, hasn't it? I mean, when you think about all the things that woman was going through, and how it ended for her? You can't function normally, can you, at a time like this? You'd have to have a heart of stone.' He agreed to reprint all one hundred programmes for collection by lunchtime on Friday. This tricky negotiation concluded, Peter and Gavin found themselves in a pleasant part of town, on a sunny evening, with a bit of time to spare. They wandered down to Soho and chose a pub and took their drinks out onto the pavement with the rest of the crowds. All around them, the conversations seemed to be about Diana, and people were reading newspapers with front-page banner headlines saying, 'WHERE IS OUR QUEEN?' There was increasing outrage that, as thousands continued to make the pilgrimage to Kensington Palace bearing flowers – the carpet of flowers laid outside the gates being many layers deep by now – the Queen had not even returned to London from Balmoral, and the flag at Buckingham Palace was still not being flown at half-mast. The national mood was growing restive: grief was turning to anger.

Gavin and Peter did not talk about Diana, however. The men (they were always men) who Chiara somehow managed to persuade to volunteer as her page-turners, baggage-carriers and general factotums tended to have certain features in common: they were handsome, they were charming, they were in their mid-twenties, and they were usually out-of-work musicians. And indeed Gavin conformed to all of these prerequisites. But he did not conform to the most important one of all: he had not fallen in love with Chiara. Stubbornly, this new recruit had resisted her undoubted charms, and instead, during rehearsals, it had always been in Peter's direction that his eyes seemed to stray whenever they were not fixed on the music. At first Peter didn't notice this; then he thought his imagination must be deceiving him; then he tried to ignore it; and then, finally, he found himself more and more intrigued by this good-looking young man whose gaze seemed to be paying him the compliment of such unexpected, flickering attention. They had found themselves talking to each other more and more, whenever a break in the rehearsal permitted it; walking together to the Tube station or the bus stop, even when that involved a small detour; and this evening, now that they had contrived to end up having a drink together, they had no intention of wasting it by discussing the late Princess of Wales. They began by talking in general terms about how Saturday's performance was shaping up. Another drink, and they were talking about Gavin's years at the Royal Northern College of Music, where he'd studied composition and acquired the reputation of being a virtuoso on the French horn. Another drink, and Gavin was telling Peter how lucky he was to have a salaried position with a major London orchestra, and Peter was agreeing, but saying the same thing could happen for Gavin too, and offering to put a word in for him if he wanted to apply to the brass section. Another drink, and they were talking about how Gavin had messed up his final year at college, and failed his exams, by having an affair with Nikos, a young percussionist from Greece, which had ended disastrously. Another two drinks, and Peter was telling him that he'd been married for seven years but things were pretty bad with his wife at the moment: she was having an affair which was more or less out in the open and he was pretty sure she'd gone to France with her lover and not with three of her girlfriends. And all the while, it was dawning on Peter that Gavin was not good-looking at all, nor was he handsome: he was beautiful, there was no other word for it, and there was nothing he wanted to do more at that moment than reach out and touch his face, trace the curve of his cheek, feel the roughness of his stubble beneath his fingers, and while this should have been an amazing, even shocking feeling, there was really nothing amazing or shocking about it at all, it felt like the most natural feeling in the world. And yet, however natural it felt, however desirable, however much Peter yearned to reach out and touch this beautiful young man who was paying him so much attention and whose eyes were like pools of azure that he wanted to dive into, he still knew that he wouldn't be able to do it. If he was able to do something like that, he would have done it years ago, five years ago at least – was that how long it had been since he'd slept with Olivia now, five years? – so there was no point, this whole evening had been a waste of time, and it was a racing certainty that he would be going home alone, as usual, back to an empty bed and a night of stupid, feverish fantasies . . .

There were more drinks. Somehow it got dark, and late. Peter was very drunk, that was for sure. He was standing on the corner of the street saying goodbye to Gavin, and he couldn't remember how they got there.

'See you on Friday, then,' Gavin was saying.

'Friday,' Peter repeated, swaying slightly.

'Final push,' said Gavin.

'Final push,' said Peter, and then suddenly leaned forward and kissed him full on the mouth. After a second or two Gavin recoiled, but only in surprise, not in repulsion: moments later he put his hands to Peter's face and kissed him back, and this time it was a long kiss, their mouths open, their tongues rolling against each other. But soon it was Peter's turn to break away.

'I can't do this,' he said, breathing heavily. 'Fuck. I can't do it. *I can't fucking do it.*' And then he walked off, without saying goodbye, without looking back. Gavin called after him but there were people on the street, hundreds of people, all talking about Diana, and Peter didn't hear him.

*

At four o'clock in the morning, an hour before dawn, Peter opened the sash window in his bedroom and looked out onto the street. He was sweaty, tired, and either hungover or still drunk or perhaps both. He was filled with anger and contempt for himself. Another opportunity missed, another chance let slip. The sense of loneliness, of impotent rage, was overwhelming, and what began as a long sigh, delivered to the night air, gradually swelled in volume and intensity until it became a prolonged ululation, somewhere between a moan of emotional and sexual frustration and a howl of bottled-up fury. When it was over there was a moment of silence and then, to his embarrassment, he realized that it had been heard by a passer-by, some early-morning shift worker or crazed insomniac, because a man's voice rose up from the other side of the street, and shouted: 'I know, mate! I know! We murdered her, didn't we? We killed her. We're all to blame.'

Peter slammed the window shut and hurried to pull on some clothes. He decided that he was going to make a journey.

Two and a half hours later he was on the outskirts of Keyhaven. His mother and father would still be there, and his brother Jack, and Ange, and their children, Charlotte and Julian. It would be strange, after three days in London, to return to that romantic old house and find the family holiday still in full swing. Now that he'd arrived, he realized that it was much too early to wake them all. He parked his car in a seafront car park above Milford on Sea and the spreading sunlight and gently breaking waves lulled him into fitful sleep for a couple of hours. After that he found a café and ate a croissant with two strong black coffees. The town was quiet, most of the holiday-makers seemed to have gone home, and he had the place almost to himself. He started to feel a little better, a little clearer in the head.

It was ten-thirty when he pulled up in the tree-lined, loosely grav-elled driveway outside the front door of the house. The door was unlocked. He wandered in and found Jack at the kitchen table, drinking tea and reading the paper. Today's headline was: 'YOUR PEOPLE ARE SUFFERING – SPEAK TO US, MA'AM.'

'My God,' Jack said. 'Look what the cat brought in. What are you doing here, bro?'

'Well, I had a free day and nothing much to do,' Peter said, with-out much conviction. 'Seemed a shame not to take a bit more advantage of this place. Where is everybody?'

'The kids have been up for ages. We're not ready to take them to the beach so Ange has stuck them in front of a video. I think Mum's watching it with them.'

This turned out not to be the case. When Peter left the kitchen he found his mother in the hallway, putting on her walking shoes.

'Hello, love!' she said, getting up, wide-eyed, every bit as sur-prised and delighted as he might have expected. 'What are you doing here?' After he had stumbled through the same explanation he had given to Jack she said: 'Oh, it's *lovely* to see you! Come on, you must be tired after that drive. Let me make you a coffee.'

'No, it's all right, I had one in town. Where were you going?'

'I just wanted to get out for a bit. I was thinking of going for a walk on the Marshes.'

'Great, I'll come with you.'

They set off together, past the rose garden, skirting the tennis court and finding the footpath that led from the back of the grounds across a meadow, a meadow filled with red clover and ragwort and evening primrose, which brought them out in a narrow lane of red-bricked cottages, and from there to the main road. Soon they were walking around Keyhaven's tiny harbour, the yachts and fishing boats bobbing almost imperceptibly on the water this morning, the sea breeze creating the most subtle of noises in their rigging, a soft, occasional, infinitely soothing tinkle. They followed the public footpath, tracing its curve around the modest headland, Hurst Castle and the Isle of Wight to the right of them, nothing but open marshland and blue sky ahead. Gulls circled. Insects darted from flower to flower. As they walked on, Mary said:

'Isn't it funny? I can't stand watching that film.'

'Which film?' Peter asked.

'That video they were all looking at. *Pinocchio.*'

'I never saw it,' said Peter.

'Grandma took me to see it, during the war,' said Mary. 'I was just a little girl. And in the middle of the film, there was an air raid. Just after he was swallowed by the whale, it was. I was frightened enough already, and then we could hear the planes. Everyone dashed for the exits, and then we ran home . . . We ran home in the dark . . . Holding on to Grandma's hand, I was, for dear life . . . Ugh! Horrible! I never want to see that film again.'

They came to a halt and, glancing across at his mother, Peter could see that her eyes were closed in recollection. When she opened them again she stared sightlessly over the long path ahead of them, a broad lake of salt water to their left, to their right the grasslands and mud flats stretching down towards the sea. She said: 'When people tell you that we all had a good time during the war, don't take a blind bit of notice. No one who was alive when it happened will tell you that. We were petrified, most of the time . . .'

On they walked, for twenty minutes or so, until a wooden bench with a view over the sea proved too tempting a prospect to pass by. Peter was beginning to flag, in any case – unlike his mother, who still thought nothing of spending three hours on the golf course several times a week. He sank down onto the bench, panting slightly. Mary sat beside him and took a packet of mints from her pocket. Passing one to her son, she said:

'Is Olivia still away?'

'Yes.'

'Shame she couldn't come at the weekend. I would've liked to see her.'

'Well, I tried to persuade her, but . . .'

'I know she doesn't really like us. Still, it would only have been a couple of days.'

Peter was on the point of saying, 'Of *course* she likes you,' but since it would have been a lie, and a transparent one, he remained silent.

'Everything all right with you and her, is it?' Mary asked.

'Sure.'

'Still no kids on the horizon?'

Instead of answering this, Peter merely stated, in a grim, matter-of-fact tone: 'I think she might have found somebody else.'

'Oh.' Mary looked across the water at the grey, formless bulk of the castle. 'Oh dear.'

'And actually I'm starting to wonder,' Peter continued, every word feeling more and more effortful, heavier on his tongue, 'that it might all have been a horrendous mistake. Not just with Olivia but . . . all the women I've been with.'

Mary squeezed his hand. 'These things happen, love. God knows, everyone makes mistakes. But you're a smashing fella. You'll find someone else soon enough. And she'll be the right one, this time.'

'Maybe,' said Peter. And then he launched himself into the abyss: 'Although I'm not sure the next one *will* be a she. Not necessarily.'

A bird alighted on the low slate wall in front of their bench. Probably a sandpiper, Mary thought. It cocked its head and nibbled away at the feathers on its belly, cleaning itself in nervous, fastidious movements. There were thousands of birds on these marshlands: turnstones, dark-bellied geese, brilliant white egrets, all looking for food along the broad stretches of mud bordering the Solent. Mary thought that she could happily see out the rest of her life just sitting here, watching the birds. She understood what her son was trying to tell her, but to her momentary surprise she realized that it did not disturb her especially, she was there already, and instead she felt a deep, unexpected peace stealing over her.

'I wanted to ask you something,' Peter said, discomposed by her silence, unable to fathom it. 'It's about something you said when I was really little. We were in the car, driving, the five of us. I don't know where we were going. It's almost my earliest memory.'

'Well, go on,' said Mary.

'You were talking about gay people, and the way you described them . . . You used this phrase. You said that they were "the lowest of the low".'

Rather than contemplate these words, rather than let them hang in the air, Mary shook her head quickly, and said: 'I've no idea, love. You can't expect me to remember what I said all that time ago. Anyway, so much has changed since then. We didn't know what we were talking about, half the time. We were ignorant. *Ignorant*, is what we were. You're talking about *years* ago . . .'

'Thirty years,' said Peter.

'Well, there you are! We live in a different world now. Things have moved on. Everything's different, isn't it? Gay rights, and all that caper.'

Peter smiled at the phrase. He put his arm through his mother's, and drew her towards him.

'You don't need my permission to do anything,' she said.

'I know that. I didn't come down here to ask for permission.'

'Then what did you come for?'

He sighed. 'I don't know. Maybe . . . advice? . . . I don't know.'

There was a long silence between them now. The sandpiper finished its ablutions, looked from side to side, making a rapid survey of the area, and launched itself into flight. Mary helped herself to another mint, and offered one to Peter. Then she said an unexpected thing.

'Did you know that David's writing poetry now?'

Peter frowned. 'David who?'

'David Foley. Sylvia's lad. You remember – you were quite pally with him when you were a boy.'

'Oh, David! Yes, of course.'

'He's published two or three books now.'

'Yes, I think I did know that. I should get back in touch with him, really.'

'Yes, you should. I saw him a few months ago. Sylvia phoned me up and asked if I wanted to go with her to the Hay Festival. Have you heard of it? It's a book festival in Hay-on-Wye. It's a bit of a strange idea – authors come along and they read bits of their books out loud to the audience and then afterwards they sign them. I don't really know who that's supposed to appeal to, but there were quite a few people there. Well, I say quite a few. David was reading from his book of poems with two other people and there wasn't much of a crowd for that, I can tell you. Apart from me and Sylvia there were probably only about twelve or fifteen of us. Still, he put a brave face on it and he read very well, I must say. Very clear, he was, you could hear every word. Afterwards he took us for a coffee and we had a nice little chat. It was good to catch up. Did you know he was teaching at the university now, in Keele? English Lit, he teaches. Well, you can't make money by writing poetry, can you? Especially not his sort of stuff. I did ask him to explain what some of the poems were about but I can't say he enlightened me very much. Went right over my head, it did. But it was a nice day out with Sylvia, I hadn't spent a proper day with her for a long time, so that was good. The meetings with the authors are held in a little school next to the car park. So afterwards we had a walk around the town – though there isn't very much to see, it's nearly all bookshops – and got back to the car park and we were getting ready to drive home when I thought I'd better go to the loo first, so I went back into the school. And there was such a crowd there, you've never seen anything like it! One of the authors had just finished speaking and now he was signing his book and there was a queue halfway round the building. In fact there were so many people there that at first I couldn't see who it was. He was an elderly chap – I mean, I know your father and I are getting on a bit now, but he looked older than that – he was almost bald, and looked very frail. So I got a glimpse of him and I thought he looked vaguely familiar and then when I was in the ladies I realized who it was. At least I thought I did. But then I thought, "No, it can't be," so I went back to take another look at him. And then I knew it for a certainty. It was Kenneth. My old friend Kenneth Fielding. Do you know who I mean? Quite a well-known journalist. Well, he used to play me and your father at tennis back when we'd just started courting, and then when I was a student at Dartford, we saw quite a bit of each other. We used to meet up in London and go to the theatre and what have you. I think we saw *The Mousetrap* in the week it came out, can you imagine that! But, my God, he did look old and ill! He looked terrible! Well, that was what his book was about mainly – I bought it a couple of weeks later. Some of it was political essays and things like that – I just sort of skimmed through those – but the last two chapters were about his cancer. I had no idea about any of that. Well, I thought about buying the book there and then, and getting him to sign it for me, but I didn't really have the nerve, I thought it could be embarrassing for him, in front of all those people, but anyway I got the chance to see him close up a bit later. Sylvia and I decided to get some fudge before we set off home – just something to see us through the journey – and when we were coming back from the shop there he was. There *they* were, actually, because he had his wife with him. I think she was a bit younger than him – my age, more or less – very glam, rather beautiful actually. He'd finished signing and she was helping him walk through the car park. I passed this close to him – just a couple of feet away – and he looked right at me, and looked as if he recognized me, or thought he did, or thought he should remember me from somewhere, but he didn't say anything, and neither did I. To be honest I was more interested in looking at *her*. You see, the last time we met – Coronation Day, it was – Kenneth sort of . . . well, I don't know what to call it, I suppose he . . . *proposed* to me, or at least . . . he asked if we could walk out together, that sort of thing, but I was already engaged to Geoffrey by then . . . Now don't get me wrong, I've got no regrets about marrying Geoffrey, of course he irritates me sometimes – that's just marriage, isn't it, you have to take the rough with the smooth – and I wish he'd be nicer to Bridget, but he's always been prejudiced like that, he's never been able to get over it – and I wish he'd . . . just show a bit of *emotion* sometimes, instead of locking himself up with his books all day. Do you know he never cried when Nana died? Didn't shed a single tear – his own mother – the same with Grandad too, all those years ago, but as I say, we've been happy, on the whole, we've rubbed along together very well, and of course if it wasn't for Geoffrey *you* wouldn't be here, or Jack, or Martin, and I can't imagine that, can't even think about it, so . . . No, I've got no regrets on that score, it's not as if I envied this woman, but I did look at her, for a moment or two, and think to myself, *Yes, that could have been me* – my whole life could have gone in another direction if I'd reacted in a different way at the Coronation, and coming face to face with her in the car park like that – it was like seeing . . . I don't know, like seeing another version of yourself. Very strange.'

'Your doppelgänger,' said Peter.

'My what?' said Mary, who didn't know the word. Peter didn't try to explain, so she continued: 'Of course, she's on her own now. Poor old Kenneth died a month or two after that, in July. And I've still got Geoffrey, so . . . I feel sorry for her now, more than anything else.'

'Perhaps you should write her a letter,' Peter suggested, 'to say that you knew her husband, and she has your sympathy, and so on . . .'

'Yes, that's not a bad idea,' said Mary. 'She must be devastated, poor thing. Perhaps I'll do that.'

(But she never did write the letter.)

'I suppose I've had a small life,' she said. 'Maybe if I'd gone with Kenneth it would have been different. Pa always used to tell me that I'd play the piano at the Royal Albert Hall one day. That never happened, did it? I just play "Jerusalem" for the local WI once a week. I'm glad you've done so well. Playing with the BBC Symphony Orchestra! I tell all my friends about you, you know.'

'Don't say that,' said Peter. 'Don't say you've had a small life. For one thing, it's not over yet. Not by a long way. And when it is . . .'

'When it is?' said Mary, turning to look at him, intrigued to know where this conversation was heading.

'I . . . Well, I know this is morbid, but sometimes I think about what your funeral's going to be like.'

'Really?' She stared at him, her half-smile a challenge. 'And?'

'And it will be *amazing*. I mean, it will be terrible as well. That side of it – the grief – I can't even begin to imagine. I'm not talking about that, obviously. I'm talking about the hundreds of people who are going to come, and the love that's going to be in the room. All the friends, all the work colleagues. Everybody you ever knew is going to be invited, and they're all going to come because they all love you so much. It will be . . . such a celebration. That's what we'll make it. I promise.'

'You can promise whatever you like,' said Mary, in her laconic way. 'I won't be there to enjoy it, will I?'

Peter could hardly contradict that. All the same, he could see that his mother was moved. Not wishing to show it, she looked at her watch and said: 'We should get back. They'll be wanting me to help them with lunch. You will stay for lunch, won't you?'

'Yes, of course.' They both stood up. 'And thanks for telling me that story. I think I know . . . I mean, I think I understand why you . . .'

And then, for the first time in a long while, Peter hugged his mother, and she hugged him back. He clung to her and wouldn't let go, closed his eyes and as he did so saw a quick, shimmering vision – vivid as any hallucination – of snowflakes settling on the sleeve of her fake fur coat as they walked together in the dark along a London street one January night, far in the past – then opened his eyes and saw only the path leading across the marshlands, and the silvery water across which the gulls and waders called to each other while the distant engine of a fishing boat could be heard miles out to sea. Otherwise all was quiet in that eternal, suspended moment.

'Do whatever feels right, love,' Mary said, finally breaking loose. 'Whatever makes you happy.'

VI.   Dance of Fury, for the Seven Trumpets

At eleven o'clock on the night of Friday 5th September 1997, Peter and Gavin were walking along the South Bank in London, heading towards Westminster Bridge. That afternoon's final rehearsal had gone well: they'd run through two complete performances of each piece, and now all four players felt confident. Afterwards, by tacit agreement, Peter and Gavin had left together. They had dinner in a restaurant near Waterloo and then drinks in the bar at the Royal Festival Hall. Now they were about to cross the river, heading north into Westminster. Again, they had not discussed what was going to happen next. However, Peter's flat lay in the opposite direction. This was the way to Pimlico, where Gavin was currently living, in a small rented room in a mews house owned by an American couple, both bankers. Peter could have said goodbye at any point, jumped on any one of the southbound buses that would have taken him home. But he didn't.

'So your father's retired now?' Gavin was saying.

'Yes, retired five years ago. Worst thing that ever happened to him, I think. He doesn't know what to do with himself any more.'

'Doesn't he have any hobbies?'

'He reads a lot. Thrillers, that sort of thing. Bit of Latin poetry, occasionally – he was a Classicist, back in the day. And he and my mother play golf. For the last twenty years, they've played golf. When they're not playing it, they're talking about it. When they're not talking about it, they're watching it on television.'

Gavin laughed. 'So I'm guessing you're not close to your parents.'

'Close enough. It's not about what you have in common with them, really, is it? Or what you agree with them about. Jesus, look at all these *people* . . .'

As they were walking across Westminster Bridge, they found

themselves part of a swelling, densely packed human tide, heading in the direction of Parliament Square and Westminster Abbey. Where had it come from? Soon Peter and Gavin had come to an almost complete halt, and they were having to shuffle forward with cramped, tiny steps. They were hemmed in by people on all sides: teenagers, pensioners, families, couples, groups of friends and solitary mourners carrying cards and placards with handwritten messages, not to mention teddy bears and the inevitable flowers. The mood was sombre. Everyone inched forward in near-silence. Some were crying.

'This is so weird,' Gavin said. 'I'd no idea it was going to be like this. It's going to take us ages to get home at this rate.'

'It's incredible. Do you know how long people have been queuing to sign the Book of Condolence? Six hours, I read. Half the country's come to London for this funeral.'

When they finally reached the end of the bridge, the crowd was able to spread out slightly, and progress became easier. Nonetheless, it was still going to be difficult crossing Parliament Square.

'And you've got . . . two brothers, is that right?' Gavin asked.

Peter nodded. He felt self-conscious: they were not just the only people having a normal conversation, they seemed to be the only people having a conversation at all.

'That's right. Two older brothers.'

'And what are they like?'

'Well, one of them's called Martin, and he works for Cadbury.'

'Cadbury's chocolate?'

'Yep. He's a solid, middle-of-the-road sort of guy. And then there's Jack, who . . . Well, I don't know how to describe Jack. He's all right, really. He likes to think of himself as the life and soul of the party. Hasn't really moved with the times, though. Still calls women "girls" and tells Irish jokes.'

'He sounds a nightmare. Sorry, but he does.'

'Oh, he's not so bad. There's no malice in him.'

Stepping carefully over a young man and woman who were stretched out on the pavement in sleeping bags, they made their way across the road into the centre of Parliament Square, where an impromptu campsite had sprung up in the last few days, to join the ones already established in Green Park and St James's Park. Some people had actually put up tents, others were taking advantage of the warm nights to sleep out in the open. Torches and candles were everywhere, punctuating the darkness and imparting a mournfully festive atmosphere to the scene. Peter and Gavin squeezed their way past two young girls – they couldn't have been more than fifteen – who had fashioned a giant illuminated capital 'D' out of candles. Next to them on their blanket was a pile of chocolate bars and packets of sweets, their nourishment for the next few hours presumably. Peter found his eyes drawn to this detail, which seemed very touching and reinforced his view that they didn't even look old enough to be out on their own. But the girls thought he was staring at their candles.

'It's a D,' one of them explained. 'D for Diana.'

'Oh, right,' he said. 'Lovely. Beautiful.'

As they walked on, Gavin took him by the arm and sniggered, whispering: 'Well, what else is it going to stand for?'

'I don't know,' said Peter, feeling suddenly transgressive. 'D for Dead?'

It maybe wasn't the wittiest remark, but Gavin had been drinking, and his burgeoning relationship with Peter was making him euphoric, and he let out a bark of high-pitched laughter. It only lasted a few seconds, but it was rather loud, and it cut very noticeably through the murmurous quietude of the campsite. And before they knew what was happening, a stocky, well-dressed man had sprung up from the ground, where he had been sitting with his girl-friend on a sheet of tarpaulin, and had seized Gavin by the collar of his shirt and was looking straight into his face with cold, furious eyes.

'What the hell do *you* think you're laughing at?' His accent was clipped, Home Counties.

Gavin laughed again, this time with nervous incredulity.

'What are you doing? Let go of me.'

'I *said*,' the man repeated, 'what were you laughing at?'

'My friend said something funny, that's all. Will you let go of me?'

'Something funny? Do you know what we're here for, you nasty little cretin? Do you know why we're here?'

'Of course I know.'

'Then show Diana some bloody *respect*, God damn you!' And with that, he pushed Gavin to the ground and kicked him savagely between the legs, and would probably have kicked him again had his girlfriend not intervened and pulled him back, saying: 'Come on, let him go, the little twat isn't worth it.'

Gavin lay there at first, clutching his genitals, flattened by the pain and in a state of shock. Then Peter helped him to his feet and, without looking back at his attacker, they began walking slowly through the groups of campers, Gavin hobbling in agony, his arm around Peter's shoulder. What with the crowds, and the throbbing pain, it took more than an hour to walk the three-quarters of a mile to their destination.

*

They arrived at a small, very elegant house in a small, very elegant mews in the heart of Pimlico. The house appeared to be empty.

'Aren't the owners here?' Peter asked.

'No. They're in the States.'

Gavin sank down onto the sitting-room sofa, wincing and rubbing his groin.

'Do you want me to take a look at it?' said Peter. 'There might be bruising or swelling or something.'

'Fuck off,' said Gavin. 'Do you honestly think the first time you see my dick I want you to be giving me a medical examination?'

They both laughed at that, and their laughter seemed to lead naturally into a long kiss. After which, Peter helped Gavin upstairs to his little attic bedroom, they undressed each other, got into bed and then, comfortably entangled, fell into a deep and chaste sleep.

VII.   Tangle of Rainbows, for the Angel who Announces the End of Time

Peter slept very late the next morning. When he awoke, the space next to him in the bed was empty, and he could hear sounds of activity in the kitchen downstairs. Not wanting to present himself in his unwashed and tousled state, he found the bathroom and had a quick shower. Then he realized that he would have to put on yesterday's clothes. This wasn't an appealing prospect, but since he saw a white bathrobe hanging on the bathroom door, he slipped into that and made his way to the kitchen. There was an enticing smell of fresh coffee, and Gavin was making something elaborate involving eggs and green peppers.

'Good morning,' he said, looking up from the frying pan.

'How are you feeling?' Peter asked.

'Absolutely fine. Apart from the incredible pain in my bollocks.'

'It's still hurting?'

'Do you want to go through into the other room?' Gavin asked. 'I've turned the TV on.' Peter didn't understand at first. 'The funeral coverage,' he explained. 'It's started.'

'Oh God,' said Peter. 'I'd forgotten. You're right, we're going to have to watch it.'

Last night, in his slightly drunken and very agitated state, he had not taken much notice of what the house was like. But now, glancing around, it was very obvious that the people who owned this property were wealthy. Peter had always liked the idea of mews houses: he realized that this enthusiasm went back (like so much else) to his childhood, when he used to watch the film *Genevieve* on television with his mother, who normally didn't like watching old films but made an exception for this one because it reminded her of going to the pictures when she was still a teenager, before her marriage. One of the couples in that film, played by John Gregson and

Dinah Sheridan, lived in a mews house somewhere in London (probably not far from Pimlico) and to Peter their house had always looked like the epitome of bohemian glamour. Back then, it seemed, a couple living on one modest income could afford to buy such a home and live in it fairly comfortably. Nowadays this place would be worth at least a million pounds. Maybe more. The proportions were small but the antique furniture, the original artworks on the walls, the lush, textured wallpaper, the fancy stereo, the complicated lighting system which allowed for every possible combination of overhead lighting and standard lamps, all suggested the hand of an exclusive and costly interior designer. Peter settled himself into the low, miniature but very welcoming sofa which owing to the smallness of the room was only a few feet from the television screen. The BBC's cameras seemed currently to be trained on the funeral cortège as it passed through the gates of a London park. For a moment Peter wondered if the commentator, whoever he was, had nodded off, because there was nothing to listen to: just the monotonous clip-clopping of horses' hooves on the tarmac as the coffin was pulled on its way past the unimaginably large crowds of wordless mourners lining the street.

'What's going on?' Gavin asked, bearing two mugs of coffee as he limped over from the kitchen.

'Not a lot.'

But just then David Dimbleby began to speak. His voice was very quiet, reflective. At first he seemed to be talking in broken phrases rather than complete sentences.

'The cortège . . . moving at a slow walk along the south side of Hyde Park . . . It came in at Queen's Gate, it's now coming up towards Alexandra Gate, heading eastwards, parallel with Rotten Row . . . where the Princess herself used often to ride . . . on its way up to Hyde Park Corner . . . The Albert Hall, in the background there . . . where she herself went quite recently to hear Pavarotti sing for one of her favourite charities . . . Draped in black.'

'Very good acoustics, the Albert Hall,' said Gavin.

'Agreed,' said Peter. 'Better than the RFH, if you ask me.'

'It was here in Hyde Park, too, that she listened in the pouring rain to

that famous concert of the three tenors with Pavarotti . . . And a huge crowd twenty deep or more is lining the route at this point.'

'Twenty deep! Jesus.'

'This is huge, isn't it? I mean, we've known all week that it was going to be huge, but this is . . . HUGE.'

The cameras cut to Westminster Abbey itself.

'The gates of the Abbey here at Westminster are just opening, and the first members of the congregation filing in through the West Door . . . During the past week they've been finding the Princess's friends, people who were known to her through her work, and contacting them and asking if they could come here today . . . But it's the millions of others that are lining the route who are perhaps the real congregation . . .'

'That's a very democratic point of view,' said Peter. 'Perhaps things really are changing.'

' "People's Princess", innit,' said Gavin, not entirely scornfully. 'Come on, breakfast's ready. They'll be a long time getting her to the Abbey at that speed.'

*

Gavin had been making allowances for Peter's inexperience, but he couldn't wait for ever. After breakfast, when they were watching the funeral service itself, he sat close to him on the sofa. He was acutely conscious that, beneath his white bathrobe, Peter was not wearing any clothes. The thought made him wildly aroused. He moved his hand in the direction of Peter's thigh as the BBC commentator announced:

'And now, the Prime Minister, Tony Blair, reads the Hymn to Love from First Corinthians.'

Tony Blair stood in the pulpit, and began reading the lesson. His delivery was practised, measured, supremely professional.

'Though I speak with the tongues of men and of angels, and have not love, I am become as sounding brass, or a tinkling cymbal.'

Tentatively, Gavin took hold of the hem of Peter's robe and drew it back. He looked eagerly at Peter's exposed genitals and laid his hand on them.

'And though I have the gift of prophecy, and understand all mysteries,

and all knowledge; and though I have all faith, so that I could remove mountains, and have not love, I am nothing.'

Peter registered the touch of Gavin's hand between his legs and felt his penis spring up in response. He looked down in fascination as Gavin began stroking it.

'And though I bestow all my goods to feed the poor, and though I give my body to be burned, and have not love, it profiteth me nothing.'

Gavin stopped for a moment. He slid off the sofa and sank to the floor, kneeling in front of Peter. He parted Peter's legs again, and inclined his head forward.

'Love suffereth long, and is kind; love envieth not; love vaunteth not itself, is not puffed up, doth not behave itself unseemly, seeketh not her own, is not easily provoked, thinketh no evil; rejoiceth not in iniquity, but rejoiceth in the truth; beareth all things, believeth all things, hopeth all things, endureth all things.'

Gavin parted his lips and took Peter's erect and swollen penis into his mouth. He took it as far towards the back of his throat as he could and then began to suck its full length, slowly and gently.

Tony Blair continued to speak.

'Love never faileth: but whether there be prophecies, they shall fail; whether there be tongues, they shall cease; whether there be knowledge, it shall vanish away. For we know in part, and we prophesy in part.'

Peter closed his eyes and slid further down on the sofa, thrusting his groin in Gavin's direction. He felt as though he was going to faint with pleasure. He had never experienced anything so beautiful.

'But when that which is perfect is come, then that which is in part shall be done away.'

Gavin began sucking harder, his head bobbing up and down.

'When I was a child, I spake as a child, I understood as a child, I thought as a child: but when I became a man, I put away childish things.'

Peter felt the first stirrings of his orgasm, deep in his body.

'For now we see through a glass, darkly; but then face to face.'

Peter squirmed and let out a helpless moan as the sensation began to build.

'Now I know in part; but then shall I know even as also I am known.'

Finally Peter came, arching his back and raising his hips and crying out in joyful release. Gavin didn't move, holding him still in his mouth, as Peter screwed his eyes shut and the force of the orgasm set off a mad carnival of images in his brain, as if his closed eyelids were a screen and onto the blankness of that screen was projected the most brilliant, the most dazzling lightshow. In that delirious instant he thought that he could see a carnival of fireworks, a chaos of beams and flashlights, even . . .

'And now abideth faith, hope, love, these three; but the greatest of these is love.'

. . . a tangle of rainbows.

VIII. In Praise of the Immortality of Jesus

In a church in south-west London, two musicians are playing the closing bars of Olivier Messiaen's *Quatuor pour la fin du temps*. This section of the piece, *'Louange à l'immortalité de Jésus'*, is an intense, rhapsodic duet between the violin and the piano, incredibly demanding on the violinist. At the end, the melody tails away to the faintest of *pianissimi*, as the final note, at the very upper end of the instrument's register, fades into nothingness, into oblivion, like the soul of a dead person vaporizing and floating up to heaven. The silence which follows this final note lasts for almost a minute, as Peter and Chiara sit, tense and motionless, with their eyes closed, still trapped in the universe of the music, until the audience slowly relaxes and, emerging from their almost mesmerized state, they break into applause, tentative and scattered at first, then loud and prolonged and ecstatic, punctuated by cheers and cries of *'Bravo!'* The four musicians smile and look at each other, replete with emotion, slightly incredulous that they have reached the end of the work, a journey which seems to have taken months or even years rather than the fifty-five minutes that have actually gone by. Peter catches the eye of Gavin, sitting beside the piano, and they hold each other's gaze as the applause rolls on, and on.

*

At the same moment, in the sitting room of a spacious, comfortable but characterless house, on an estate made up of identical houses, just outside Redditch in the West Midlands, a man is handing his wife a cup of tea.

'How are you feeling now?' Jack asks.

'Better,' says Angela. 'I think everyone's feeling a bit better, after the funeral. It was very . . .'

'Cathartic?' says Jack.

'Exactly,' says Angela. 'We all needed to get that out of our system, didn't we? Give her a proper send-off. Have a good cry.'

They sip their tea in contemplative, respectful silence. Then Jack says:

'Do you remember how young and innocent she looked, the day she got married?'

'I never saw the wedding,' says Angela.

'Yes, you did. You saw it with me, at my brother's house.'

'No. I wasn't even here. I was out of the country.'

'Oh yes, that's right,' says Jack. 'That was somebody else.' God, *her*! What was her name? Pauline? Paulina? Patricia, that was it. What a miserable, sour-faced little piece of work she had been. Quickly, he moves on: 'I was just thinking what an amazing transformation since then, in the last sixteen years. From nothing, to . . . *that*.'

'Diana hardly came from nothing,' Angela says.

'I know she was from the aristocracy, sure, but she was just a kindergarten teacher, wasn't she, when she met him? Just an ordinary teacher going about her business. No one had heard of her. And today . . . Celebrities from all over the world. Millions of people in the streets. Doesn't that make you think . . . well, that you can achieve anything, anything at all, if you put your mind to it?'

Angela nods. 'Yes, I suppose it does.'

'I think, if her life is going to mean anything, we should all take that lesson from it. That we can achieve anything.'

'Yes, I agree, but . . . what are you saying, Jack?'

Jack takes a deep breath.

'I think we should cash in our PEPs, cash in our Premium Bonds, put this place on the market and put in an offer for that house. The one just outside Bewdley, with the swimming pool and the stables.'

Angela puts down her mug and draws him into a delighted embrace.

'Yeah, let's do it,' she says. 'It's what she would have wanted.'

★

At the same moment, in the garden of a house in Bournville, a married couple are sitting on a bench, looking at the debris of toys and books left behind on the lawn by their children, who have now all gone inside. They cannot yet quite summon the energy to clear everything away.

'Do you remember,' Martin is saying, 'when we all watched the wedding together?'

'Of course,' says Bridget. 'In that little rented house in Pine Grove. We had everybody round. Bit of an ordeal, if I remember rightly.'

'There was that nice couple who brought the Indian food, and nobody wanted to eat it.'

'Well, that's your family in a nutshell . . .'

'Today was different, though, don't you think?'

'Yes. Just the five of us. Much nicer.'

'I don't mean that,' Martin says. 'I mean the event itself. I know you're more cynical about this than I am, but in a way that funeral was quite something.'

'Well, I suppose it's impressive,' Bridget says, 'that somebody was able to pull the whole thing together in a week.'

'But also,' Martin says, 'the royal family were there. They didn't want to be there. They didn't even want it to take place. But they had to do it, in the end. The establishment had to cave. Has that ever happened before? She forced them into it.'

'The people forced them into it.'

'Yes, of course,' says Martin. 'Which just goes to show that change *is* possible.'

Bridget knows her husband well enough to suspect that this is merely the preamble to an announcement. She wonders if this is one of those rare occasions in his life when he has come to a decision.

'Where is this leading, I wonder?' she says.

'The chocolate war will be done and dusted in a couple of years,' says Martin. 'I think that would be a good time for me to leave Cadbury.'

'And?'

'And maybe stand for the European Parliament.'

'You mean, try to become an MEP?'

'Yes. I don't know what the system is, exactly. I suppose I'll have to get someone to put me forward . . .'

'When are the next elections?'

'Two years' time. What's the matter, don't you think it's a good idea?'

Bridget has gone very quiet, and is looking very thoughtful.

'Think about it,' he continues. 'I've been going to Brussels for four years now. I understand how that place works.'

'I know.'

'Well, of course you know. You've helped me out every step of the way. You've read all the reports and draft resolutions, you've given me legal advice, you've helped me to write the presentation papers. So after all that, can you honestly say there's anyone round here who knows the ins and outs of those processes better than I do?'

'Yes,' says Bridget. 'Me. For precisely those reasons.'

Martin is taken aback. 'Meaning . . . ?'

Bridget smiles. 'Once they can go back into Europe,' she says, 'the company's going to need you, Martin. Need you more than ever. No way can you leave them now.'

'So I shouldn't stand for the Parliament?'

'No,' Bridget answers. 'Definitely not. But maybe I should.'

*

Later, in a pub in south-west London, the Coffrini Trio, plus their guest clarinettist Camille, plus their temporary assistant Gavin, are all sitting around a table, drinking and celebrating the success of the concert. On a large TV screen at the back of the pub, the BBC are replaying highlights of Diana's funeral service in a programme called *Farewell to the People's Princess*. Most of the other drinkers, still caught up in the collective solemnity of the occasion, are watching intently. Occasionally they glance in the direction of the high-spirited musicians in the corner, trying to shame them into silence with disapproving glances.

At around 10.45, shortly before closing time, the first person gets up to leave. It is Peter. As he is gathering his possessions – including his violin case – Gavin stands up too, and takes him to one side.

'Wait a minute,' he says. 'Aren't you coming home with me?'

'Olivia's back from France,' Peter tells him. 'She got back a couple of hours ago. I'd better go home and see her.'

Gavin looks at him, waiting for something more, for some certainty, for some reassurance.

'We've got a lot to talk about,' is all that Peter says, and then he offers his goodbyes to everybody, leaving the pub in a flurry of confused hugs and handshakes. Gavin stares anxiously after him, watching him disappear through the door.

*

Finally, in a house halfway up Rose Hill on the outskirts of Birmingham – a house that is by now much too big for the two people who are still living in it – Mary Lamb dozes in front of the television. Just after ten o'clock, she awakes with a start, looks at the clock on the mantelpiece, and realizes that she has been asleep for almost two hours. When she nodded off, she had been watching a performance of Fauré's *Requiem* from the Proms in London. Now she sees Meryl Streep wearing a safari suit and wandering through some desiccated African landscape. Mary looks around for the remote and turns the television off.

The house is almost silent. They returned from Keyhaven yesterday, and she is trying to adjust; trying to adjust to the loneliness, after being surrounded by her sons and her grandchildren for a few precious days. Of course, she is not quite alone. Geoffrey is with her, as always, and that is some consolation. He may not have much to say to her, they may not even spend much time in the same room as each other, but she can sense his presence always, and that is better than living all by herself, in an empty house. Nothing could be worse than that.

The house is almost silent, but not quite. Mary rises from her chair to go into the kitchen and as she does so, from upstairs, she can hear a strange noise. It is such a strange noise, in fact, that at first she can't identify it, and then it begins to frighten her. It sounds as though there might be some animal up there, some animal in distress, trapped and trying to escape. There are sounds of whining and snuffling. Nervously she climbs the staircase and pauses on the landing. The noise is coming from her left, from the room which used to be Martin's bedroom and which is now used by Geoffrey as his study. Now that she can hear it close up, it is a terrible noise: a dreadful suppressed sobbing, the like of which she has never heard before. She pushes open the door, and says, 'Geoffrey?'

He is sitting in front of his portable TV set, doubled up, his hands over his eyes. On the screen there are images of Princess Diana's funeral. Geoffrey's shoulders are heaving and he is racked by long, convulsive sobs. When Mary takes hold of his hands and gently pulls them away from his face, she sees that his eyes are red and swollen, his cheeks glistening with tears, his mouth contorted into an obscene rictus of grief. Geoffrey is crying like a baby. Tears are pouring from him: the tears he never cried for his father, nor for his mother; the tears that nothing else, nothing that has happened to him or to Mary or to his children, has ever managed to draw from him in the last seventy years.

SEVEN

The 75th Anniversary of VE Day

8th May 2020

I.

Sunday 15th March 2020: Morning

Peter slept badly. He was oddly disturbed by his mother's tales of VE Day, of Doll and Sam, of Carl Schmidt, and all the stories that came after, all the memories she had stirred up during a long, uncharacteristic evening of shared reminiscence. Gavin! It was ages since he had thought about Gavin. That misjudged yet blissful fling had only lasted a few months. Then there had been other men, four or five of them, and then the relationship with Teddy, which had spanned more than a decade and had brought him as much solid happiness as he had ever known or expected to know. And since then, nothing.

He was up at 6.15 on Sunday morning, but Mary was up before him. He found her in the kitchen, sifting through an enormous backlog of post, most of it junk mail, some of it opened and some not. In the background the kettle was boiling in readiness for what would no doubt be the first of the day's several dozen pots of tea. After a while she found what she was looking for.

'I meant to show you this,' she said. 'Last night reminded me. What do you think? Should I go?'

She handed him the letter, which was from a Mrs Hassan of the Bournville Village Trust. It was about their plans for the anniversary of VE Day in May. *'We are contacting all those people who lived in Bournville at the time of the original celebrations,'* she had written. *'Unfortunately there are not very many of you! Would you care to join a street party in Birch Road, where I believe you lived in 1945, and share your memories with the current residents? I'm sure there would be interest from the newspapers and perhaps even local radio.'*

'Sure,' said Peter. 'Why not?'

'Do you think so? Maybe I should go, then. I've been thinking about it. I just wanted your advice.'

This had become the normal state of affairs between them, ever since Geoffrey had died: Mary could not make even the smallest decision without consulting her sons, and Peter in particular. They had been amazed to find, in the early months of her widowhood, how helpless this strong, dynamic woman was in many respects. She had never filled her car up with petrol before, or taken money out of a cash machine, and they'd had to lead her through these processes step by step. It had been her sons' idea that she should acquire a cat for company, but Peter had been required to go with her to the cattery, select the kitten and even choose his name. (And even now he wondered if he had chosen the right cat, because Charlie was a shy, reclusive animal with anger issues, although you could not fault his devotion to his owner.)

'How would I get there, though?' Mary asked.

'They'd probably send a car for you,' said Peter.

Mary nodded, but Peter could see that a cloud had passed over her face at the raising of this practical difficulty. Eighteen months ago her doctor had told her that she was no longer allowed to drive. He had notified the DVLA and she'd had to surrender the driving licence she had held for more than sixty years. She had been bitterly upset, and it was one of many things that she held against her aneurysm: that, and the fact that it was probably going to kill her one day.

2.

Susanne had been unable to book direct flights home from Leipzig for either of them. They both had to change planes at Frankfurt, and it was there, in one of the airport cafés, that they had their final coffee together.

'I suppose we're lucky these places are still open,' said Mark. 'You won't be able to go for a coffee anywhere soon.'

'Really, you think so?' Lorna said. 'The UK's going to lock down?'

'Of course it is. I had three gigs lined up in Scotland. All cancelled in the last couple of days.'

'We'll play together again, though, won't we?'

'Sure, I hope so. And make another record.'

Those were the last words Mark spoke to her before his flight to Edinburgh was called. Just before disappearing out of sight in the direction of his gate – where his enormous bulk would strike fear into the other passengers, all praying that they hadn't been given the seat next to him – he turned and smiled and waved, and Lorna's heart swelled with fondness. She would not see him again for more than a year, and it would be longer than that before they played another concert together. Mark would survive Covid, but it would have a terrible and lasting impact, leaving him with tremors in his hands so severe that he could not possibly play the guitar, with breathlessness so extreme that he could not walk more than a few yards unassisted, with cognitive impairment so far-reaching that he would remember almost nothing about his twenty-five-day induced coma, or the three months he spent in hospital after that, or even the names or the faces of the staff who had looked after him. For some time he would remember none of these things, although he always said that he retained a diamond-sharp memory, strangely enough, of Lorna's closed eyes and rapturous, transported face as she played her bass solo at their Hamburg concert; and also, sharper even than that, of the magnificent *Schnitzel* that had been placed before him late one happy night at the Café Engländer in Vienna.

3.

Tuesday 17th March 2020

He had almost reached Betws-y-Coed when the rain turned to sleet, and then the sleet turned to snow. That was when he decided it had been a mistake to drive across the mountains. He had thought this route might afford him some scenic views. In the summertime, maybe. Not in mid-March, when there was less than an hour of daylight left. He had made a terrible choice.

The snow intensified as he began his slow descent, leaving Snowdonia behind, heading for England. Visibility was dreadful, and he drove at around twenty-five miles an hour, craning forward to look through the windscreen, terrified of coming off the road or even running into an errant sheep. By the time he reached the lowlands of the Dee Valley and the snow had eased off, he was exhausted and in need of a break.

It was shortly after eight o'clock when he arrived in Llangollen. Not knowing the town at all, he drove aimlessly for a few minutes until he reached the riverside, and saw a pub across the water that looked warm and welcoming. It was called the Corn Mill.

*

David ordered himself a tonic water, although he really needed something stronger. He was half-inclined to stay overnight here if he could, and settle in with a whisky or two. The pub was not busy. Already there was a weird apprehension spreading through the country, an eerie sense of foreboding and uncertainty, to which people were starting to react by staying at home. If they did come out, they brought strange new accoutrements with them: rubber surgical gloves, bottles of hand sanitizer. They no longer hugged when they met, but touched each other with their elbows. Normal human contact, it seemed, was rapidly becoming taboo.

Here at the Corn Mill, however, the scattered patrons still seemed fairly relaxed. Apart from some solitary drinkers, the main bar was dominated by a table of four – three men and a woman – who sounded like long-standing friends. They were loud, and it was impossible not to overhear their conversation, but David was not really listening to it: he was thinking, instead, about his visit to Bangor University, about the nervousness of the young student for whom he'd been acting as external examiner, the typically awkward atmosphere in her viva, the untypical anxiety, as they said goodbye, that one or more people in the room might have been carrying the virus, and might have passed it on to the others. Professor Strachan, who had supervised the PhD, was not a healthy man: late sixties, overweight, asthmatic. What would his chances be, if he were to catch it? They said that it stopped you breathing. That it felt like someone sitting on your chest, or your lungs filling with water. David shuddered. He wasn't in great shape himself, these days. Time to start that exercise regime he had been putting off for months. Time to dig out the treadmill that was lying somewhere behind piles of debris in the garage.

Just then, he heard a name mentioned: a name that he recognized. He glanced across at the table of four, and realized that a celebration was in progress, and that the celebration had something to do with a person he had once met. One of the four was quite a bit younger than the others – he seemed to be in his thirties, and the others all looked twenty or more years older than that – and his friends were making a fuss of him. They had bought a bottle of champagne and kept refilling his glass. It appeared that he was a journalist – so were some of his friends, by the sound of it – and he had just been shortlisted for an award, for a series of pieces he had written. It was the name of the award that had caught David's attention.

'The Kenneth Fielding Award,' the woman was saying. 'Now that's proper prestigious, that is. That's really something to be proud of.'

'To be honest, I never heard of him before today,' said one of the men. 'I must be very ignorant.'

'When I made the mistake of going to London,' the woman continued, 'and working for a certain newspaper that I'd rather not mention, he was the only person I met there who resembled a human being.'

'Well, that's not setting the bar very high, is it now, Sioned?'

'No, it's not. I can tell you, take every horrible image you have about those people, multiply it by ten, square it, multiply it by another thousand, and you'd still be nowhere near realizing what a bunch of absolute shits they are.'

'But our Ken was a saint in human form, was he?'

'I didn't say that. He had an open mind, that's all. I mean, you'd think that would be the first thing you'd find in a journalist, but I can assure you it's not. I never met a more bigoted, closed-minded lot than that rabble.'

'Still scarred by the experience, I see.'

'There was a piece I really wanted to write. I had a bee in my bonnet about MAC, back then, and I wanted to do something about them, digging deep into the history, finding out not just what they did but what they were fighting *for* . . .'

'I'm sure that endeared you to the editor. No wonder you didn't last long.'

'Yeah, obviously they weren't going to touch it with a bargepole. But *he* was helpful. Ken Fielding. He gave me the money to work on it for a few weeks. Even came with me on a couple of trips. I've still got all that material somewhere. The thing is, he was . . . fair.' Having used the word she paused for a moment, appraising it. 'Yes, that's how I'd describe him. You know what they say about English fair play? Well, it does exist. It just happens to be *incredibly* rare . . .'

'My God, did you hear that, boys? She's crossed over to the other side. Sioned has become an English nationalist.'

'Well, cheers, Harri,' she said to her young colleague, ignoring the others' mockery. 'To get on the shortlist for a prize like that is an incredible thing. "For journalism that promotes the cause of social justice". Brilliant. Which you certainly have done. As well as putting a few landlords out of business. Let's hope the judges— Yes, can I help you?'

She was addressing the man who had walked across to their table and was now standing over her.

At first it had been Kenneth's name that made David consider introducing himself. He had been planning to tell them that he, too, had met Kenneth Fielding once, shortly before he died – in the green room at the Hay Festival in 1997. That evening the three of them (Kenneth's wife had been there too) had gone on to spend a very convivial, rather drunken few hours together at a nearby restaurant, and then in some pub afterwards if his memory was accurate. But that was by the by. Now, it seemed, he had an even more personal reason for making himself known.

'Your name's Sioned, right?' he asked.

The woman nodded.

'I think I remember you,' David said. 'I think we may have met before. Ages ago.'

'Could be,' Sioned said. 'I meet a lot of people.'

'This was when we were kids. Did your father have a farmhouse outside Llanbedr? And he used to rent it out for holidays?'

'That's right.'

'That's amazing. I stayed there. Remember me? David?'

Apparently she didn't. 'Hundreds of people stayed there, over the years,' she said. 'D'you expect me to remember all of them?'

'But we hung out together. You came on trips with us.'

She shrugged her shoulders.

'You even asked me to marry you.'

Sioned's friends, who had been following this exchange with interest, erupted into laughter at this point.

'Well, now we've heard everything,' Harri said.

'We all knew that somebody would end up suing you one day, Sioned. But we never thought it would be for breach of promise.'

There was more laughter at that. David was becoming worried that the import of this occasion was going to be lost among the hilarity.

'I wrote a story,' he said, making a final bid to jog Sioned's memory. 'It was called *The Underwater Village*. You said it was the worst thing you'd ever read.'

Hearing this, her whole demeanour changed. She slowly put down her champagne glass and looked up at David, searching his face for any resemblance to the young boy she had met, briefly, back in the late sixties. And yes, it was there. Faint, certainly; almost faded out of existence. But his face was a palimpsest, and beneath the features of a man in late middle age she could just about read the memory of that younger, half-erased person.

'Jesus Christ almighty,' she said. 'Yes. You're David. Thomas's son.'

Such was the emotional heat of this moment that it did not occur to David, for now, to wonder why she remembered his father's name as well.

'Wow,' he said. 'This is incredible. Do you mind if I join you? Can I get you all a drink?'

'Of course you can,' said Sioned. 'We'll have another bottle of champagne, please. Decent stuff, not the rubbish Aidan bought last time. And you can bring an extra glass for yourself if you like.'

Having attended to this, and having settled in at the table, David squeezed next to Sioned and, while the other three talked among themselves, they quickly exchanged résumés of the last fifty years. Their stories, in fact, were not dissimilar: both divorced, both with single children. David's daughter, Amy, now in her mid-twenties, was living in Australia with her mother. Sioned's son, Rhys, was in his first year at Manchester University. But for her brief flirtation with the English press in the early 1990s, Sioned had been working continuously in Wales, and was now writing features for the *Daily Post*. David was part of the English department at Keele, and had recently been made full Professor. His seventh volume of poems, *Breath of Stone*, had recently appeared and been warmly reviewed.

'So, you kept going with the writing, then,' Sioned said. 'My critique of your story didn't put you off altogether.'

'I was devastated,' he said. 'It's one of my worst memories of childhood. And you don't remember *anything* about us staying with you, apart from that?'

'Oh, I remember it very clearly now,' she said. 'Your father especially. As it happens you look quite like him.'

David smiled sadly and said, 'He died,' and there was something about the way he said it that made Sioned think he was not talking about a distant event.

'I'm sorry,' she said.

'Just three weeks ago. The funeral was last week.'

'Oh.' She put her hand on his arm and squeezed it.

'He was a very good age. No complaints there. Ninety-four! He'd been living with my sister for ages, and then two years ago he went into a care home. His mind was going but physically we thought he was in good shape, so it was a bit of a shock. Very sudden. They said it was pneumonia.' He took a sip from his champagne and added, as an afterthought: 'Third one in the same home that week, actually.'

Sioned pondered this information but said nothing directly in response. However, it seemed to guide her thoughts in the direction of the pandemic and, looking around the pub, she said, to the table in general: 'Well, lads, how long before this place has to close down, do you think?'

'I didn't think the pubs were closing yet,' said Aidan.

'They don't have to. But if Boris is "advising" people to avoid them, they won't be doing much business for the foreseeable future, will they?'

'That's typical fudge coming from him, that is. "Advice", indeed. We'll need a bit more than that soon, if Italy's anything to go by.'

'I still can't believe it,' said Harri, shaking his head.

'European countries going into lockdown, you mean?'

'No, I can't believe it's *him*,' said Harri. 'I can't believe he's the one in charge when this happens.'

'The thing is, you see,' Aidan began to explain, turning to David, 'that this place has something of a history with Mr Johnson. Back in 1997 he stood for election here. Naturally enough we sent him packing. A few months ago he was round here again, in his capacity as Prime Minister, no less – *Prime Minister!* – talking about his bloody oven-ready Brexit deal (in Welsh, I should add, or his own atrocious version of it) and bugger me if this time it didn't work. Clwyd South has gone Tory for the first time in history. And incidentally, I have a distinct memory that madam here –' he pointed at Sioned – 'once said she would give me a blow job if the people round here ever voted Conservative. And she still hasn't done it.'

'Dream on, Aidan,' Sioned said. 'Dream on.'

'To be fair,' said Harri, 'it must have seemed like a safe bet. None of us thought that could ever happen.'

'No indeed,' said Aidan, draining his glass. 'And yet happen it did. These are the end times, all right.'

*

Lying awake at two in the morning, David reflected on what a difference a few hours could make. Not long ago, he had been struggling to drive through the thickening snow outside Betws-y-Coed, thinking of nothing but whether he was going to reach home safely, and whether it should be lasagne or chicken jalfrezi that he slammed in the microwave when he got there. Now, he was lying in bed next to Sioned, the creamy light from the street lamp outside filtering through her curtains and softly illuminating the upper half of her body: the beautiful curve of her shoulder, the graceful valley between shoulder and hip. Unable to resist, he curled forward and planted a gentle kiss in the small of her back. Her skin was incredibly soft and warm. Sensing the kiss, she let out a little purr of pleasure, then stirred and turned towards him. She put her arms around him and drew him towards her until their faces touched.

'Not much social distancing going on here, is there?' she whispered.

'A shocking disregard for government advice,' he agreed.

'Well, they can't police what we do in our own homes.'

'Not yet.'

*

'There was something I meant to ask you,' Sioned said to David, later. 'A favour, if you will.'

On the point of falling asleep again, David said, without thinking: 'Of course. Anything you like.'

'It's about your father.'

'My father?'

'I know it's a painful subject for you right now, but . . . I suppose he must have left some stuff behind. Some papers, and so on?'

'Yes, of course. Gill's got all that.'

'Were you planning to look through them at any point?'

'Probably, yes, some time over the next few months.'

'Well, if you find something that you think I might be interested in . . . will you share it with me?'

This question was surprising enough to pull David back from the edge of sleep. He raised himself onto one elbow and said: 'What?'

Sioned repeated her request; and somehow, it made even less sense to him the second time.

'Wait a minute,' he said. 'This is my *father* we're talking about, right?'

'Of course.'

'Well . . .' He was lost for words. 'No offence, but . . . what the fuck are you on about? What does my father have to do with you?'

Sioned looked at him, her eyes gleaming in the dark, and then her hand went to her mouth. 'Oh my God,' she said. 'He never told you.'

'Told me what?'

She sat up and turned on the light, then pulled the duvet around her, suddenly conscious of her nudity. She thought for a while, then looked at David directly and repeated her words, as a question this time: 'He *never* told you?'

'I've no idea,' he said, 'literally *no idea* what you mean.'

'OK.'

She got up, pulled on a single item of clothing – a long white T-shirt that came down as far as her thighs – and started pacing the room.

'Many years ago,' she began, 'when I was down in London, I started working on a big piece that never got published. It was about MAC – Mudiad Amddiffyn Cymru. Have you heard of them?'

David shook his head.

'Also known as the Movement for the Defence of Wales. They were around in the sixties.'

'I've heard of the Free Wales Army,' he said, helpfully.

'This was a parallel movement. Connected, but separate. But they were doing similar things. Bomb attacks on reservoirs, and the like. More people know about the Free Wales Army but it was always MAC that I was most interested in.'

'Why was that?'

'Because my uncle was a member.'

The words gave David a jolt.

'Your uncle?'

'My Uncle Trefor. There's a good chance you might have met him because he was always hanging around the farm when I was a kid. And I know for a fact he was there the week you came.'

'Yes, of course, I remember him,' David said. 'I remember my father talking to him. In Welsh, rather bizarrely.'

'OK,' said Sioned. 'So let me tell you about my Uncle Trefor.' She stopped pacing, and sat down on the bed beside him. 'First off, he's dead now. More than twenty years ago. But before he died I told him I wanted to do an interview with him.'

'Did you already know he was part of this . . . movement?'

'Oh yes. That was an open secret in our family. Always had been. All sorts of dodgy characters used to come to the farm when he was staying there. They used to sit in the kitchen and plot away in low voices while Mum made them cups of tea. It was small-scale stuff, mostly, but they scored a few hits. They used to target the Elan Valley pipeline to Birmingham, and in '68 they managed to bomb quite a key part of it, in West Hagley, near Stourbridge. But the really big thing, what it was all building up to, was Prince Charles's investiture . . .'

'Hang on a minute,' said David, as a powerful recollection was triggered. 'Did you say West Hagley?'

'That's right.'

'Shit . . .' He stared into space, as the memory came into focus. 'I remember that happening. I was at school. We were told not to use any water if we could help it.' It was the day he'd gone around the toilets with Tony Burcot turning all the taps on, and they'd been caught red-handed by Auntie Mary. The shame of it had never left him . . . But *that* was the reason for the water shortage?

'It was one of their rare successes,' Sioned said. 'Generally speaking they were a bit unreliable. There was usually something wrong with the bombs they made, and also their security left something to be desired. Information tended to leak out. So that's why, when they started planning to bomb the investiture, the British security services found out and sent someone along to try and talk them out of it. A little bit of gentle persuasion.'

David waited for her to elaborate, but she didn't. Instead she stared intently at him, willing the penny to drop. Which it finally did.

'That "someone",' he said, the words coming slowly, 'it was my dad?'

'Exactly. My uncle told me that one day he took them on a fishing trip – him and my father – somewhere along the river, and that was when he di it. Told him the cat was out of the bag and he should give up any thought of trying to disrupt the ceremony.'

'It was the last day of our visit,' said David, with absolute certainty. 'In fact, we stayed on an extra day for it. I can remember them heading off, and then Mum took us all to Shell Island. You came too. Jesus, I can't believe it. My dad was . . . a *spook*? And he was doing it under our noses?' He shook his head. The images from that week were still clear in his mind. 'And did it work? How did your uncle react?'

'Well, whatever your father threatened him with, it must have been pretty effective, because a few days later he went to the guy who was running all these operations – John Jenkins, his name was – and told him that he wanted out.'

'And that put a stop to it?'

'Sadly not. Two other men were tasked with planting the bomb instead. They were supposed to put it on the railway line at Abergele, the night before the investiture. But something went wrong and it blew up in their faces. "The Abergele Martyrs", people called them. Uncle Trefor always used to shiver when he talked about it and said it could have been him. So in a weird way your father saved his life.' When she saw that David was too stunned to reply, she concluded: 'I should have written that piece, but it's not too late to do something with all the research. I've decided now. I'm going to make a book out of it.'

David wasn't listening. He was lying flat on his back, his hands to his temples, looking up at the ceiling and trying to make sense of all this. Everything he had assumed about his first meeting with Sioned, all those years ago, was wrong. Everything.

She turned off the light and lay beside him. He could feel the soft pressure of her breasts against his body. She rested her head on his shoulder and he kissed the warm tangle of her hair. They lay like that for a long time, silence hanging between them.

'I suppose you'll be leaving in the morning,' Sioned said at last.

'I suppose so. Wednesday's normally a teaching day, but . . . well, everything's up in the air at the moment. This bloody virus.'

'I know. I think I'm going to bring Rhys home this week. Most of his friends have gone home already. Poor kid. He was just getting into the swing of his first year. They all were. Now he'll be back with his mum again.'

'God knows what's going to happen. My neighbours have been stocking up on toilet roll and tinned tomatoes. Should I be stocking up on tinned tomatoes? None of us know what's going on.'

'I hope we can see each other again,' said Sioned. Then added, with untypical nervousness, 'If you want to, that is.'

David clasped his arm around her more tightly. 'I want to,' he said.

Silence fell again, as they luxuriated in wordless intimacy, in the warm, musky air of hope and happiness that this unlooked-for encounter had brought them tonight.

Sioned had only one more question.

'Did I really ask you to marry me?'

'Actually, no. You *told* me that you were going to marry me.'

'That's more like it. And what did you say?'

'I honestly don't remember.'

'Well, that's very hurtful, David. Very hurtful indeed.' She eased herself away from his shoulder and said: 'But it won't stop me from *telling* you – telling you, not asking – that I'm going to come and visit you at the weekend.' And with that she said, 'Goodnight,' and turned away from him, but not before slipping the T-shirt off and offering the gift of her smooth, slender back for him to rest against.

*

Saturday 21st March 2020

Sioned came to see David at his house in Newcastle-under-Lyme on Saturday, and in the afternoon they drove to the woods at Hanchurch. It looked as though it was going to be a beautiful spring. Long beams of sunlight cut through the leafy canopy above them, casting golden patterns on the trunks of birch trees, aspens and Scots pine. The woods were quiet, almost ghostly. Where was everyone? They walked for two hours and couldn't have seen more than half a dozen people. They felt like outlaws: going out for a walk was already starting to seem like a transgressive act. Maybe everyone else was heading to the supermarkets instead, to stock up on household items and non-perishable food. The day before, the Chancellor had announced a furlough scheme, whereby employees would be paid 80 per cent of their wages if they couldn't go in to work, and the Prime Minister had ordered all pubs, restaurants and cafés to close until further notice. The country seemed to be entering full emergency mode. There had been more than seven thousand cases of the virus now, and almost two hundred deaths. These figures suggested that Britain was lagging only about two weeks behind Italy which seemed in a matter of days, judging by the television news, to have transformed into an eerie landscape of empty streets and deserted city squares.

'We're going to be locked down too, any day now,' Sioned said. 'Sod's law, isn't it? I finally start a passionate affair with someone and immediately afterwards I'm not allowed to leave my house. Have you ever tried virtual sex?'

'Can't say that I have,' said David. 'What does it involve?'

'I think we sit in front of our computers and talk to each other while we play with ourselves.'

'I suppose we could try it,' said David, doubtfully. 'Or there's always online Scrabble.'

'Yeah, bit less embarrassing when your son comes into the bedroom without knocking, to ask where his dinner is.'

They walked on. On the rare occasions when somebody passed them in the opposite direction they swerved slightly to avoid them, and turned their heads away so that they weren't breathed on.

'So I've been thinking about my father,' David said, 'and the security services. I was wondering if he did anything else for them besides the stuff in Wales. He used to go to Eastern Europe a lot in the sixties. Prague especially. He always said it was for work but that doesn't make much sense. And I know he was at the World's Fair in Brussels in 1958. We used to have a little model of the Atomium in our living room. That was another episode you could never get him to talk about.'

'Maybe when you can start going through his papers . . . ?' Sioned said, hopefully.

'Anyway, last night Gill phoned up. She said she had some news about him.'

Sioned turned, more expectant than ever. 'And?'

'She'd just been to see Dad's solicitor. It seems there was a letter. A letter he'd written to us both a few months ago. She asked if I wanted to come down and open it with her, because it was addressed to both of us, or was I happy for her to read it out over the phone. So I said that's fine, go ahead and read it.'

'Don't tell me – he was giving you the instructions to find a manuscript locked away in some bank vault. *Confessions of a Master Spy*. "How MI5 recruited me to fight Welsh terrorism."'

'Ah, you'd love that, wouldn't you? But no, it was something quite different.'

He kept her waiting.

'So it turns out . . .' David began. A large Airedale terrier had bounded up to greet them, panting and eager. He knelt down to pat it on the head. Animals, at least, were not supposed to carry the virus. He nodded a cautious hello to its owners and then, standing up again, said to Sioned: 'So apparently, it turns out that Dad had another daughter. I've got a sister I never knew about. In Italy.'

4.

March – April 2020

'*From this evening I must give the British people a very simple instruction – you must stay at home.*'

'Well, we all saw that coming,' said Bridget. 'Not before time.'

'*You should not be meeting friends. If your friends ask you to meet, you should say no.*'

After more than twenty years in Brussels, Bridget had found herself out of a job when British MEPs had officially departed from the European Parliament at the end of January. Starting with a week's holiday with Martin in Cornwall – from which they had just returned – she had been putting together a busy programme of social activities to fill the days ahead, but that would all have to be scrapped now. She didn't relish being confined to this house, a house they had bought for its proximity to the airport and to Birmingham International station, but which neither of them had ever warmed to. Still, they were better off than most, and she was not going to complain about it.

'*You should not be meeting family members who do not live in your home.*'

'*You should not be going shopping except for essentials like food and medicine – and you should do this as little as you can. And use food delivery services where you can.*'

'My folks will be all right,' said Bridget. 'They've got neighbours all around them. What about your mum? Has she worked out how to use that tablet yet?'

'*If you don't follow the rules the police will have the powers to enforce them, including through fines and dispersing gatherings.*'

'Oh yes, and how's that going to work?'

Martin did not appear to be joining in the conversation, so she let

Boris Johnson make the rest of his speech uninterrupted. She tried to focus on what he was saying, but it was difficult because his manner was so distracting. It felt as if he was trying to sound like Churchill making a broadcast to the British people during the darkest hours of the Blitz, but this mode of speech was so alien to him – so far from his normal rambling, off-the-cuff manner, full of bad jokes and barely relevant Classical allusions – that there was something disturbingly weightless about the performance, as if the nation was being addressed by an empty vessel, a hologram of a Prime Minister rather than the real thing.

'*No Prime Minister wants to enact measures like this,*' he insisted.

'*I know the damage that this disruption is doing and will do to people's lives, to their businesses and to their jobs.*

'*But at present there are just no easy options. The way ahead is hard, and it is still true that many lives will sadly be lost.*

'*I want to thank everyone who is working flat out to beat the virus.*

'*Everyone from the supermarket staff to the transport workers to the carers to the nurses and doctors on the front line.*

'*But in this fight we can be in no doubt that each and every one of us is directly enlisted.*

'*Each and every one of us is now obliged to join together.*

'*To halt the spread of this disease.*

'*To protect our NHS and to save many, many thousands of lives.*

'*And I know that as they have in the past so many times.*

'*The people of this country will rise to that challenge.*

'*And we will come through it stronger than ever.*

'*We will beat the Coronavirus and we will beat it together.*'

When it was over, Martin could find nothing to say. Bridget, who had lived with her husband for almost forty years, knew exactly what he was thinking. His mind was going back, as it so often did, to those days in Brussels in the early 90s, when he was still fighting the chocolate war and everyone was talking about this shambolic but already celebrated journalist who had found a funny new way of writing about the European Union.

'He's Prime Minister, love,' she reminded him. 'He's there. It's happened. There's nothing you can do about it. Just try to get over it.'

6.—(1) **During the emergency period, no person may leave the place where they are living without reasonable excuse.**

Mary was alone. She had been widowed now for more than seven years. Two of her sons were nearby – half an hour away, in different directions. Her youngest son was two hours away, in London. These were not great distances, in the larger scheme of things, but to Mary it now felt as though her children (she still thought of them as her children, her sixty-year-old children) were living on different continents.

She and Geoffrey should have sold this house years ago and moved somewhere more suitable. But they hadn't, and now she was eighty-six, and she would never move house again. It was too big for her to look after by herself. Once every week a cleaner came: but she would not be coming from now on, because of the lockdown. Once every fortnight, a gardener came: but he would not be coming from now on, because of the lockdown. Once every three weeks a hairdresser called Deborah came to do her hair: but she would not be coming from now on, because of the lockdown.

Mary was alone, but she could not be silent. She had to talk, it was a basic need for her. In the absence of human company she talked to Charlie, her cat, and she talked to her aneurysm. She didn't give it a name, she did not want to humanize it to that extent, but every morning she would roll up her jumper and her T-shirt and stare at the spot just beneath her heart where she knew it was festering and give it a good telling-off, just as she used to tell off the disobedient boys and girls at school. She would tell it to stop growing and not to burst and generally to leave her in peace so that she could enjoy a few more years. The unthinking will to stay alive was still strong in Mary, even if her parents were gone and her husband was gone and she didn't see enough of her sons or grandchildren. (They were the ones, really, her grandchildren, who gave her a reason to go on living, determined as she was to follow the progress of their lives and to welcome the great-grandchildren who were slowly, finally, starting to arrive.)

And she talked to Peter. Every evening, at around nine o'clock, she would call him and they would talk for a few minutes. It was never more than that, because in reality they had little to say to each other. It was ironic that the son to whom she had the least to say was also the one she most needed to talk to. But it had been like that for seven years now, ever since Geoffrey died. She had spoken to Peter almost every day since then. 'I just want to hear your voice,' she would say to him, and then they would chat about something they had seen on the news or on one of the TV quiz shows they both liked to watch. Today they talked about Boris Johnson's address to the nation and Mary lamented the fact that Peter wouldn't be able to come and see her for weeks now and then she got morbid and said what if she died in that time and would he take Charlie and look after him and Peter said of course he would and anyway what are you worrying about, you're going to be with us for years yet and everything is going to be just fine.

*

5.—(1) A person responsible for carrying on a business, not listed in Part 3 of Schedule 2, of offering goods for sale or for hire in a shop, or providing library services must, during the emergency period—

(a) cease to carry on that business or provide that service except by making deliveries or otherwise providing services in response to orders received—
    (i) through a website, or otherwise by on-line communication,
    (ii) by telephone, including orders by text message, or
    (iii) by post;
(b) close any premises which are not required to carry out its business or provide its services as permitted by sub-paragraph (a);
(c) cease to admit any person to its premises who is not required to carry on its business or provide its service as permitted by sub-paragraph (a).

'So that's it,' said Jack, after he had locked up the showroom for the last time, bidding a mournful farewell to the rows of Porsches and Mustangs and Alfa Romeos which still looked, in his eyes, more beautiful than any display in any art gallery. 'Thirty years I've kept that place open, apart from bank holidays, and now it's shut until God knows when. All because some bloke in China ate a bat that he picked up from some filthy food market.'

'I can't believe Boris is doing this to us,' said Angela. 'Literally locking us up in our own homes. We could be stuck here for months.' She looked out from the upstairs landing window, across the lawns, the pool, the thatched guest apartment above the garage, her gaze roaming as far as the orchard which was just beginning to lose the last of the evening sunlight. 'I mean, it's almost like we're living in a totalitarian state, isn't it?'

*

(2) For the purposes of paragraph (1), a reasonable excuse includes the need—

(a) to obtain basic necessities, including food and medical supplies for those in the same household (including any pets or animals in the household) or for vulnerable persons and supplies for the essential upkeep, mainten-ance and functioning of the household, or the household of a vulnerable person, or to obtain money, including from any business listed in Part 3 of Schedule 2;

(b) to take exercise either alone or with other members of their household;

Peter's house in Kew was tiny – only two bedrooms – but there was a small rectangle of outside space at the back (you couldn't really call it a garden) and for that he became intensely grateful over the next few weeks. In fact, although he felt keen pangs of liberal guilt admitting it to himself, he had to say that he really liked lockdown.

True, his financial position was not great. Peter's salary from the orchestra was modest at the best of times, and now he would only be getting a portion of that, and of course all performances were cancelled until further notice. But most features of lockdown suited him. As well as licensing his more sedentary pleasures – reading, watching movies, listening to music – it actually inspired him to take more exercise than ever before. Day after day, in perfect weather, he walked along the south bank of the river, from Chiswick Bridge to Richmond Lock and back. Sometimes he would detour to the super-market, putting on a face mask before he went inside: he'd bought himself a pack of twenty such masks online, and it seemed that more and more people were starting to wear them now, even though the government's chief scientific advisor, Sir Patrick Vallance, said that the evidence for their effectiveness was 'weak'. In the early days of lockdown Peter's obsession, whenever he visited the shops, was to try to find some bread, of which there seemed to be an acute shortage. Then he started to follow the trend for baking your own, although at first it was almost impossible to buy flour. But soon sup-plies started to trickle back and social media became saturated with images of home-baked sourdough and pitta. He found an organic wholesaler in the West Country which delivered to London and began to order huge quantities of fresh fruit and vegetables. Some-times, when the boxes arrived, he would try to engage the delivery drivers in conversation but they usually didn't want to linger, either because they had busy schedules or because they didn't want to be infected by him.

'It's amazing, really,' he said to Mary on the phone one night, 'how the middle classes have just sort of disappeared, gone to ground. And yet there are loads of people still out there – delivering stuff to us all, working on the tills at the supermarket . . .'

'Somebody still delivers my paper every day. I don't know what I'd do without it.'

The *Daily Telegraph* had been Geoffrey's paper of choice, and Mary had never seen fit to change it since his death. Every day she spent an hour or two on the crossword puzzles and Code Words. She sometimes glanced at the news pages, but didn't read the com-ment section at all. She watched the television news, though, as well as the Prime Minister's daily teatime press conferences, and when Boris Johnson caught the virus himself, and ended up in intensive care at St Thomas' hospital, she followed the story closely.

'What happens if he dies?' she asked Peter. 'What happens then?'

'I've no idea,' said Peter. 'Someone even worse will take over, I suppose.'

'If I die,' his mother said (and Peter groaned silently at the other end of the line, thinking: here we go again), 'you will look after Charlie, won't you?'

'Of course I will, Mum. I've told you that.'

'He's a good little cat, you know. He sleeps on top of me every night. Lies there purring, looking straight into my face.'

'I'll look after him, don't worry about that. But it's not going to happen.'

'At Christmas, you know, I had this feeling . . .'

'I know, Mum, you told me.'

'. . . that it was probably the last one. It was such a shame Bridget wasn't there. Why didn't she come?'

'Jack and Bridget don't talk to each other any more.' He had told her this many times. She didn't seem to want to take it in for some reason. 'She won't even be in the same room as him.'

'All because of Brexit? How stupid.' (Mary herself had no strong feelings about Britain's membership of the European Union. Her approach to the 2016 referendum had been to phone her grandchildren and ask how they would like her to vote, since the outcome would affect their future, not hers.) 'Fancy falling out over a little thing like that. You'd think they could have made it up, for the sake of our last Christmas together.'

Peter sighed and repeated, 'How many times do I have to tell you, Mum? It *wasn't the last one.*'

The note of confidence in his voice was not entirely genuine, even so. He did worry about her. He had discussed her situation once, with a friend, a retired GP, who had asked whether his mother kept any morphine in the house. Peter didn't know. 'Why do you ask?' he had said, and his friend had told him that the rupturing of an aortic aneurysm, although relatively quick, was also an extremely painful way to die.

*

8.— (1) A relevant person may take such action as is necessary to enforce any requirement imposed by regulation 4, 5 or 7.

(2) A relevant person may give a prohibition notice to a person if the relevant person reasonably believes that—

    (a) the person is contravening a requirement in regulation 4 or 5, and

    (b) it is necessary and proportionate to give the prohibition notice for the purpose of preventing that person from continuing to contravene the requirement.

(3) Where a relevant person considers that a person is outside the place where they are living in contravention of regulation 6(1), the relevant person may—

    (a) direct that person to return to the place where they are living, or

    (b) remove that person to the place where they are living . . .

(12) For the purposes of this regulation—

    (a) a "relevant person" means—
        (i) a constable,
        (ii) a police community support officer.

Lorna really liked her Uncle Peter, but he was starting to annoy her. Every time she Skyped him or they spoke on the phone, he told her that the British lockdown was no big deal compared to what was happening in France and Spain and Italy, where you could only go out for an hour at a time and had to fill in paperwork to prove that it was for a good reason. It was fine for him. He had one of the loveliest stretches of the River Thames to walk along, and he had a little back garden where he could sit all afternoon in the sunshine reading his books and his magazines. Lorna and Donny Simes lived on the seventh floor of an eight-storey block just south of the Soho Road in Handsworth, a couple of miles from Birmingham city centre, and while it was a comfortable flat, the rooms were small (it didn't help that there was a double bass permanently stacked against the wall in the living room), there was no outside space apart from a tiny balcony, neither of them was allowed to go in to work and after a few weeks they were beginning to get on each other's nerves. The most liberating thing they did every week was the bizarre Thursday-evening ritual of going out onto their balcony and 'clapping for the NHS'. Some of the block's other residents were even more enthusiastic about this, and brought an assortment of pots, pans and other kitchen utensils out with them, and for the next ten minutes the air would be filled with clapping, whooping, cheering and the clanging of wooden spoons against frying pans and Dutchies and Balti dishes. Wherever the idea had come from (after a few weeks nobody could remember) and however much it carried a whiff of empty symbolism, the general feeling was that it also created a sense of community, allowed everyone a rare but welcome glimpse of their neighbours, and at the very least added a weekly punctuation mark to the otherwise identical days, which had begun to slide by in an amorphous, unmemorable stream.

One afternoon in late April, about five weeks into lockdown, Lorna looked out from her balcony and decided that she would have to escape for a few hours. For the last few days the weather had been taunting everyone. It was no longer spring-like: high summer had arrived early in Britain that year. News reports suggested that people were making their own free interpretations of the lockdown rules and driving out into the countryside or even to the coast. Widely circulated pictures of crowded beaches were drawing cries of indignation from lockdown purists. Lorna's ambitions did not go as far as that. All she wanted to do was sit out in the sun by herself and read a book for a few hours. Bernardine Evaristo's *Girl, Woman, Other* was just out in paperback, and having bought a copy (from an enterprising local bookshop which was offering click and collect) she was keen to get started. Handsworth Park was her destination, and she set off along Soho Road, heading east.

The traffic here was getting heavy again. For a few weeks there had been a welcome absence of exhaust fumes but now the buses, trucks and cars were once more out in force and the air was thick and humid. Two cars were waiting next to each other at a set of traffic lights, both with their stereo systems turned up to the max, and Lorna noticed that one was pumping out Bhangra and the other one Grime in a way that was setting up an unintended cross-rhythm so fascinating that she had to stand and listen to it for a while. But the street was still relatively empty of pedestrians, and most of the shops remained closed. This area had the reputation of being unsafe after dark but during the daytime Lorna had always loved it: there were shops and cafés run by Sikhs, Muslims, Bengalis, Jamaicans . . . Poles too, until recently. There used to be a little Polish shop which sold the most incredible *Krakowska parzona* but it had closed down a couple of years ago. You didn't hear Polish spoken round here so much any more, not as much as Punjabi, Urdu or Somali. Her favourite shop was the Sanjha Grocery Store, which had stayed open all through lockdown and was still run by a sweet old grey-haired guy called Rakesh who had come to Birmingham from Punjab with his parents way back in the 1960s. She would stop off there on her way back, see if they had any of that lime pickle that Donny liked . . .

Lorna left Soho Road behind, reached the park after about five minutes' walk, found an empty bench and began reading. She made slow progress, not because she wasn't enjoying the book but because it was so tempting just to close her eyes every now and then, tilt her face towards the sun and bask in the simple pleasure, made even more intense by the spread of the virus, of being alive, free and in good health. On the grass opposite her, a young woman with a spectacular Afro had laid out a rubber mat and was performing yoga exercises, and some of her serene vitality seemed to be transmitting itself in waves across the park and making Lorna herself feel even more energized.

She had been there about ten minutes, and was just about to turn a page, when a shadow fell on the book and she sensed the presence of someone standing over her. She looked up. It was two people, in fact. Two men: police officers.

'Do you think you could move on, please?' one of them said.

She didn't understand. 'What?'

'You're allowed to leave your place of residence for the purpose of exercise. Not reading.'

'Are you kidding me? I can't sit on a park bench and read?'

'Are you going to go home by yourself, or are we going to have to come with you?'

'But – what about her?' said Lorna, indicating the young woman on her yoga mat not ten yards away.

'She's exercising,' said the second constable.

Lorna sized up the situation. They were quite serious, and quite inflexible. Without another word she gathered up her book and her can of energy drink and started walking back along the path in the direction of the estate. She glanced back and the policemen were no longer watching her; they were just laughing and talking between themselves. Her eyes pricked with tears of righteous anger.

'Did you hear what happened to Lorna today?' Peter asked his mother, during their phone call later that evening. He described the incident to her and she immediately said:

'How ridiculous. What harm was she doing to anyone, sitting on a bench and reading? Is it worth it, do you think? Is this blessed lock-down doing any good?'

'I'm sure it is,' Peter said. 'We have to stop the hospitals being overwhelmed.'

Mary sighed. 'I suppose so. It just seems so . . . wrong. Not being able to see anyone, not to be able to talk face to face. The last time I saw Bridie' (this was her eldest great-granddaughter, aged five) 'all I could do was look at her through the window and wave at her. Susan wouldn't bring her any closer. It felt . . . it felt *awful*. And that was more than a month ago! You can't believe how much I miss everyone. Talking on the phone just isn't the same.'

'What about Skype?'

'Oh, I can't get the hang of it. I can never see anyone properly. And they're always complaining that I'm holding it at the wrong angle.'

'Martin and Jack come round, don't they? I thought they took it in turns to shop for you.'

'Yes, and then they just leave the stuff on the doorstep and wave at me through the window and drive off.'

'I know it's hard, but I don't suppose it will be for much longer.'

'I'd give anything to see you again. Just for a chat. See you in person.'

'I'll come up as soon as it's allowed. It'll be the first thing I do.'

'You promise?'

'Promise.'

And after that there was nothing more he could say. He hung up and poured himself some wine, and tried not to think too hard about his mother sitting alone in her house, surrounded by the souvenirs of half a century of family life, then climbing the stairs, putting herself to bed in the bedroom where he had once been conceived and born, lying awake in the dark, feeling the cold green eyes of Charlie upon her as he lay on her chest, purring mechanically as together they journeyed into the very dead of night.

*

7. **During the emergency period, no person may participate in a gathering in a public place of more than two people except—**

(a) where all the persons in the gathering are members of the same household,

(b) where the gathering is essential for work purposes,

(c) to attend a funeral,

(d) where reasonably necessary—

    (i) to facilitate a house move,

   (ii) to provide care or assistance to a vulnerable person, including relevant personal care within the meaning of paragraph 7(3B) of Schedule 4 to the Safeguarding of Vulnerable Groups Act 2006,

   (iii) to provide emergency assistance, or

   (iv) to participate in legal proceedings or fulfil a legal obligation.

'. . . so I'm afraid that all our plans have had to be cancelled,' said Mrs Hassan, 'which is a shame, as we had six of you coming to take part in the celebrations, and all the residents were looking forward to hearing your stories, but under current regulations we can't do it, people are just going to sit in their front gardens in family groups, or come to their front doorsteps, it will be a bit low-key, I think, not really what we were hoping for, I hope you aren't too disappointed, or maybe you're relieved in a way? This way you can have a quiet day at home by yourself and watch the celebrations on television, nowhere near as stressful for you . . .'

5.

Friday 8th May 2020

It was another beautiful day. The weather itself seemed to be mocking her. She had lunch in the garden but she didn't like to spend too long out there because Charlie was sitting behind the French window, staring out at her longingly, and it broke her heart. Still, she refused to let him come into the garden, she was terrified that he would just run off and never be seen again. Now she was bored and lonely and she had done all the crosswords and puzzles and had nothing more to occupy her. She went inside, sank into her regular chair, scrambled around for the remote control on the coffee table, found it, and unmuted the television. Charlie had arrived at her feet and was watching her closely. He was torn between resentment at the fact that she had been outside for so long and relief that she was back with him now. Once he saw that she was settled he decided to forgive her, jumped onto her lap and began his full purring, kneading and clawing routine.

The BBC were showing random shots of the muted anniversary celebrations around the country. The iconography was all too familiar by now: flags, bunting, tablecloths and paper plates all in an overwhelming sea of red, white and blue; royal regalia and paraphernalia; mugs and T-shirts emblazoned with the wartime slogan 'Keep Calm and Carry On'. Mary was not particularly keen on these trappings but the smiles on people's faces as they enjoyed themselves with their families made her feel like Charlie staring out of the French window at a paradisal world to which he was denied access.

Then it was back to the studio and time to listen again to Winston Churchill's VE Day speech, exactly as broadcast on the radio in 1945. Mary turned up the volume on the television. Presumably she had heard this speech, on the day. She must have been listening to it with her parents. Would it stir any memories?

'Hostilities will end officially at one minute after midnight tonight, but in the interests of saving lives the ceasefire began yesterday to be sounded all along the front, and our dear Channel Islands are also to be freed today.

'The Germans are still in places resisting the Russian troops, but this should not prevent us from celebrating today and tomorrow as Victory in Europe days.'

She didn't remember any of this. The voice was familiar, of course, but that was all. Nor could she picture herself sitting in the front room of number 12 Birch Road, listening to the speech with her parents. Maybe she had been imagining that.

The telephone rang. It was Martin.

'I was just ringing to see how you were today.'

'Oh, I'm fine, love. Just a bit bored. Where are you calling from? You sound like you're in the car.'

'I'm in the supermarket car park. Bridget's gone in to do some shopping, so I'm just waiting for her.'

'Today, perhaps, we shall think mostly of ourselves. Tomorrow we shall pay a particular tribute to our Russian comrades, whose prowess in the field has been one of the grand contributions to the general victory.'

'You rang in the middle of Winston Churchill. They're playing his speech again. The one from VE Day.'

Martin tutted. 'Who on earth wants to listen to that again? Honestly, this country and its Second World War fixation. No other country in Europe is obsessed with that war, you know. They've all moved on.'

'Oh, give over. I know we overdo it a bit sometimes, but . . . I was supposed to be going to a street party today, you know. Really looking forward to that, I was. And now all I can do—'

'Oh, look, here's Bridget. Sorry, Mum, got to go. Just wanted to check that everything was OK.'

So Mary was left alone again: just her, Charlie and Winston Churchill.

'We may allow ourselves a brief period of rejoicing; but let us not forget for a moment the toil and efforts that lie ahead. Japan, with all her treachery

and greed, remains unsubdued. The injury she has inflicted on Great Britain, the United States, and other countries, and her detestable cruelties, call for justice and retribution. We must now devote all our strength and resources to the completion of our task, both at home and abroad. Advance, Britannia! Long live the cause of freedom! God save the King!'

Following these phrases the broadcasters had mixed in the sound of cheering crowds, and it was these cheers that inspired Mary with her first serious pang of nostalgia. But it wasn't nostalgia for 1945: it was nostalgia for the first two months of 2020, for the days (already far distant) when it was possible to leave your house and enjoy the company of other people. She pictured Martin sitting in his car in the supermarket car park, and suddenly the very idea of such an open space, however ugly, however banal, filled her with yearning. She would give anything to be sitting in a supermarket car park.

Mary rose to her feet, unceremoniously dislodging Charlie who gave an angry miaow and retreated to a corner of the room to lick his tail. She walked over to the windows which looked out over the front drive.

Her car was still parked in the driveway. It was a little white Toyota Aygo, purchased soon after Geoffrey had died. Mary had always been a good driver, and had always loved driving: to her it symbolized autonomy and personal freedom and independence – qualities which she had managed to regain in the years since her husband had died, but slowly (so slowly!) and with great difficulty. When the GP had told her that because of her growing aneurysm she would have to surrender her driving licence, it had been a crushing blow: Peter thought it had aged her by years, and she cried many tears of frustration in the days after putting the little plastic card in the post. But even after that, Mary had refused to sell her car. The keys were still hanging on a hook in the kitchen, and every week, on Monday mornings, she would turn the engine over. Its presence out there on the front driveway fulfilled a psychological need. It was not just that she wanted to be able to use it in an emergency. For somebody to take it away would be an act of violence, like an amputation.

She was staring at the car, irresolute at this point, when the telephone rang again. This time it was Jack.

'Howdy doody!' he trilled at her. 'Where do you think we are? You'll never guess.'

In the background she could hear a medley of voices, and some distant music.

'Weston-super-Mare!' he said, without waiting for her answer.

'You've gone to Weston?' Mary could not have been more astonished if he'd told her he was standing outside the Sydney Opera House. 'What brought this on?'

'We couldn't stand being cooped up in that garden any longer,' he explained. 'Ange said that she'd literally die if she didn't see the sea again. So we thought, what the hell. Jumped into the car and here we are. Took a couple of hours, mind you. Dreadful traffic on the M5.'

'What about the lockdown?' his mother asked.

'Well, Boris more or less told us we could relax a bit now, didn't he? Half the Midlands seems to be here today. They're squashed together like sardines on the beach.'

'I don't know, really I don't. Are we all supposed to—'

'Oops, got to go, Mum, I can see a parking space. Take care, have a good one!'

He hung up.

*

She turned the key in the ignition and fastened her seat belt, with Charlie watching her phlegmatically from the house, having taken up his spot on the windowsill. Mary's heart was pounding now, as she reversed into the main road and set off down the hill. This was the most risky and most rebellious thing she had ever done in her life. It wasn't that she had forgotten how to drive, or was in danger of having an accident. But she had never once, in all her eighty-six years, knowingly broken the law. Luckily she had no idea how many concealed cameras were mounted on the roads between Lickey and Bournville, so she could sustain the happy illusion that she was driving unobserved. She moved rapidly up from first gear to fourth, enjoying the feel of the gear lever in her hand and the powerful thrust of acceleration as she coasted down towards the roundabout.

Along the Bristol Road, where the speed limit was mainly thirty miles an hour, she sped up to fifty. She weaved her way in and out between slower cars, driven by much younger drivers. She had lost none of her skill or alertness. She began to feel something returning to her, some core element of her identity that had been mislaid for the last eighteen months.

Mrs Hassan's address was in Acacia Road. Mary knew exactly where it was. She pulled up about twenty yards from the house and sat in the car for a while, calming herself, allowing the adrenaline rush to subside. It was late in the afternoon and the whole street was suffused with a delicious, kindly, hospitable light. It was years since she had been to Bournville and she had almost forgotten how verdant it was, what a soothing green enclave it formed almost at the very centre of Birmingham. There was a fair sprinkling of flags and bunting along the street, and most of the little front gardens were occupied by family groups eating and drinking at makeshift tables, but the atmosphere was not exactly boisterous. Someone had brought a portable speaker into their garden and had put on a playlist of 1940s hits – Glenn Miller, Tommy Dorsey and the like. One or two men had kitted themselves out in battle dress of the period, complete with field service caps and canvas gaiters. Mary thought this was a peculiar thing to do, on the whole, but each to their own. She made directly for Mrs Hassan's garden and guessed that she must be the attractive, dark-haired woman sitting between her husband and two slightly embarrassed-looking teenage boys nibbling their way through a plate of samosas.

'Hello,' she said. 'I'm Mary Lamb.'

Mrs Hassan, visibly startled, rose to her feet and brushed her hands down on an apron bearing the slogan 'Make Do and Mend', which she was wearing over a colourful sari in vivid yellow and blue.

'Mrs Lamb! We weren't expecting you to come today. Of course, it's wonderful that you're here, but as I think I explained on the telephone . . .'

'Yes, I know all that,' said Mary. 'But I had to come. I just knew that . . . this was where I wanted to be today.'

'Well, yes, I'm sure there must be a *lot* of memories for you, associated with this place, and this day.' She turned to her sons. 'Boys, this lady was here – here in this very spot – on the original VE Day, seventy-five years ago. How old were you, Mrs Lamb?'

'I was eleven years old.'

As the boys made polite noises of interest, Mrs Hassan resumed her apologies: 'I'm so sorry that we can't really offer you anything. Of course, there was no public health crisis back in 1945 . . .'

'Oh, don't you worry,' said Mary. 'I just wanted to come and introduce myself, and see the old village again. Nothing much has changed here, I can tell you. I was going to drive up and look at my old house later.'

'Ah yes – Birch Road, wasn't it? Number twelve?' She turned to her husband. 'Can you remember who lives there now?'

'Yes, yes, of course. That's where Mr and Mrs Nazari live.'

'That's right. They came here from Iran a few years ago – as refugees, you know. They've done very well for themselves since. A very nice couple. You should really go and say hello. They'd be delighted to see you.'

'Well,' said Mary, uncertain. 'Maybe later. I think I'll walk down to the Green now. It was lovely meeting you!'

The walk to the Green took just a minute or two, but it was tiring all the same. Mary was glad to find herself a bench and to sit watching as children and adults played and laughed and danced on the grass in the sunlight. The atmosphere was very restful. Suddenly she felt happy here, profoundly at home. To her right was the Bournville carillon, set in a small stone belfry on the north-west corner of the tower of the village school. Ahead of her was the row of shops she remembered so well, and behind them, the rising bulk of the chocolate factory, benign and reassuring in its red brick. All that was lacking in the scene was somebody to share it with. What would she and Geoffrey have talked about, if he had been sitting next to her? Nothing, probably. They would have enjoyed the afternoon in settled, companionable silence. And what about her boys? Martin? He would have grumbled, no doubt, at the sight of the factory. Talked about how Cadbury's wasn't the same after some American company had taken it over a few years ago – that was when he had resigned in protest – and how most of the chocolate bars weren't even made there any more. Where were they made now? Eastern Europe somewhere, Poland or Hungary or somewhere like that. What a strange state of affairs. Why make chocolate bars in Poland and bring them all the way back to England? It didn't make any sense. The rest of the factory was a kind of theme park now, Cadbury World. She had gone there once, many years ago, with Jack and Ange when their children were still young. The kids had liked it, but she had felt stupid, sitting in a little car called a Beanmobile and being driven through all the different zones with their fake scenery and special effects. She could remember thinking what a good thing it was that her father had never lived to see any of this, and afterwards Julian had bought far too much chocolate in the shop and had been sick in the car on the way home. Jack had made light of it as usual, the way he made light of everything. If Jack was sitting with her this afternoon, he'd probably find something to crack jokes about. Sometimes his optimism raised her spirits, sometimes it got on her nerves. Martin was so gloomy by comparison, but on the whole she trusted him more to explain what was really happening in the world. He didn't like the direction things were taking and she suspected he was right. How had she managed to raise two boys who were so different? And then there was Peter. How lovely it would have been to have Peter here, right beside her on this bench, her arm through his. He would have asked endless questions about her childhood, about the old days, and today, for once, she was just in the mood to talk about them.

She sat above the Green for a long time, almost an hour, lost in these thoughts, and then she knew that it was time for the final stage of this pilgrimage. She walked back to her car and drove the few hundred yards to Birch Road. She parked a few doors along from number 12, not wanting to park directly outside it, then walked to the front gate of the house itself – which, like the other houses in the street, was draped with straggles of Union Jack bunting. Mary had expected to feel a sudden onrush of memories as soon as she saw it, but to her surprise, the sight of her parents' old house left her strangely untouched. The shape of the front porch, the mottled ochre of the brickwork, the distant glimpse of back garden: she might have expected these things to carry her back in time, back to her infancy, but no, you couldn't escape the present. Somehow Mary could not connect with the eleven-year-old girl who had lived there once. She was an eighty-six-year-old woman now, tired from the day's excursion and beginning to yearn for her own empty house and the weight and warmth of a loyal cat on her lap. She was about to start walking back to her car when the front door opened and a man and a woman appeared on the step. They were in their thirties, good-looking, dark-skinned. The man's hair was on the long side, and he had refined, delicate features. His wife was pretty, too. Tall. And very poised. A strikingly handsome couple.

'Hello,' the woman said. 'Can we help you with anything?'

It was very obvious that Mary had been staring at their home, and she felt quite embarrassed, but could not resist telling them: 'I was just looking at my old house, that's all.'

'Oh really?' said the woman. 'You lived here once?'

Before she could stop herself, Mary was confiding in them both, telling them far more than she had intended: how she had grown up here as an only child, how she had lived here throughout the war, how she had still been living here when she met her husband.

'I was married from this house,' she told them.

'That's amazing,' said the man. 'I wish we could invite you to come in and have a look around.'

'Yes,' said Mary, 'it's not allowed, is it?' There was a note of disappointment in her voice, but in truth she was quite relieved. She would have been afraid to go inside. The thought of what she might find in that house frightened her.

'But you must come back and visit us,' the woman said, 'when all these restrictions have been lifted.'

'Well, that's very kind . . .' Mary started to back away. She was breathing heavily and was craving the safety of her car. 'But I'm not sure that I . . .'

What was she trying to say?

She looked at them directly, one last time, and found herself speaking these words, without knowing where they had come from: 'No, I won't be coming back, I don't think. It's yours now.'

*

'I speak to you today at the same hour as my father did, exactly seventy-five years ago. His message then was a salute to the men and women at home and abroad who had sacrificed so much in pursuit of what he rightly called a "great deliverance".'

The telephone rang. It was Peter. Mary was happy to hear from him, of course, but his timing was dreadful.

'The Queen's on,' she said. 'What did you call now for?'

'I didn't realize.'

'Of course you didn't. At least Jack would know when the Queen was on, I'll give him that. Martin phoned during the middle of Winston Churchill. You're as bad as each other.'

'Shall I call back later, then?'

'No, I don't suppose she'll say anything very interesting.'

'The war had been a total war; it had affected everyone, and no one was immune from its impact. Whether it be the men and women called up to serve; families separated from each other; or people asked to take up new roles and skills to support the war effort, all had a part to play. At the start, the outlook seemed bleak, the end distant, the outcome uncertain. But we kept faith that the cause was right – and this belief, as my father noted in his broadcast, carried us through.'

'I drove to Bournville today,' she said. 'I went to see if there was a street party going on.'

'You *drove*?' said Peter. 'Mum, that's illegal. You could have been arrested.'

'There were lots of people about. Most were in their gardens, some were in the street. It was all quite pleasant, actually.'

'You do know that we're in the middle of a pandemic?'

'Don't put a dampener on it. Nobody was doing any harm.'

'Never give up, never despair – that was the message of VE Day. I vividly remember the jubilant scenes my sister and I witnessed with our parents and Winston Churchill from the balcony of Buckingham Palace. The sense of joy in the crowds who gathered outside and across the country

*was profound, though while we celebrated the victory in Europe, we knew
there would be further sacrifice. It was not until August that fighting in the
Far East ceased and the war finally ended.'*

'We're just worried about you, Mum, that's all. We don't want
you to catch this thing. It's really nasty.'

'Well, you've got to die of something, haven't you?'

'I mean, were people social distancing?'

'Of course they were. Well, most of them. Some of the time.'

*'Many people laid down their lives in that terrible conflict. They fought
so we could live in peace, at home and abroad. They died so we could live
as free people in a world of free nations. They risked all so our families and
neighbourhoods could be safe. We should and will remember them.'*

'I've seen clips on the news,' Peter said, 'with people doing all
sorts of stuff at these parties today. Doing the conga up and down
the street.'

'Ooh, that sounds fun. I like a conga. Is that allowed?'

*'As I now reflect on my father's words and the joyous celebrations, which
some of us experienced first-hand, I am thankful for the strength and
courage that the United Kingdom, the Commonwealth and all our allies
displayed.'*

'Of course it isn't allowed. We're still in lockdown. The trouble is
nobody knows what the regulations are. They've been giving out
signals that we can all relax, and we *can't*. But you can't expect Boris
to give us proper guidance. He's so fu— so bloody useless.'

'Oh, you're always criticizing him. He's doing his best. He didn't
know this virus was going to happen.'

'Doing his best? People's lives are at stake.'

*'The wartime generation knew that the best way to honour those who
did not come back from the war, was to ensure that it didn't happen again.
The greatest tribute to their sacrifice is that countries who were once sworn
enemies are now friends, working side by side for the peace, health and
prosperity of us all.'*

'You can die of all sorts of things, you know. I reckon people can
die of loneliness.'

Peter didn't want to hear this.

'Did you watch *Genevieve* last night?' he asked.

'I caught the end of it.'

He sighed. 'I *told* you when it was on.'

'*Today it may seem hard that we cannot mark this special anniversary as we would wish. Instead we remember from our homes and our doorsteps. But our streets are not empty; they are filled with the love and the care that we have for each other. And when I look at our country today, and see what we are willing to do to protect and support one another, I say with pride that we are still a nation those brave soldiers, sailors and airmen would recognize and admire.*'

'Well, I saw the last ten minutes. Oh, it is a lovely film. The music! Larry Adler, that was. We had the record, you know, your father and me. It was one of the first films we saw together. Did you watch it?'

'Of course. I always do. I love the mews house at the beginning.'

'I'll tell you something, though. When it was over I changed channels and . . . well, I've never seen anything like it. It was one of those dating shows, and all the people on it were completely naked. Starkers. The camera went in and you could see all these chaps' dangly bits. They'd shaved every bit of hair off, as well. Who wants to see that on a great big wide screen? Fancy going from *Genevieve* to that!'

Peter laughed and said: 'Well, Mum, I don't know . . . You've seen some changes, haven't you, over the years?'

'Changes? I've never seen anything like it in all my life!'

6.   *The Top of My Mother's Head*

It's become one of those pieces of music we no longer think about, because we hear it so often. It is in 4/4 time. Two three-note phrases: the first interval being a perfect 5th (E flat and B flat), the second an augmented 5th (D natural and B flat again). Primitive but impossible to get out of your head. Millions of us hear it every day: the little fragment of sound that announces the beginning of a Skype call. When I am calling my mother, I hear the phrase repeated at least fifteen or twenty times. This is how long it takes her to respond. I am on the point of giving up when the screen at last flickers into life. At first the image shakes and wobbles, and then, when it stabilizes I find that I am looking at something I don't recognize. A rectangle of pale grey, viewed from below at a strange angle. It takes me a while to realize what it is: one of the cupboards in my mother's kitchen.

'Mum,' I explain, patiently. 'Your camera's pointing in the wrong direction again.'

'I can see you,' she replies. 'I can see you perfectly.'

More adjustments take place, until we arrive at a compromise. She props the tablet up against some object on the kitchen table – a fruit bowl, maybe, or a cake stand – and now my screen still mainly shows her kitchen cupboard, but I can also see the top of her head. It's not perfect, but it's good enough to start the conversation.

My mother, eighty-six years old, is not used to being apart from her family for this long. None of us have been able to visit her for more than three months. Every night, she and I talk on the telephone, and two or three times a week, we talk via Skype. We have nothing very much to say, but the purpose of the talk is not to exchange information. It is to achieve a kind of closeness, to huddle together for warmth.

While she's talking to me, I study the top of my mother's head.

It is a part of her body I never really noticed, before the pandemic started and these calls became our only way of communicating. I had not realized, for instance, that her forehead was so high, and her hairline had receded so much. The greyness of her hair is visible now, because for several months she has not been able to receive a visit from her hairdresser and have her hair dyed blonde, as she has always done for the last twenty years or more. I can see the flaky, uneven texture of her scalp. It seems odd that this part of her body should have become so familiar to me in recent weeks, that I should be seeing more of it than I see of her eyes and her mouth, because she does not know how to angle the camera on her tablet correctly.

The tablet was a present for her eightieth birthday, but she has never really learned how to use it, and has only now started to use it at all because it is the only way she is able to catch a glimpse of me and the rest of her family. The last time I saw her in person was just before the beginning of lockdown. March 2020. Back then, the world was just beginning to wake up to the existence of this virus. How long ago it seems, already. How naive we all were. We had seen images of the lockdown in Wuhan and had been telling ourselves the story – a comforting story, but also a slightly racist one – that these were scenes that could happen in Asia but not here in Europe. Then it was announced that the virus was spreading all over the north of Italy and the whole country was going into lockdown. In the UK, larger gatherings were being discouraged in order to promote something called 'social distancing' – a new phrase, two words which no one had put together before, but a phrase which, soon enough, everybody was using as if they'd known it all their lives. This was the situation beginning to unfold when my niece Lorna, a jazz musician, flew to Vienna for a short tour: Vienna on Monday, then Munich, then Hanover, Hamburg, Berlin and Leipzig. Everywhere she went, public events were being cancelled and venues were being closed down. She told me there were discussions before every concert, while people tried to decide whether it was still legal to perform. Everyone's behaviour was starting to change. Nobody was wearing masks, but people were wearing gloves on the trains, and for some reason buying huge quantities of toilet paper. They weren't hugging each other any more, they were touching each other with their elbows.

Suddenly, contact with another human being – real physical contact – was a source of fear, of disgust, something to shrink away from. When Lorna's sister, Susan, visited their grandmother, and took her little daughter, Bridie, with her, they were scared of infecting her with the virus, and wouldn't go into her house. They stood outside the window, and talked to her on the telephone.

'I *hated* that,' my mother told me afterwards. Whenever she expressed her feelings, she always used as few words as possible, but I knew exactly what she meant: being able to see her great-granddaughter only through a sheet of glass, being able to talk to her only on the telephone, even though she was just a few yards away, was a source of agony to her.

Once lockdown started, I didn't see my mother again for three months. Just the top of her head, on my computer screen. The greying hair, and the flaking scalp.

*

The first weeks of this new reality begin to pass.

During this time, I sometimes find myself asking: what does it mean, this pandemic? To me, and the people around me? And I realize that the answer to this question depends, to a large extent, on the relationship that you have with your own body. For my own part, I learn that I am not an especially tactile person. I do not really miss hugging people. My own body has never interested me very much. To me, it is just the shell that contains my consciousness, the suitcase in which I carry around my thoughts and my feelings, and I pay no more attention to it than you pay to the suitcase which you put away in a cupboard when you come back from a holiday. So although I cannot work, and start worrying about whether I will soon have enough money to survive, the pandemic in other ways changes nothing essential for me. But it is different for other people: different for the people who are still going out to work, delivering the things the rest of us are relying on; different, too, for the young people who have been snatched away from their friends at school and university, whose lives have been brutally interrupted. It is different for my mother, who was always an athlete, a sportswoman, whose body is an intrinsic part of her being, and who believes, in her heart, that the true value of a conversation with someone depends upon both people occupying the same physical space. For her this confinement, these enforced separations, are a kind of torture.

Somehow, the weeks go by. Spring turns into summer, and slowly, tentatively, we begin to emerge into the daylight again. Travelling between cities is once again a possibility. On 1st June, our government announces that from now on members of different households are allowed to meet not just in public spaces, but in private gardens (as long as we don't have to walk through a house to get there). I call my mother and tell her that I can come and see her at last. Not Skype, this time, not in the virtual world, but in the real world. 'Tomorrow?' she asks, eagerly, and I say, 'Yes, why not.' The next morning, however, dawns cold and rainy. I look at the weather app on my phone, and see that in two days' time – Thursday 4th June – the weather in Birmingham will be sunny again. So I tell her that I'm putting off my visit by two days. Is that OK? Her response surprises me. Of course she agrees, but she sounds strangely daunted by the request, as if I am asking her to exert some enormous effort of will by waiting an extra forty-eight hours. I put it down to her emotional fragility, to her old age.

On Thursday morning, I get into my car, and drive from my home in Kew to my mother's home on the outskirts of Birmingham. This drive, from London to Birmingham, takes about two hours and I used to find it impossibly boring. You never leave the motorway. The landscape seems unchanging. But today is different. England is bathed in sunlight and everything – the tower blocks on the edges of London, the motorway service stations and interchanges – looks fresh and beautiful.

Birmingham looks beautiful too, so much so that, seized by a nostalgic impulse, I make a detour to take a look at the house where my grandparents used to live in the 1960s, in a quiet backwater of south-west Birmingham once known as the Longbridge Estate, now called the Austin Village. Three parallel roads are lined with white weatherboard bungalows, shipped over from America more than a hundred years ago. My father's parents used to live in one of these, and visiting them was always a treat: I remember the cold lunches of strange semi-Germanic food, and the joy of playing in their Anderson shelter which always reminded me of Bilbo Baggins's hobbit-hole at Bag End. Their bungalow is still there, unchanged, although there are now blocks of flats encroaching upon the garden, and the Anderson shelter is long gone.

The detour makes me half an hour late to see my mother, but why should that matter? There will be many more visits, many more occasions like this.

When I arrive, she comes quickly around the corner of the house to greet me, smiling. Maybe I'm imagining it, but there seems to be a little more effort behind the smile than there used to be.

For the next three hours, we sit in her garden, beneath the shade of the sumac tree which has been there for as long as I can remember. The first thing she gives me is a cup of tea and a Cadbury's Creme Egg. I am fifty-nine years old, but whenever she sees me, my mother always gives me chocolate. She can't help herself. This time I demur at first, but she says, 'Oh, come on – when a man's tired of chocolate, he's tired of life. Who said that?' I tell her that it was Dr Johnson, and he said it about London, not chocolate, but she just laughs and says it still applies. I notice that she doesn't eat any chocolate herself, today. She seems to have very little appetite.

Over sandwiches in the garden, we talk a lot about the past. Maybe it's because of my age, but I'm starting to get interested in my family history, and she is almost the only one left now with a clear memory of relatives who died in the 1940s and 50s. We talk about the future, too, about her grandchildren and great-grandchildren and what she hopes they will do with their lives. A musician herself, she especially likes to hear about Lorna. And of course we talk about the pandemic. But what we talk about doesn't really matter. It is the fact of talking that is important. And even more important, the fact that we are together, in the same space, each of our bodies picking up energy from the other's proximity.

As I leave, I promise that I will come back in two weeks, and try to bring Lorna with me. My mother smiles but she looks uncertain, as though she doesn't quite believe me.

I set off for home at five o'clock. It's a drive that should take two hours, but I allow it to take three. I leave the motorway and make my way along small roads through the Oxfordshire countryside in the evening sunshine. On the rare occasions when I can persuade her to visit me in London, I always pick my mother up from her house and drive her down this way. She hates motorways as much as she loves these winding A-roads with their gentle undulations and chintzy houses in mellow Cotswold stone. As I drive, I recall fragments of our conversation. We talked only of everyday things but there was nevertheless something momentous about it. I think back on my lifetime of knowing my mother, the strange mixture of distance and intimacy between us. I remember one moment, long ago, one very untypical moment, when I felt an incredible closeness to her: it was a winter's night in London, I was very young, and we were listening to a performance of the *Hymnus Paradisi* by Herbert Howells. Maybe the saddest music ever written. I put the same piece onto the car stereo now, as I drive through Oxfordshire. There is a synchronicity between the curves of the road, the rise and fall of the landscape, and the melancholy of the music which suits my mood so well because there was something melancholy about that conversation with my mother, too, despite our joy at being together again. I feel both wildly happy and desperately sad at the same time.

Later, at eight o'clock, I phone her to say that I've arrived home safely.

One hour after that, at nine o'clock, my brother Jack phones me, to say that my mother called a few minutes earlier, saying that she had a terrible pain in her stomach.

My brother, who lives closer to her house than I do, drives over to see what is happening. My other brother, Martin, is already there. An ambulance has arrived and Mum is being attended by paramedics. We know that she has an aortic aneurysm, a tiny balloon-like swelling in one of her arteries very close to her heart. It can't be operated on, and for some years she has lived in fear of it bursting, an event which would inevitably be fatal. Martin explains this to the paramedics but they assure him, confidently, that this is not what has happened, my mother simply has a bad infection. They are insistent upon this, and they are insistent upon another point: Martin and Jack cannot come into my mother's house to comfort her. Covid regulations do not allow it. They have to stand outside, in her front garden, and watch through the window as she clutches her stomach in pain. Through the window they can see her cat Charlie circling her, agitated, as the paramedics do their work. Her sons have to communicate with her using their eyes, and on the telephone.

After a while, my mother is put to bed, and the paramedics get ready to leave. They assure her that she is going to be all right, but she tells them that she is in agony, so they suggest to my brothers that they get some prescription painkillers from her GP in the morning. The paramedics themselves are not authorized to give her any now, just some paracetamol. So then Jack and Martin, too, go home, knowing that their mother is in terrible pain. They have not been allowed to speak to her in person, they have not been allowed to touch her.

Shortly before midnight I phone her. It's a very short conversation. I ask how she feels. She says she is in too much pain to talk, and hangs up. A few minutes later I try calling again but the line is engaged. It is engaged for the rest of the night. I worry that she is alone in the house, quite alone, apart from her cat, who sleeps on her bed every night and will probably be there with her now. That's some comfort, at least.

Still worried, and still unable to get any answer from her telephone, I drive back up to Birmingham at dawn the next morning, but I am only halfway there when Martin phones to tell me that she died during the night.

*

This pandemic, of which we are perhaps seeing only the beginning, has already been full of cruelties. Families separated by huge distances, unable to see each other for much longer than I was unable to see mine. And of course, millions of unforeseen, premature deaths. Millions of lives cut short when people thought that they still had years, perhaps decades ahead of them.

And so I try to be grateful. I try to be grateful for the fact that my mother willed herself to stay alive for long enough to have one last conversation with me, in the sunlight, beneath the shade of the sumac tree in the garden which was not just her garden, for almost fifty years, but mine as well, the setting for so many of my childhood games and childhood fantasies. That memory will never go away, at least. It was a precious gift that she saved for me.

But I cannot forgive the cruelty either. The cruelty of the fact that the last time my brothers were able to see her, it was through the window of her house. The last time her grandchildren saw her, it was also through the window of her house. Her great-grandchildren too. The fact that most of the conversations we had with her, during her last few months of life, took place on our computer screens.

These screens, these windows, are the barriers, made of glass and silicone and plastic, that the pandemic has raised between us. They have forced us apart and they tease us with ways to communicate which are pale imitations, sometimes mere parodies, of real human contact. I regret now that my mother and I never wrote letters to each other during those last few months – we hadn't written letters to each other for years – because I feel that being able to see her handwriting, today, would perhaps be the only thing that might bring me closer to a sense of her living presence. Meanwhile, I cling to the image of that last afternoon, that last conversation. Something I will always be thankful for. Without it, after all, what would my final memory of her consist of? Nothing. Just the little fragment of melody that announces the beginning of a Skype call, and a view of the top of my mother's head.

7.

Before getting into his car, David took Peter by the arm and said:

'I liked that piece you wrote, by the way. Very much.'

'Thanks, David.'

'I mean, I wouldn't say it was great literature, exactly, but it was . . . from the heart.'

Peter nodded and smiled. 'Maybe too much.'

'I thought you might have read it at the service.'

'I thought about that, but . . . it didn't seem the right thing to do, in the end.'

After the funeral, in the absence of a proper reception, a few of them had come down to the miniature boating lake, stopping at a sandwich shop on the way to buy refreshments. They'd laid out rugs on the grass near to the water, and sat together for an hour or two. The funeral itself had been bizarre. Only twelve mourners had been allowed, sitting on chairs which were widely spread out around the chapel, yards of empty space between them. A few people had been watching the service outside the crematorium, on a CCTV screen. Presumably more people had been watching it on Zoom: Peter had imagined a few dozen of Mary's friends sitting at home, peering at their laptops, struggling to get on top of this new software which probably their sons or daughters had had to install for them. All three of Mary's sons had given addresses (Martin had spoken about her teaching career, Peter about her life in music, Jack about her love of sport) to an audience consisting solely of their wives, sons and daughters. That made ten altogether, so in addition David Foley had been invited, along with his sister, Gill. Gill's husband had waited outside, watching on the screen, as had David's new girlfriend, Sioned. Now David and Sioned were about to drive back to Wales.

'I know this is a weird thing to say,' she said to Peter, 'but it's been nice seeing you again. I'm so sorry for your loss.'

'Thank you. It's a bit of a strange way to reconnect. I'm amazed you still remember me.'

'It's not easy to forget a kid who plays Bach on the violin outside their caravan in the middle of a field.'

Peter laughed. 'I suppose not.'

Once they had gone, he walked back towards what remained of the picnic party. There were only five people there, now: Angela had taken a carful of the younger family members to New Street station (calling at a newsagent's on the way, because there was a story in the *Mail* she was desperate to read, about Meghan Markle and her jealousy over Prince Harry's allegedly too-close relationship with the singer Adele). This left just the three brothers, and Bridget, and Lorna. Which meant that they had a dilemma. Jack and Bridget had not spoken to each other for four years, and although everyone had assumed that if anything could bring their feud to an end it would be Mary's funeral, they were still not speaking to each other now.

'Well, do you think that went off all right?' Peter asked.

'As well as could be expected, under the circumstances,' said Martin.

'Shame we couldn't have a proper spread afterwards,' said Jack. 'Private room in a pub, something like that.'

'I like it here,' said Lorna. 'Out in the open air, in the sunshine. I think Gran would have liked it, too.'

Looking around him, Jack said: 'Remind me why we came here, again?'

'I just thought it would be nice,' Peter said, 'if we commemorated her somewhere that was . . . you know, important. In our family history.'

Martin and Jack nodded in solemn approval, and didn't speak for a while. Then Jack said:

'I don't think I've ever been here in my life before.'

'Me neither,' said Martin. 'I didn't even know it existed. Are you *sure* Mum used to come here?'

'Of course I am.' Irritated by his brothers, Peter traced a finger unconsciously along the groove of the long, painful scratch that ran almost the length of his forearm, from wrist to elbow. Charlie had been living with him for three weeks now, and their relationship was proving tricky to say the least.

'Well, at least they allowed us to sit here in peace,' Lorna said.

There had been some discussion as to whether this funeral picnic, if that's what it was, had constituted an illegal gathering.

'Crazy, isn't it?' said Martin. 'I find it really hard to see where all this is going to end. Is this virus just supposed to go away now that the sun's come out?'

'Oh, it'll fizzle out, soon enough,' said Jack. 'Something else will come along to take its place, and in a couple of years we'll be wondering what all the fuss was about.'

'I wish I was an optimist, like you,' said Martin. 'Must be nice.'

'I'm not an optimist,' said Jack. 'I'm a pragmatist. Big difference. The important thing is not to waste energy worrying about things you'll never be able to change. Life's too short. No disrespect – I mean, none of us are looking our best today – but you two' (and yes, it did seem that he was including Bridget in his comments) 'are beginning to show your age a bit.'

'Is that so,' said Martin, flatly.

'It's because you worry too much. And you don't worry about the little things like getting the plumbing fixed or getting the car serviced, because you're on top of all that. You worry about global warming, or the future of the BBC, or what's happening in Palestine, or what's happening in Syria. Things you can't do anything about – and mostly things which have got *nothing to do with you*. The world would be a better place if we all just tended to our own little patch, because trying to interfere with stuff like that always just makes it worse. *That's* why people like Boris Johnson, by the way. Because he lets people get on with it and doesn't interfere.'

Martin snorted at that, but said: 'I suppose Pascal would agree with you, anyway.'

'Who?'

*

'Blaise Pascal. He said that "All the trouble in the world comes from people who can't sit quietly in their rooms."'

'Very well put. The British philosophy in a nutshell.'

'He was French.'

'Well, even the French get it right occasionally.' Jack glanced across at Bridget. Clearly it was needling him, even now, that she was not engaging with any of this. 'I mean, take Brexit. I voted to leave, you all voted to stay. Fine. We can have a civilized disagreement about it. All the British MEPs lost their jobs and their perks. Well, they're pissed off about that. I don't blame them. But at the end of the day, nobody knows how it's going to pan out, do they? Maybe it'll turn out to be a mistake. That's not the point. The point is that we made a choice. We made a choice and we just have to stick with it and see what happens. And in the meantime we can still all be friends.'

After a few moments Peter said, reflectively: 'You know, even right at the end of her life, Mum didn't know whether she'd made the right choice or not.'

Jack turned to him, puzzled. 'What do you mean?'

'Marrying Dad.'

'Why?' said Martin. 'There was never anyone else, was there? I thought they met when she was still at school.'

'There was someone else. She told me about him a few times.'

'Really? Who? What was he like?'

'Very different to Dad, from what I could gather. Different enough that her whole life might have gone another way.'

And as Peter stared across the little artificial lake, the lake around which his mother and Kenneth had once walked together, decades earlier, lifetimes ago, he suddenly felt so consumed with grief that he couldn't trust himself to say any more. Only Martin seemed to notice. He patted his brother on the shoulder and said, 'Let's pretend we're here to do some exercise, shall we?' and then the two of them went off to walk around the lake, leaving Jack and Lorna and the ever-silent Bridget alone.

A gust of wind rose up and sent ripples across the water.

'Maybe we should go soon,' Lorna said to her mother. 'It's getting a bit chilly.'

There was a long pause. When Bridget finally spoke, it was not in response to this suggestion.

'Jack, you're full of shit,' she said.

Jack turned. These were the first words his sister-in-law had spoken to him since June 2016.

'My God,' he said. 'The oracle has spoken. Her mouth has opened. Words have come forth.'

Still not looking at him, her face turned away at a defiant angle, she repeated: 'Full of it.'

'Would you care to elaborate?' he asked.

'No,' Bridget said. But she did not mean that she didn't care to elaborate, she meant this: 'No, we can't be friends. It's a pity, but we can't.'

He laughed dismissively. 'Blimey, talk about an overreaction. It was just a bloody referendum, Bridge.'

'That's not it.'

The silence was long enough now for Jack to find it unnerving. 'Oh, come on,' he said, 'we've known each other now for – what? – nearly forty years . . .'

'Yes.' She turned and looked at him directly for the first time. 'Exactly. We've known each other for nearly forty years. And do you know another person I knew for a long time? Almost as long as that? Your father.'

'Dad? What about him?' His voice with steely with bravado, not conviction.

'I was part of your family,' she said, speaking slowly, choosing each word with care and pronouncing it without emphasis. 'I went on holiday with you. I had dinner with you. I came to your weddings and your christenings and funerals. I gave them grandchildren, Geoffrey and Mary. Thirty-two years, he and I knew each other. *Thirty-two years*. And in all that time, do you know what? He never once – not *once* – looked me in the eye. He couldn't do that. He couldn't bring himself to do it. Not even at the end, when me and Angela were looking after him, when we were bathing him and getting him dressed, and . . . clearing up after him. And all that time, the rest of you . . . Yes, sure, you've always been nice, you've always been kind, you've always been friendly, but you *knew*. You could see it. *All* of you. And you never did a damn thing about it. Not a damn, fucking thing. You closed ranks. You never said a word to him and do you know what that means? It means you *took his side*. So it's got nothing to do with who voted for what – I mean, maybe the referendum was the last straw but to be honest who cares whether you want to be part of the European Union or not, who gives a shit about that. It just made everything clearer than ever, that's all. Where we stood. Where *you* stood. And Mary, too. Let's not forget about Mary. Jesus Christ, I loved that woman, don't anybody start telling me that I didn't love her – I was the one, for fuck's sake, I was the one who went into the house that morning and tried to save her, I was the one who pumped her chest, I was the one who opened her mouth and tried to get her breathing again – but let's tell the truth about this, Jack, let's be honest, even she, *even Mary*, never stood up for me against him. Not really. Christ, she never even talked to him about Peter, he died not even admitting that his own son was gay, and all so that . . . what? All for a quiet life. All so the sacred family could be preserved, as if there was nothing underneath the surface that stank. Stank to high heaven.'

She stood up, brushed a few blades of grass away from her trousers, and said to her daughter: 'Come on, love, let's go home.'

'Where've the others gone?' Martin asked, when he and Peter returned from their walk.

'Your Mrs gave me a piece of her mind,' said Jack, 'and then they stormed off.'

'You mean she spoke to you?' said Peter, incredulous.

'I'll say. Gave me a right old earful.'

'How am I supposed to get home?' Martin wanted to know.

'Don't worry, mate, we'll see to it.'

'An earful of what?' asked Peter.

Jack rummaged in the paper bag they had brought from the sandwich shop and took out a bar of Dairy Milk.

'Ah, she's just upset. I don't think she even knew what she was saying. Grief can do strange things to you, can't it? Especially a woman, at her time of life.' He unwrapped the chocolate, broke it up into separate chunks and offered them around. You know,' he said, putting a piece into his mouth. 'The menopause, and all that caper.'

Lorna had never seen her mother so angry. She couldn't believe they'd just driven off and left her father to fend for himself.

'Oh, he'll be all right,' said Bridget. 'We can cook him something nice for dinner later. When were you thinking of going home?'

'I'll have to call Donny, but I thought I'd stay with you two tonight, if that's OK. We could do with a bit of time apart, to be honest.'

'I can imagine. Well, they'll have you back in to work again soon, I should think. Offices will have to start reopening.'

'Didn't I tell you? I got a letter this week. A dozen people have been laid off. Including me.'

They left Bournville's green spaces behind, began driving through the blander, more conventional suburbs of Stirchley, King's Heath and Hall Green.

'I don't agree with what you said about Gran, by the way,' Lorna said. 'I don't think you can fault the way she lived. She had a blameless life. Totally blameless. That's enough, isn't it?'

Bridget changed gears abruptly. The car gave a complaining judder.

'I used to think so. But these days I don't think you can stay neutral for ever, that's the thing. There comes a time when everybody has to pick a side.' She accelerated through some traffic lights just as they turned red, and added, in such a low voice that Lorna assumed she was talking to herself: 'We'll all have to do it, pretty soon.'

8.

The banging noises from under the roof were quite alarming, and when the plumber came downstairs he looked grimy and flustered. The cuffs of his shirt were black with ancient dust and there were cobwebs in his hair. He told Shoreh and Farzad that in his opinion no one had looked at that water tank for about eighty years. The outlet pipe and valve had almost rusted away, the overflow pipe was blocked, every single joint and washer needed replacing and he wasn't sure if half the parts were even obtainable any more. The biggest supplier he knew was in West Bromwich and the best thing he could do would be to drive out there this morning and see what he could find. Oh, he said, and I found this, wedged between the tank and the rafters, and he handed them a small cardboard box about the size of a shoebox.

After he had departed on his errand, they sat down at their kitchen table and took the lid off the box. The rest of it fell apart as they did so. There was not much inside: two pocket diaries, for the years 1943 and 1944; a signed black-and-white photograph of a striking young man whose name seemed to be John Miller; a small, sharp triangle of dull bronze metal.

'Probably shrapnel,' said Farzad. 'If these things are from the war.'

There was also a name written in the 1944 diary: Mary Clarke, 12 Birch Road, Bournville. Age: 9 years.

'The old woman who came here on VE Day,' said Shoreh. 'These must belong to her. How amazing. We'll have to try and find her address and give them back.'

At the bottom of the box was a strip of pale yellow cloth, covered with brownish stains. It looked very unsavoury. Farzad picked it up between his finger and thumb and dropped it in the swing-bin.

Then it was time for him to leave. His shift at the hospital started at eleven.

Alone in the house now, Shoreh remained at the kitchen table, sifting through these fragile, meagre relics of a world long gone, turning them over very gently, for it felt as if the diaries might disintegrate in her hands. Mary had only written a few words for each day. School and piano lessons seemed to have dominated her thoughts. These scribbles didn't tell you much about her daily life but surely they would still be of sentimental value. It would be nice to return them, to see the glow of recognition and remembrance lighting up the old lady's face.

Shoreh got up and went to the swing-bin. She opened it and took out the fragment of cloth her husband had thrown away. She held it up to the sunlight that was beginning to stream through the cloudy glass of the verandah. (It really was time to do some proper window-cleaning.) Were those rust-coloured blotches really stains, or was there some sort of design there? Either way, she did not believe this was simply a rag. Looking more closely, she saw that there was a tiny label sewn onto it at one end. It looked like something you might wear beneath your collar: a neckerchief or tie. There must be some reason, after all, why Mary had decided to keep it, and to hide it in this secret place. Shoreh laid it carefully on the windowsill.

*

She was still pondering the mystery of this cloth when she went outside to sweep the front doorstep. It was a quarter to eleven and for a few minutes, as she swept, she found herself savouring the habitual, resonant silence of Bournville at this time of the morning. Then, from a few hundred yards up the road, she heard the ringing of a handbell, and realized that it was many months since she had heard this bell, which used to ring out regularly, at this same time every day. Of course: the schools had closed during lockdown, and now this one was open again. It was the first day of term.

A few seconds later, she heard the gradually rising babble of high-pitched voices, muffled and indistinct at first, then suddenly full-throated as the main doors of the school were thrown open and more than a hundred children thundered out into the playground. Shoreh loved the silence that blanketed her village for much of the day, but she loved the sound of the next fifteen minutes even more. She loved the sound of the children calling out each other's names, the shrill cries of over-excitement, the chanting of nursery rhymes and taunting songs and skipping games. Not that any of these elements could be heard distinctly, or separated one from the other: everything merged into one chorus, a lovely, chaotic medley of infantile voices. Standing on the front doorstep with her broom in hand, listening to the distant sound of children's voices, Shoreh felt that she was at once inhabiting the past, present and future: it reminded her of her own childhood, her own schooldays, more than twenty years ago, the little school in Hamedan, an ancient but vivid memory, but it also reminded her that these shouting and singing children would be the ones carrying the next few years on their shoulders. Past, present and future: that was what she heard, in the sound of the children's voices from the playground at mid-morning break. Like a murmurous river, like the incoming wash of the tide, a distant counterpoint to the swish, swish, swish of her broom on the step, a disembodied voice whispering in her ear, over and over, the mantra: *Everything changes, and everything stays the same.*

Author's Note

Although *Bournville* is a novel, and a work of fiction, the character of Mary Lamb is based closely on my late mother, Janet Coe. However, any connection with my own family story ends there. In particular there is no resemblance between Mary's husband, Geoffrey, and my father, Roger Coe, a convivial, much-loved family man whose working life was spent not at a bank but at Lucas Industries, where he was engaged in designing ever more efficient car batteries. Similarly, all the other members of the Lamb family depicted in the book – Jack, Martin, Peter, Angela, Bridget and Lorna – are fictional creations, and while I have placed their story in real Midlands locations familiar to me from my childhood, the things that happen to them are all invented: so too is the character of Kenneth Fielding. As for the tousled-haired 'Boris' who first appears in the Brussels section, even though he might, of course, seem familiar to some readers, whether he's a fictional character or not remains hard to determine with any certainty.

*

In 2011 the French director and screenwriter Julie Gavras asked me to work with her on a script called *The Chocolate War*. We wrote several drafts together, and although little of that material has made its way into this novel, I must thank her for alerting me to the narrative possibilities of this curious episode in EU history, for the fun we had working together, and for giving me permission to draw on our joint efforts for the section of *Bournville* called 'The Abyss of Birds'.

*

This novel is intended to stand alone, but is also part of a loosely connected series of books I've been writing for some years under the general title of *Unrest*. The other ones are:

Each of these books contains some reference to Thomas Foley, his wife, Sylvia, and his children, David and Gill, although only in *Expo 58* does Thomas take centre stage. I hope to write one more book in the series at some point.

⋆

Special thanks are due to Ralph Pite, Janine McKeown, Charlotte Stretch, John Dolan, Andrew Hodgkiss, Duncan Cadbury, Julia Jordan and Fenella Barton. Also to my daughter Matilda, who helped me with research; to my agent, Caroline Wood; and to Mary Mount and Isabel Wall at Penguin for their excellent editorial suggestions. For the third part of the novel, set during July 1966, much valuable information was gleaned from 66: *The World Cup in Real Time* by Ian Passingham.

⋆

The section entitled 'The Top of My Mother's Head' was originally written to be read aloud at the Massenzio Festival in Rome in July 2021. Although I have made some small revisions in order to adapt it to the character of Peter Lamb, it is otherwise a faithful account of the death of my own mother in the early hours of 10th June 2020. Driving home through the Oxfordshire countryside after my final visit to her, I listened not to Howells's *Hymnus Paradisi* but to a beautiful song called 'Silence', by the singer-songwriter Dos Floris. Almost two years after the event, it still saddens and angers me that my mother died alone, without pain relief, and that members of her family were allowed no personal contact with her as it happened. But then, like thousands of families up and down the country – and unlike the occupiers of number 10 Downing Street at the time – we were following the rules.

London, 21st April 2022

MIDDLE ENGLAND

Set in the Midlands and London over the last eight years,
Jonathan Coe follows a brilliantly vivid cast of characters through
a time of immense change and disruption in Britain. There are
the early married years of Sophie and Ian who disagree about the
future of Britain and, possibly, the future of their relationship;
Sophie's grandfather; Doug, the political commentator; and
Doug's Remaining Tory politician partner, who is savaged by the
crazed trolls of Twitter.

And within all these lives is the story of England itself:
a story of nostalgia and irony, of friendship and rage,
humour and intense bewilderment.

As acutely alert to the absurdity of the political classes as
he is compassionate about those who have been left behind,
this is a novel Jonathan Coe was born to write.

Praise for *Middle England*

'Brilliantly funny'
Economist

'A pertinent, entertaining study of a nation in crisis'
Financial Times

'A copper-bottomed masterpiece'
Barney Norris

Winner of the Costa Novel Award 2019

MR WILDER AND ME

A young woman named Calista meets the famed Hollywood director Billy Wilder in the sweltering summer of 1976. She knows nothing about him or his work, but this chance encounter will change her life for good. But while Calista is thrilled with her new adventure, Wilder himself – struggling to raise the money for his next feature film – is living with the realization that his star may be on the wane.

In his new novel that is, by turns, funny, tender and profoundly truthful, Jonathan Coe turns his gaze to the nature of time, fame, family and nostalgia. When the world is catapulting towards change, do you hold on for dear life or decide it's time to let go?

Praise for *Mr Wilder and Me*

'As good as anything he's written – a novel to cherish'
Observer

'Absolutely wonderful'
Nigella Lawson

'A tender portrait'
Daily Telegraph

NUMBER 11

This is a novel about the hundreds of tiny connections between the public and private worlds and how they affect us all.

It's about the legacy of war and the end of innocence.
It's about how comedy and politics are battling it out
and comedy might have won.
It's about how 140 characters can make fools of us all.
It's about living in a city where bankers need cinemas in their
basements and others need food banks down the street.
It is Jonathan Coe doing what he does best – showing us
how we live now.

Praise for *Number 11*

'An incredibly Dickensian novel'
Tom Holland

'Often satirical, always compassionate'
Tatler

'This is first-class entertainment'
Evening Standard

THE ROTTERS' CLUB

Jonathan Coe's widely acclaimed novel is set in the
1970s against a distant backdrop of strikes, terrorist attacks
and growing racial tension. A group of young friends inherit
the editorship of their school magazine and begin to put their
own distinctive spin onto events in the wider world.

A zestful comedy of personal and social upheaval,
The Rotters' Club captures a fateful moment in British politics –
the collapse of 'Old Labour' – and imagines its impact on the
topsy-turvy world of the bemused teenager: a world in
which a lost pair of swimming trunks can be just as
devastating as an IRA bomb.

Praise for Jonathan Coe

'Probably the best English novelist of his generation'
Nick Hornby

'Hugely readable, moving, richly comic'
Daily Telegraph